D0340693

MOSCOW TWILIGHT

MOSCOW TWILIGHT

WILLIAM E. HOLLAND

POCKET BOOKS

New York   London   Toronto   Sydney   Tokyo   Singapore

POCKET BOOKS, a division of Simon & Schuster Inc.
1230 Avenue of the Americas, New York, NY 10020

Holland, William E.
    Moscow twilight / William E. Holland.
        p.   cm.
    ISBN: 0-671-74643-X
    I. Title.
    PS3558.O3492S4   1992
    813'.54—dc20   91-31317
                                        CIP

First Pocket Books hardcover printing July 1992

10 9 8 7 6 5 4 3 2 1

To Lisa and Cindy, with love.

Dad

Acknowledgments

Thanks to Misha and Volodya for their expert comments, and to my wife, Olga, for her knowledge, advice, and support.

Contents

· I ·

MOSCOW

· 1 ·

Wednesday, January 18, 1989
3 A.M.
Lenin Prospect

THE TELEPHONE FINALLY DRAGGED CHANTURIA FROM HIS SLEEP, UNWILLING as he was to leave it. The scratch in the voice on the other end might have been the connection, or might have been the time of night. No reasonable person functioned quite right at 3:00 A.M. "Comrade Captain Chanturia?"

"Yes."

"Captain Novikov here. I'm the duty officer. You have been assigned to an investigation. Lieutenant Orlov will be at your apartment with a driver in fifteen minutes. Meet him downstairs."

"I'm not on duty," Chanturia mumbled. The part of him that was awake knew it would do no good.

"You are now. By personal order of Comrade Colonel Sokolov."

"Shit. All right." He felt the other side of the bed. It was still warm where Tanya had been. He found the light switch and enjoyed the several minutes he wasted blinking at the glare before getting up to dress.

He stumbled over Tanya's nightgown on the bathroom floor. She had by nature the ways of a true princess: her discarded garments she would leave lying for the girl to pick up—although there was no girl and never had been one and never would be.

Orlov was already waiting outside in the car. Chanturia kicked the snow from his boots and got into the back of the Volga beside him.

3

"You look happy this morning, Comrade Captain," Orlov said, using Chanturia's title with ironic politeness—he was friendly enough with Chanturia to address him by his name and patronymic, Sergo Vissarionovich, or even just "Sergo" if he was feeling self-confident. Chanturia was not much older than Orlov, and they had once been lieutenants together, when Chanturia was stuck in grade as a lieutenant. Now he expected Orlov would catch him again.

"Of course I'm happy. Work is joy. What's going on?"

"It's a wild story. A gang broke in at one of the late-night cooperative cafes. The one out on Prospect Mira. Cut up some of the patrons and then torched the place."

"Why has the colonel got me out of a sound sleep for a Mafia attack on a cafe? Have all the militia died of boredom?"

"It seems there were foreigners in the cafe."

"Who else would be able to afford it?"

"Cooperative owners, Mafiosi . . ."

"Yes, of course."

The car went quickly through the snow-choked back lanes around Chanturia's apartment bloc east of Lenin Prospect in southern Moscow. Nothing was moving. Even Lenin Prospect, when they turned onto it, was deserted. Ignoring the two inches of new snow on the street, and of course ignoring the speed limit, the driver set the speedometer needle at 120 kilometers per hour and held to the inner lane toward the center of the city. Chanturia would have told him to slow down, but he knew it would be a waste of time. The driver was young, just out of school; and drivers had their own rules—even KGB drivers.

The cooperative cafe Come In and Taste was located on the ground floor of a nine-story stone building of Stalin's time—square, solid, and ugly. The heavy front door, specially built up with boards to present a luxurious and formidable appearance, was standing open to the cold.

A militia captain met them at the door. He saluted, although they were not in uniform, his precise correctness as good as a sneer to show the policeman's disdain for the representatives of the Committee on State Security. All the policemen Chanturia had ever known were convinced that the KGB thought themselves superior to mere militiamen; and all the KGB men he knew did think so. He thought so himself.

"What do we have here, Captain?" Chanturia asked.

"Murder. Arson. The investigator is in the main hall. I will tell you what I can of the scene here in the front premises." The captain stepped back into a small anteroom—little more than a wide part of the hall with a small desk, and behind it a coatroom that was only a narrow closet.

"The assailants, reported to be five in number, entered through the front door," the captain said. "They had already cut the telephone wires. They tried to knife the manager, there"—he pointed to a few dark spots on the floor, apparently the blood of the manager shed in defense of the cafe's business—"and then proceeded to the main hall, where they methodically attacked the guests. It was like a military operation." He turned and led them through the narrow front hall of the cafe, to the "main hall" in back, which was hardly a hall at all, but a low small room just large enough for seven tables. A curl of soot licked across the ceiling. Inside there still hung the sour smell of gasoline smoke and soaked drapery. The bold-painted wall murals—they looked like Georgian scenes—were startling in their brilliance, except near the door, where a blaze had brought the paint off in curls like dying fingers.

A tall man in a dark blue suit came from the far side of the room. "You're the investigator?" Chanturia asked.

"Yes. Filin, from the Procurator's office." Filin had a lean face, topped by wild blond hair—no doubt he'd been called from bed too— and a skinny neck that didn't fill his shirt collar. His red tie hung slack in his collar.

"How many guests?" Chanturia asked the militiaman, ignoring the investigator.

"Fifteen in all, it appears."

"What did the intruders do here?"

"They produced bottles of benzine, smashed them on the furnishings, and lit the fuel with a pocket lighter."

"A brave action. If not completely wise. Were any of the attackers burned as a result?"

"Not to our knowledge."

"That's a pity," Orlov said. It was nothing personal: a burned assailant might show up at a hospital.

"How many persons injured?" Chanturia asked.

"Five of the guests. The service personnel were all in the kitchen at the instant of the attack." The investigator pointed out through the door of the "main hall," to another door only two steps away. "When they saw what was happening, they barricaded themselves in the kitchen. The assailants were unsuccessful in breaking in there, and departed quickly once the fire was started."

"How many foreigners were here?"

"Six of the fifteen. A German and a Finn, three Japanese, and one other." He hurried to add, "Three were injured. Two of the Japanese, and . . ."

"Other? What do you mean by 'other'?"

"We don't know. He didn't have any papers."

"What?"

The investigator shrugged. It wasn't his job to keep track of foreigners. Let the Committee on State Security worry about it.

"How serious were the injuries?" Chanturia demanded. "Are they all at the hospital?"

"The two Japanese sustained superficial cuts on the arms and hands trying to defend themselves. They were taken to the hospital. The other one is over there." He pointed to a bundle covered with two tablecloths. "We saved him for you."

"Many thanks."

They uncovered the body. "Male of European ancestry," Orlov said, taking notes for the report. "Name unknown—'Mister X.' Height about 180 centimeters."

"That's standing up," Chanturia said. "As is, about, oh . . . twenty centimeters."

"Weight maybe eighty-five kilos," Orlov continued. "Hair brown, eyes brown. What'd he die of?" he asked the investigator.

"You'll get the autopsy report. As of now, I'd say he died from the stab wound in the right lower rib cage. Probably it cut the heart." The investigator motioned toward the body, and the policeman, using a handkerchief, pulled open the dead man's shirt, which was unbuttoned. He used the handkerchief to avoid touching the bloodstain that spread over the right side of the shirt. The wound had been wiped clean, however, probably by the ambulance crew, and was only a thin red line on the man's pale side.

"He had no identification at all?" Chanturia asked.

"None."

"Where were his clothes made?"

"A mixture of European countries. English suit, Italian shirt and tie, German shoes."

6

"Underwear?" Orlov asked.

The investigator smirked. He wasn't about to be caught so easily. "Italian. Boxer shorts."

"No credit cards?" Chanturia asked.

"No. Only cash. Some American dollars, some Finnish marks, some German marks, a few Italian lira. A lot of rubles. Also a French wristwatch—Hermès; an English fountain pen; a fine Irish linen pocket handkerchief; no rings or other jewelry."

"Not Italian, then," Chanturia said. "There's always jewelry. The underwear had me excited for a minute." He stood at the corpse's feet, studying the face. "What do you think he is?" he asked the investigator.

The investigator shrugged again. He didn't think for a minute that the KGB gave a fart for his opinion. "Could be anybody. You see one foreigner, you've seen them all."

"Well, he's not African."

"Might as well be," the policeman said. "He's not Russian."

Orlov, out of the side of his eye, looked at Chanturia. Chanturia was Georgian, both on his father's side and his mother's. But Chanturia showed nothing. "Was he with anyone?" he asked.

"Yes," the investigator said. "He was with a Russian woman. Age about thirty, blond, strikingly beautiful, according to the waiters."

The bitch, the policeman thought.

"Well, then?"

"She disappeared before we got here. The kitchen staff escaped out the back windows, but the alarm had already been turned in from the next building—the watchman called in. No one dared go back inside until our men arrived. By then the woman was gone. No one else knew her. None had seen her before."

"Did the raiders kidnap her?"

The investigator didn't answer at first: he hadn't thought of that possibility. Finally he shrugged. "Could be. No one knows anything. None of the other clients knew either her or the dead man."

Chanturia pulled the tablecloths back over the corpse. "Have him taken to the lab," he said. "What about the citizens? Who were they?"

"Two whores with the Japanese. Plus a birthday party of six. Three men, three women."

"This place was a regular menagerie, wasn't it?" Chanturia said. "There was one of everything. Well, where are they all?"

7

"I took statements and told them all to report to us in the morning."

"All right. We'll want them for interrogation. Send them to us first." As he turned away, Filin, the investigator, only stared. The policeman saluted again—more a wave than a salute.

"Not much there," Chanturia said to Orlov as they went out.

"Except for one asshole investigator."

"Ah, that's his job. Getting up at two in the morning to look at dead bodies."

"You'd think he'd want to share them, instead of keeping them for himself."

"Everybody wants to hold on to all of his job that he can these days, Lyosha."

"Do you think he'll make a decent job of it?"

"On his own? What does he care about a dead foreigner? He'll file his report and forget it. For that matter, what do I care about a dead foreigner? If our Comrade Investigator knew who the foreigner was, we'd never have heard about it either. And I wish we hadn't. I'd rather be in bed."

"With anyone in particular?"

"Not your business, Lyosha." Although said lightheartedly, it was a rebuke.

"What do you make of it, Sergo Vissarionovich?" Orlov asked. He used the formal address in reaction to Chanturia's words, despite their tone. "What was a foreigner doing here with no identification?"

"Maybe he left his hotel without his passport, by mistake."

"And also without his hotel card and his wallet?"

Chanturia sighed. "Did you ever notice, Alexei Ivanovich"— Chanturia used the formal address too, in reaction to Orlov's use of it—"that no one ever understands irony? And in a country with so much of it!"

"Oh."

"I don't know what he was doing here, other than spending an expensive evening with an apparently beautiful Russian woman."

"The son of a bitch."

"Ah, Alyosha, why begrudge our fellow creatures their pleasure when it doesn't lessen our own?"

"Maybe *I* could have been out with this beautiful woman, if it weren't for this foreigner."

"You'd have a hard time explaining to the Comrade Colonel how you could afford a meal at a cooperative cafe on a lieutenant's salary.

8

In the morning we'll see who *can* afford such a thing. Now let's get some sleep. We'll need our wits sharp. But first, call in and have someone contact all the foreigners' hotels in the morning."

"I can have that done right away."

"No. In the morning. By then the maids will know who didn't come home tonight."

· 2 ·

Wednesday, January 18, 1989
9 A.M.
The Lubyanka

CHANTURIA LIKED TO START WITNESS INTERVIEWS WITH THE SMALL FRY and work up to the bigger fish. He often got useful background information that way before the important interviews; and it let the main characters worry a little longer. Worry was a useful activity for a witness.

In this case, he started with a warm-up.

"Maria Petrovna Popova," Chanturia read from the woman's identification card. He looked across the table at her. She was dressed this morning in American blue jeans and a West German sweater that would cost three months' wages from a street trader, although certainly she hadn't got hers from any *fartsovshchik*. There was a lighter streak, perhaps natural, in the mass of dark blond hair that framed her head and shoulders. Her carefully unkempt coiffure gave her a wild look. There were lines at the corners of her blue eyes, and the eyes were tired. She was not used to being up so early. She looked back at him steadily at first, but then the eyes switched away to one side. They always did, sooner or later. She had lasted longer than most.

"Are you still living on Warsaw Prospect?" he asked.

She looked back at him. "That's what it says, isn't it?"

"I didn't ask that."

She waited a while. "You know I'm not."

He made a note. "Are your parents still living there?"

9

"Yes."

"And you?"

Again a pause. "I rent an apartment at 156 Svobodny Prospect."

"You live alone there?"

"Yes."

"How much are you paying?"

"A hundred fifty rubles a month."

Half of a KGB captain's salary. "Who owns the apartment?"

Maria Petrovna's back stiffened. "She's just an old woman. She needs the money. Her pension wouldn't pay for bread and tea, let alone sausage. She went to live with her daughter."

"Her name?"

"She's got nothing to do with this."

"Her name?"

A pause. "Kuzina. Varvara Mikhailovna."

He made another note. "When was the last time you reported to the Committee?"

"I'm sure you have a record."

"When was it?"

Her eyes were icy. "Two nights ago. I gave a report to your officer at the International Hotel. I was with a German."

He made a note to have Orlov look for the record, although he was sure it would be of no interest.

"Is it all right if I smoke?" she asked.

He didn't answer. She started to take a pack of Marlboros out of her bag, then put them back. The bag was black leather, probably French. About two months of his salary there. Another two months, he supposed, for the simple black leather shoes. Simplicity you couldn't buy in a Soviet shoe store.

"What time did you arrive at the cafe last night?"

"About eleven."

"Who were you with?"

"You know that already."

"Who were you with?"

"My friend Elena."

"Her patronymic and family name?"

"Elena Semyonovna Smolenskaya."

"Who else were you with?"

"We were with three Japanese men. I don't know their names. Yukio and somebody and somebody."

"Had you known them before?"

"No."

"Where did you meet them?"

"At the International."

"What were the circumstances?"

"Elena and I were in the bar. One of them came over to talk to us, and then he asked the other two to join us. Then we decided to go out for a late supper."

"Why weren't there three women?"

"We couldn't find anyone else."

"Everyone's busy? Business must be good."

"It's not. You know how expensive it is for us to get into the International now. So we couldn't find anyone else."

"When you arrived at the cafe, who was there at the time? What guests?"

"I didn't notice, really. A group at the big corner table, six or seven. A birthday, I think."

"Soviet or foreign?"

"Soviet. And there were two foreigners at another table."

"Describe them."

"Men. Forty years old. They were speaking German, but one of them wasn't German. His German was terrible."

"Do you speak German?"

"Yes."

"What were they talking about?"

"Us, at first."

"Us?"

"Elena and me."

"What did they say?"

"We were beautiful girls, we shouldn't be out with yellow men . . . the usual things. The German told the other one he probably couldn't afford us, and it was a crime the amount of money the yellow people were making out of this country, and the other one said, 'No more than the Germans are,' and they both laughed."

"Do you speak Japanese?"

"No. *Arigato, sayonara* . . . that's all. Two of the Japanese spoke some Russian, and the other one spoke English."

"Do you speak English?"

"Yes. Not too well."

"You specialize in Germans?"

"I speak German best."

"Was anyone else in the cafe when you arrived?"

11

"Just the staff."

"Describe them."

"The old man guarding the door. The manager. I saw only two waiters. It's a small restaurant."

"Did you know any of the staff?"

"I'd seen them all before. I don't know them."

"Were these all people you'd seen before?"

"Yes."

"Do you go often to this cafe?"

"One or two times a month."

"It must be costly to you."

She looked at Chanturia and smiled. It was a knowing smile, and not friendly; but even so, when she smiled, she was an extremely beautiful woman, and he wondered for an instant how it would be to be able to take such a woman to any cafe in Moscow and not think about the cost.

He asked, "Did anyone else arrive after you?"

"Yes. A man and a woman."

"Describe them."

"She was Russian. Blond, hair longer than shoulder length. Quite beautiful, though her nose was a little long. I don't think she was thirty yet. Her clothes weren't very nice—all Soviet. Maybe she was a patriot."

He ignored the irony. "How was she dressed?"

"Purple trousers, a lavender blouse, horrible imitation-leather shoes. She didn't look as if she belonged with such an expensive man."

"Did you know her?"

"I'd never seen her before."

"Had you seen him before?"

"No."

"Describe him."

"Light-haired, tall, quite good-looking. Thirty-five years old. Wearing a gray wool suit, European. Striped silk tie. Expensive gold wristwatch."

"Was he Russian?"

She laughed. "Where would a Russian have got those clothes? Don't be stupid."

"Where do you get yours?"

"From friends. My girlfriends in the West send them to me."

Chanturia decided not to waste time on this. "So if the man wasn't Russian, what was he, then?"

"I don't know. He spoke Russian to the waiter. But he wasn't Russian."

"What did they talk about—the man and the woman?"

"I couldn't tell. They talked in low voices, but I don't know what about. They weren't in love."

"They weren't in love?"

"That's right. They weren't in love."

"How do you know?"

"I'm in the business of love." She stared at him. She didn't say it, but her eyes did: even a whore can know about love. Chanturia noticed again the lines starting around the corners of her eyes, and he knew—and knew that she must know—that she had not many more years in her present occupation.

"Nothing from the hotels," Orlov said when Chanturia stopped at his office after the first interview. Orlov had a pot of tea and a plate with two Sverdlovsk rolls sprinkled with white powdered sugar. Chanturia's stomach growled. As usual, he hadn't got up in time to eat breakfast.

Orlov dug into a drawer for another cup and pushed the plate across his desk to Chanturia. He always ordered an extra roll for his captain.

"*Spasibo*," Chanturia said. He took a roll and bit into it with his head cocked to keep sugar off his uniform. "Nothing at all?"

"There was an American at the Ukraine who didn't stay in his room last night, but it appears that he went to Stavropol to visit a collective farm and just didn't check out of his room."

"Americans!" Chanturia said. "Who else would keep a hotel room just to leave their luggage in? But are you sure he went to Stavropol?"

"The Agro-Industrial Committee says he got on an airplane with one of their foreign-relations people yesterday evening."

"So we don't know of any missing foreigners."

"Not all the reports are in yet, though. The Kosmos—there's two thousand foreigners there. Always sleeping in each other's beds. Did you learn anything from the interrogation?"

"I learned that the missing girl wasn't a whore, or was just starting to be one. No fancy clothes, and the two with the Japanese didn't know her."

*   *   *

13

Yukio Fujiwara, one of the two Japanese businessmen injured in the attack, turned out to be the Moscow representative for the Kawamoto Corporation. He lived in the apartment building attached to the International Hotel. The other injured Japanese was his assistant. They appeared together to be interviewed. One had a badly cut hand, the other some minor cuts on the forearms and a black eye where he had been knocked to the floor. The third, uninjured, Japanese did not appear. He was uninjured because these two had inserted themselves between him and the assailants. He was a high official of the Kawamoto Corporation, and the Kawamoto Corporation was a supplier of electronics items of such potential importance to the Soviet Union that his tranquility was to be disturbed no more than necessary. Submission to a KGB interview was beyond the necessary.

Chanturia did not mention the whores to Fujiwara or his assistant. He asked, "Did you recognize any of the men who attacked you?"

"No," Fujiwara said with a shake of his head. He looked to his assistant to confirm this. "No," the assistant said.

"Did you recognize anyone else in the cafe?"

"No." "No."

"There was a couple, a man and a woman, seated not far from you. A Western man and a blond Russian woman."

"Yes, I remember the woman." "Yes."

"Had you seen either of them before?"

"No." "No."

"Did you hear anything they talked about?"

"No." "No."

"You know the man was killed?"

"I thought so. It is most unfortunate." "Most unfortunate."

"Did you see him killed?"

"No. We struggled with the men. And then when they were gone, we tried to put the fire out. Then we saw that this man was lying still on the floor." The assistant nodded vigorously.

"Very well. I think that's all. Thank you for your cooperation."

"A pleasure. I understand, by the way, that your organization will make no report of this to the Japanese Embassy or to our company."

"So I understand."

"It would be most appreciated if this is so. And if you need anything . . . some Scotch whiskey, perhaps, some small thing . . ."

"Thank you. I am a person of few needs."

"Ah, I see. So, thank you, then."

"Thank you for your cooperation."

"Thank you." "Thank you."

Statement of Ivan Petrovich Stonov

My name is Ivan Petrovich Stonov. I am 32 years old. I was born on January 17, 1957, in Moscow. I work as a waiter at the restaurant Uzbekistan.

On the night of January 17, 1989, I was at the cooperative cafe "Come In and Taste" on Prospect Mira. I don't often go there, but it was my birthday, and a friend who is a waiter there had arranged for me to have a small birthday party at the cafe. There were six in our party. They were Vyacheslav Fedorovich Arkanov and his wife Vera, Alexandra Ivanovna Syerova, Svetlana Kalinina, and Maxim Nikolayevich Gradski.

At some time after midnight I was startled by the sound of shouting in the entry hall to the cafe, outside the room we were sitting in. I heard a man shouting, "Stop!" and then a scream. Then four men burst into the room. They were wearing black hoods over their faces. Two or more of them were carrying knives. When they came in they slashed out at the people sitting at the tables nearest to them. The closest man was badly stabbed. There were some Asiatic men at the second table from the door, and they jumped up and tried to fight back. They got their arms cut badly. Two of the attackers went to the kitchen door but couldn't get it open. After they banged on it for a few seconds, one of the others told them, "Let's go, let's get out," or words of that sort. He had some kind of accent. I think it was probably Georgian. He and at least two of the others then took bottles of benzine out from under their coats and smashed them on the tables and lighted the benzine. The four of them escaped out the front door.

The fire spread so fast that we couldn't do anything to stop it. My girlfriend tried to call the fire department from the manager's phone, but the phone was not working. The manager was out in the front hall and had been stabbed, but not badly. He got everyone out the front door—all the guests. The kitchen staff must have escaped out the kitchen windows, as they were out in the front when I got outside.

I don't have anything else to add.

(signed)
Ivan Petrovich Stonov

Chanturia looked up from the statement. "So, Stonov, is that your signature?" He showed the waiter the statement.

"Y-Yes."

"You didn't see much, did you?"

"Everything I said there."

"These four men, how tall was the tallest one?"

"Oh, not very tall, I think. Let me see . . . a meter eighty, I would say."

"And the shortest?"

"Not very short. Perhaps a meter seventy."

"The others?"

"In between. Yes, definitely."

"Tending toward the taller, or the shorter?"

"The shorter, I think."

"And how much did this tallest fellow weigh, do you think?"

"Well . . ." Stonov scratched his chin. A real bumpkin, this one, Chanturia concluded. How had he ever got a Moscow residence permit? Bribery, no doubt. The world couldn't be that desperate for waiters. Or could a Muscovite be born a bumpkin?

"Well?"

"Well . . . eighty kilos?"

"Is that a question or an answer?"

"An answer, Comrade Captain, sir. Eighty kilos."

"Not extremely heavy, then?"

"Not extremely. But not extremely light."

"And the others?"

"The same, in proportion. Not extremely anything."

"So, these extremely average persons—what were they wearing?"

"Hoods. As I've said." Stonov put his finger on the line of his statement, turning his head to try to read it upside down—he didn't dare try to turn the paper.

"So you have. And otherwise, they were naked?"

"Naked? Of course not! They were dressed like men!"

"What sort of men? Workingmen? Men ready for a restaurant dinner? Policemen?"

"Policemen? Ha, that would be good! No, no, of course not, Comrade Captain! Like honest workingmen, that's how."

"Honest workingmen dressed to repair a street, or . . . ?"

"No, no. For an office, maybe. I really don't remember: it was such a shock, what they were doing, that I looked at that, and not their

16

clothes. But I didn't see anything to notice, if you understand me. They were all dressed very much alike, very much like everyone else."

"Except for the hoods."

"Yes, of course, except for that."

"This one who spoke—which one was he?"

"Not the tallest, not the shortest."

"Did he seem to be the leader?"

"Only in that he spoke. Otherwise, they all seemed to have assignments. Two came forward, and two stayed back by the door at first. As if guarding it."

"The one who spoke. Anything at all unusual about him?"

"Yes. As I've said"—the waiter's finger tapped at the paper again, and he looked for the spot—"his accent. He wasn't Russian. He sounded . . ." The waiter stopped, looked up from the paper, though his finger did not leave it. He looked at Chanturia's face.

"He sounded . . . ?"

The waiter did not answer, so Chanturia took the paper from under the waiter's hand and read from it. "Georgian."

"Yes." The waiter didn't look up. His hand still rested on the desk where the paper had been.

"Do you know a Georgian accent when you hear it?"

"Yes, of course. I hear all kinds of people in my work. Your Russian is, of course, much better than his was, Comrade Captain. I don't know if I'd say you had an accent, even. But he was Georgian. I'm sure of that."

The sweet bluntness of the Russian peasant, Chanturia reflected. Any sensible person, faced with a Georgian captain of the KGB, would hastily modify the rash words of his statement. But here was this waiter, sticking to it. Probably he hadn't brains enough to think up a better story. So, probably he was right. At least one Georgian was involved in this mess—besides a captain of the KGB.

"This man who was stabbed," Chanturia said; "did they single him out for attack?"

"I don't think so. It appeared that he was just convenient—he was close to the door."

"What did he look like?"

"Well, he was about the size of the biggest of the four attackers. I noticed that when he got up."

"When did he get up?"

"After he was slashed the first time. He stood up, and then the man stabbed him in the side, and he just doubled over and fell."

"Did he say anything when he was stabbed?"

"Something, but I didn't hear what it was exactly."

"What language did he say it in?"

"Oh, it was in Russian. He was a foreigner, of course; but he spoke good Russian."

"How do you know he was a foreigner?"

Stonov adopted a hurt look. "I am a waiter at the restaurant Uzbekistan, as my statement says. I have seen foreigners."

As punishment for the tone of Stonov's voice, Chanturia asked, "How much do you earn as a waiter?"

Stonov answered cautiously: "A hundred fifty rubles a month."

"Is that enough to pay for a party for six at a cooperative cafe?"

"Well . . . as I said, I have a friend there."

"And you earn a little extra in tips, I suppose?"

Stonov shrugged. Tips were not exactly legal; but, of course, everyone got them, and there was no use denying it.

"And sometimes some hard currency?"

"No. I wouldn't keep any of that, of course. It's against the law."

"Of course. Now, this foreigner, what did he look like? You started to describe him."

"Well, he was nice enough looking. Though the woman with him seemed not to care about him especially."

"What did he look like?"

"Didn't they let you see the body?"

"What did he look like?"

"Well . . . he had light brown hair. Regular features—strong chin, I think. Nice enough looking, as I've said. He had on an expensive suit—nice wool. You couldn't get one like it for a thousand rubles."

"Is that all?"

"I don't recall anything else."

"What country do you think he was from?"

"That's harder. He was dressed European, but he didn't seem European, really. He might have been American."

"Why do you think so?"

"Well . . . he was friendly with the waiters. Europeans, they order waiters around, think they're too good to have to be considerate. Americans are more like us; everybody's all on one level . . . even if they do have more money than we do."

"Do you speak English?"

"Not much. Enough to wait on people who speak English."

"Did he ever speak English, that you heard?"

"No."

Chanturia tapped his pen against his notepad. "You said the woman didn't like him?"

"I said she didn't like him *especially*. Maybe they didn't know each other well. She was friendly enough, but not warm. Not . . . familiar."

"Was she a foreigner too?"

"Oh, no! She was Russian."

"What did she look like?"

"A beauty. Blond, dark eyes. Nicely dressed—sort of lavender pants and blouse. Not dressed like a whore, you know, but like a good Russian girl. And a real beauty." Stonov closed his eyes and smiled. "She had a butt like a peach. You know?"

Chanturia pretended not to know. "When he was stabbed, what did she do? Did she call out a name, or . . . ?"

"Well, that was a little strange. No, she didn't call out or anything. She looked around . . . she might have been looking for help, but it was more as if she was looking to see who was watching. And then she ran out."

"Out where?"

"Out the door. Right past the two men there, and out the door. I didn't see her again after that."

Chanturia turned again to Stonov's statement. "These other people in your party—who are they?"

"Well . . ." Stonov pointed to his statement for its support. "There was Shura . . ."

"That would be Alexandra Ivanovna Sycrova?" Chanturia asked, scanning the names in the statement.

"That's right."

"Tell me about her."

"Ah!" Stonov said, rolling his eyes. "Talk about a peach butt! And *siski* like melons! And—"

"That's not exactly what I meant."

"No? Oh. Well, she's a meter sixty-four tall . . ."

"No. What's her relationship to you?"

"Relationship? We're not related. Oh, I see what you're asking. Sure, she'll do it once in a while. Worth the effort, too."

"She's your girlfriend?"

"Right."

"How long have you known her?"

"Nine months. I met her in Pushkin Square. Slava said to me, 'Look at the *siski* on that one,' and I looked, and . . . it was love at

19

first sight. Took me three months to get her into bed, she was that stuck on herself; but it was worth the effort."

"Slava would be Vyacheslav Fedorovich Arkanov?" Chanturia asked, again referring to the statement.

"That's right. He's a waiter. Like me. We went to waiter's school together. He works parties at the Kremlin. He got me on there once, but I told him I'd rather work at the Uzbek as a general thing. The glory is nice, of course, at the Kremlin, but . . ." He seemed not to know where to go from there.

"But you can't eat glory?" Chanturia prompted him.

"You understand the workers, Comrade Captain."

"Where does Shura work?"

"She's a hairdresser. The shop across from the telegraph office on Gorky Street."

"All right. And the other people in your party? There was Arkanova, she's Slava's wife?"

"Yes, of course. Vera."

"What does she do?"

"She keeps a floor at the hotel Friendship of the Peoples."

"A foreigner's hotel?"

"Yes . . . but from socialist countries only. No capitalists."

"Maybe someday she'll get a promotion. The Ukraine. The Intourist."

"Why not the International, as long as we're dreaming?" Stonov said. "She has a friend who manages a floor there. The gifts that woman gets from *biznesmen* . . . pantyhose, cosmetics! One single Western lipstick—a week's wages. And she doesn't even have to do anything for them!" He stopped, then added hastily, "She doesn't sell anything, of course. That would be illegal."

"Of course. And these other two in your party?"

Stonov was suddenly shy. "Ah. I don't know them so well. Sveta . . ."

"That would be Svetlana Kalinina?"

"Yes. She's Arkanov's cousin. She was going to be a ballet dancer, but she broke an ankle, and it didn't heal correctly at first, and now she's an English translator."

"For whom?"

"The Chemicals Institute, I think. She translates technical articles. Sometimes she does work for foreign businessmen. To make ends meet, you know. She's divorced, she's got a boy by her marriage, she has to support him."

20

Chanturia made a note. Then he asked, "The man she was with wasn't her husband, then?"

"No. She should be so lucky."

"Maxim Nikolayevich Gradski? What's lucky about Max?"

"His father's the First Deputy Minister of Machine Building."

Chanturia wished life could stay uncomplicated; but somehow it never seemed to. "What does this First Deputy Minister's son do for a living?"

Stonov was suddenly cagey. "I don't know exactly."

"How did you meet him, then?"

"I just met him at my party. He came with Sveta."

"Sveta whom you don't know so well?"

"Well, she's Arkanov's cousin. So of course she was welcome."

"Of course. Still, a party at a cooperative restaurant . . . Every guest adds a little bit to the reckoning?"

"I was glad to do it for her."

"And for her friend, the First Deputy Minister's son."

"Of course."

"Of course. You don't know *exactly* what this First Deputy Minister's son does for a living. What do you think he does, approximately?"

"I don't know."

"You spent all evening with him, consuming three bottles of champagne and two of vodka among the six of you, and he didn't mention anything about what he does?"

His statement hadn't specified any liquor consumption, and so it made Stonov apprehensive that the captain had the numbers right, as close as Stonov could recall. "I think he said he was an engineer. It wasn't important. I didn't press him. It would have been impolite."

As it happened, Chanturia had only estimated the number of bottles of drink consumed at Stonov's birthday party. Not that it was any great feat: at any occasion involving three Russian men, two bottles of vodka would have gone down in the course of the evening. And any birthday party demanded champagne.

Svetlana Kalinina turned out to be a dish. She moved like an ex-ballet dancer. She had red hair but Oriental eyes—some Tatar heritage there, not too many generations back.

"I'm glad to see your ankle has healed," Chanturia said as she took a seat across the table from him.

"You know about that?" she asked, without surprise, but obviously uncomfortable with his words.

21

The trouble with his job, he reflected for the thousandth time, was that any show of personal knowledge about someone always made them nervous. "Your friend Stonov mentioned it."

"My cousin's friend," she said.

"How well do you know him?"

"Not well. Mainly through Slava."

"Slava is your cousin, Arkanov?"

"Yes." She was cautious with her words, and she clearly thought his effort to put her at ease was a ploy—which, of course, it was. At the same time, it was genuine. That was the hard part of his work—staying real in a job that demanded that he pretend to be real.

"Where do you work, Comrade Kalinina?" he asked, becoming more formal than necessary in the hope that it would make her more comfortable. But she was certainly entitled to the formality: she was a Party member.

Instead, she seemed to take is as hostility. She said stiffly, "I am employed by the Scientific Research Institute of Organic Chemistry."

"You're a translator there?"

"I am."

"Where do you normally work?"

"I work at home. I go to the Institute to receive texts, but I do most of the work at home. I have a good library there."

"You're fortunate."

"No. It's taken me eight years to build it up."

"I believe you also work as an interpreter for foreign businessmen?"

"On occasion I do, at the request of the U.S.S.R. Chamber of Commerce and Industry."

"How often do you work for them?"

"That varies greatly. Sometimes several days a week, sometimes once a month."

"I suppose the foreigners you work for are mainly in the chemicals industry?"

"Not really. Interpreting isn't often technical work. Presently I'm working with a company trying to sell shoes here."

"What is this company's name?"

"United Shoe. An American company."

"Whom do you work with from this company?"

"Their international sales chief, and his assistant."

"Their names?"

"Ronald James is the chief, and his assistant is Jeff Millington."

"Ridiculous names these foreigners have. Don't any of them have fathers?"

"Presumably. But they don't memorialize them in the children's names."

"When did you last see either of these men?"

"Last week. They come and go. They're to return in four weeks."

"What success are they having?"

"None. Our country can't afford foreign shoes, as you know." Suddenly she spoke heatedly. "It's a scandal! It's a worse scandal that we should need to buy foreign shoes. 'Arrange to buy something from us,' our buyers tell the foreigners. 'Then we'll discuss buying your shoes.' But what do we have that a foreign company will buy? Nothing! Exactly nothing! It's a scandal, but it's so."

He was surprised at this outburst, which seemed to have caused her to forget her discomfort. "It seems that you take your business engagements quite personally."

She snorted. "I take my shoes quite personally, that's all." She turned sideways in her chair and put one foot out beyond the side of the table so that he could see it. "I broke a heel on my boot, on our socialist sidewalk, just outside here on Kirov Street. Our sidewalks are in terrible repair."

"Our climate is not equable, of course."

"I worked for a year at our consulate in Canada, where the climate is no more equable. The sidewalks aren't falling apart *there*, I can assure you."

Chanturia resolutely put aside any thought of discussing the West. "How did you come to be at the cooperative cafe Come In and Taste last night?"

"My cousin invited me. His friend Stonov was giving a party and wanted me to come."

"Since Stonov is not your friend, as you said, why did he want you to come?"

"I don't know."

"Did it have anything to do with your friendship with Maxim Nikolayevich Gradski?"

She looked him in the eye. "I don't know."

"How long have you known Maxim Nikolayevich?"

"About a year."

"All right. Tell me what you observed at the cafe."

She described the events briefly and, from what he now knew,

23

quite accurately. "The attackers were entirely precise," she added. "It was like a military operation."

"Have you seen military operations?"

"Of course not. That's merely a figure of speech. If it disturbs you, just say they were precise. Methodical."

"The man who was killed, had you seen him before?"

"I had not."

"Did anything about him make an impression on you?"

"I'm not sure what you mean. He was a foreigner, of course . . ."

"Are you sure?"

"Yes, of course."

"What sort of foreigner?"

"Not German—he didn't have a German accent. His Russian was very good, but I believe he was an English-speaker. He had that accent—something of a sweet sound in his u's. But, of course, I didn't listen closely to him. There was no reason to."

"What did you hear him say?"

"Just orders to the waiter."

"How did he act with the waiter?"

"What do you mean?"

"Was there anything strange about it? Anything that would make you think he was from one country or another?" It was a hint Chanturia had picked up from Stonov. Maybe it was nothing; but even from clay, sometimes a clever man could make something.

"Oh, I see." She thought, and thinking seemed to relax her. "He didn't act like a German or an Englishman with the waiter. I think he was American."

"Why do you think that?"

"Americans are like Russians: not too proud to be friendly with waiters."

Chanturia made a note. "The woman who was with him, was she a foreigner?"

"No, she was Russian."

"What did she do during the attack, and after?"

"I didn't see, especially. I wasn't watching her: I was watching the men with the weapons and torches. She screamed . . . not screamed, exactly, but gave a little shriek, a gasp, when they stabbed him. I don't know what happened after that. We all pushed to get outside, and I didn't see her there."

"The attackers—can you describe them?"

"I see you have my statement. I described them for the investigator."

"Yes; but think if there's anything you can add."

She shook her head.

"One of them reportedly spoke with an accent. Did you observe that?"

"Yes."

"Would you say it was a Georgian accent?"

She looked at him. There was in her eyes—what? Not fear. Caution. "I don't know."

"You're a translator. You must have an ear for language. Yes, I am Georgian too. But I ask only your professional opinion."

She almost smiled. "I would say it was a Georgian accent."

"I appreciate your cooperation." He made a note.

As he was writing she said, "Oh, and there was one other thing."

He looked up. "Yes?"

"The Georgian—if he was. He limped."

Chanturia looked at her thoughtfully. "No one else has mentioned that."

"He was trying not to show it. But I'm quite sure." She did smile. "It's my professional opinion. I'm a dancer. I was a dancer."

He smiled back. "You've been very helpful, Comrade Kalinina." He made several notes, then returned his attention to her. "Now, about your friend Gradski."

Her smile was gone. She waited.

He waited too. At length she asked, "What about him?"

"You said you've known Gradski for a year?"

"Approximately."

"What's the nature of your relationship?"

"We're friends." She had seemed to hesitate.

"What does 'friends' mean?"

"Friends means friends."

"You're divorced?"

"Yes. Does that mean I can't have friends? Is my personal life part of this investigation?"

As Chanturia watched her friendly attitude toward him turn and vanish, he regretted his occupation yet once more. "I'd like to understand why Gradski, who was unknown to Ivan Petrovich Stonov, was invited to Stonov's very expensive birthday party."

"He wasn't. I was invited, and told I could bring a guest."

"Stonov is a generous man. And was Gradski the nearest friend you could think of to invite to this expensive party?"

"I don't often go out since my husband left me. Maxim is a friend."

25

She said this with great force. He wished she had looked him squarely in the eye when she said it.

"He was supposed to be here this morning for an interview, along with you and others. He hasn't come. Do you know why?"

She looked away. "No. No, I don't."

It was hard to understand Orlov with his mouth half full of a salami-and-cheese sandwich. Chanturia couldn't face a salami-and-cheese, and even the KGB cafeteria couldn't seem to do better than that these days. This part of winter was when longing for Georgia became physical—a food-longing, a desperate desire for a little bit of fresh fruit and maybe a tomato. His longing made Chanturia angry. "Don't talk with your mouth full," he said. Then he regretted sounding like Orlov's mother; but Orlov was used to obeying superior officers. He swallowed and repeated himself: "Maxim Nikolayevich must think Papa will protect him. He got the same notice as everyone else." But Maxim Nikolayevich Gradski, who had got the same notice as everyone else in the cafe, still had not arrived to be interviewed.

"If he thinks that," Chanturia said, "he will learn that he is wrong." He longed for a pomegranate.

"What happened? Some witness didn't show up?" This from an old man who had sat down at the same table with them. Chanturia knew him slightly. He was a pensioner, a captain long retired who had been tossed a consulting task which he used as an excuse to come into headquarters for the cheap meals and a chance to talk shop.

"*Some witness* is right," Orlov said. "Son of a First Deputy Minister. What do you expect?"

"Nothing," the old man said. "I expect nothing, these days, with the country going to ruin. First Deputy Minister! In my time I'd have had the son and the old man both in a holding cell. And now a Committee man can't even be safe in his own home! What times these are!"

"What do you mean?" Orlov asked.

"What do I mean? Let me tell you. I live back on Dorogomilov Street, not far from the Kiev Station—an old house, true, but always quiet and peaceful. Built for the Committee, in fact. I moved there right after the end of the war, and every head of family in the building was with the Committee. And now?" He swept his hand downward, a sign of the fallen state of the world. "All gone but me. And the rest of the people there now, they're long-haired punks. I get notes under

26

my door; threatening. My wife's afraid to go out at night. We have to double-bolt the door to get a nap of sleep. That's what the world's come to! Ignoring a notice to appear! Who could have imagined?''

Nobody could have imagined, Chanturia knew. The KGB had no official power to summon witnesses, of course: that was a power of the Procurator, the state investigator. But that was only a nicety. In the old days, nobody would have ignored a KGB request to appear. Almost nobody. There was the case of the militiamen who had killed an officer of the KGB—off duty, true—and the two bureaucracies had fought it out for months before the investigation actually proceeded; but that was different. Maxim Gradski didn't have a police ministry behind him. He was just the spoiled kid of a high official, a spoiled kid who needed a little salutary fear.

Chanturia was instantly ashamed of the thought. The thought of a true KGB man, he reflected. How his mother would mock him if she knew of it.

· 3 ·

Wednesday, January 18, 1989
4 P.M.
The United States Embassy

AT THE WINDOW OF AN APARTMENT IN THE NEW RESIDENTIAL SECTION OF the American Embassy, Ben Martin sat leafing through a Soviet newspaper, trying not to look out at the snow sifting down over the Moscow River, and wondering when it would stop, and knowing the answer was several months away.

Rollie Taglia knocked at the door. Martin knew it was Rollie by the knock: the first half of "shave and a haircut"—no bits.

Rollie came in without waiting for an invitation, which was standard. Rollie was the Deputy Chief of Mission, second only to the Ambassador, but he didn't stand on ceremony. He showed no surprise at finding Martin there. "Hello, Professor," he said. "Where's Hutch?" The apartment belonged to Charles Hutchins.

"I was hoping you could tell me."

"How can I tell anything to a professor from a major Eastern university?"

"*Near*-major Eastern university," Martin corrected him, smiling. "The only way to be offensive is to keep the facts straight."

"He said he'd be here at three-thirty."

Martin didn't need to look at his watch to know the time. Dark was settling over Moscow. At this time of year, that meant 4:00 P.M. After a year and a half thinking about it, Martin still couldn't find a sufficient excuse for dark to fall at that hour, at any time of year. "He's not in his office," Martin said. "I checked there. His number two said he's 'out.' "

"Number two? Who's that? Number two what?"

"Denson. Number two spook."

"You're not cleared to know that."

"Excuse me. 'Assistant Agriculture Attaché Denson' says his boss, the agriculture attaché, is out."

"That's better. *That* you might be cleared to know."

Martin was an irregular at the Embassy, an assistant cultural attaché by special appointment, and after more than a year there he knew he would never be cleared to know anything, let alone where the spooks were hidden on the Embassy staff. At least he wouldn't be cleared to know anything officially. Actually knowing was a different matter. It was impossible to be the friend of a man like Hutch and not know how he earned his living. Hutch was agriculture attaché at the Embassy, a grown-up kid from Des Moines, Iowa, who knew all about corn and cows. But Martin had come to realize that Hutch also knew a lot about Soviet politics for a grown-up kid whose specialty was corn and cows. Hutch didn't talk about his work, other than the corn and the cows; but even a special assistant cultural attaché with no specialty other than Russian literature found it hard to miss the point.

Martin was never sorry he liked Hutchins so much, but teaching Russian literature at a near-major Eastern university wasn't a background that made it easy to be friends with a probable spook. He consoled himself by supposing that Hutch was an improbable probable spook. For one thing, he really was an expert on corn and cows, from Des Moines, Iowa; and who could dislike a guy like that? Still, he wasn't a guy you could introduce to your friends at a near-major Eastern university. Friendship with him was a guilty pleasure, which Martin justified by concluding that if Hutch was an improbable spook, he himself was an improbable diplomat, even for an irregular by special appointment.

Martin considered his special appointment one of those strange fates that happen to people when they should have been being careful.

At the university where he taught Russian literature, an emergency faculty senate meeting had been called to ward off approaching calamity: a student group had invited the President of the United States to speak at the university, and the President had shown the poor taste to accept.

Martin was the only faculty member to oppose banning the President, against the multitudes who urged that an evil-doer (*exempli gratia*, the President of the United States) should not be allowed to disgrace with his presence such a center of learning and civility as theirs. The university overruled the student group's invitation.

A year later, Martin had been astonished to find his name on the short list of persons being considered for appointment to an experimental program of cultural exchanges between the embassies of the United States and the Soviet Union. The program was a professorial exchange—one Soviet specialist in American literature for one American specialist in Russian. The two were to study freely, to absorb the ambience of their respective countries of destination, to promote other scholarly exchanges and programs, to spread goodwill and scholarly fellow-feeling, and to help the staffs of their respective embassies better appreciate the artistic life of the host country. Being of a different political persuasion from his government, Martin was not only surprised to find his name on the list, but even more surprised to be informed that he had been chosen. He did not know the reason until later.

"What's in *Izvestia?*" Rollie wondered. "Anybody getting into Raisa's knickers?"

"If so, they haven't reported it." Martin tossed the paper to Taglia and got up to stretch. Winter evening in Moscow could be a lead weight on the soul. "Moscow Nights": the song was a lot better than the reality. The test of true art, he supposed. He wandered along the opposite wall of the room, looking at the pictures Hutchins had hung there. Martin had seen them all before—had been at the buying of many of them. They were all recent and anonymous. Hutchins liked to find live artists to buy things from. "If it's more than forty years old, you can't take it home without an export permit," he would say, "and why should they give one to an ag attaché? Anyway, it's our

29

duty to fan any spark of creativity we see in the darkness." On the same theory, he also bought only cheap stuff. "Artists need appreciation. If it's expensive, it's already appreciated. Let's help out the guys nobody is looking at." Nevertheless, what he had ended up with was an art gallery.

"Wow, did you see this?" Taglia asked from deep in the back pages of *Izvestia*.

"I didn't see anything that exciting. What is it?"

"Arson. Murder. Criminality. Everything but sex, dammit." He read with Tagliaesque dramatics:

Assault with Arson; or, Drama on a January Night

In the night of 17–18 January, at 0045, several persons unknown rang at the door of the cooperative cafe Come In and Taste on Prospect Mira in Moscow. This cafe was working in the regime as late as any client stays. We mean it *was* working; because after that night visit unfortunately it is not possible to have guests there anymore.

Unknown persons to whom the door was opened tried to apply knife wounds to the administrator on duty at the time. . . .

"Wait!" Martin said. " 'Apply knife wounds?' "

"That's what it says," Taglia told him.

Martin looked at the paper and shook his head. "Go on. What happened to our unfortunate administrator?"

Rollie continued to read:

He fortunately ducked and got only a small cut. After that the assailants wounded with knives several foreign guests of the cafe (payments in the cafe are made not only in rubles but by credit cards as well) and pushed them into the closet. Next they broke into the main halls and threw bottles with gasoline. The fire started . . .

Trying to escape the assault, the personnel (mainly women were working in the cafe that day) blocked themselves in the kitchen. They could not call for help anywhere—the telephone was already cut off . . .

When, breaking the bars on the windows, the personnel got out into the back yard, the assailants were already gone, firemen and policemen were standing at the entrance, the fire was being controlled. The wounded were hospitalized, their lives were out of danger. As the chief of the department of the state fire brigade of Moscow fire security, E. Lobanov, said, the alarm about the fire in the cafe came in at 0051. Within nine minutes, the fire brigade of six machines was at the scene. At 0123 the fire was localized and at 0132 liquidated.

As E. Lobanov said, in recent times this is the second case of setting a fire in a cooperative cafe. The first one was in December of last year in the October district of the capital.

"As best we can tell, we got in the millstone of clarifying relations between two hostile criminal groups," said the chairman of the cooperative, Anatoli Rutkovski. "Otherwise, it's difficult to explain the vandalism that burned our cafe. I think that the investigation will clarify all this and will establish the purpose of the assault on our cooperative.

"The purposefulness of the actions of the assailants is astonishing, everything was being done as if by a score. I'm deeply convinced that those who destroyed the cafe have been here before more than once: they oriented themselves very well, knew where to cut the communication lines, how to block the exits.

"We will redo the cafe exactly as it was. And it was one of the most beautiful and popular places in the capital. The interior alone was very valuable: in Russian, Georgian, and maritime styles. We'll have to rebuild all this. The district authorities are helping us, the bank is giving credit, we are supported—we'll continue to work as a trader-buyer and production cooperative. And we're sure the cafe, after the reconstruction, after two months, will again host guests, including foreigners. Also, we don't reject the establishment of a planned Soviet-Finnish service joint venture. In short, we will not allow any kind of bandits to triumph!"

The investigation of the case of the firing of the cooperative cafe Come In and Taste is being performed by the office of the Procurator of the Dzerzhinsky district of Moscow. Here the opinion is that it is too early to make any preliminary conclusions about what happened. The investigation is being performed in close coordination with departments of MUR (Moscow criminal investigation department), expert institutions, and other organizations.

"Other organizations!" Martin said. "Are they *still* afraid to say KGB?"

"A cautious person is protected by God," Taglia answered, quoting a Russian proverb. "But what do you think about it?"

"I think your Russian is definitely improving. Unfortunately, your English is execrable. 'Working in the regime as late as any client stays'—is that what it says? 'Apply knife wounds to the administrator'?"

"Don't talk like a professor," Taglia said. "Nobody likes professors."

"Where I come from, everybody likes professors."

"In Wis*con*sin?"

"Being from Wisconsin isn't a lifetime occupation. Now my home is the world of learning."

"New *Jersey?*"

"Wherever I am."

"Wherever it is, it sounds like a good place to be from and not at. I'm glad I missed the occasion. Even if I did miss the chance to learn beautiful Russian."

"Your Russian's not bad. It's creative."

"It's not my fault anyway. It's the damn Soviet influence. I can't help the way Soviet Russian is put together."

Martin picked up the paper and scanned the article. "Well, you've got a point," he admitted. " 'Clarifying relations between two hostile criminal groups!' There's nothing like a Molotov cocktail to clarify relations. What do you suppose it was really about?"

"I'd say *Izvestia* is telling half the truth."

"As usual?"

"Different. No political motive for leaving out half, this time."

"Hutch says there's always a political motive."

"Yes, but this isn't the usual political motive. No propaganda purpose. They just failed to see the fact, or didn't want to admit it."

"This unseen, or unseemly, fact being . . . ?"

"That there was only one 'hostile criminal group' involved."

"You mean it's the protection racket, rather than a gang war."

"Sure. Wealthy cooperative refuses to pay, and gets burned out. What else?"

"I don't know," Martin said. As an irregular at the Embassy it was his prerogative to admit ignorance without any penalty. He walked back to the window, where he stood looking out on the gray twilight of Moscow at four o'clock in the afternoon. At first, through the falling snow, he could see only the lights of the office building of the Russian Republic, a white tombstone planted on the near bank of the river, just across the street. For a moment the veil of snow

32

parted, and over the shoulder of the Russian Republic building he could make out the shape of the Ukraine Hotel tower across the river, a kilometer distant. He had been there within the past week. He thought with a chill of the little clutch of long-distance trucks from sister socialist countries that had been huddled, as always, at the hotel's feet in the wind-swept parking spaces along the Shevchenko Embankment. Then the veil fell again, blanking out not only the hotel and the river, but even the lights of the Russian Republic building. The snow had been falling since Thanksgiving and was likely to continue till the Ides of March, he supposed. After which it would turn to a foot of slush, to be tracked into the depths of every building in Moscow. As a boy in Wisconsin, he had loved winter, the bright cold of the birch woods bound in snow. It was one of the things—what foolish things a life is made of!—that had drawn him to Russian literature: the vast empty cold of the *les,* the Russian forest. But now he saw that Russian literature about winter wasn't really about winter.

The blizzard cries like a gypsy violin, the poet Yesenin said—but that poem was really about a woman. *The birch trees dressed in white cry in the forest*—that about death, the poet's own. *A funereal blizzard cries at the window.* The sadness of the Russian soul, trapped in winter. The point wasn't winter; it was sadness. Winter was the real world read as metaphor.

Now he hated winter. No, not hated it—was desperate for it to end. In only his second year, by this time of year in Moscow, he was desperate for winter to end.

He turned away from the cold darkness. "What were you asking?"

Taglia pointed to the newspaper. "What could it be, if not the protection racket?"

"I don't know."

Taglia took the paper. "Here the opinion is that it is too early to make any preliminary conclusions," he translated again.

Martin ignored this little joke. "The foreigners—who were they?"

"Lnu Fnu," Taglia said. "Last name unknown, first name unknown. *Izvestia* doesn't seem to care. You seen one foreigner, you've seen 'em all." He folded the paper and put in back on the chair where Martin had been sitting. "It's got to be protection. A cooperative starts to make real money, and the Mafia comes wanting its share."

"A bit cheeky of them, though, to begin by taking out foreigners."

"We don't know where they *started*," Taglia pointed out. "They may have been making low-level threats before this. This is just the

33

first thing to make the papers. And a year ago, it would never have been published at all."

"A year ago, the cooperative wouldn't have existed," Martin said.

"It does my capitalist heart good," Taglia said.

"To see a new generation of Communist millionaires being made?"

"No. To see the authorities admitting that crime does exist in the Worker's Paradise. Not one, but two—or more—*competing* 'hostile criminal groups'! It's just like New Jersey."

Martin ignored the remark. "Ask Hutchins who did it," he suggested. "He gets paid for knowing this sort of thing. At least maybe he'll know who the foreigners were. Where is he when we need him?"

"Out making indigenous contacts, I hope. Looking at cornfields, like a good agriculture attaché. You're right: the CIA should do something about things like this. Racketeers slaying foreign citizens in the heart of Moscow!"

· 4 ·

Wednesday, January 18, 1989
Evening
Lenin Prospect

HIS APARTMENT SMELLED OF FRESH-MADE BORSHCH: TANYA HAD LET HER-self in. She called from the kitchen, "Supper's almost ready." He was surprised she was there—she didn't often come two days in a row—but glad. Otherwise, supper would have been yesterday's bread.

While they ate, she talked about the successes of her day: "Marina had some new mascara in her department; she owed me six boxes, so I took two and then I went to Yeliseyev's and got the chocolates the manager's been holding for me. Sonya wants some, and she'll have spring hats soon. He would have taken more mascara and given me a credit, but I think I can do better with it. But he was saving some nice sausages, so I thought we'd have them in borshch while they're still fresh. Do you like it?"

He did.

Another thing Chanturia liked about Tanya, perhaps the thing he liked best of all, was that she had absolutely no curiosity about his work. She had met him through his work, and she didn't care to think about it any further.

He had been assigned to investigate illegal foreign currency trading. Soviet citizens were reported to be exchanging things for hard currency (that is, for foreign, non-socialist, money). A witness had connected Tanya to the sale of an icon for American dollars.

She was ordered to appear at his office for questioning.

Typical of Russian women in their thirties, she had more of everything than she once had; but nothing was out of proportion. She was round as a ball, but muscular rather than fat. Her short curled hair, currently blond, set off an appealing face.

It was evident at a glance—Italian sweater and earrings, smell of French perfume—that she didn't live on her salary as a cosmetics saleswoman at the Central Universal Store. But she denied having sold any icons. There was no hard evidence. Eventually the case trailed off into nothing, and Chanturia closed his file.

He would never have thought of her again if he had not gone to a restaurant with friends on a Saturday night a few weeks later. When he first came up to Moscow, he spent most of his free weekend nights in restaurants; but he had grown tired of it and lately rarely left home. But this week a friend was visiting from Tbilisi, and entertainment was required. The Tbilisi lad's highest goal was to get laid by a Russian woman, and so they went to the Arbat Restaurant for the broadest selection.

The usual drill was for several men drinking together to look around the room for a table of two to four women looking around the room. With eye contact established, a distant toast was offered to the women, and if it was accepted the waiter was sent over with a bottle of champagne. The champagne was followed by an offer to dance, discreet discussion of pairings, and a consolidation of chairs.

But tonight, before they had a chance even to study the room, a bottle of champagne appeared at their table. Chanturia looked around in surprise and found himself caught by Tanya's eyes a few tables over. She raised a glass to him.

His friends whooped and pounded his back.

He had no choice but to invite her to dance. By the time they returned to her table, his friends had moved in. The numbers matched; the pairings seemed to be acceptable; there was nothing he could do but continue to dance.

She was light on her feet; she was volubly friendly; her sense of humor matched her figure—copious, but not out of proportion. After some time they went back to his table and sat alone there. "Are you still chasing icons?" she asked him.

"People are in danger of prison any day now."

"Well, I haven't any myself. You can come search my apartment if you don't believe me."

Not much later, his friends waved goodbye from the other table.

Later, he did go to her apartment. She had no icons. What she had was an apartment that put his own to shame—three rooms in the middle of Moscow, full of Finnish furniture, Czech crystal, and wardrobes full of clothes. He tried to back out then; the only source he could imagine for her wealth was prostitution, and he said so. She laughed at him. "I don't need men's money," she said. "I have my 'deficit exchange club.' "

"What's that?"

"For a KGB officer," she said, "you're not very well educated."

Tanya worked selling cosmetics. Cosmetics were always in deficit— customers wanted more than the Union produced or imported. Good products were sold out within minutes. So Tanya and her fellow workers regularized supply and demand. Tanya saved back a few things for her friends; and in exchange her friends supplied her with the goods they had access to. One had Italian sweaters, one had winter coats, one had access to mayonnaise. It took years to build a network of dependable contacts. Tanya was still building hers—a business within the business of the Central Universal Store.

Her speculation was on the edge of legality; but it wasn't a KGB matter. It was what people did to live.

Chanturia, as he soon came to understand, was part of her business plan. Chanturia had access to the Party stores reserved for special people, including the KGB.

Not that Tanya was all business. She didn't want another husband—one boss at a time was too many for her—but she did want a friendly man in her bed from time to time. It was a business principle which she carried over into her personal life to give more than she got, as Chanturia soon discovered. She made sure he never felt that he was just another part of her deficit exchange club.

She took to coming one or two nights a week to his apartment and made him welcome to come to hers. But, except for goods from the Party stores, she kept him separate from her business life, and kept herself from his. She wanted life regular but unencumbered.

36

· 5 ·

Thursday, January 19, 1989
10:30 A.M.
The Lubyanka

THE CAFE MANAGER, LEV BOK, MIGHT HAVE BEEN TREMBLING FROM THE cold. He had been kept waiting all the previous day and part of this morning in a bare, windowless room in the Lubyanka. It was a cold room, but the Lubyanka—the KGB headquarters, and prison—was a building that made Muscovites uneasy just to pass by.

Bok's hands still trembled a barely noticeable amount as he sat across the table waiting for Chanturia to finish reading his statement given to the militia. Chanturia, however, had read the statement before he entered the room, and now instead of reading it he secretly watched Bok's hands, which shook in a small rotary motion on two-second cycles: three quick jerks and a pause, three quick jerks and a pause.

Without looking up from the statement, Chanturia asked, "How many of these raiders did you recognize?"

"How . . . how many? Not any! It doesn't say there that I recognized any, surely?"

Chanturia looked up. "It's your statement, is it not? Here is your signature at the bottom. Is that your signature?"

Lev Bok affirmed that it was. "But I didn't tell the officer that I recognized any of them!"

"We're not discussing what you told the officer. I asked how many of them you recognized."

"But they were masked, hooded . . ."

"A mask doesn't disguise someone you know well, however."

"Why would anyone I know attack my cafe?"

"I don't know the answer to that. I'm only asking how many of them you recognized, and you're not answering my question."

"I've told you that I didn't know any of them."

"No, you haven't. Is that your testimony?"

37

"It's there in my statement, I'm sure."

"But is it your testimony now?"

"Yes, of course it is."

"Very well. Let's proceed, then. And if you cease evading my questions, this will go much more quickly, Citizen Bok."

The pause in Bok's trembling hands had shortened from two seconds to one. "But I assure you I wasn't trying to evade answering! I was simply—"

Chanturia cut him off. "What Mafia group do you pay for protection?"

The manager's hands stopped still. "I don't understand." The hands resumed their movement as he spoke.

"You're an educated man, Citizen Bok. Surely you understand plain Russian. Whom do you pay for protection against attacks such as this one?"

"It is the duty of the security organs to protect the citizens of the state," Bok said stoutly.

Chanturia laughed. He had worked a long time to perfect a scornful laugh, and he very much enjoyed using it. "Yes, of course it is. And it is my duty and that of the Committee on State Security to protect the security of the state. And if this were only a disagreement on price between you and the criminal elements, then it would be left to the militia to regulate. But if there may be some conspiracy that endangers the state, then we can hardly leave the matter in such hands. And so I'm afraid you are going to have to tell me about your protection arrangements, whether you prefer to or not. So, now, to whom do you pay protection?"

Bok bowed his head. He spoke, after a moment—speaking into the table top. "He's called Tooz."

Tooz. The word meant "ace." "What's this ace's real name?"

"I don't know that."

"Is he Georgian?"

Terror crossed Lev Bok's face. His voice was almost a squeak. "No! He's Russian! Russian!"

"Any Georgians in his gang?"

"I don't know of any."

"Who does he work for?"

"I don't know that either."

"Well, who do you think he works for? You're an intelligent man, Citizen. You wouldn't pay protection to anyone working on his own, would you?"

Lev Bok's hands were shaking steadily, and his face became quite pale. "Please. You must understand. I could be killed for saying anything, even as much as I have."

Chanturia looked at the man steadily. "We know who these gangsters are, Citizen," he said, not even pausing to wonder if it were true. "We know who all of their groups are. And although the Union would be a better place if it were our mission to control them, that is not our mission. So, again, tell me for whom this Tooz works."

"I don't know," Bok said. "If you know all these groups, then you know who he works for; but I don't know. And I didn't recognize any of the men who attacked my cafe. I tell you this sincerely." And he would not say any more.

Chanturia sat nursing a cup of tea and staring at his notes. "There is someone they fear more than they fear us," he said to Orlov. *And that is going to be a problem. Maybe not today or tomorrow; maybe not in connection with this investigation. But soon enough: it is going to be a problem soon enough.*

· 6 ·

Thursday, January 19, 1989
3 P.M.
The Lubyanka

MAXIM NIKOLAYEVICH GRADSKI CAME TO HIS INTERVIEW, A DAY LATE, dressed in a blue suit of Soviet make, gray shirt and blue polyester tie, and gray imitation-leather shoes. The shoes—chosen not to overdo the part, Chanturia supposed—were Czech, but not the good Czech stuff. Except for his expensive haircut, hard to undo on short notice, Maxim Nikolayevich looked like a good Soviet worker right out of some back office.

"That's a nice suit," Chanturia said, just to see what Max Gradski—rather than his suit—was made of.

Gradski looked to one side and then the other, as if suspecting ambush. He looked as if he would have turned completely around to secure his backside, if he dared. Then he seemed to make a decision to be annoyed. "Did I come to give answers about my suit?" he asked.

"Oh, no. Of course not. It was only an observation. So. Your father is First Deputy Minister of Machine Building?" It was better to get that over with at once.

"Yes. Am I here to answer questions about my father? Or about machine building?"

"I hope it's not inconvenient for you to be here." He had come soon enough after the Committee contacted his father. The First Deputy Minister of Machine Building had lived through too much of the history of the Soviet Union to get crosswise with the Committee in his old age. But as for his son . . . It was a new world, for sons.

"Certainly it's inconvenient for me to be here. Do I have a choice not to be here?"

Chanturia said nothing for a moment. He waited. Max Gradski waited too, even after the silence dragged out for a long time. Chanturia knew then that Gradski had been educated about police interviews. Gradski knew that to say anything was a mistake. Uneducated people always said something eventually. "Of course you have a choice," he said. "But you know you can be held responsible for noncooperation. You know this investigation involves a murder."

"No, I didn't know. I knew someone was hurt. I'm sorry to hear he died. Who was he?"

"A foreigner who was in the cafe. But perhaps you can tell me about that?"

"What would you like to know?"

Chanturia took out a paper. "Let's start with your name."

"Maxim Nikolayevich Gradski."

"Where do you live?"

"Bersenyevskaya Embankment 20/2, apartment 182."

It was a building of large apartments, originally built for Stalin's bureaucrats. "Who lives with you there?"

"My father, my mother, and my sister."

"Your education?"

"I have a master's degree from Moscow Pedagogical Institute, in literature."

"What is your place of work?"

"The Department of Roads."

Chanturia paused a moment, then wrote it down. "What work do you do there?"

40

"I'm a roadmaster—shift manager for maintenance of the Circle Road, southeast quadrant."

"Isn't that an unusual job for a pedagogue whose father is a First Deputy Minister?"

Gradski shrugged. "Perhaps so."

"How do you happen to work there?"

"I enjoy working with real workers. It's useful work. Our country needs it done."

"Very commendable. And how did you obtain this position?"

"I don't see what this has to do with the subject of a murder."

"Nothing at all. But it's interesting to me."

"Pardon me, but I believe that I'm not required to be here to satisfy your personal interests."

"You're quite right. So, what do you remember about the evening of January 17, continuing to the morning of the eighteenth, at the cafe Come In and Taste?"

What Gradski remembered corresponded closely enough with what everyone else remembered. It added nothing; it contradicted nothing. Chanturia wrote it all down. He said, "You recall this well, considering the amount of drink you had consumed."

"I don't believe I have testified as to the amount of drink I had consumed."

"Your host comrade Stonov mentioned two bottles of vodka and three of champagne, I believe."

"Then that is his testimony and not mine."

"Of course. And how much drink had you consumed?"

"I don't recall. But I drink very little. I would not want my statement to reflect otherwise."

"All right. Read this."

Chanturia handed over the notes he had made into a statement. Gradski read slowly and thoroughly. Gradski requested changes in several of his answers. Chanturia made them. At length, after reading it again, Gradski signed the record of his interview.

"Very interesting." Orlov handed Gradski's statement back to Chanturia. "So he came to his interview as a worker, did he? The militia report said he was dressed in a Western coat and tie at the cafe. He didn't buy them on his roadmaster's salary."

"Maybe his father bought them for him abroad," the Peasant suggested. Kupinski, the Peasant, was the section's seven-by-eight, a Ukrainian farm boy who had got into the Committee on the strength

41

of his achievements as an Olympic shot-putter. Bulk had its uses. Kupinski didn't mind being known as the Peasant. It was what he was, and no shame to a Soviet man.

"First Deputy Ministers don't make that kind of money," Chanturia said. Of course, First Deputy Ministers didn't have to make that kind of money. They didn't have to buy things abroad: things were bought for them. But no one wanted to say that. "I don't think it's papa's wealth he's living on," he said.

"No?" the Peasant asked. "What, then?"

"Easy money. But I don't know what kind yet."

"Do you think he's connected with the arson attack?"

"Well, what do we know about him? He's a First Deputy Minister's son who has a nothing job, yet dresses expensively—except when he wants to impress us with his working-class sympathies. Who's he kidding? He could have any job he wants. He has expensive tastes, so he clearly wants money—more than this job can pay him. Not even much chance of graft in that job, that I can see. So what does he get out of it?"

The Peasant shrugged. "Free time?"

"Exactly!" Chanturia said, waving a finger at the Peasant, who beamed in pleased surprise at having got a right answer for once. "Free time. The law requires him to work; but it doesn't make him work every day. In this job he works one day—twenty-four hours straight—and is off three. Free time. But for what?"

"He's got a girlfriend," the Peasant mused.

"An English-speaking girlfriend," Orlov observed.

"Right. And maybe that fits too," Chanturia said. "But free time for what? Not for Svetlana: he isn't spending that much time with her. So for what? For his 'easy money' business, whatever it is. But maybe it does fit with his English-speaking girlfriend, who is a translator of chemical treatises and works at home, on her own schedule, and has a perfect excuse to meet with foreigners."

"But he wasn't at the cafe with any foreigners," the Peasant observed.

"Or not obviously. But what was he doing there? A First Deputy Minister's son, at a waiter's birthday party? Sure, his girlfriend is a cousin of the waiter's friend. But that's not much of a connection, to be invited to a party that cost what that one cost."

Orlov said, "Our waiter had plenty of cash. Not surprising, as he works at a restaurant that has plenty of foreign customers. Probably he has a stash of foreign currency. He might have wanted to do some kind of deal with Gradski."

"Or with someone else, someone who wanted to meet with him— maybe with both of them—without being seen to meet with them. So he takes a different table at an expensive cafe."

"Ah," Orlov said.

"I don't get it," the Peasant said. "They *didn't* meet. Nobody saw them together."

Chanturia waved a hand impatiently. "So they went to the men's room at the same time. Or one of them danced with the foreigner's girl, or he danced with one of theirs . . . they could have done it a dozen ways."

"Done what?" the Peasant asked.

"A drug sale," Orlov suggested.

"We don't know that yet," Chanturia said. "But let's get someone to follow our friend Gradski for a few days."

"And Gradski's girlfriend?" Orlov asked.

Chanturia pondered that. "No. We're too short-handed. But check with our representative at her Institute. See what he can tell us about her."

· 7 ·

Thursday, January 19, 1989
4 P.M.
Suvorov Boulevard

A GANGSTER KNOWN AS TOOZ WAS IN FACT IN THE COMMITTEE'S FILES, AND in the militia's. Valentin Petrovich Morozov was his name. His file photo showed a thick-necked but handsome young Valentin Petrovich with a black look in his eye. In 1980 he had been Champion of the Russian Federation in the heaviest weight class of boxing. For a few years after that he held a series of positions with the Russian Sport Committee, from which he departed after beating up the chairman of the Commission in a disagreement concerning certain aspects of behavior of the chairman's wife. The police files had him involved after that in three minor assaults and suspicion of a burglary. The KGB itself had later interviewed him twice in connection with thefts of state property from a machine-tool factory where he had been on the payroll for three months—although he had never appeared for work. He had since retired completely. Early retirement—that is. not working—was a violation of Soviet law, but it did not appear that Morozov had ever been arrested or tried on this charge. He was believed now to be associated with a criminal group of undefined extent.

Orlov took the Peasant and Timur Iskakov, half Tatar on his father's side and therefore known as the Tatar, to pick up Morozov. Ordinarily Orlov would have wanted two seven-by-eights for this work. The Peasant was one, but the Tatar was barely half that size. The Tatar, though, had reckless courage enough for any two bigger men.

They found Morozov at his group's usual place of business, the cafe All Food to the Soviets, on Suvorov Boulevard.

Morozov was drinking vodka at a table with three other men. All of them wore dark blue knit-wool track suits and East German running shoes. They paid no attention to the three KGB men until Orlov spoke to them: "So, Citizens, you appear to be ready for exercise."

All four turned toward Orlov. After a moment Morozov alone answered. "It's not a crime to be fit." It was clear that he knew they were law-enforcement people, and that he didn't much care.

"Then we won't arrest you for being fit," Orlov said, showing his KGB credentials. "We'll think of something else."

"I didn't know whether he was going to come along or not," Orlov said to Chanturia later. "I think he thought I was militia, and he was going to tell me to go to Benya's mother. Then he saw I was with the Committee, and he still thought about telling me where to go, until the Tatar started to break his fingers off. What's going on in the world?"

"Life's getting more complicated," Chanturia said.

"When a punk gangster even thinks about telling an officer of the Committee where to put his credentials, it's time we started making life simple again, Captain."

Chanturia agreed; but he wondered who—if anyone—had the power to make life that simple anymore. "What did you learn from Mr. Tooz?"

"Nothing worth knowing. And maybe none of it true. He doesn't know who torched the cafe. He'd like to find out, because the cafe

44

is his territory, and it's bad for business to have unpleasantness happen to his customers unless he causes it himself. Not that he does anything illegal, of course."

"Of course. But how he makes his living isn't our business, as long as he's registered for an officially approved job—which he isn't. Did you remind him of that?"

"I did. That was when he decided to talk to me."

"So where does this leave us?"

"Nowhere that I know of, Captain."

"Nowhere that I know of either."

"Comrade Colonel Sokolov's not going to be happy."

"Well, we didn't invent the world."

· 8 ·

Thursday, January 19, 1989
5 P.M.
The United States Embassy

"WHERE THE FUCK IS MY AG ATTACHÉ?" THE AMBASSADOR DEMANDED. "Nobody else seems to know. Do you?" The Ambassador was a large, profane, long tall Texan who thought that for public personas Lyndon Johnson had had it just about right, and he cultivated the same one. The professional diplomats mostly thought him profane and vulgar, which he was. He wanted to be known as a man who could pour shit from a boot without needing instructions stamped on the heel; and he was. Russians liked him.

Martin liked the Ambassador too, for the same reason. Living in the Soviet Union had a strange effect on Americans, even the professional diplomats, let alone civilians like Martin: they began to value most what was most blatantly American, even if at home it would have made them wince. Liberal sensitivities (Eastern liberal bullshit, as the Ambassador would put it) found no resting place in Fortress America on Tchaikovsky Street. Not even with the special assistant cultural attaché, Martin reflected ruefully. Before he returned home next year he would have to try to work back into a frame of mind politically acceptable for academics. He said to the Ambassador, "Your ag attaché is reported to be up-country somewhere counting beef cattle. Stavropol *krai,* I think." Stavropol was a general cover destination used to refer to the location of anyone whose real whereabouts shouldn't be spoken aloud. Martin didn't know where Hutchins was. Hence, for practical purposes, he was in Stavropol.

The Ambassador made a production of it. "What's Hutchins gone to Stavropol for? The CIA still trying to get a handle on beef production in this worker's paradise? Tell 'em to look at their damn satellite pictures. Count the legs and divide by four. Won't take 'em long, because they ain't enough cows in this fuckin' country to make a good roundup on my back ranch. If we held a barbecue here, we'd have to send west for ribs. Matter of fact, that's what we did last Fourth of July, isn't it?"

Martin laid a finger on his lips and looked ceilingward as a reminder to the Ambassador: they were not in a safe room, and so they had to assume that the KGB was listening to whatever they said. Hutch was always reminding Martin of it, by the same gesture. The Ambassador, however, did not consider himself bound to pamper the feelings of eavesdroppers and regularly said whatever he wanted to as long as it was opinion and not fact. Facts might be secret: his opinions were not. If the Soviets objected to his opinions, they never said so.

"Damned expletive-deleted stairways!" the Ambassador muttered—another opinion he didn't mind sharing with the Soviets. Martin and the Ambassador were winding through one of the hall-stairway passages of the old Embassy, which was an ant's nest of tiny rooms and winding, climbing, descending passages stuffed into a converted Stalin-era apartment building. A complete new Embassy building, with wide, straight American hallways, stood empty next door; but the new Embassy, except for the living quarters, was deemed unusable because it was known to be bugged throughout, whereas the old one was not known, but only suspected, to be.

They came to the special assistant cultural attaché's office, a windowless cubicle, bookshelf walls stuffed with books to the ceiling—books standing, books lying on the top of standing books, books sliding to the floor. Most of them were cheaply printed and nearly all of those were in Russian.

"You got anything decent to read in here?" the Ambassador asked, looking doubtfully at the shelves. "Spy novels? Shoot-em-ups?"

46

"*War and Peace,*" Martin said. "There's a fair amount of action in it."

"I've read it," the Ambassador said. He in fact had a good working knowledge of Russian—in which he had no Texas accent—and was widely read in Russian literature. "Not a bad book."

"Tolstoy would be grateful for your opinion."

"Probably. Yeah, it's a lot like *Dallas*—the TV show, not the city. You could make a great soap opera out of it. Will Natasha run off with the wicked Kuragin? Will Count Pierre survive the battle of Borodino? Will Kuragin's father's fortune survive Kuragin's gambling habit? Tune in next week . . ."

"I never thought of it that way."

"Well, think about it. You'll agree."

"I sincerely hope not."

"You better not think about it, then. Cause if you do, you'll see my point." Martin sat down behind his desk, and the Ambassador sank into the chair on the other side of it and pushed the door shut with his foot. "You think they got the bugs out of this place?"

Martin shrugged. "It's swept every year, whether it needs it or not."

"Well, it'll have to do until somethin' better comes along." The cubicle had started life as one corner of a standby safe room developed after the official safe rooms—even the Communications Programs Unit, the very heart of Embassy security—were found to have been penetrated by the KGB with the help of lovesick Marine guards. Eventually the original safe rooms were rehabilitated; and when more space was needed and the new Embassy still unavailable, the room had been divided up. Martin had been stuck into this part of it for lack of other space, but it still had a residual air of safety about it. Now people dropped into his office for private conversations. Even if the KGB got new bugs into the rest of the Embassy, who would bother to bug a special assistant cultural attaché?

"*Do* you know where Hutchins is?" the Ambassador asked seriously. "I'll tell you he didn't sign out to be gone this long. And he sure as hell ain't supposed to be anywhere without someone knowing where he is."

"He signed himself out on something he didn't want to tell me about," Martin admitted. "But he didn't say anything about being gone this long. Might be overnight, he said."

"You think he's got hisself a woman somewhere?" the Ambassador asked.

"He's not the type."

"Everybody's the right type sometime, if you find the right woman. Did he tell you what he was working on?"

"Not me. I don't work for his company. They don't tell me any secrets. Did you ask Denson?"

"Sure I asked Denson. I wouldn't be talkin' to you if Denson knew. But you're Hutchins's best friend—talk about odd couples! So I thought he might've said something to you that he didn't say to his staff. He's got 'em worried this time. There's nobody else he'd've told. As far as I know. Me, I'm just the fucking Ambassador. Nobody tells me doodley-squat."

"Maybe it's a joke." Hutchins was well known as a practical joker.

"Some joke."

· 9 ·

Thursday, January 19, 1989
7 P.M.
The Lubyanka

FROM HIS WINDOW IN THE BUILDING ON DZERZHINSKY SQUARE, COLONEL Sokolov could just see the red neon *M* of the metro entrance on the opposite side of the square, facing the statue of Felix Dzerzhinsky, the founder of the KGB himself, on his pedestal in the middle of the traffic that swirled around him day and night. The lights of the cars drifted up through the snow, washed as pale as Sokolov felt himself at this stage of winter. The red light of the metro sign was diffused by the fine, hard powder snow and reached him only as a red blur. Of the crowd that he knew poured in and out of the station he could see nothing at all.

He turned back into the room. He had left the investigator Captain Chanturia to his own thoughts long enough to have made any sensible person nervous, although he wasn't sure it had been enough in Chanturia's case. Well, sometimes imperturbability was enough to make up for lack of sense. Sometimes.

Sokolov took from his desk a copy of *Izvestia* and tossed it at Captain Chanturia. "You've seen this?"

Chanturia smoothed out the paper and studied it in a fashion that Sokolov considered insolent. He knew Chanturia had read the paper. Everybody in the building had read it.

"Yes, I've seen it, Comrade Colonel."

"It's in the newspaper! The newspapers are printing our unsolved cases! I remind you, Comrade Captain, that we have a duty to the People. How can it be," Sokolov asked, "that out of twenty-three people on the premises, none of them can give a useful description of one missing woman, admitted to be strikingly beautiful; not to mention that none of them can give a useful description of any one of the assailants?"

"Three factors, Comrade Colonel. The suddenness of the attack, the lateness of the hour, and drink. Not necessarily in that order. And, in several instances, the language problem. The German and one of the Japanese do not speak Russian, and the other two Japanese only badly." He bided his time, knowing that the Colonel would not come to the important point first.

"And in this whole organization we have no interrogators competent in Japanese or German?"

"We have, of course. But the business is not efficient through a translator."

"I said interrogators, not translators."

Chanturia lit a cigarette and breathed in the smoke slowly. "I judged it necessary to have the questioning done by one person, to minimize the risk of overlooking some small thing that might be significant."

"It appears, however, that no small significant thing was found, nevertheless."

Chanturia waited.

"And how can it be, Captain, that a foreign person with no papers can sit drinking champagne for a whole evening with a Russian beauty, and ultimately get himself fatally stabbed, and still a day and a half later no one has the slightest idea who he is? What is the Party going to think the Committee on State Security is doing? Sleeping?"

Chanturia breathed the smoke out slowly. It was a useful technique, when being interrogated, to smoke: the slower the better. He did his best to discourage it in persons he was questioning. "To identify a person totally without papers, and totally out of context, is quite difficult, as the Colonel knows."

"The Colonel has *some* experience in these matters." The Colonel's tone made Chanturia resolve to control his sense of irony. No one ever understood irony. The Colonel went on, "Difficulty is not an excuse for failure."

"Of course not, Comrade Colonel. And we will not fail. It's a difficult puzzle; but we'll solve it." The rubbish we have to put out for the higher-ups, Chanturia thought regretfully.

Why do we have to put up with such rubbish? Sokolov thought. In the old days this captain would have been sweating blood. "Tell me what you know of the deceased Mr. X so far," he said.

Chanturia did not look at his notes. "Height 181, weight 84 kilos, in reasonable physical condition, age about thirty-five. Dressed in a mixture of European clothes, quite expensive. Capitalist luxury goods, in fact. Of European descent, no prominent scars, smallpox vaccination of European or American type, on the shoulder. Only one dental filling." *Not Russian, then,* they both thought.

Chanturia smiled as he read the thought in the Colonel's eyes. Of course the smallpox vaccination also made non-Russian identity probable—Russian ones were normally low on the upper arm.

He went on: "Not apparently Slavic—more the Nordic type. Blood type O positive. Did not smoke—lungs were clear of tar. We are checking the fingerprints—nothing concluded yet. He died"—here Chanturia opened a file he was holding and consulted a paper, not because he needed it, but to show that he had it—"of a stab wound to the heart, in the right chest." The paper was an autopsy report showing the outline of a human body in two views, front and back. The report showed only one wound, neatly marked in red pencil on the front view. The margins were covered with the pathologist's notes.

"Do you draw any conclusions?" the Colonel asked.

"None firmly. No witness remarked on it, but the location of the wound is consistent with the assailant having been left-handed."

The Colonel grunted. "Go on."

"The deceased may have recently traveled outside the Union, as he had a variety of money on him. Although of course"—Chanturia added this before the Colonel could—"that could be a ruse to conceal identity rather than revealing it. Or he could have got it as change in a hard-currency store. As you know, the cashiers tend to treat all non-socialist currencies as interchangeable."

"Also he had sound taste in women," the Colonel said.

"Apparently." Chanturia had not wanted to mention the woman again, although he had supposed it inevitable.

"And this particular woman—who might she be?"

"I'm afraid I have to report to the Colonel that we don't know yet."

"Let's not say 'we,' shall we, Comrade Captain? This is *your* investigation, after all, not mine. I'm not expected to know, until you tell me."

"I have not yet ascertained the woman's identity."

"Isn't she a whore?" He didn't need to say, *Who else would be consorting with foreigners?* Chanturia could read that thought too.

"Apparently not. Her description doesn't match anyone who reports to us. And neither of the two prostitutes with the Japanese knew her."

"And the staff of this cafe—they hadn't seen her there before?"

"They all say she had not been there before. She was the kind of woman a waiter would remember, according to all the testimony. They were quite sure she had not been there before."

"What did she look like?"

"Blond, long hair, dark eyes. Quite pale. Full figure, but slender. Age not more than thirty. No wedding ring—one of the waiters was quite sure of that."

"Your typical *russkaya krasavitsa.*"

"Not typical enough, unfortunately." Chanturia knew it was risky to trade remarks about "Russian beauties" with Colonel Sokolov, but after a day of getting nowhere, he felt he owed it to himself. And certainly there were some good-looking Russian girls; but few of them stayed that way at close to thirty.

"I would not expect a handsome young officer to suffer a shortage of beautiful women," the Colonel said. "Especially an officer from Georgia."

Chanturia did not reply. He knew he was on dangerous ground. The Colonel was a Russian; and when a Russian man mentioned Georgian men, it was best for Georgian men to be careful.

"This 'foreigner,'" the Colonel said.

"Comrade Colonel?" Chanturia spoke warily. He was relieved to have the subject changed; but the Colonel's voice sounded thoughtful, as if he were considering a new idea; and Chanturia did not care to hear any new ideas on a subject on which his own had led to nothing concrete.

"How do we know he's a foreigner?"

51

"Everyone has said so from the beginning, Comrade Colonel. All of the testimony is that he was a foreigner. All of the waiters, the cafe administrator . . . they were quite convinced. Two of them believed he might be American."

"American." Sokolov had a way of mixing scorn and doubt in everything he said. It gave a sad tinge to his voice—sadness at the foolishness of subordinates. "Why did they think he was American?"

"The way he sounded; the way he acted with the waiters—a certain equality in relationships."

"Ah. Great egalitarians, these Americans." More scorn than sadness.

"And of course, his clothes, his personal effects . . ."

"Yes. But there's no proof, is there? I've read your report. There's no proof he was a foreigner. He had no documents. None of the hotels for foreigners is missing a guest. He does not match the visa photo of any recent arrival. Everyone *has* said so from the beginning—but suppose everyone was wrong? Did he say to anyone that he was a foreigner? No. In fact he spoke exclusively in Russian, so far as anyone recalls. Good Russian, though accented. What accent? No one is sure. So what proof is there? His accent, and his clothing and effects. But of course, the Union is full of people who speak accented Russian. He was of the Nordic type, you say: but why not Lithuanian or Estonian? As for the clothing and personal items, there are many citizens now who can afford such things, and who buy them when they can. The manager of this very cafe, Come In and Taste, for instance, is reported to have a fortune of a million rubles. Perhaps our 'foreigner' also manages a cafe, in Riga or wherever he learned his good Russian. So then, the unusual assortment of origins of his personal effects does not seem strange, does it? It would be expected that a foreigner would own mostly items made in his own country; but a Soviet citizen buying foreign goods buys what he can."

"That's true . . ."

"Yes, Captain, it is true. And it makes a great deal of sense out of what otherwise seems quite senseless—that this office cannot identify a foreigner who was slain in a senseless attack on a cooperative cafe in the middle of Moscow."

"If he is not a foreigner, of course, this is not the business of the Committee on State Security," Chanturia said.

What might once have been a smile passed across the lips of Colonel Sokolov. "Precisely."

Chanturia thought a moment. "Then the remains and the personal effects should be transferred to the Procurator's office for further investigation."

"Not for *further* investigation. For investigation. There has been no investigation, as this is a matter outside our authority."

"Yes, sir."

"That was slick," Orlov said, laughing. "Sokolov didn't get to be a colonel by lack of imagination. The *Procuratura* are going to shit when we turn this mess back to them." He continued to box up the personal effects that the evidence room had tagged. "Too bad this has to go." He turned the Hermès watch carefully under the overhead light. "Some interrogator's assistant will think this is his lucky night." He wrote down the number on his property list and tossed the watch into the box.

It was true, Chanturia assumed, that before the night was over, someone would be wearing a very fine wristwatch—although not where it would be seen by any of his superiors—but that was a matter for the Procurator to worry about.

"Let's sign the late citizen out and have him on his way to the *Procuratura*," Chanturia said. "Bring his stuff." He went down the hall, Orlov following with the box under his arm.

But not everything seemed quite right to him.

They waited for the elevator to the morgue. "Tell me, Lyosha," Chanturia said as they listened to the elevator in its shaft creaking its way up toward them, "have you ever heard of any Italian underwear for sale in Moscow?"

"No. But that's no surprise: Italian underwear is a deficit commodity. Even Soviet underwear is a deficit commodity. There probably is no commodity more in deficit than Italian underwear. It would be gone in seconds."

"Seriously."

"Seriously, no. But of course, there are Italian tourists. They'll sell anything."

"Even their underwear?"

"Probably. Maybe *especially* their underwear."

"And English wool suits? Does a tourist who can afford a suit like that sell it for rubles on the street, like a hippie? To someone whom it fits perfectly?"

"Am I to understand that you are doubting the Colonel's conclusion, Comrade Captain?"

"Not in the least. The Colonel, I have to admit, has come to a

53

brilliant conclusion, one that gets this mess, as you call it, off of my desk and onto our friend Filin's, who certainly deserves it more than I do."

The elevator rattled to a stop at their floor, and Chanturia slid open the cage door and held it for Orlov. He pressed the button for the basement floor. The elevator rested for a few seconds and then with a groan started back down.

In the morgue, the clerk found the papers for the body and presented them to Chanturia. "Number 542. Will you want to see the body, Comrade Captain?"

"Yes. Let's make sure we deliver the correct remains to our comrades at the *Procuratura.*" There had been a case a year or two before where the remains of two deceased prisoners were interchanged. It had caused no end of troubles for the officer in charge.

"This way, please, sir." The clerk took a set of keys from his desk drawer and led the two of them back through a separate door into a high room that had one wall covered floor to ceiling with square, metal-plated doors. The clerk searched through his keys, found one, and unlocked door 542, which was at shoulder height. He pulled open the refrigerator-style handle and slid out a metal tray from the opening in the wall. On tray number 542 was the ex-foreigner. The face was stark white under the fluorescent lights. The upper teeth showed behind the pulled-back lips. "Not much the worse for the autopsy," Orlov said.

"If he's the right one, I'll take the papers, sir," the clerk said.

Chanturia signed the papers and handed them back to the clerk.

"Do you mind if I ask who he was?" the clerk asked.

"Some Lithuanian," Chanturia said.

"Really?" the clerk said. "I'd have sworn he was a foreigner. He just has that look, you know? Well, I'll get him on a trolley and roll him out to the ambulance stop."

At the morgue counter, Captain Solodovnik was waiting. Solodovnik was chief of another section, currently assigned to embassy watching. Chanturia greeted him: "Are you here to view the results of one of your interrogations, Solodovnik?"

"I was about to ask you the same."

"No—I'm transferring an unauthorized body."

"Unauthorized? What are we doing with an *un*authorized body? And who authorized the transfer, then?"

"We're getting rid of it. Orders of Colonel Sokolov. Of course only an officer who unauthorizes a body can authorize its transfer. Didn't you know?"

"I remember the regulations, of course."

"I was sure you would." Solodovnik remembered every regulation that had ever existed, along with many that never had. "So how are our sharp-eyed colleagues spending their winter? Have you seen any exciting departures? Heard any interesting conversations?" Embassy watch was not glamorous duty, nor strenuous.

"As it happens," Solodovnik said, "we're keeping the motherland safe from the prying eyes of foreign spies disguised as diplomats, who would be free to come and go as they please if not for us. Interesting conversations? Is it interesting when a foreign ambassador can't find his chief of intelligence?"

"I'm not surprised. Some ambassadors can't find their way to the toilet without a map. The question is, can our embassy watchers find his chief of intelligence?"

There was a loud rattling and banging as the clerk appeared from the door to the back room pushing a hospital trolley bearing a corpse under a sheet. The trolley had bad bearings in one wheel and constantly swung to the right as if trying to make an escape through the wall. The bearing rattled and the trolley banged continuously along the wall, whomp, whomp, whomp.

"Perhaps we can see this unauthorized deceased person?" Solodovnik asked. He was wondering, Chanturia supposed, by what right a person deceased without authority. Solodovnik pulled back the sheet. He gasped and stiffened. "Him!" He turned to Chanturia. "How . . . how did he come here?"

"Do you know this corpse?" Chanturia demanded.

"Certainly I know him! Haven't I watched for him every day at the American Embassy for a year and a half?"

"At the American Embassy?" Chanturia felt a cold stone sinking through the middle parts of his hot-blooded Georgian body.

"Of course at the American Embassy. He's Hutchins—the CIA station chief!"

55

· 10 ·

Friday, January 20, 1989
9 A.M.
The United States Embassy

PROMPTLY AT NINE O'CLOCK A BLACK VOLGA STOPPED AT THE UNITED States Embassy on Tchaikovsky Street. The streetlights, still on, did little to improve a dark morning's disposition: through the sifting snow they barely illuminated the two Soviet militiamen on guard outside the building. Officially, the militiamen were there to protect the Embassy. In fact, they were there to stop Soviet citizens trying to enter.

A man wearing a dark heavy overcoat and a fur hat emerged from the back seat of the car. A student of such things could read the man's status in the fur of his hat, which was mink, but not all mink: only the front and back panels and the tied-up ear flaps were mink; the inner part, the hat itself, was suede leather, so that when in really cold weather the flaps were put down, the exposed crown was not mink but suede. This, said the hat, is a man who knows quality, and aspires to it, but can't yet afford as much as he deserves. Someday his hat will be all mink.

The man walked to the guards and presented his identity card to one of them. Although the man was not in uniform, the guard saluted him. The man then walked past to the guard post inside the Embassy entrance. To the American marine there he handed an envelope. Then he turned on his heel and walked back to the waiting car as the Soviet militiamen saluted his back.

"What's the news?" the Ambassador asked. He didn't look up from his desk at first. He was studying last night's cable traffic from Washington.

"Bad news," Taglia said.

The Ambassador looked up. "Worse than what those assholes in Congress are up to?"

56

"Maybe." Taglia handed the Ambassador the note he was holding. At the top it said in embossed Cyrillic letters, MINISTRY OF FOREIGN RELATIONS OF THE UNION OF SOVIET SOCIALIST REPUBLICS.

The Ambassador read the note slowly and completely, then read it again. "Well I'll be go to hell," he said. He read the note again. "Do we know any more than this says?"

"No, sir."

"Well, they offered us a briefing. Get your ass over there and get it. Take somebody with you."

"Hutch's deputy?"

"No. We don't need a spy for this. Why give them a chance to identify any more Agency people? Take Martin. He's Hutchins's buddy." He looked at the note again. "We regret to inform you—I bet they do. We regret . . . that a person accidentally slain—accidentally slain, get that!—has been determined to be an employee of your Embassy, Mr. Charles Hutchins, agriculture attaché. You are requested to confirm . . . bm, bm, identity . . . bm, bm, circumstances of this matter are being further investigated . . . we will of course brief your. . . . What is this, Rollie? Do they think we came in on a load of shit? You get over there, and you brief me the minute you get back, you hear?"

Rollie Taglia, the Ambassador's deputy, was a Texas Italian—Italian by genetics, Texan by chance, he liked to say, the chance being that his Philadelphia father had taken shore leave from the Navy at Galveston during the war and met a Texas beauty who didn't hanker to live where it snowed. So Rollie was born and raised on the shores of the Gulf of Mexico. He did not owe his Moscow position to the Ambassador. At forty-five, he had twenty years in the Foreign Service and had been posted to Moscow before the Ambassador was appointed—although being a fellow Texan didn't hurt, they both liked to say.

Rollie was fluent in Italian, but he hadn't learned a word of it from his father, who had enough trouble trying to learn to talk Texan to a woman who spoke no Italian and didn't want to learn. Rollie learned Italian the easy way, by sleeping with Italian women while on shore leave from the Navy at Naples, where he spent his Vietnam War years. The Mediterranean warmth was so congenial that, after the Navy, he went into the Foreign Service, which promptly posted him to Moscow for his first tour of duty. He learned Russian—though not, to his regret, as pleasantly as he had learned Italian. After the standard Foreign Service course, he put in two more years of hard slogging at the Embassy under the tutelage of an iron-corseted, red-haired old woman from Toledo, Ohio, secretary to the commercial attaché. She had an unconquerable suspicion of Italians—a suspicion which, in Rollie's case, with respect to her, was not even well-founded. Consequently, he still had not come to grips with the more intimate Russian expressions. On the other hand, he knew enough Russian and enough about Russians to believe he knew when he was hearing *blyadoslovye,* which was what he believed he was hearing from a Deputy Foreign Minister of the U.S.S.R.

"Please accept our government's condolences on this unfortunate incident," the Deputy Foreign Minister said. Although he did not have a paper to read from, his condolences were in the form of a speech. "It must be a shock to you," he continued. "Certainly it was to us. We very much regret that incidents of this nature occur, although of course they are not specific to our society. We regret even more that foreign nationals have been involved, and you may be assured that our state organs are making every effort to see that the perpetrators are brought to justice. We have the preliminary report of the police and the Committee on State Security, both of which will be made available to you. We do, of course, wish you to conclusively identify the body; although we have no reason to doubt, as our police have ascertained, that the deceased is indeed your agricultural atta-ché. There is also the matter of transfer of the body, which we will, of course, arrange at your convenience."

"And what is the condition of the body?" Taglia asked.

"The cause of death was a stab wound to the heart. Otherwise, the deceased was not badly injured in the attack."

"Then we can expect to find no other marks on the body?"

"I am informed only that the deceased was not otherwise badly injured in the attack."

"Not badly injured except for a fatal wound."

"Precisely." The Deputy Foreign Minister had been ordered to be unfailingly polite and sympathetic, and he was not about to do other-wise, although personally he did not care for the sarcasm in the voice of the Deputy Ambassador.

"We will be very interested in the content of your investigators' reports," Taglia said. "And, of course, we wish to be kept informed of the progress of the investigation."

"Of course."

"I wonder," said Martin to the Deputy Foreign Minister, "if we

58

could offer our assistance in the investigation." Taglia shot Martin a look of surprise: Martin had no brief to speak. Martin found himself surprised: he didn't know why he said it. He had no brief to speak; but he hadn't been ordered not to, either. It was what had got him to Moscow in the first place—talk first and reflect later.

The Deputy Foreign Minister said, "I'm sure the investigation is quite under the control of the proper Soviet investigative organs."

"I'm sure it is," Martin agreed. "Still, we have more than the usual interest in this case. And it might be that we could provide information which could be helpful."

The Deputy Foreign Minister seemed interested. "Yes ... you might." He pondered. "I will forward your suggestion."

Chanturia banged his head against his desk. Then he got up and banged it against one wall, spun away, and at the end of two complete pirouettes slammed his back against the opposite wall. He staggered back to his chair and pulled his hair with his hands. "Whose fuck-your-mother idea was *this?*" he screamed. " 'Cooperate with American organs!' Do they mean to invite the CIA into our files? Bad enough that we don't know what this fuck-your-mother CIA station chief was up to! Do we expect *them* to help us find out?"

Orlov reflected, for more than the hundredth time in his career, that Chanturia was not an average KGB officer. Not even an average Georgian, he suspected, although in truth Orlov hadn't worked with many. On the other hand, Orlov felt about this order exactly the way that Chanturia apparently did, although he wasn't about to show it.

So, for that matter, did Colonel Sokolov, judging from Chanturia's description of their conversation: "I am sure, Captain Chanturia, that our superiors have carefully thought through what might be gained and what lost in such an exchange," he had said dryly; "and if their assessment of the balance is different from yours and mine, then no doubt it is based upon superior information. But if I find that in the course of this exchange you provide the Americans with the slightest scrap of information about Committee procedures, then I will personally see that you are transferred to Tadzhikistan for the rest of your career."

"I'm sure," Orlov said carefully to Chanturia, "that higher levels have carefully considered all aspects of this, based upon more complete information than we have at our own disposal."

Chanturia stopped short. He was not at all sure that higher levels had considered the matter at all, nor that they had any information whatsoever or would know enough not to wipe their butts with it if they had it; but Orlov, though he was a friend of long standing, was a by-the-book officer, and Chanturia had the feeling that he had let his hair down before Orlov far enough. He subsided into the chair behind his desk.

Court Medicine Morgue Number 5, a yellow one-story building, stood alone in the snow amid bare trees on Salam-Adil Street. A technician led them through the front hall, a cold marble-paneled "farewell hall" where two small bouquets of flowers stood expecting a funeral ceremony. Behind that, a corridor led to the rear. At its end a large room, green-painted, held two dozen bare wooden tables. On half of them were bodies, seven naked men and three women and two figures under sheets. They lay heads to the wall, feet to the aisle, in neat socialist order.

The technician pulled down the sheet from one face. "Is that him?"

"Yes." Martin studied Hutchins's yellowing face, the teeth that showed just under the upper lip where it was slightly pulled back, as if in an effort to sneer.

"He looks smug as ever," Taglia said. "Right to the end. He'd have been happy to know it." He motioned for the technician to pull down the sheet, but the man didn't do it; so Martin took the top edge and pulled the sheet down to the waist.

Taglia went pale. "This is a heart wound?"

The chest and abdomen were slashed open from the throat to where the sheet still covered the body at the abdomen. The incision still gaped open; a pile of guts and other parts seemed to have been dumped inside without any thought for the arrangement. Hutchins looked like a waste disposal site.

"What happened to him?" Taglia turned to the technician and demanded, "What did they do to him?"

The man shrugged. *"Vskrytie."*

"Of course they'd do an autopsy," Martin said. He studied the corpse intently, although he wanted to vomit. He studied the face, to avoid the guts. Hutch had a silly smile on his face, as if this were one more practical joke, and he'd caught Martin falling for it.

60

· 11 ·

Sunday, January 22, 1989
2 P.M.
The United States Embassy

GATHERED IN THE BUBBLE ON THE NINTH FLOOR OF THE EMBASSY WERE five people: the Ambassador, Rollie Taglia, Martin, the defense attaché Colonel Sam Wheelwright, and Ellson Bierman, who had arrived from Washington on the Pan Am flight that same morning. Bierman did not introduce himself other than by name, but everyone in the room knew that he had come to replace Hutchins.

The Bubble was a room within a room, a floating world built of clear plastic. Raised off the floor and not touching any walls or the ceiling, it was electrically, electronically and acoustically isolated from the rest of the world and was swept daily for listening devices.

"This place is like flying IFR," Wheelwright complained. He hated being closed in. Even in an aircraft cockpit in cloud he became uneasy: he hated having to trust to instruments to know what was out in the world. To him the Embassy itself was like—was too much like—a plane in cloud, cruising on instructions from somewhere else, from someone who also couldn't see the ground, someone who knew even less about what was really happening outside. "So," he said to Bierman, "what does Washington tell us is going on?"

"That's what Washington sent me to find out. So, shall we have the postmortem? What do we know?"

The Ambassador nodded to Taglia, who began, "We know the following. Hutchins signed himself out on January 17 to meet a local contact. He gave the watchers the slip—we believe he did—by means that aren't relevant. The name of the contact was known only to himself. He expected to be back late that night but said there was a possibility he might be gone all night. He did not return that night nor the next day, and nothing further was heard from him.

"In the afternoon of January 18, an article appeared in *Izvestia* about an attack on a cooperative cafe in Prospect Mira. The attack

61

occurred early on the same morning. Several foreigners were reported injured. The perpetrators were reported to be unknown. The cafe manager suggested that the attack was connected with hostilities between two criminal groups.

"On January 20, two days ago, we received a note at 9:05 A.M. from the Soviet Foreign Ministry—hand delivered—notifying us that a person killed in the attack on the cafe had been identified as an American citizen and an employee of the Embassy. They requested that we identify and collect the body and offered to brief us further to the extent of their knowledge.

"Ben Martin and I appeared at the Foreign Ministry at 11:30 A.M. We were briefed by the Deputy, Dubinsky . . ."

"Is that normal?" Bierman interrupted.

"No, it's not. Although I can't say we have much experience with cases of murdered Embassy staff. But I would have expected somebody two or three steps down. Dubinsky is right below Shevardnadze himself."

"I know about Foreign Ministry procedures. The question is, why was Martin there? He's not cleared for Agency matters."

Martin was annoyed—but not surprised—that, although he and Bierman were old acquaintances, Bierman addressed this question to Taglia instead of to himself.

"I'm not either," Taglia said.

"You're the Deputy Chief of Mission."

"I sent Martin," the Ambassador said. "And since he was there, I decided he should come to this meeting too."

There was nothing for Bierman to say; but he wrote a note while everyone, including the Ambassador, sat. Then he looked at Taglia again. "Go on."

"Dubinsky essentially repeated the note. Polite as hell. Told us where the body was. Told us the cause of death."

"A stab wound to the heart." Bierman said this without any inflection whatsoever to tell what he thought of it.

"So they said."

"Do you doubt it?"

Martin had known Bierman for nearly fifteen years now. From as far back as freshman Russian class in college, he remembered the arched right eyebrow, the way Bierman turned his head down and a little to the left to look up under that arched eyebrow. He said to Bierman, "There is nothing to base any doubt on. Therefore, one

62

must doubt it. 'Shall we have our postmortem?' you asked. Well, the KGB had already done theirs. The body had been autopsied."

"Autopsied?" The eyebrow arched higher.

"Yes. And after that, it was impossible to tell anything about the cause of death. Doc Snyder did another, as well as he could. Hutchins could have died from any number of things. He did have a stab wound in the upper right frontal rib cage, consistent with being stabbed from the front by a left-handed person. The wound apparently occurred while he was alive. Time of death was noon the eighteenth, plus or minus twelve hours."

"And he was last seen here at . . . ?"

"Late afternoon the seventeenth," Taglia said. He consulted his notes. "Yes, sixteen-thirty."

"So they could have had him alive for a day or more."

"Could have. Or they could have collected him dead, as they claim. The KGB report and the police report are consistent in saying they did."

"They would be, wouldn't they?" Wheelwright said.

Bierman's eyebrow arched so much higher it seemed to pull him up straight in his chair. "We've *got* the reports?"

"We have. Dubinsky promised them, and the Foreign Ministry delivered them."

"When?"

"Seventeen-thirty yesterday."

"Plenty of time to make something up."

"Hell, they had two days before that," Wheelwright said.

"Yes, of course," Bierman said. "Well, I don't know that I've ever seen an actual KGB report. Where is it?"

"Here." Taglia took a stapled, three-page document from his stack of papers and slid it across the table.

In fact, none of them had never seen an actual KGB report either— if that was really what this was. And none had never thought he would. But this, Martin supposed, was exactly what he would have expected one to look like, if he had ever expected to see one. Three pages, typed double-spaced on a manual typewriter with a faded ribbon. The copy was a carbon, not a photocopy. Typos had been corrected by striking over, not by correction fluid. The paper was thick but fragile. Bierman held it tenderly on the palms of both his hands, as if expecting it to fall apart.

"It's a piece of shit!" Wheelwright growled.

"Do you think it's a fake?"

"If it's a fake, why wouldn't they do a classier one?" Taglia objected.

"*Can* they do a classier one?" Wheelwright asked.

"Maybe they think no one will suspect that miserable thing to be a fake," Taglia suggested. "The only thing that surprises me is the staples. I would have expected one of those half-size copper Soviet paper clips . . . if I'd expected anything."

Bierman read the report slowly. He had not been stationed in Moscow and was not fluent in Russian. But he did not pretend to read quickly. He read slowly, at his own pace. After several minutes he put the report down. "Is there any physical evidence inconsistent with this? Any evidence of interrogation?"

"No external marks on the body," Martin said. "He hadn't been beaten. No electrode burns. We don't know what else they can do, exactly."

"Their report says he carried no identification."

"Yes, it does."

"Is it correct?"

"They didn't turn any identification over to us. A preliminary search of his apartment here didn't turn up his Embassy I.D. There's no evidence whether he had it when he left here."

"Surely he would have carried it as a matter of routine?"

"One would think so."

"Could it have been stolen during the 'attack'?"

"Presumably. Although the report notes that he was carrying a good deal of hard currency of various kinds. That wasn't taken by the murderers. It was all returned with the body."

"Would he normally have carried that variety of currency?"

"No. But it's possible he was meeting someone he didn't want to pay in dollars, to make tracing harder."

"Is there any indication that they knew who he was?"

Martin shrugged. "The report says they identified him as the agricultural attaché."

"Yes. 'Identified from a photograph match.' I'd like to see their photo files; wouldn't you? Did someone go through all the photos of foreigners known to be in the country? How did they know for sure he was a foreigner, for that matter?"

"I'd guess they assumed he was, from the circumstances, the clothes, the currency, and went from there."

"Well. But do they know he was with the CIA?"

"Are you kidding?" the Ambassador broke in. "They know every time anybody takes a shit in this place! Of course they knew he was CIA! Don't you guys know who's KGB at their embassy in Washington? I sure as hell hope you do!"

Bierman didn't answer this. He leafed through the KGB report again, and then again, but without apparently looking for anything.

"Well, what next?" the Ambassador asked finally.

Taglia said nothing.

"I'd say we take them up on their offer to cooperate," Martin said.

"Their what?" Bierman's tone was not surprised, but hostile.

"Together with the KGB report, the Foreign Ministry delivered an offer to allow us to cooperate with the ongoing KGB investigation."

"In response to Martin's suggestion," Taglia said.

"Who gave you authority to suggest that?" Bierman demanded.

Martin shrugged. "It seemed like a good idea at the time. We don't have to do it, of course."

"Still seems like a good idea," the Ambassador observed. He had leaned back in his chair and put his feet up on the table and, arms behind his head, was staring at the ceiling. "Maybe we'd learn something."

"The only thing we'll learn from a KGB investigation is what they want us to learn. And we don't want to know that."

"That right?" the Ambassador drawled. "I never could get the hang of this spy stuff. Why don't we want to know it, exactly?"

"Because there won't be any truth in it. Or worse yet, there'll be just enough truth in it to get us to wonder if the rest is true; but the rest will be lies."

"I don't s'pose we could tell one from the other? Anyway, I don't see what it could hurt to see what they have to say. Sometimes, as Yogi said, you can observe a lot just by watching."

· 12 ·

Monday, January 23, 1989
Noon
The United States Embassy

MARTIN SAT IN HUTCHINS'S APARTMENT, UNABLE TO GET STARTED. THE LAST time he had inventoried anyone's personal effects was in the Army, and he hadn't expected ever to do it again.

Moscow television was putting out an imitation of Western rock, not bad for beginners. In one more generation they'd have it down. Meanwhile, the noise kept his mind off the man whose life he was packing away.

He launched himself reluctantly to his feet and took his list over to Hutch's desk. He knew he didn't need to worry about coming across classified papers or personal embarrassments: Bierman would have those. Martin had to admire the professionalism of the job Bierman and Denson had done ransacking the apartment in the name of "securing official papers." If Martin hadn't known the apartment and its contents well, he would have thought it untouched. He was sure the papers were "secure." Nothing was left to do but check off the remains.

There were few remains: the desk held two Fedoskino boxes and a Georgian dagger Hutchins had used as a paperwieght, now paperless. The boxes and dagger weren't valuable. Mainly, there were the paintings. Sitting at the desk, Martin looked around the walls of the apartment with its dozen or more big canvases and crowd of small ones. He tried to remember when they had each arrived, but couldn't. That rainbow of colors opposite the window—that was the first. He had introduced Hutch to Yuri Krasavitsky, the artist. Hutch had invited Martin here to this apartment for a drink the same day. But after that? He couldn't recall, even though he had been with Hutchins when Hutch bought most of the others too.

They had arrived in Moscow on the same day, on the same flight. They met on the plane. Probably if their friendship had not started

66

then, it never would have, they were so unlike: he forty-five and tired of petty academic wars—"Campus politics is so bitter because it involves so little"—Hutch thirty and eager for the challenge of "the most important job in my line of work," as he had said.

"Agriculture attaché?" Martin had reminded him, politely; and then they both laughed.

He sat for a long time staring at the wall and thinking of Hutch, and only slowly realized that the wall he was staring at held a painting, and that in the painting was a woman's face.

It was a small oil painting, a half meter square—a portrait, apparently, of a woman, but showing only the face, from chin to hairline, floating on a blank background. He recognized it, now that he thought of it. He remembered when it had shown up, sometime back in the fall. Hutchins had bought it on Arbat Street. "Cheap and good," he had said, and no more. Martin had not paid much attention to it then: it was not his taste in art. It reminded him of the Chinese theatrical masks for sale in the art galleries of half of Asia, but this was far more lifelike—except that it was done in two shades of blue separated by a line slashed diagonally across the face. The draftsmanship was skillful: the face looked almost three-dimensional; but the colors mocked any attempt to see it as a real woman. And like a mask, the eyes were blank, though behind the empty sockets there was . . . something. Not mere unpainted canvas, but something put there by the artist—or was it something seen in the model herself? He went over to the painting; but get as close as he might, he could not tell what it was behind the eyes, although he was sure it was something, or a suggestion of something. It was not a picture Martin liked. It was not realism, it was not abstraction, it was not anything he had ever seen before; and he did not like it.

It was unsigned. He took it down and looked at the back. There was no signature there either. He hung it back on the wall.

He went back to the desk and went on with his work; but now that he was aware of the painting, he kept having the feeling of someone watching him, and he looked up constantly, each time to find the woman's eyes on him.

· 13 ·

Monday, January 23, 1989
4 P.M.
The Lubyanka

COLONEL SOKOLOV SCOWLED AS HE SURVEYED THE GROUP, CHANTURIA'S section, gathered in his office. There were five of them, and under other circumstances he would have been heartily sorry to see them charged with an investigation of this delicate nature. Under other circumstances? Maybe these *were* "other circumstances." But it was too late to change anything now.

Chanturia himself Sokolov had never liked. It was not that Chanturia was Georgian—a Georgian could be effective: Stalin had been Georgian, after all. And Sokolov had been posted to Georgia as a young officer, in charge of special matters for the Tbilisi office. No, he had nothing against Georgians. But Chanturia—he wasn't serious enough to be an officer of the Committee on State Security. There was one kind of Georgian who never quite got down to business with life, and Chanturia was that kind. Orlov, Chanturia's lieutenant, had plenty of seriousness, enough for both of them. It would be better if he had more brains, but there was nothing fundamentally wrong with him. Too much intelligence was perhaps not a good thing in an intelligence officer either. Belkin, for example. Belkin was a good officer, the best of them. He would have commanded the section, if he weren't a Jew. His name didn't show it, nor did point five of his passport: but those who knew, knew. And but for his intelligence. Belkin was smart enough to understand his superior officers, but not smart enough to hide it. Kupinski, the Peasant, could get by in the Committee on the strength of his achievements as an Olympic shot-putter, but he would never head a Chief Directorate; while Timur Iskakov, the one known as the Tatar, had enough of that race's blood in him to give the shivers to men who had invested a career in fighting Asian secret wars, men who remembered when Stalin uprooted the Tatar people from their homes and shipped them to

Asia during the war because he feared they'd side with the Germans. Iskakov wouldn't prosper.

And then there was the other man in the room. Dushenkin. The Silent Death. The representative of the Inspector General.

Sokolov turned to Chanturia. "Captain, are you ready to report?"

"Yes, Comrade Colonel."

"Begin, then."

"This case involves the death of a foreign national, Charles Hutchins, an American, who was killed during an incident at a cooperative cafe on Prospect Mira on the night of 17–18 January. *Gospodin* Hutchins was the Central Intelligence Agency's Moscow station chief." Chanturia referred to Hutchins by the old Russian word for "mister," now used only for foreigners. "The American Embassy has made a request that they be allowed to 'cooperate' in our investigation. This request was made to our Ministry of Foreign Affairs verbally by Mr. Benjamin Franklin Martin, not known to have any connection with the Central Intelligence Agency. Pursuant to orders, at the request of the Ministry of Foreign Affairs, a full report on the circumstances of the death and our subsequent investigation was prepared and was given to the Ministry of Foreign Affairs for delivery to the American Embassy. It was delivered to the American Embassy Saturday, January 21, at approximately 17 hours and 30 minutes."

Dushenkin spoke. "Is this the report I have in my hands?"

"Yes, Comrade Colonel, it is."

"A rather small report."

"It was of course made sanitary before delivery."

"But the facts it contains are correct?"

"Yes, sir."

Sokolov broke in. "I reviewed the report myself before its delivery."

"Very well. Proceed."

"As the report will show, Comrade Colonel, the facts are these . . ." Chanturia proceeded to restate the case for the third time that day— first for his section members, then for Colonel Sokolov, and now for the Inspector General's representative. Chanturia was heartily sick of the facts of this matter. He wished *Gospodin* Charles Hutchins had got himself killed on someone else's shift.

Come to think of it, he had. Chanturia had been off duty when he was called. Why did these things happen to him?

When Chanturia finished, Dushenkin asked, "Why would a request for cooperation have come from an American having no connection with the CIA?"

"We don't know," Chanturia said.

"It seems highly unlikely," Dushenkin said. Dushenkin was called the Silent Death because of his cold silences. He made a habit of speaking only when he had something critical to say. He turned now to Sokolov. "Could this indicate that our information is in error? That this Martin is indeed an agent of the CIA, although not previously identified?"

Sokolov started to sweat. "Certainly it's possible. But if so, his cover has been very good. Much better than is normal for the Americans. He has been assigned to the Embassy here for over a year, as some sort of a special assistant cultural attaché; and there has been no indication that he has engaged in intelligence activities. Previously, he was never employed by the CIA, nor indeed by the U.S. government, except for two years active duty in the military after college. And he has never had any other foreign post."

"Cultural attachés always engage in intelligence activities," Dushenkin said. "What else are they good for? I suggest you concentrate a little harder on *Gospodin* Martin. Now, what is the nature of our 'cooperation' to be?"

"We have arranged a personal briefing for the designated American investigators tomorrow," Sokolov answered.

"Do we know who they are to be?"

"No. Not yet. We have asked to be notified. The Americans have not responded."

"Perhaps you will ask them why they did not ask our 'cooperation' when this man Hutchins was missing for two days."

"We'll ask," Sokolov said.

But perhaps they won't tell us, Chanturia thought to himself.

· 14 ·

Monday, January 23, 1989
8 P.M.
Christmas Convent

FOR SOKOLOV, THE SHORT WALK UP DZERZHINSKY STREET TO THE BOULE-vard Ring was a trip of fifty years.

The street was almost deserted. There were no cars, and only a few people walking, all of them in the street to avoid falls on the side-walks, where three centimeters of fresh powder covered the ice pack that a thousand boots had made of a season's unshoveled snow. He had been born at the other end of this street, within a kilometer of Dzerzhinsky Square. Those were the two ends of his world: the KGB headquarters on Dzerzhinsky Square at the near end, and at the far end, towering over the Boulevard Ring, the ruin of *Rozhdestvenskii Monastir*—Christmas Convent. It was there that he was born, in the convent.

It had been a ruin even then. Once among the grandest convents of Mother Russia, it was closed at the Revolution, but by the twenties Christmas Convent had been reoccupied by workers seeking shelter in the dilapidation of Moscow; and it was still occupied today. Still occupied, and still a ruin.

Sokolov had long ago ceased to see this street, he had walked it so often; and though he did not often come this way now, it was still as familiar as breath to him. The pale blue and yellow shop signs barely made a glow that could be seen through the ever-falling snow, but he knew them all. The smell of an alleyway open into a court-yard, a compound of boiled cabbage and damp plaster and piss—he knew that smell, now almost sealed off in winter's grave, but some-how still there, calling out of spring evenings and humanity.

He turned into the open gate of the convent, a gate not closed in seventy years now. He climbed carefully the slick cobbles of the slope to the first church. He could not see far through the snow, although the snow itself made the night white within the limits of vision; but

71

he knew the church, felt its stones before he saw it. It was marked as a state architectural landmark now. In his day it had been a mine for bricks to shore up the crumbling apartments around it, themselves once nuns' quarters, built into the inner face of the convent wall. The mine was closed, and the apartments were crumbling faster than ever. What was the world coming to? To save the ruins of old superstition, while living people shivered.

"In my day . . ." It seemed so long ago. And yet he was still alive. Still young, even.

Pavel Fedorovich Sokolov, now Colonel of the Committee on State Security, was born in 1930 in Moscow. His father was a Bolshevik who rose in the government to be Deputy Minister of Light Industry. Even as a youth, Pavel had no memory of his mother, who died of fever when he was two years old. He was born in a communal apartment built into the wall of the old Christmas Convent. Later his father could have had better lodgings, but he saw no need to raise himself above the workers.

The neighbor who shared their kitchen was a single woman, a music teacher, Vera Stepanovna. Although she had never married, Vera Stepanovna had a daughter of her own, Olga Viktorevna. Days, Pavel and Olga were left at the same day-care center. Vera liked young Pavel and began to take care of him evenings when his father worked. On the rare occasions when his father came home early, they would all sit together in the kitchen. She cooked plain *blyni* and talked about the children she taught in the neighborhood school. Pavel's father thought it was good for his boy to hear this.

It was raining that evening his father came home earlier than usual, cold rain, but instead of going to the kitchen for dinner, he asked Pavel if he wanted to go for a walk. This was something unusual, and Pavel was glad for it. He put on his galoshes and raincoat, and they went out. As they walked, his father said that he was going to tell Pavel something important. Sometimes things in life don't turn out as one wants them to, he said, and he wanted Pavel to remember, whatever happened, that his father was an honest man who gave his life to building a country that would belong to the poor people, and that all his life he was devoted to the people and to Comrade Stalin. Then they walked home.

Pavel heard a noise in the middle of that night and felt a light turn on. When he opened his eyes he saw three men in the room, three strange men, and his father putting on his clothes. One man stood by the door, another by his father, and the third was looking through some papers.

Without saying anything, Pavel looked at his father, asking with his eyes what was going on. And without saying a word, his father came to him and with a hand stroked his hair. He looked into the boy's eyes and said, "Everything will be all right." They went out, the three men and his father, and the boy ran into the corridor, where he ran into Vera Stepanovna standing in her nightgown and shawl, her eyes full of tears. She turned to him and said with a trembling voice, "Oh, it's so cold," and looked at his naked feet on the cold floor. She picked him up in her arms, and he felt his shirt wet with her tears.

The strangers left with his father, and Vera Stepanovna took him into her room, into her bed, where Olga was already whimpering. He lay like a scared little rabbit as she cried quietly. Close to morning they all fell asleep.

His father never came back.

For several years more Vera Stepanovna cared for him; but then she became sick herself, and after a few months died. Her sister and her sister's husband, by quick work, succeeded to the apartment. They took Olga with it, but they had no room for a boy they didn't know, who wasn't family; and so Pavel was placed in an orphanage where he finished school, an orphanage founded by Felix Dzerzhinsky himself. He went into the army at age eighteen, and at twenty, out of the army, he went to KGB school.

He thought often about his father, although he could remember little more than his face and the way he talked, and especially that last night. He never allowed himself to think about what happened to his father after that night. He stopped his thoughts with his father's words—that different things happen in this life, and not everything that happens is pleasant.

And that was fifty years ago. And what was the world coming to now?

There was hardly a light from the apartments. Their triple-paned windows and their outer shutters alike were closed against the cold, and the cracks stuffed with rags. Yes, that was how it had been. And still was. And dark as Hell. Light showed only where the shutters fit badly.

He walked once around the church and then halfway again. There were only his own footprints in the snow. Satisfied that no one was following him, he went to a door and knocked. He knocked forcefully—how else should an officer of the Committee knock?—but the snow muffled the sound, which seemed hardly able to force its way past his form into the night.

"Who is it?" a voice called from within. A man's voice. He was here, then.

"A visitor," he answered. He heard the bolt being drawn back.

A young man opened the door. "Good evening, Colonel. Be healthy."

"Be healthy." The Colonel stepped into the entry hall and kicked the snow off his boots. He whacked the snow out of his hat and tucked it under his arm.

"It's cold," the young man said. "Would you drink some tea?"

Through the open door the Colonel could see into the tiny living room. It had hardly changed. He supposed he could find the teapot himself, if asked. "No, thank you." But he stepped into the room. The younger man limped through the door. It annoyed Sokolov. Cripples lacked character. Sokolov closed the door behind them because he did not know who had the other room that shared the kitchen.

"The water's hot."

"I'm not staying. Is Olga Viktorevna here?"

"She's in line somewhere to buy cabbage."

"Good. You saw the story in *Izvestia?*"

The young man laughed. "Fame at last! It's too bad I can't brag about it."

The Colonel's voice cut short the laugh. "See that you don't."

The young man dropped into a chair—one of two in the room; there was no space for another. "You needn't worry."

"I am worried. I didn't think you and your friends would be stupid enough to knife foreigners."

"Is the Committee so solicitous of foreigners now? You want us to restrict our work to citizens?"

"What I want doesn't matter right now."

"Anyway, we didn't know our target wasn't there, until it was too late. What were we supposed to do? Back out with apologies?"

"There's going to be a joint investigation."

The young man shrugged. "The militia aren't going to bother *us.* We've dealt with them for years."

You mean your father has, Sokolov thought; but he didn't bother to say it. What he did say was, "It's not the militia. It's the Americans. The CIA, in short."

The young man opened his eyes wide. "The C . . . I . . . A?"

"The one you killed was an American agent."

The young man laughed. He laughed sitting down, and then he stood up and hugged himself and laughed standing up. "The fuck-your-mother CIA! He won't believe it!" He spun twice around and nearly fell off his bad leg, but ended facing Sokolov. "And the KGB is going to cooperate?"

"Such are my orders."

"It's good you're in charge of the investigation, then."

"To the extent anyone is in charge, now. It would be useful if you left Moscow. You and everyone involved in any way."

The young man grew serious. "It's not a convenient time."

"Make it convenient."

"He won't be happy to see me go just now."

"Then he'll have to be unhappy."

"I can't promise he'll approve leave for me. The others, no problem, but I have the rendezvous to coordinate."

"Understand that I'm not asking anyone's approval of anything. I'm suggesting what would be best. For your health. It's nice in Tbilisi, this time of year. In Moscow, not so nice. Tell your father what I said. He'll understand." Sokolov said this in a flat voice—not an unpleasant voice, but the voice of a man who didn't customarily have to say anything twice.

The young man, very serious now, sucked at his upper lip.

The Colonel put his hat back on. "As you know, it's also not very nice in Siberia. Good night."

He closed the door to the living room behind him but paused a moment in the hall. The same wooden coat-pegs in the wall, the gaps in the floorboards, the same smell from the toilet past the kitchen. Nothing changed.

But now everything had changed.

What was the world coming to?

75

· 15 ·

Friday, January 27, 1989
2 P.M.
The Lubyanka

THE EMBASSY CAR LEFT MARTIN, BIERMAN, AND ROLLIE TAGLIA ON THE sidewalk at 2 Dzerzhinksy Square. An officer in uniform was waiting for them. "It's a good thing Felix is looking the other way," Taglia muttered, referring to Dzerzhinsky's statue, the genuine Iron Felix.

They entered the tall oak front door and were in a different world.

The grimy misery of Moscow was outside. Inside was a soft-carpeted floor, a winding stairway, a crystal chandelier reflected on marble walls.

They signed a register watched over by a scowling green-hatted guard. Their guide led them down marble stairs to check their coats at a garderobe which was Soviet standard except that it was manned by a young KGB recruit instead of a grandmother. After a jolting elevator ride, another young guard led them along beige-walled halls lined with tall dark wooden doors, all closed and unmarked, and led them at last through a narrow anteroom—empty, except for an empty coatrack, an unused desk with a telephone on it, and a single chair—and into the conference room, where they were left alone.

The conference room, large enough for two delegations of twenty-five to face off across the table in the center, was paneled in new gloss-finished blond plywood. The windows were hung with dark red velvet drapes over venetian blinds angled so that it was impossible to see anything outside. The room had the unfinished look standard to official Soviet spaces, even the best of them. The wall paneling did not quite fit at the bottom, where it just failed to make contact with an uneven floor of not-quite-smooth oak strips laid in a slightly uneven herringbone pattern. The only furniture was the long conference table and the chair on its two long sides. At the center of the table a metal tray held several bottles of fruit-flavored drink made from mineral water, several glasses, and a bottle opener.

76

At Bierman's advice, to reduce the feeling of being on the enemy's ground, the Americans staked out their claim on the side of the table with their backs to the window, where they could see anyone who entered the room. They sat down at the middle of that side and, although they sank into lolling American attitudes, they talked in low voices.

The door they had come through opened, and four uniformed KGB officers entered. They entered in order of rank, led by a full Colonel, with a Captain at the rear. The Colonel introduced their party from across the table. No one made an attempt to come around or reach across to shake hands. Introductions were made through the third man of the Soviet delegation, a Major, who spoke flawless American. His name, he said, was Miroslavsky. The others were Dushenkin, Sokolov, and Chanturia. Miroslavsky waved off Bierman's attempt to flatter him for his command of English: "I had good training; but there are more important skills."

"If you'd prefer, we could speak Russian," Martin said in Russian. "It might make things move faster."

"We accept your offer," Dushenkin said. But the translator, Miroslavsky, stayed, nevertheless.

"Please sit down," Dushenkin said. Chanturia, the junior officer, opened a bottle of the drink and poured a glass for each of the Americans. He offered it also to the other Soviets, who all declined. Chanturia took a glass himself and sipped at it.

Dushenkin spoke first. "We regret the circumstances which bring us together here," he said. "It is of course embarrassing to our government when untoward situations develop. You have seen our report, I believe? Then we should be ready for concrete discussions. Our investigation has been hampered by lack of certain information, which may be available to you. We would like to know what theories you may have as to the reason for the attack on Mr. Hutchins—if indeed it was an attack on Mr. Hutchins, and not merely on a cafe at which he happened to be present. To begin with, it would be useful to our investigation to know how Mr. Hutchins happened to be there that night. Where he had been, who he had spoken with, and who he was with when the attack occurred."

This introduction was followed by a long silence during which, it seemed to Martin, each side had determined on the spur of the moment to stare down the other. Certainly, he knew, the American side had made no such plan; but it was a long and determined silence which followed. Martin broke it at last. His designation by Bierman as the American spokesman had been for the simple purpose of confusing the Soviet side, who would expect the new CIA station chief to be part of the delegation and would look for clues to his identity. It was, Martin knew, a sacrifice Bierman did not relish but yet in a way enjoyed, the enjoyment of the insider secretly in charge. He believed that Bierman, if forced to choose, would rather be in charge secretly than openly. As it was, Bierman was the note-taker for the American side—an assignment that let him control the history of the meeting.

This was the silence that Martin broke. He said, "We don't know how Mr. Hutchins happened to be there. We have no information on where he had been or who he was with."

This time it was the Soviet side which sat silent. It was the silence of a chess match. Their opening had been to go directly to their highest priority in this meeting—to determine the CIA's mission in sending Hutchins to what turned out to be his death. Dushenkin personally considered the American counter, a bare-faced denial, to be quite unimaginative—so much so that it almost made him wonder whether this delegation in fact included any CIA personnel of sufficient stature to have been trusted with knowledge of the deceased's mission. He was all but sure, of course, that Bierman was an agent of the CIA: Bierman had arrived at the Embassy immediately on the heels of the news of Hutchins's death. He was not the only American diplomat to do so, to be sure; but the North American Department—so they claimed—had been able conclusively to filter out all the others as mere screens for the movement of Bierman—who was, significantly, the only one of the lot who had come to this meeting, so perhaps the North American Department was right. But still, Bierman might be a mere messenger or low-level investigator. Taglia, as a career diplomat, certainly must be supposed to be CIA, and if so, the paucity of information on him in the Committee's files testified that he was an important person indeed. But on the other hand, American career diplomats—for reasons Dushenkin could not imagine—were not always trained by the CIA. So it was possible that Taglia was indeed merely a career diplomat without a significant intelligence role. That would leave Martin; but if the special assistant cultural attaché, after a lifetime outside apparent government service, were an agent of sufficient stature to head this delegation, Dushenkin would think *that* the most unnerving item of information to have surfaced in this bizarre case. It would show a level of subtlety never before imagined in CIA deep planning and covert capabilities. Also, if Dushenkin were playing the American side of this game, he would not let the man in charge do the talking in this meeting; but again, of course, a deeply covered agent might be given the assignment for exactly that reason.

"It's most surprising," Dushenkin said at length, "that you don't require your personnel to report their plans and whereabouts." *Especially,* he thought, *that you didn't inquire about him for two days after his death—not until we informed you of it, in fact.*

"That's the difference between our system and yours, I suppose," Martin said. "Our people are free to do what they want on their own time."

"I believe you have certain rules concerning fraternizing with Soviet citizens, however? Rules which it appears Mr. Hutchins was violating."

"We have rules for our security guards, as it appears that there has been a consistent effort on the part of your Committee to distract their attention from their duties through the use of Soviet citizens," Martin responded. "Attractive citizens, as I am told. But Mr. Hutchins, as agriculture attaché, was not privy to classified information, so of course there was no need to extend those rules to him. Although it does appear from your report that he was in the company of an attractive person of the female persuasion who most probably was a Soviet citizen."

Chanturia watched this exchange intently. But he watched also the Americans not involved in it. While he admired Martin's sparring, it seemed clear enough that of the three Americans the one most intent on following the Soviet side of the discussion was Bierman. And he had no doubt that the CIA would be far more interested in the workings of the Committee than in the loss of their station chief. Certainly he knew that the Committee, if it were suddenly so blessed as to have a team wandering the halls and conference rooms of Langley, would have that team ready to jump through their assholes to make the most of the event, no matter who had died to get them there.

For him, Bierman was the man to watch.

"The citizenship of Mr. Hutchins's female companion has not been determined," Dushenkin said. He sounded annoyed.

"But your report shows that the witnesses uniformly believed her to be Russian."

"True. Which is *proof* neither of her heritage nor of her citizenship."

"I suppose you would grant that it is some evidence?" Martin asked. "But we'd rather discuss what you know of the identity of the killers. It seems that you have even less evidence on that point, unless your investigation has produced something since your report was written." And so Martin ended up at the point most important to him—and, he suspected, to the Ambassador. Bierman believed that the KGB had killed Hutchins, and Martin was willing to assume that Bierman was right; but unlike Bierman, he was not interested in what mission the KGB might have been carrying out, except to the extent that it had resulted in Hutchins's death. Martin suspected, however, that Bierman's view was simply the obverse of Dushenkin's: that the main thing was to discover the involvement of the opposite agency. All else was simply intelligence data bearing on that goal.

Dushenkin replied with great gravity, "Our report stated our data and conclusions as of its date. We have continued our investigations, and we will continue to provide you with a full statement of our results, as our Foreign Ministry promised you. I regret to say that we have not yet advanced our conclusions beyond the point reached in the report, although there are developments which give us reason for cautious optimism. We are of course grateful for your offer of cooperation and are intensely interested in receiving whatever help you can provide to us."

"Could you summarize the steps you've taken to reach this 'cautious optimism'?" Martin asked.

Dushenkin turned to Chanturia. "Captain Chanturia has immediate responsibility for Moscow field activities. Captain, your report."

Chanturia reluctantly left off watching Bierman. With a serious face he nodded to Dushenkin and proceeded to spin out a line of gossamer designed to inform the Americans that several of the witnesses were being surveiled, without revealing—which could be political dynamite, and for the CIA an intelligence coup of the highest value—that a First Deputy Minister's son was the subject of suspicion. Imagine what the CIA would do with that bit of information: perhaps build an attempt to turn not only the son—if they did not have his soul already—but the First Deputy Minister himself to their purposes! Considering the instability of the present politics in Moscow, the insane fears that were developing around the elections going forward for the new Congress of People's Deputies, nothing was beyond possibility.

"There are also certain activities being conducted outside Moscow," Chanturia concluded, "which are not under my personal direction."

"Colonel Sokolov will address those," Dushenkin said. "Thank you, Captain. Colonel Sokolov; please."

The CIA's local files reviewed in preparation for this meeting had contained nothing on Captain Chanturia; but they had some sketchy information on Sokolov. He had joined the KGB not long after World War II and so was a product of the Stalin KGB, the real KGB, when the Committee was at its purest and most powerful. Most of his career had been spent on internal security, not foreign intelligence: he was a breaker of dissidents.

Sokolov had the manner—either natural or cultivated—of the blunt man of action. "Captain Chanturia's investigations indicate that one of the assailants may have been Georgian. One witness stated that this assailant walked with a noticeable limp—although the witness's statement was not clear as to whether he favored the left leg or the right."

"We may conclude that he was a nonpartisan assailant, then?" Martin wondered aloud. Taglia and Chanturia laughed; Bierman, Dushenkin, and Sokolov did not.

Sokolov looked at Martin with the unamused look of a man who takes his business seriously and disapproves of those who do not. "This is the only physical evidence as to the identity of any of the assailants," he went on. "Our information does not reveal any person of this description associated with known Moscow criminal elements. We suggest that it may be useful to look beyond Moscow; and we have requested our forces in the Georgian Republic to identify persons having these characteristics. We are, in fact, turning Georgia upside down to find such a man. I have no doubt that if he is there, we will locate him."

Martin saw that Chanturia's and Sokolov's elaborate police jargon was a screen to hide the fact that they were saying nothing. The KGB had not identified the killers. They had no theory to account for the attack, other than Mafia extortion: but the manager's testimony—fragmentary as it was—indicated that the cafe was already paying protection. They had not identified the woman, the vanished mystery witness.

Or, in the alternative, they were lying. Bierman had already told the American side what he thought: that it was a KGB operation, disguised to look like a Mafia attack; that the woman was the KGB's own agent, whose identity would never be discovered; and that this "cooperation" was only another stage of a charade, intended now to discover whatever could be learned about CIA methods.

It was perhaps in the nature of the meeting that the clearest truth told by each side was what seemed to the other to be the greatest lie; while the small shadings away from strict truth which they both introduced seemed to the other to be the most likely clues to the "real" truth. (Both sides had been directed by their authorities to cooperate with the other; but both would "of course" interpret their orders in such a way as to protect their respective agencies' reputations.)

Thus, because the Americans could not admit what the Soviets knew (could not admit it even though they were almost certain that the Soviets did know it)—that Hutchins was the CIA station chief, someone who simply would not have been out on his own on a frolic with a Soviet woman—the Soviets doubted the truth they were being told, that the Americans had not the slightest idea what Hutchins was up to nor who his companion was. The Soviets assumed that the woman must be an agent of the CIA.

Conversely, because the Soviets could not admit what the Americans knew—that the Soviets did know that Hutchins was the station chief—the Americans supposed that the Soviets had aimed a torpedo at him in the form of a beautiful woman.

So, a great castle of doubt, the cooperative work of both sides, was erected on the suspicion that, fundamentally, the truth must be something other than what was being said by the other side.

It was a castle in which both sides enclosed themselves: and they looked for truth only within its walls.

Nevertheless, they each had a mission to perform. Two missions, really—first, to investigate the death of Charles Hutchins, and second, to find out what the hell the other side was after.

In pursuit of those missions, they were bound to run a three-legged race, kneeing and elbowing one another all the way to the goal—or tripping one another short of it.

"And now," Dushenkin said, "we would like to hear your suggestions for further investigation."

"It would be best," Martin said, "if we could interview the witnesses ourselves. Your work was quite professional; but sometimes a new point of view can result in additional information."

Dushenkin answered: "In principle this would be possible; but practically speaking, there are serious difficulties. As to the foreigners, the Committee has no authority to interfere with their lives; and as to the citizens, since they have already given up working time to be interviewed once, their employers may be unwilling to free them a second time. They are, after all, working people—like everyone in the Soviet Union."

Martin offered to go to their places of work to conduct a short interview.

"That would be so inconvenient for you," Dushenkin said. "Let us try to arrange a place for you to meet with them. But of course, we must involve our Foreign Ministry authorities in the question, and you know how slow bureaucrats can be."

"Yes, bureaucratic sloth is a pity," Martin answered.

"We will do our best," Dushenkin said. "But as to other avenues. American technical proficiency is of course well-known throughout the world. There may be many approaches which we have overlooked. We have, of course, sealed the cafe premises for the course of the investigation, and I believe you will find it quite undisturbed."

"It's a pity you didn't take the same care with the body," Martin said.

"Could you explain your meaning, please?"

"I mean that if the body had not been autopsied, we might be able to find some information about the cause and manner of death, and perhaps about the killer."

"An autopsy is required by Soviet law in cases of violent death. We of course conducted one. You have the full notes and report."

"Which is not exactly the same as having the body intact."

"It is, unless you think that the doctor who conducted the autopsy has lied," Sokolov said in a voice colder than the winter outside the room. "Is that what you are saying?"

Martin didn't answer this, but Dushenkin said smoothly, "I'm sure Mr. Martin means that their additional technical resources might have yielded additional information. We too regret that this is no longer possible. But we were in possession of a body—we did not know whose—and needed to preserve what information we could. If we had been notified promptly of the disappearance of Mr. Hutchins, then, of course, we would have proceeded otherwise. It is regrettable that this was not done; but it was not, and we must go from where we now stand. As to the premises, they are intact. It is also regrettable that time has passed; but still, if you wish to make any technical investigations—blood tests, chemical tests, I don't mean to limit you, but I am not sure what to suggest—you may be sure of our full cooperation."

"We'll want to inspect the premises," Martin said. "Perhaps we can make recommendations thereafter."

"We can arrange for you to go there immediately. Shall we meet tomorrow, then? At that time we can consider a continuing schedule of meetings, based upon the investigations you wish to make."

"What shall we call this joint operation?" Bierman asked, bending over his notes.

"We first labeled our inquiry 'Investigation X,'" Dushenkin said. There had been an investigation number, of course; but he didn't care to reveal that: no hint of Committee procedure would ever pass from him to the CIA. "For 'Mister X'—although now we know the name."

"Then I suggest that the joint inquiry be named 'Operation X,'" Bierman said.

"Agreed."

Bierman made his note.

One shading of the truth on the part of the KGB was to maintain that the report given to the American side was complete. Of course it was not. It had been sanitized in ways which were necessary to make it politically acceptable.

One was the elimination of any reference to Maxim Gradski, son of the First Deputy Minister of Machine Building.

· 16 ·

Friday, January 27, 1989
5 P.M.
The KGB

"GRADSKI. WHAT DO WE DO ABOUT GRADSKI?" CHANTURIA DID A FAIR imitation of Colonel Sokolov as he glowered at the members of his section. "I don't know what the son of a bitch is up to, but if the Americans start asking about him, we're dead. How are we going to convince them we're trying to solve this crime when we've been ordered to lay off our prime suspect?"

"Well, you can't have an investigation of the son of a First Deputy Minister, can you?" This was from the Peasant. From most people it would have been irony; but Chanturia knew the Peasant had no more irony in him than a brick wall. The Peasant just couldn't conceive of a country in which the sons of First Deputy Ministers weren't exempt from the rules.

"You didn't report that you've been staking out his papa's dacha, did you?" Chanturia asked Orlov.

"No one's asked yet. But we'll have to account for that time somehow."

"Hell, tell them you've interviewed every hooligan in town looking for limping Georgians. It's damn near true. What's going on at the dacha? If there's not something soon, we *will* have to pull people off there."

"Tatar, what's your report?" Orlov asked.

Timur Iskakov stood. He was always conscious of being shorter than the others, and in compensation he tried always to stand straighter than anyone else. His report was sharp and concise, although his impressions were not. Timur was a romantic in a profession that offered little scope for romanticism. He tried to keep it well hidden. "He's worried," Iskakov said.

The country home of Comrade First Deputy Minister Gradski was one of some two dozen built by the state for its best workers—that is, for high Party officials and government ministers—in a forested valley not far outside Moscow. They were solidly built sprawling houses of one or two stories, fit for year-round living, with furnishings from special factories dedicated to making fine things for discriminating customers. The servants lived in smaller quarters adjacent, but the groundskeepers and special medical staff stayed at central facilities well out of sight of any of the houses. There was a danger that the general population, entering such a place, might become confused by what they saw, and so the sector where these houses were located was surrounded by a tall fence of barbed wire patrolled by special guards. From the houses themselves, the guards could not be seen, nor could any house be seen from any other. The impression from each was that it was located alone in an idyllic valley, where in winter the moon shone on unbroken snow and in spring the flowers spread unhindered over storybook meadows. Timur Iskakov, dressed as a member of the special guard, greatly enjoyed the views down the long still valley. He chose a location where he could see the house but could not be seen, and he waited. It was cold, but Iskakov was used to that. When his shift ended, he was replaced by another agent of the Committee, and so on around the clock, around the days.

Max Gradski, son of the First Deputy Minister of Machine Building, seemed not to be a lover of fine views: by day and by night he kept to the house, where he had come directly from his interview with Captain Chanturia. Timur didn't know exactly what the captain had said to Gradski, but he knew the actions of a worried man when he saw them. Or the inactions of a worried man when he didn't see them. A man gone to ground as solidly as this was very worried about something.

· 17 ·

Friday, January 27, 1989
5 P.M.
The United States Embassy

"ALL RIGHT, WHO'S DOING THIS BRIEFING?" THE AMBASSADOR ASKED. "Rollie, I guess you're the ranking officer here, even if you're not a genuine spook. What did the Ivans tell you? What are they after?"

"I'd say it was a high-level welcome," Taglia said. "We were welcomed by two long-faced junior officers and two long-faced Colonels. They might have been chipped out of the same stone. We all stared at each other and tried to say nothing meaningful first. 'You show me yours, and I'll show you mine.' The short of it is, we have the right to interview the known witnesses, they are eager for us to bring in the CIA's Magicians to dust the place for fingerprints or do whatever else Magicians do—they're really keen to see what that might be, having presumably emptied the place of any answers; we'll have more meetings as seems appropriate, at which we will exchange any and all information developed; and we'll all live happily ever after and never get to the bottom of this. But we'll say we're glad we tried."

"You sound hopeful," the Ambassador said.

"When you're playing in the other guy's yard, under his rules, with his mom watching, it saves a lot of disappointment not to be hopeful."

"Yeah, I suppose so. Does the other side have any theories?"

"The same one everybody would have, if it was Joe Blow who got in the way of the knife: a Mafia action to enforce the protection racket."

"What about you, Bierman? Are you surprised at the organized-crime theory?"

"Only that they'd admit the possibility to a foreigner. But it's not much of an admission for them, anymore. Crime is in the papers all the time. Even the KGB must get used to the idea that it exists."

Taglia said, "All those years they succeeded in keeping crime off the streets and in the government. New competition is always the hardest to take."

"Well, you've seen the premises, Bierman," the Ambassador said. "What do you think? *Are* there any CIA Magic things we ought to be doing? Fingerprints, blood tests, secret rituals, scans for spiritual plasma?"

"The place has been burned out, cut up and walked over," Bierman said. "It's doubtful that there's anything to find. If we were in this on our own, there are some things we'd try, but nothing that would offer any hope without getting into some serious Magic—things we certainly won't show to the Committee. Even low-grade help would take a week to organize."

"Maybe real help would help find the people who killed Hutchins," Martin said.

"In our business, Martin, the mission comes before the men, especially dead men. And our business is to learn Soviet secrets, not to give them ours."

"Then I'm glad I'm not in your business."

"All right, cool it," the Ambassador said. "We're supposed to be cooperating in this investigation, so let's cooperate. Figure out the best we can do without compromising anything, Bierman, and let's get it going. If it's not going to tell us anything new, then we don't mind if it takes a while to organize—Magicians from the states, whatever. What's next?"

"Who's going to interview witnesses?" Taglia asked.

"I'll do it myself," Bierman said. "I've already tried for the foreigners, of course. I've seen the two Japanese. They agree with what's in the KGB report, and they seem to be telling the truth. The German and the Finn have left the country. Our people outside will talk to them; but I don't expect anything new. No, the lie here is not in the witnesses' stories. It's woven in more deeply than that." He sat back and stretched his arms along the back of the couch. "No, I think there really was a woman," Bierman said. He closed his eyes, as if to see hidden truth more plain. "They got to Charles with a woman, and now they're trying to see if we're onto them. And trying to see what else they can get out of us."

"You think they lured him into a cafe at two in the morning and stabbed him to death?" Martin asked.

Bierman opened his eyes. "Do you think he just happened to be sitting in a cafe, when in walked the Mafia and offed him by accident? Sheer, stupid coincidence? Coincidence can be stretched only so far." Bierman seemed offended that anyone—at least, any red-blooded American—would think that an operative of the Central Intelligence Agency could be affected by anything so mundane as coincidence.

"But why would they go to all that trouble? Why not just knife him in a dark alley, or at her apartment, or . . . ?"

"He would display *some* caution, after all," Bierman said. As if to say, even a blundering brother in the art should be left a certain minimum of self-respect. Even if he was too dead to enjoy it. "And, of course, the blatancy of it would deflect suspicion from the Committee."

"That part of it doesn't seem to have worked," Martin observed. "Or is that not suspicion I detect in your voice?"

"It's professional jealousy," Bierman said. "No, you've got to hand it to them. This was one slick job. They left us without any grounds for *official* suspicion at all. It was one slick job."

· 18 ·

January 27–February 3, 1989
The KGB

IT TOOK A WEEK FOR CHANTURIA'S CREW TO DIG MAX GRADSKI OUT. MAX wasn't moving, but he might have been talking, so they applied for permission to put a tap on the house's telephone. The application was refused, but by that time a little discreet listening had been done anyway. Gradski had telephoned three foreigners—two of them Finns working on the reconstruction of the Metropol Hotel, and the third, a German who was the resident agent for a West German machine-tool manufacturer. They were careful conversations on Gradski's part, clearly made with the possibility of eavesdroppers in mind, constructed in a kind of code: which meant they had to be important conversations, to be made at all. They were about meetings postponed, delivery of goods delayed.

"What's he up to?" Chanturia asked.

"Selling stolen equipment, most likely," Orlov said.

"Buying equipment, more likely," Belkin said.

"Buying equipment?"

"In a manner of speaking." Belkin spoke with the patience of a good teacher helping problem students. "This kid's old man is First Deputy Minister of Machine Building. His ministry spends a hundred million in hard currency with foreign companies every year. A few words in the right places determine who gets the contracts. Do they want Max Gradski to be their friend?"

"Does the wild bear shit in the woods?" Chanturia asked.

"So Max helps the ministry buy the 'right' equipment," Belkin said. "Everyone's better off. Some more so than others, of course."

Still, no one higher up had the guts to make the argument that the son of a First Deputy Minister might be talking on his father's telephone to foreigners about matters of state security (any conversation with a foreigner was by definition a matter of state security), so the tap was denied; but a search of his apartment in the city was authorized. This apartment was not at Bersenyevskaya Embankment 20/2 where Gradski had stated he lived with his parents and sister. Interviews with Gradski's friends had turned up a bachelor apartment not far from Arbat Street.

The search of the Arbat apartment turned up the names and addresses of nearly a hundred foreigners resident in Moscow and, in the same file, names and addresses of more than twice that many Russian women.

"Now what the hell is this about?" Chanturia asked at the section's meeting. "Max Gradski knows a lot of foreigners: that I can understand. But all these women?"

"Where you've got men and women together," the Tatar said, "there's one thing going on. Let's talk to his friend Sveta, the translator."

Their conversation with the Committee's officer at her Institute had turned up nothing suspicious about Svetlana Kalinina, the translator.

She was a member of the Party, outspoken for a woman, and not overly strict about attendance at Party meetings, but apparently hard-working professionally and respected by the officers of the Institute.

Chanturia's cure for outspokenness was to turn Svetlana over for questioning to Orlov, who enjoyed these things more than he did.

Svetlana talked to Orlov.

"Timur was right," Orlov reported. "It's love."

"She's in love with Gradski? What a waste of a good woman. I guess the proverb's true, 'A woman may love even a billy goat.' "

"It's not quite that kind of love. More in the line of business."

"She's no whore."

"No. Just a *biznes* person." From Orlov's tone, Chanturia could tell that he didn't see much of a distinction.

"What's her story?" Chanturia asked. He asked it sad at heart.

Svetlana's story was that she was a source of introductions to Western businessmen for Max Gradski, who was in turn a source of introductions for Western businessmen to Moscow girls wanting the standard of living they deserved—a standard of living which, in Moscow, was available only to people with access to real money (which meant Western money—"hard currency")—that is, to high officials, criminals, and any and all foreigners. For a suitable gift, Max Gradski would arrange an introduction between the deserving Moscow girl and the desiring foreign man.

Chanturia shook his head. "What a sorry business." He sighed. "Have you confirmed it?"

"Not yet. But I don't doubt it."

"I don't either. Shit, I don't either. Well, let's do it."

Chanturia set out to confirm Gradski's business by interviews with a random sample of the people in Gradski's address books. They were in various degrees distressed by this rude exposure of their living arrangements; but they confirmed it.

It was time to go back to Max Gradski.

Faced with the witness statements from his girls, Gradski gave up his story, but not his arrogance. Why had he been at the waiter's birthday party at the cafe? He shrugged. "A waiter at the Uzbekistan sees a lot of girls and a lot of foreigners. Now, if you want to arrest me, find something illegal," he said.

"Have you read Article 226 of the Criminal Code?" Chanturia took from his desk a small gray-bound book and leafed through it.

" 'Procuring sexual connections for profit.' It's worth up to five years of your life."

"Where's the profit? These are just girls having a good time. There's no law against that. Anyway, I don't get money from them, or from their friends. Sometimes I get a gift—a little sign of appreciation. Sometimes I don't."

"That's not their story. Sometimes they get paid hard currency. That's worth three to eight years. Article 88 of the Criminal Code. Want me to show you?"

"It's their three to eight years, then. I don't receive their hard currency. If they get any."

"No? Where did you get the leather jacket you were wearing that night at the cafe?"

Max shrugged. "It was a gift."

"A gift from the foreign 'friend' of one of your girls?"

"A gift from my father, actually. He bought it on a trip to Italy. Would you care to ask him about it?"

"Witnesses have reported paying you hard currency for introductions. That's your three to eight years, not somebody else's."

"If you believe these witnesses, write up your report. And then see if you get permission to arrest me."

Max had a point—maybe even two points. The labor of his girls was easy, fun work, but that was not illegal in itself. Its occasional result—receipt of real money by a Soviet citizen—was illegal; but that was their problem, not Max's. Prostitution was a misdemeanor; but it wouldn't be easy to prove that what they were doing was even prostitution. Judges weren't going to stretch to find a woman guilty of prostitution just to have the pleasure of sentencing the son of a First Deputy Minister. Even the possession of real money was not likely to support the arrest of the son of a First Deputy Minister.

"This woman," Chanturia said. "The one who was with the foreigner in the cafe. Did you introduce them?"

"I'd never seen either of them. I wish I had. For a woman like that, I could get a thousand dollars for a one-year contract," Max said. "Let me know if you find her."

"I should turn the son of a bitch over to the Procurator's office on general principles," Chanturia said. "Screw his father."

"Easy for you to say, Sergo," Orlov said. "It'll be some investigator's career on the line; and you know how he's going to decide it. What's the point?"

The Tatar said, "You know, Captain, this Gradski's business has interesting possibilities."

"Interesting for a guy too short to get laid," the Peasant laughed.

The Tatar ignored him. "Why not go into business with him?"

"I'm not a *biznesman*," Chanturia said. "And if I were, I wouldn't like Max Gradski's business."

"Think of the connections he's got: a hundred good home-grown girls sleeping with foreigners. And all of them owing him a favor."

"So how do we get them to do *you* a favor?" the Peasant persisted.

"I am not interested, Timur," Chanturia said.

"Why not?" Orlov asked. "This is an *idea* Timur has. Why not go into business with our Max? Who can tell, maybe next time Max really will be able to place one of his girls with the CIA head of station."

"I am not interested," Chanturia said.

But some ideas are too strong to die. If Chanturia wasn't interested, others were. Sokolov himself took an interest in this one when he heard of it.

And so Max Gradski came out of the dacha and continued his business with a new partner. After some carefully explained delays and the manufacture of a better cover story than he had given to the KGB, Max was even interviewed by Bierman. He was not identified to Bierman as the son of a First Deputy Minister of the U.S.S.R. Bierman found nothing interesting about Max Gradski.

· 19 ·

Monday, February 13, 1989
11 A.M.
The Lubyanka

CHANTURIA IN COLD FEBRUARY IN HIS SNOW-BOUND OFFICE DREAMED OF spiced meats, of steaming *khinkali* with Georgian wine, of *khachapuri* and *shashlik* and golden sunshine and . . .

"Captain, the Colonel wants to see you. On the double!"

Being called to Sokolov's office was always unpleasant. It was worse than unpleasant on the first day of the fourth week of nothing to report. Chanturia walked slowly, to make the hall last as long as possible.

If smiles could be made of ice, Sokolov had one. Chanturia supposed it was a smile: he had never before seen the Colonel move his mouth into this shape. The Colonel had an unsuspected treasure trove of two gold teeth on the left side of his upper jaw.

"At twenty hours today the train arrives from Tbilisi," Sokolov said. "It is carrying prisoners. Your orders are to meet the train and receive the prisoners for transfer to the Procurator of the Moscow Region."

Prisoners. Why was the Colonel so jovial about prisoners?

"You're to be congratulated, Captain. And your section."

"Thank you, sir. May I ask why?"

"You may. Because we have fulfilled our duty to the People. These prisoners are assailants who killed our late friend *Gospodin* Hutchins. The message just arrived from Tbilisi. The murderers have been found; they have confessed; the documents are on the way, along with the prisoners. I call that neat, Captain. Everything in one package. And all based upon the information you and your section developed—perfectly in accord with it. The Americans, the black devils take them, can keep their fancy methods they don't care to show us. We've got the criminals."

"They confessed?" Chanturia asked.

"They confessed. There's no question left. You'll see them. Here, take a look at the message. Well done, Captain."

The gold teeth were still showing as the Colonel dismissed Chanturia with a waved response to his salute.

The prisoners came off the train hugging themselves against the cold. On the bitter wind the steam of their breath blew from them like old luck leaving, like fond dreams of the south they had left thirty hours before, not dressed for Moscow winter. They hugged themselves and cursed and shivered.

Their guards, three KGB sergeants, one handcuffed to each prisoner, handed over the papers and took Chanturia's signature and then the signature of each prisoner before they unlocked the cuffs. The guards were dressed for the weather in military greatcoats, but they were happy to be staying on the train for the trip back south.

One prisoner was Georgian, but the other two were Russian, although they had all come from Tbilisi. The Georgian—Akaky

Shetsiruli, according to his papers—looked Chanturia over. "Is it always this cold in Moscow?" he said in Georgian.

"It's no worse than last month when you were here," Chanturia answered. He spoke Russian, not wanting to set himself apart from the others with this prisoner.

"No? I'm glad of that." Shetsiruli's Russian had the accent of Georgia.

He stumbled a little on the stairs from the station platform going out to the van. He did have a limp. He noticed Chanturia noticing. "Afghanistan," he said. "Stepped on a mine. A good Soviet mine. Took two toes, but it missed the leg bone."

"That's lucky."

"There's all kinds of luck."

"You had more than the American did. Which one of you killed him?"

The man smiled a little, looked Chanturia in the eyes. "I did."

"Any particular reason?"

The man shrugged, still smiling. "It's a job." He added, "I didn't know he was American. Next time we'll ask for papers first. Nobody gets this excited if you kill citizens."

"Fucking Americans can't take a joke," one of the other prisoners said. He and the other two prisoners were locked in the back of the van with two guards, and Chanturia rode in front with the third guard driving.

Moscow was cold and deep in snow. Chanturia wondered where these three would be going from here. Somewhere even colder, probably. He didn't think about it long.

· 20 ·

Thursday, February 16, 1989
3 P.M.
The Lubyanka

CHANTURIA WAS LAST IN LINE FOR COLONEL DUSHENKIN'S CONGRATULA-tions, and until he had actually felt the handshake, he doubted that it would happen. He had the feeling that Dushenkin doubted it too. But it went very well, like something as inevitable as winter, and then he and his team retired to his own office to taste a bottle of Georgian champagne—much to the distress of the Peasant, as drinking during duty hours was contrary to the recent admonitions of his President, M. S. Gorbachev.

After the others left, Chanturia sat down at his desk and reread the report from the Tbilisi office:

Investigation based upon information from Moscow led to identification of suspect Akaky Shetsiruli, age 30, known Mafia relationships. Suspect suffered injured left foot during military service in Afghanistan due to explosion of antipersonnel mine. Suspect was absent from Tbilisi during subject dates, believed to have traveled to Moscow. During interrogation, suspect confessed to arson attack upon subject cafe, motive to enforce payment of protection money. Intention was to kill one or more patrons to impress cafe management with delicacy of its business situation. Suspect stated that he was hired by Moscow criminal organization because he was unknown to Moscow authorities. Accomplices have been identified, and two are in custody. A third is deceased as result of intraorganized crime activities. Suspects have been transferred to Moscow City Procurator for prosecution.

Chanturia laid the report back on his desk. It was a successful conclusion to an important investigation, made possible, as the two colonels Sokolov and Dushenkin had duly pointed out in reports, by information developed by Chanturia's section. Now there was only the final meeting with the Americans—another celebration—to get through, and he could put all this behind him. He wished he could decide what he didn't like about it.

There was a knock at his door, and Belkin stepped in, looking for the briefcase he had left on Chanturia's desk. He glanced at the report next to it. "Wonderful work, that, eh?" Belkin didn't sound as though he thought it was wonderful.

"A woman might love even a billy goat," Chanturia responded— "if it's the right goat for her."

"You don't like the report of our fraternal Tbilisi office?" Belkin affected surprise, but cautiously. Belkin was older than Chanturia, and it was not officially clear why he had not been promoted to head of the section; so relations between them had always been "correct."

"I can find nothing wrong with their report," Chanturia said.

"Neither could I," Belkin said.

"Why don't I like it, then?" This was a rather bold thing to say, even to a directly junior officer, about an official report of any office of the Committee.

Belkin seemed to take Chanturia's openness as a personal compliment. "I don't know, Comrade Captain. I haven't figured out why I don't like it, either; but I don't." This was Belkin's first departure from correctness that Chanturia could remember. They had both taken a kick at the System. In the Union, where all relationships were supposed to flow through the System, all personal friendships had an element of conspiracy.

"Well . . . in April I'll be going on vacation," Chanturia said. "I haven't seen my mother in a year."

"As I remember, she lives in Tbilisi."

"That's right."

Belkin smiled. "The spring air of the Caucasus will clear your mind of all this wintry pile of troubles. I wish for you new thoughts, and clearer vision. But Captain . . . be careful."

96

· II ·

TBILISI

· 21 ·

Friday, April 7, 1989
Tbilisi, Georgian S.S.R.

AS THEY TRAVELED TO HER APARTMENT FROM THE AIRPORT, HIS MOTHER'S voice melted Sergo with memories of childhood. Listening to her was like being a child again: the voice was still the same. But when he looked at her, it was then that he wondered where youth went. Although she had still the warm eyes and soft hands he remembered from his youth, her face was filling with lines. He wished he could protect her somehow from the age that was eroding her face.

Maria Ashvili was the daughter of a once wealthy Georgian family. Her father was an architect, creator of all of the finest buildings in Tbilisi in the thirties; but he died in the Great Patriotic War, leaving a daughter so young she hardly remembered him. When Maria was twelve, her mother died of pneumonia, and she went to live with her mother's sister and her husband.

All she inherited from her father was his talent and his friends, who were delighted when she too became an architect (although as a woman she could not expect to have the career her father had) and distressed when at twenty-four she married Vissarion Chanturia, who was twenty-six, strikingly handsome, and, in their view, essentially worthless. It was no comfort to any of them when they were proved right. Vissarion's idea of marriage was the traditional Georgian one, in which the husband's obligation is to drink, entertain his friends, womanize, and be head of the family. The view of marriage of Maria's aunt and uncle was also in the Georgian tradition—that once a marriage was made, it was forever, and the woman had better make the best of it. She was not welcome to come back to them. So she stayed with Vissarion. After a few years a child came, and she hoped life would get better; but it didn't.

Maria taught her son to love literature and history. They read and played the piano together. Sometimes young Sergo heard quarrels between his parents when his father came home drunk. His father would complain that the mother was making the boy weak—he should be out with his friends instead of hanging at her skirt. She never made any response to this.

One night when Sergo was eight he woke to such an argument going on in the next room. Then the words stopped, and he heard a crash. He rushed out of his bedroom and found his mother fallen against the wall, bleeding from the mouth. He stood over her to keep his father back, and his father laughed and tried to hug him—for Sergo to protect his mother was the act of a man, and his father loved it—but then when Sergo persisted his father got angry again and hit him too.

Maria Ashvili did an untraditional thing. She moved out into a room of her own, taking her son with her; and when her husband came after her, she knocked him down the stairs with a broomstick and then, on her word never to tell anyone of it, got his agreement to leave her alone. After that she raised her son by herself. All her family was angry that she left her husband. For months they came continually to try to talk her into turning back. Sergo kept his fist for her, and when no one saw him he said a little prayer that she would not go back. How had he learned to pray? He didn't know.

He learned to be independent.

Vissarion Chanturia was not a man strong enough to keep his word entirely. The presence in Tbilisi of his wife, living well enough without him, drove him to occasional fits of manly self-assertion, including attempts to kidnap her and charges that she had stolen money from him. Sometimes Sergo heard his mother crying in the night, and knew that she was afraid. But she never went back.

When Sergo was fifteen years old, his mother fell ill. Her illness could not be diagnosed in Tbilisi, and so, through the influence of friends, she was sent to one of the central clinics in Moscow, directed by Chazov, the Minister of Health. Chazov's Clinic was situated in downtown Moscow, in a narrow, short street called Petroverig Lane, where it occupied an old building that had been a military college before the Revolution. All the rooms and corridors had high ceilings and the look of ages. His mother was placed in one of these rooms with five other women. Sergo stayed behind in Tbilisi with the famous Georgian singer Nino Gukushvili, a friend of his mother.

His mother had expanded her father's circle of artistic friends in Tbilisi during the years they had lived apart from his father. On Thursdays Nino had an open tea evening. At one of these evenings, Georgi Mikadze suggested to Sergo that the two of them go to visit his mother.

Sergo knew Mikadze well. Sergo's father had never liked Mikadze, and while his parents lived together Sergo rarely saw him; but in later years Mikadze and his wife, Sophia, famous for her beauty, often came for coffee in the evening. They would all sit in the tiny kitchen as Sergo's mother made coffee for the three grownups in three separate small coffeepots and a cup of warm milk for Sergo. When it was ready she would take the box of hot sand from the oven and set the pots in it to stay warm as they talked through the long evening. Sergo had fallen asleep so many evenings to the sound of those voices, but he remembered most of all the voice of Georgi Mikadze, the most famous voice in Soviet Georgia; for Mikadze was a great writer and poet—although, it was said, his finest poems and writings were never published.

Georgi and Sergo went to Moscow on the overnight train. They stayed several days at a hotel near the clinic. Although his mother had been hospitalized for two months, her illness had not been diagnosed. She seemed to have internal damage to her spleen. "Perhaps she had a fall, in earlier years?" a doctor suggested to Georgi.

"Very likely," he said.

Although the doctors proposed no cure, the rest seemed to benefit her, and eventually she returned home, restored if not cured.

During this visit with Georgi Mikadze, Chanturia often walked through central Moscow while the clinic was closed to visitors. He discovered the street of Bogdan Khmelnitski, named after the Ukrainian chieftain who first agreed to union with Russia, a street full of little stores selling flowers, candies, and other small items. The candy store was in an old building covered with ornate carvings in the traditional Russian style. Behind it the state had built ugly new boxes for people to work and live in. They were buildings Sergo hoped his grandfather would have been ashamed of.

One day Sergo walked with Mikadze to the children's department store not far from the end of Bogdan Khmelnitski Street. Mikadze had no children of his own, but he enjoyed buying gifts for the children of his friends. He and Sergo walked up a broad boulevard with a park in its center. At the end of the park was a vast open square in which automobile traffic swirled about a statue. The square was dominated by a building on its far side, a building whose lyrical colors—pale yellow accented by rust-brown, set onto a base of massive gray granite—seemed strangely ill at ease with its shape, massive and powerful and secretive.

"What building is that?" Sergo asked.

"That?" Mikadze laughed. "That's the Lubyanka."

It was not a name most men laughed at, even then, with Stalin fifteen years in his grave. It was the prison headquarters of the KGB, the Committee on State Security. This terrible building was named for a peasant's splint basket, *lubok,* the old name of the street the building stood on, although the street had now been renamed after Felix Dzerzhinsky, the founder of the original secret police, the Cheka, the forerunner of the KGB.

"Let's go that way," Sergo said.

Mikadze was amused. "All right."

Sergo easily spotted the plainclothesmen around the building, men who were not part of the crowd but walked back and forth as the crowd washed around them. He looked with interest at the men in military uniform who came and went from the building, moving at a serious pace with quick and firm steps. And he knew that if he were one of those men, his mother would never be afraid again.

It was not until five years later, after his army service, that he told his mother that he had decided to go to KGB school. She could not believe that her son would choose such a thing. She had thought of him as an architect like herself, or an artist of some other sort, like their friends. But why the KGB?

He did not tell her.

"Well," she said, using a Russian proverb, "it's better to have pain from one who loves you than from a stranger." The possibility of no pain at all never seemed to cross her mind. She was more like a Russian, that way, than a Georgian.

Sergo's mother lived now in an apartment building near the center of the city, only a street over from Rustaveli Prospect, the major avenue of Tbilisi. It was a building designed by her father. He remembered when she had moved into it at last, after he joined the KGB, how proud she had been showing him the high ceilings and the view from the windows and the courtyard with a play area for children. How proud she had been that her father had designed this.

The taxi turned off the usual route. "Rustaveli Prospect is closed," the driver said. "It's the strike."

"What can you tell me about it?" Chanturia asked.

His mother laughed. "Surely you know more than we do!" She always seemed to think that because of his work he would know everything that was going on in Georgia—everything that was going on in her life, even.

"Still, tell me about it."

"A lot of students have closed off the avenue. They have signs— you'll see them. Protesting. It's *glasnost* for sure."

"What do they want?"

" 'Freedom for Georgia,' " she said. It sounded strange to hear a political slogan from his mother, even as a quotation.

"Is that what their signs say?"

"Oh, yes. And more. One of our neighbors"—she always spoke as if he still lived at the apartment—"is a member of the Georgia Liberation Front. Tsagarcli, remember him? Probably he'll come knocking at our door to enroll you: I told him you were coming home."

"Has he forgotten who I work for?" But he knew she was only joking. "How long has this been going on—this strike?"

"Three, four days. It started with some women on a hunger strike. What for, I don't know. Something to do with the Abkhazians. They want freedom from Georgia; Georgia wants freedom from Russia; Georgia doesn't want the Abkhazians free from Georgia . . . I don't understand it. Georgi understands it. He'll be waiting for us at the apartment. Did I tell you he'd be with us for supper tonight?"

"No. You wrote that he'd been released."

"Is it all right that he comes?"

"Of course. I thought I'd have to go find him."

"He'll tell you about the strike."

"Sure. Try to *keep* him from telling me."

But even with his mother's warning, he was not ready for the Georgi he found at the apartment. He remembered the handsome tall man with flowing black hair, a man with a voice of gold. Who was this, sunken cheeked, who leaned on his cane and shook hands with a weak trembling grip?

His mother went to the kitchen, and within minutes the bread and sharp cheese smell of *khachapuri* filled the apartment.

103

"Ah, your mother's *khachapuri*!" Georgi exclaimed. "I remember when I ate it last: and it was so fulfilling I lived for ten years on that memory!" When he spoke, it was with slow, painful precision, each word a journey. "Do you remember, Sergo?"

Chanturia didn't remember. He wanted to, but he didn't. He remembered other things instead. He remembered his first home visit after he completed KGB school. He tried to put the memory from him; but it came anyway.

Home had smelled of *khachapuri*.

He had washed his hands and gone to the kitchen to eat. He and his mother ate without talking. The food was so good that at first he didn't notice the silence—unusual, because she always talked around him when he ate at home. He saw that she was worried. "What's the matter?" he asked. She said nothing, but looked with dark eyes at the window. Then, feeling his impatience, she said, "Georgi has been arrested."

It wasn't unexpected; but still it was a shock. "He published something abroad?"

"Yes. He published two articles in Paris, in *Continental*. You know no one would take them here." She started to cry softly.

He touched her shoulder. "Maybe his term will be short. A lot of things can happen."

She shook her head. "Can you do something for him?" she asked suddenly, with her head bowed, not to look at him.

He felt rising irritation. His mother had never asked anything from him, although she knew as well as anyone the possibilities that his KGB position opened to him, ways to overcome the stupid annoyances of Soviet life. She had always got by on her own, pointedly not asking; but now she was asking for Georgi.

It left him numb: the one thing she had ever asked of him he could not do for her.

He had known Georgi all his life. His earliest memory of him was of his mother telling him that Georgi was a man with a wonderful fate: he was the voice of his people. He had a gift from God.

And now he and his gift from God were arrested.

"You know there's very little I can do," Chanturia had said. It pained him to think of it now. But it had been truth. "If it had been theft—stolen cars, hooliganism, things of no importance, maybe I could help. But this is political. The little *blat* that I have won't help him. You'd have to change the law. I can't do *that*."

"But the law is unfair; and your organization is implementing this unfair law! I'm sorry. I never wanted to talk with you about things like this."

"Mother, Georgi was a member of a writer's union, and he wrote, he was published. If he couldn't publish everything he wanted, those are the rules of the game. He knew the rules, and he knew what to expect. So you shouldn't feel too sad for him. He knew what he was choosing, and he should have been ready for it."

She said, "Why is it that in Western countries people aren't imprisoned for political reasons?"

He looked at her. "How do you know they aren't?"

"I listen to the Voices at night."

It was hard for him to imagine his mother in the middle of the night sitting in the armchair at the window—the only place her radio could have picked up foreign broadcasts—listening to the Voices: the BBC, Radio Liberty, the Voice of America.

That was ten years past, and here was Georgi, whose God had left him and his gift in prison for two consecutive five-year sentences—one for anti-Soviet propaganda and the second for good measure, imposed at the end of the first instead of release, allegedly for breach of prison discipline, but really, everyone knew, just for emphasis—here was Georgi, whose name had been spoken by Sakharov in the first moment of his return from exile, in his demand for the release of all political prisoners, here was Georgi at the end of his impassioned voyage through the Russian language and the Georgian in pursuit of liberty, or his people's freedom, or . . . what? Here was Georgi, shipwrecked on the desert isle the State had made of his life, his wife dead and his health gone and his golden voice a whisper . . . here was Georgi, the fire still alight in him.

Georgi eased himself into a chair with the help of his cane. He smiled at Chanturia. "You think more highly of the pleasure of sitting when you recall being forced to stand for two days, in a box no bigger than yourself."

Chanturia could think of no response. The KGB, after all, ran the prison camps. "I guess this is a stone in *my* garden," he said lamely, quoting an old Russian saying.

Georgi laughed. "If I'd known I was going to fall, I'd have put down some hay," he responded. And then their awkwardness eased. In the old days, they had both been lovers of proverbs and peasant sayings—in Russian, in Georgian, in whatever language they happened across. Chanturia supposed he had acquired the taste from

Georgi, although he no longer remembered. Once it had been their game to lard their conversations with these old saws, sometimes to the disgust of their friends. That Georgi remembered made Chanturia easier at heart.

Georgi went on, "My friend Sakharov is running for the Congress of People's Deputies, I understand. Have you heard any of his campaign speeches there in Moscow?"

"I've not had the pleasure," Chanturia said.

"Not even in a professional capacity?"

"No."

"A pity. I would have liked to ask you what he is saying. I would be proud to live in his district, to have the chance to vote for such a man."

Chanturia didn't answer, and Georgi closed his eyes and sank back in the soft chair. "I had a friend in prison," he began. "My friend was a fine physicist. Not so fine as Sakharov, possibly. Certainly not so lucky—not so well-placed earlier in life—not so whatever is the magic that sets the great apart from the humble. I do not mean to imply that it is through mere good fortune that Sakharov is great, or that he is less than great. I merely mean to say that my friend, though a fine physicist, was of insufficient stature to be allowed to remain outside the *gulag*, although he was a man who spoke nothing but the truth. He shared that with Sakharov—but in his case it brought him not only trouble but an early grave. Still, he spoke the truth: a commodity not to be wasted in our situation. We must catch what we can of it, and try to put it to good use."

Chanturia wondered whether Georgi's remark was aimed at him in particular, as representative of the body that had jailed him, or whether it was a generalization on the state of society. Probably both, he decided. Georgi had been a writer of great power and subtlety, whose work was understood at more than one level. In part that was his downfall, arousing the suspicions of men who wanted everything plainly put, with no possibility of meanings they might miss. "You yourself speak the truth, as usual," Chanturia said.

"But very little of it, nowadays. Still, one does what one can. I have been invited tomorrow to address a meeting at the Government House. You might care to come. Out of professional interest, of course."

"Does this have to do with the strike on Rustaveli Prospect?" Government House was located on that avenue.

Georgi smiled. "I should have known I couldn't take you by surprise. Yes, it does; although 'strike' is perhaps too ambitious a description. They have closed the theaters, the museums, and the schools. Will we bring this giant to his knees by refraining from amusement or education?" He looked at Chanturia as if he expected a considered answer to this question. After a moment, he said, "Well . . . we do what we can do."

After dinner Chanturia's mother brought in the box of sand with the little steaming pots of coffee. Georgi looked a long time at the coffee pots. There were still three pots, but now there was no little cup of milk for the vanished boy Sergo. Chanturia was afraid that Georgi was going to comment on the fact that there were three— afraid, because Sophia, Georgi's wife, had died while he was in prison. But he said nothing. He poured the coffee into his tiny cup and drank it, as always, without sugar, bitter as it was.

"What do they want, these strikers of yours?" Chanturia asked Georgi, to change the thoughts of his own mind. He did not know what Georgi was thinking.

"Not 'of mine.' They are not mine, any more than a grapevine belongs to the peasant in whose garden it grows. He may claim it; but it has its own purposes. It cooperates with him so long as their purposes agree. Might as well call him its peasant; but he doesn't belong to it, either."

Georgi, Chanturia noted, still clung to the homely fables that had formed his work before prison.

"In a way," Georgi went on, "we could take that as our text for a discussion of what these strikers want. It's the same with Georgia and the Union, you see. The Union calls Georgia 'its' republic; but of course, Georgia doesn't really *belong* to the Union, any more than the Union belongs to Georgia. They cooperate, so long as their purposes agree." He stopped for a moment and looked at Chanturia with a twinkle in his eyes. "I assume no one is listening to this, other than persons authorized to hear such things? Men have gone to prison for less than suggesting that Georgia doesn't *belong* to the Union—though not, of course, since *glasnost* broke out. But, to continue my figure of speech, these free-minded strikers began by protesting against the wish of the Abkhazian Autonomous Republic to be free of us—of you and me, of Georgia—at which time our good Georgian Communist government supported them. But they rapidly moved on to the idea that we Georgians should be free of Russian domination, an idea

107

definitely not supported by the Georgian Communist Party. In short, the strikers have concluded that there is a Georgian nation whose purposes no longer coincide with those of the Union of Soviet Socialist Republics, and that the ownership should therefore be terminated.''

"They're Georgian nationalists?'' Chanturia said.

"You sound surprised! You, of all people, should know what a seething pot of nationalisms this Union is.''

"The Baltic republics, yes. But Georgia . . .''

"Human beings too: guilty as charged. Balts, Ukrainians, Georgians, all those Islamic republics . . . all the old nationalisms that Lenin and Stalin put down, rising up again to haunt us.''

"Nationalism is a dead end of history,'' Chanturia said, and then blushed because it sounded so much like a propaganda lesson from some KGB school or other. But despite the blush, he believed what he said. "Without the Union, what would any of these republics be? What would Georgia be? There would be war up and down the perimeter of the Union, if not at its heart. Already we're on the edge of civil war in a dozen places. Look at Nagorno-Karabakh; at this very minute only the army keeps the Armenians from massacring the Azerbaijanis, or vice versa. Look at Georgia itself. The Abkhazians live in mortal fear that we Georgians will murder them in their sleep, if the Russians will let us. I can't believe that nationalism is such a wonderful medicine, in a world where people who hate each other are so mixed together.'' Except perhaps for Russia, practically a continent in itself, none of the fifteen republics of the Union would amount to much alone. The Baltic republics, for all their energy, were tiny, little more than counties. And Uzbekistan, Azerbaijan, Kazakhstan . . . without the civilizing influence of the Union, they would drift off into darkest Islam, their people condemned to poverty and squalor and ignorance.

But Georgia? He had never thought of Georgia as an independent state. Nor, he supposed, had the Russians.

"No, nationalism is not necessarily a wonderful thing,'' Georgi said. "But at least it's something, in a time when we've been given nothing else for support. That's the problem, as I see it: that the rest of what we're asked to believe in is lies. Our nationality, at least, isn't a lie. There's something there that can't be manufactured, can't be fed to us like slops for hogs. We *know* we are Georgian, and that this is our native land around us; and nothing the Party tells us can convince

108

us otherwise. The terrible thing is that we have been reduced to believing no more than that.

"I believe as you do, you see. I believe that humankind is one thing, and that one man's death diminishes all of us. I believe that we should all live in peace and harmony, without distinctions between us; and when I say 'we,' I mean all human beings. But the problem is, those who rule us do not believe it, although they say that they do. The state has tried to crowd out nationalism; but it has tried to crowd out everything else too; and people cannot be left with nothing. So they cling to what they know is true; and one thing our neighbors can truly know is that they are Georgian and not Russian.

"*Nations* and *states*, you see, are two different things. They may have the same boundaries; but still they are two different things. The Union insists that we are all one nation: by which it means, we must all cling together while the Union's problems are being solved. But of course, we are not all one nation: the boundaries of this state were established by force and not by consent. It is natural to such relationships that force must continually be reasserted. And when sufficient force is no longer available, such states break up into their constituent nations, which *are* defined by consent."

"Surely you don't say that being Georgian is a matter of choice?" Chanturia insisted, not sure how far Georgi was serious.

"Yes, of course I do. I am Georgian because I say I am. Or, to put the matter in the proper frame of reference, *we* are Georgian because we say we are. It is a matter of mutual consent, of mutual recognition, and not merely of one person's will."

"And if a Tatar claimed to be a Georgian?"

"He would be one if everyone—including himself—thought he was. That's the definition of nationhood. All nations, of course, are fuzzy around the edges. What about someone who has a Georgian mother and a Tatar father? Is he Georgian? He is if we think he is. But the true fact of nationhood is not the edges, but the core. If there is a core that knows it is a nation, then it is a nation.

"We are Georgian, you and I. We are not Russian. We know it, and the Russians know it. We are both one state—at the moment. The Russians are saying, 'We are all one nation.' But of course, we are not. We are all one state—a different matter altogether. They are saying we are one nation in order to keep hold of us, but otherwise they don't act as if we were one nation. In fact, the problem goes deeper than just Georgians and Russians. The problem is the Party, your Party, which acts as if it were a conquering nation ruling a state

109

made up of subject nations. It is the problem of 'we' and 'they,' sliced in a different direction. Do you want to know where I first became aware of this? It was in the *gulag,* where the state insisted at every moment that I be aware who was 'we' and who was 'they.' 'We' was myself and my fellow prisoners; and 'they' was everyone else, and particularly the organs of the Soviet Union. It didn't matter then that the prisoners were Georgians or Russians or Chukchis or Uzbekis. And the result? We were a nation, the prisoner nation. But we were a nation by consent. We were prisoners by the will of the state; but we were a nation by our own consent.

"It is a truth this state has yet to discover, unfortunately. Force, no matter how long maintained, does not substitute for consent."

"But how do you get consent?" Chanturia insisted. "You can't ask every citizen every day, 'Do you consent to be a part of this state?' "

"Of course you can't," Georgi agreed. "You can build lasting consent, by lasting care. By government for the benefit of the governed. There is no other way. And you can lose it in a day, by the application of uncaring force. But there is no other way. Government is organization for the benefit of the governed. What we have is organization for the benefit of the governors—that is, organized crime.

"The problem," Georgi said, "is that our law does not work. Or rather, that we have no law. The people have a duty to obey the law; but the rulers have no duty to the people. We are not a law-ruled state, but one ruled by force, and accustomed to it. But in the absence of law in the state, there is still the law of honor. It is what nations live by; because honor is nothing but adherence to a code, and those who agree on the code are a nation—they define themselves to be so. It was what we lived by in the camps. The regime tried to make us live by force; but, in fact, we lived by honor. Not perfectly, but in principle. But even in the absence of a nation—a group agreeing on the code—a man may live by his honor. Maybe that is the highest form of living."

After Georgi left, Chanturia and his mother talked, but only of old times; neither had much to say, and most of that better left unsaid. He went to bed early, and woke once in the night to the rumble of something powerful moving, but went again to sleep.

· 22 ·

Saturday, April 8, 1989
10 A.M.
Rustaveli Prospect

MOSCOW STILL STRUGGLED WITH BITTER WINDS, WITH DAYS OF GRAY FREEZ
ing drizzle following sifting fine snow following freezing drizzle that
melted and froze and melted and froze. Winter's accumulated grit
and dirt and salt followed feet everywhere, into every shop, every
office, every apartment. While Russia heaved its weight against the
weight of winter that even in April seemed unlikely ever to end,
while spring was yet too far to dare a hope—an idea to be held for
a time yet only in distant memory—in Tbilisi, in the Georgian Soviet
Socialist Republic, the leaves of the trees on Rustaveli Prospect were
pale golden-green in the morning sun.

Chanturia stopped where an old woman was selling golden mimosa
flowers from a bucket outside a *khachapurnaya*, a cafe that sold Georgian fast food and was doing good business with small groups of
young people of high school or university age. Chanturia was dressed
in clothes he had worn here when he was a student at the university
before KGB school—old gray trousers, an old blue jacket and an old
gray polyester shirt open at the neck. His mother had cried when she
saw him wearing them that morning. "You haven't aged at all," she
had said. "You could be starting again at university. You could be
anything you want to be."

"If I could decide what I want to be," he had said, ". . . when I
grow up."

The old woman held up a bunch of flowers to him. "From my
garden," she said in Georgian. "From a fine young man such as you,
there must be a girl who wants these flowers."

"I'll buy them for my mother," he said, and only then thought of
Tanya, in gray Moscow.

"Your mother will be glad," the old woman said. She fumbled in
a tiny cloth bag for kopecks in change for his three-ruble note. There

111

was no paper money in the bag. "Keep your kopecks, please," he said with formal politeness. "For good luck." When she smiled at him, her teeth were bad, and her face was lined as the Georgian mountains; but it was a happy face. Happy as the Georgian mountains.

He walked on up the avenue carrying his flowers.

All along the avenue he came upon more and still more groups of young people. Militia were all around but not interfering, and it wasn't until he noticed the flags that Chanturia realized that these kids were the strikers. Almost all of them were carrying flags. Most of the flags were tiny, and he didn't realize what they were until he came upon two people waving one two meters square that had been sewn up from dyed bedsheets. It was dark red, with a black bar and white bar in the upper left quarter.

It was the flag of Georgia before the Union.

He wandered out into the avenue. There was no traffic; the avenue was closed somewhere beyond the street that led back to his mother's apartment. He could see for blocks, and now for the first time he saw what it was that he had heard in the night: three tanks and a half-dozen armored personnel carriers were parked along one side of the avenue under the trees. A squad of soldiers with rifles lounged beside one of the APCs. An officer stood in the turret hatch of one tank, but none had its engine running. Not far from them, a few protesters with placards were talking to one another and ignoring the soldiers, and the soldiers were ignoring them. It was like the warm-up for a military parade on the anniversary of the Revolution, when tanks filled the streets of central Moscow, except for the wording of the placards. They were crude things done on whatever scraps of board could be found, or on bedsheets, in housepaint and in cut-out paper letters. Chanturia had monitored a hundred public demonstrations in support of the regime, but he had never seen such crummy signs. It was certain they hadn't come from the Party's propaganda shops. One said, "The Russian Empire Is Dead and Rotting and It Stinks." Another said, "Army of Occupation, Get Out of Georgia;" and a third, simply, "Russians Go Home."

A young woman sitting on a bench under the trees away from the street, beside twin babies in a pram, asked him the time as he walked past. "It's eleven-thirty," he told her. "And do you think it's safe to have the children out here with all this going on?"

She laughed. "There are plenty of soldiers to protect us."

He couldn't tell whether she was being ironic. "What do you think of the strike?"

"The same as everyone. The Russians should get out and leave Georgia to us." She included him in "us," he could see.

"But then who'd protect the children?"

"Then they wouldn't need protecting."

"Well, those are fine-looking children. Maybe a flower will keep them from harm?" He took two sprays from his bouquet and handed them to her.

"I wouldn't want to rob someone special of your flowers," the woman said, smiling.

"Someone special, certainly; but she'll be glad to part with two. They're for my mother, and she loves children. And while I'm giving away flowers, here, one for the children's mother."

"Thank you; I'll give it to her."

"Ah. They're not yours?"

"They're my sister's."

He managed to feign a little embarrassment. He had seen that she wore no wedding ring. "In that case, let's add flowers for the baby-sitter. It's only fair." He made a show of choosing the best spray of flowers and handed it to her. She thanked him and, without expressing any invitation in words, moved over on the bench to leave a space for someone to sit down.

Chanturia sat down. He said some nice words about her sister's children and then asked about their mother and their father and then about herself.

Her name was Lamara. She had a smile that showed even in her eyes. As she talked with him she was continually adjusting the children's blankets to keep them warm and the hood of their pram to keep them shaded. She was, as the Russians said, as kind as fresh bread.

The protesters with the signs gave up pointedly ignoring the soldiers and came down the avenue past Chanturia and the girl. Some of the protesters waved as they passed. One of them, a girl, called out: "Lamara, are you coming this afternoon?"

"Of course I'll be there!" she called back. "After I take Elena's kids home!"

Chanturia wanted to ask who they were. He also felt that it was his duty to ask who they were. But if he got answers he would have to write a report, and he did not want to write a report.

"They're my friends from the university," Lamara said, answering

113

the question he was not going to ask. "We've been carrying water to the hunger strikers. The strikers are brave women."

"Women?"

"Yes. A hundred and fifty of them."

"And what do they expect to get by their hunger strike?"

"Freedom for Georgia." She said this looking him in the eye, as an open challenge. "You don't seem to know much about our movement," she said. "Don't you read the newspapers? Don't you come downtown?"

"I live outside the city," Chanturia said.

"Oh? Where do you live?"

"Moscow."

He didn't expect her to be impressed, and she didn't appear to be. Tbilisi was an older city than Moscow, with far longer traditions of culture and art. "And what do you do in Moscow?"

"I'm an administrator," he said automatically. "Ministry of Internal Affairs." It was his standard cover story. He had an imaginary office, imaginary work which he could describe in full detail if necessary, and a real telephone number that would be answered correctly by a hypothetical secretary, actually a KGB employee sitting in Dzerzhinsky Square; but he didn't think it necessary this time to elaborate on the details. "Paper, paper, and more paper—that's my work. But no Georgian newspapers."

She laughed again. "You need an education in local affairs, then."

"Reeducation. I grew up here. My mother still lives just two streets away. Perhaps you'll reeducate me. Maybe we could find some lunch; and then you can introduce me to your friends and your ideas."

"I wish I could," she said, sounding as if she meant it. "But I'm responsible for these two until evening." She nodded at the twins. "But I could meet you after that."

He agreed to meet her at the corner of Government House; and they parted outside the cafe.

Government House was a new building with a cut-stone facade of narrow arches that towered five stories high, with a column of windows behind each arch. Before it, stood one of those monuments of Soviet monumentalism, genus *Soviet worker*, species *victorious*, featuring one each, male and female, striding forward boldly. The man's hand was upraised in triumph; the woman modestly carried the fruits of harvest at her bosom. A statue of Stalin had once stood in the vicinity; but Stalin was gone now, though Lenin still lurked nearby.

114

Between the monumental workers and the long flight of low stone steps leading to Government House washed a sea of real workers, men and women together. They faced the building.

At the top of the long stone steps, facing the workers of stone and the workers of flesh, a man stood alone. Behind him, along the front of the building, stood nearly a hundred gray-clad police, the People's Militia, Georgian boys already in light summer uniforms, but they did not interfere. More militiamen were in the crowd. It was hard to tell why any of the militia were there, either in the crowd or on the steps—whether to prevent or to protect or to listen. A woman and several men also stood on the top step, close to one another but several meters distant from the man alone. Nothing marked the place where he stood. It was as if this had been done intentionally, for emphasis. There was no dais, no speaker's platform, no podium to stand behind, to separate *speaker* from *spoken to*.

The man was Georgi Mikadze. He stood leaning on a cane, both his palms pressed against its curved top with his arms stiff in front of him; if the cane had been kicked away, his body would have fallen forward. He was a small man, and old, and he seemed of little significance in the high empty arch of the massive building.

He began to speak softly in Georgian. As he spoke, his voice grew.

"Who is it?" someone arriving at the back asked one already there.

"It's Mikadze. Hush."

No other voice competed. His voice was low but resonant, and in the still evening it carried to the farthest reaches of the crowd. As he spoke he stood straighter by degrees and began to walk back and forth, then leaned the cane against one of the columns near him and walked away from it.

"I am told there is a Decree," Mikadze said. He held up a piece of paper, cheap paper covered with dense printing. "A Decree of April 8, 1989. A Decree which is the law of this country, the law over you and over me. And what is this law? It is a law which prohibits 'calls for changing the social and state system.' And what is the purpose of this law? The purpose, according to those who defend it, is to protect the 'process of democratization.' To protect, we must therefore suppose, the right of the people to discuss the form and effect of their government and their social system. But we must further suppose that, having carried on such discussions, the people may not decide that their government and their social system should be in any way changed, or if they decide so, they may not say so; for to say so

115

would be to 'call for change in the social and state system'; and that is prohibited.

"Who initiated the adoption of this Decree? That, it appears, is a state secret. No one claims to be the parent of this child. Although this child totally without parents seems to have arrived in the world vigorous and well enough defended.

"Who is it that defends the Decree? For one, the Ministry of Internal Affairs, charged with defending the laws of our country. And what does the Ministry of Internal Affairs say? It says that our state must be kept safe from its people. 'The first duty of the state is to defend itself.' Not, 'the first duty of the state is to defend its people.' 'The first duty of the state is to defend itself.' And how does the state defend itself? Apparently, by prohibiting anyone from suggesting that this state of affairs should be changed!"

And as he spoke, voices began to rise from parts of the crowd, a few scattered outbreaks of applause, and then from somewhere a call: "Georgia free!" The crowd had swelled until it almost filled the square.

Chanturia, from his position partway up the steps at one corner of the building, looked out across the crowd and saw it build steadily. He had thought the square was full when he arrived; yet as Georgi spoke, more people pushed in, and still more. He saw, too, militia interspersed in the crowd and behind it. Several of the militiamen at the back carried two-way radios, and they made a show of calling one another and looking official; but they did nothing.

Farther away, a handful of men in civilian clothing walked the edge of the square well back from the crowd. They spoke to one another when they met, but they did not seem especially interested. Chanturia watched these more closely than the militia. He knew they were officers of the Committee. They were not Georgian but Russian—most Georgians had been forced out of the KGB at the fall of Beria, the Georgian head of the KGB, after Stalin's death. Chanturia himself was one of the few Georgians to trickle back into the ranks of Committee officers. He knew, too, for the first time now what Belkin's oblique remark to him had meant when they had talked of his vacation in Tbilisi: "Try to keep out of trouble." There was more going on in Georgia than even the KGB was telling its people.

At the call, "Georgia free," these men suddenly disappeared from the square.

"Georgia free"—the words became a chant that slowly died away as Georgi spoke again.

"Yes, Georgia free!" Georgi said, echoing the call. "But not only that. These faceless people who believe that the state must be protected from its citizens, let them come out and show their faces. Let us see who they are. Let us speak with them about their reasons. And as for us, my friends, let us speak our minds clearly. Freedom for Georgia, yes. But not only freedom for Georgia. Freedom for people. The time has come when every one of us must raise his voice for that, or freedom will never come. We stand here today within sight of the spot where once there stood a monument to Josef Stalin. Stalin was a Georgian, as you and I are. And it is for that reason that I say to you, our call must not be simply for the Russians to go home. We want freedom from the Russian Empire—but not only that. We want freedom. The Russian Empire itself is a monument to Stalin, a monument of living fear and not of stone. But like the stone monument that so recently stood in this square, this monument will be removed, if we are brave enough to demand its removal. We have only one thing to fear, and it is not Stalin in the grave: it is Stalin in us. We have been too long afraid to demand what is the right of every Georgian, every Soviet citizen, every person. Now we demand it."

The chant in the Georgian language began again somewhere at the back of the crowd and rolled around the square, surging closer and louder with each repetition. It was the echo of what Georgi had said; and yet not all of it; for a shout can be echoed, but not an argument. What came back was not the argument, but a shout, the simple declaration that divided "them" from "us." The rest was lost between the heart and the mind. "Georgia . . . free!" the chant said. "Georgia . . . free! Georgia . . . free!" And Chanturia found his own heart falling into the rhythm: Georgia. Free. Georgia. Free. Georgia.

An army officer appeared on the top step from between two columns a little way to one side of Georgi. The officer's lapels carried the colors of the special Internal Security Forces, the internal army of the Union. He carried a power megaphone at his lips, aimed like a weapon at the crowd. "Quiet!" he commanded, and the artificial power of his voice met the massed voices of the crowd. He was used to command. The crowd was not, and fell silent.

"I am Lieutenant Colonel Baklanov," the officer said. He spoke in Russian. His voice of steel and electrons boomed across the square.

"My division of the Internal Security Forces of the Motherland has been requested to carry out its duty to the People . . ." A low noise began to issue from the crowd; ". . . to carry out its duty to the People in suppressing counterrevolutionary threats to Soviet power . . ." The noise took form, a rhythmic cadence, a chant; ". . . threats to Soviet power in the Georgian Socialist Republic . . ." The chant in Georgian surged around the Colonel's voice like waves crashing on a rock. It surged, receded, surged again, and swept away the Colonel's Russian words. The chant said: "Russians . . . out! Russians . . . out! Russians . . . out!" The Colonel put down his megaphone, let it dangle from a lanyard around his neck. He stared into the crowd as if trying to memorize faces, though of faces there were thousands. And then the chant died slowly away, and from the crowd there began a song. Chanturia felt the hair on his neck rise. The song was a church hymn in the Georgian language. It was a hymn of Georgia free.

The Colonel backed away from the step and vanished between the columns.

The singing continued late that night on Rustaveli Prospect. Chanturia could never think of it afterward without coming near to tears. It was the voice of a nation—a voice not heard in over sixty years.

He added his voice to the singing, although he had never sung a hymn before.

He was singing when Lamara found him. She slipped her hand under his arm as if she had known him all her life. "Mikadze is magnificent!" she whispered, and joined in the song.

They went from group to group in the crowd. Everywhere, Lamara seemed to know someone. Bottles of wine were open, Georgian wine flowing like blood among brothers. There were toasts, elaborate Caucasian toasts that branched and grew like wild untrimmed plants hung with flowers. There were more songs and laughter.

> Bliss was it in that dawn to be alive;
> But to be young was very heaven.

Sergo Chanturia and Lamara Kacharava stood close together in the shadow of one of the columns at the top of the steps of Government House, out of the light of even the dim lamps of the square. They spoke softly to one another, listening half to one another and half to

118

the songs and voices from the crowd which still packed the square at this darkest hour of the morning, not wanting to let this night end.

At the back of the crowd a commotion began.

From the front it was impossible to see at first what was happening, even from the steps. Then the crowd at the back of the square parted, people running everywhere, and beyond them Chanturia saw a dark mass moving into the crowd. He could not see what it was. He stood his ground as the crowd began to press against him. He was pushed against the column, as if by the force of a moving tide; but there he clung, as the dark mass pushed closer, resolved itself.

It was a phalanx of soldiers.

They advanced like the heroes of a thousand Soviet battle monuments, soldiers of the Motherland advancing through a sea of enemies; but the sea they pushed through was a sea of their fellow citizens. The faces of the troopers were emotionless, goggle-eyed gas masks. Each soldier carried on his left arm a curved black shield half as long as his body, and in his right hand a sharp-bladed trenching shovel. Those in the front rank swung the shovels without mercy: the phalanx cut its path through the crowd in a trail of blood.

There were shouts, cries of anger and of pain, and then from somewhere a white cloud drifted down across the square. Chanturia got a whiff of it, and knew its reek. "Gas!" he shouted. "Get away! Get away!" He did not know who he was saying this to; but he started trying to push along the steps in the direction of the troops, against a stream of bodies trying to push in the opposite direction. The stream carried Lamara away from him. He struggled to the top step where there was more space, but then the gas cloud rolled over him. Nausea overcame him, and he sagged retching against the wall of the building.

Chanturia forced himself to stand and move in the direction the gas had come from. The square was suddenly a formless void, with only a few figures struggling in the other direction, downwind, away from the gas; because of that, he guessed that there would be no more gas released. He bumped into a woman who half-collapsed against him. He had met her in the last few hours, but couldn't remember her name: at first he didn't even recognize her—she had been laughing and singing, and now blood was running down her face from somewhere in her hair, and her hair was clotted with it. The blood smeared across his shirt. "Help me," she said. He put an arm around her and supported her until they struggled clear of the crowd.

All across the square, figures were scattered. Some were people on all fours puking violently; here and there individuals wandered, streaming blood from gashes in the head or upper body; but most lay unmoving—strange surrealistic sculptures in shapes of death.

The woman gasped against his shoulder: "Murderers!" she whispered. "'Murderers!"

Not knowing what else to do, he hugged her and kept her moving out into the square.

From one of the side streets, an ambulance hurtled into the square. A dozen men or more jumped out even before it stopped. They fanned out among the bodies and began conducting a hasty triage. Chanturia steered the woman toward the nearest of them, a young man dressed in blue jeans and a white shirt and necktie. He had turned over a man lying contorted on the pavement and was giving mouth-to-mouth resuscitation to him even though the man had vomited. "Who are you?" Chanturia asked in Georgian. The man didn't look up or break his rhythm. "I'm a doctor. What are your symptoms?"

"I'm all right. This woman has a bad wound."

The man looked up. His eyes went quickly over the woman. "She'll live. Lay her down so she doesn't go into shock. Get her a blanket from the ambulance, if there are any. Then come help me." He turned back immediately to his first patient.

The ambulance stood empty, as if abandoned. The doors were open. There were no blankets in it. Chanturia started back to the doctor, stepping over bodies he could not walk around. He saw a woman coming across the square: it was Lamara. He motioned for her to meet him where the doctor was still working on the man on the ground. But before either of them got there he saw the soldiers coming back. They were driving the living before them out of the square. He saw the young doctor argue with them, and then one soldier raised his trenching tool and smashed the doctor to the pavement. He was going to hit him again, but Chanturia ran and caught his arm from behind.

He took his KGB credential out of the inside pocket of his jacket and held it up for the soldier to see. Behind the dark plastic lenses of the gas mask, Chanturia saw fear in the startled eyes of the soldier. "Leave him alone," Chanturia said. "He's a doctor." He said this in

Georgian, but he saw that the soldier didn't understand, so he repeated it in Russian.

"We're ordered to clear the square," the soldier said. His voice was muffled by the gas mask, as if he were speaking from inside a fortress.

"Where's your officer?" Chanturia demanded.

The soldier gestured back across the square. "Over there."

Lamara had come to them. Chanturia told her to go to the ambulance: he couldn't leave her alone in the open square—he didn't know how long his order to the soldier would last.

Instead of moving, she said, "You're KGB."

"Yes, I am. Could we discuss it later?"

"There's nothing to discuss." She turned and ran toward the other people who were leaving the square.

Chanturia started after her, then turned back. Although his lungs were aching from the gas, he forced himself to run. At the far side of the square an army Captain in a gas mask was arguing heatedly in Russian with a Georgian police sergeant. Chanturia produced his credential again. The policeman came to attention. The Captain stiffened, but as he and Chanturia were of equal rank, he resisted the impulse to follow the policeman's example. "What are your men doing, Captain?" Chanturia demanded. He was glad he hadn't found the Lieutenant-Colonel, who would not have been cowed by any Captain, not even one of the KGB.

"They're killing people!" the policeman blurted out.

"They're carrying out this unit's orders to clear the square," the captain responded curtly.

"I just stopped one of your men trying to kill a doctor," Chanturia said. "Is that what you were sent here for?"

"Then your 'doctor' is an enemy of the people," the officer said. "We were told what to expect."

"I'm telling you otherwise. You," he said to the police sergeant. "Where have the militia gone?"

"We were ordered back by the army commander," the sergeant said. He was a man in his early twenties, and he was near tears.

"Well, I'm ordering you back into the square. You're to separate these soldiers from the civilians and then form lanes to evacuate all civilians. There will be no interference with the activities of medical personnel. Is that clear?" Chanturia added in Georgian, "Do it fast."

The sergeant snapped a hasty salute to Chanturia and ran for the rear where the militia had been ordered back.

The Captain of special troops was furious; but he did not dare to

121

interfere with a KGB order. Within minutes Georgian militiamen were cordoning off sections of the square.

Chanturia ran in the direction the crowd had been driven. He kept finding faces he had met earlier, but he could not find Lamara for a long time. Someone told him that a group of people had been chased into the Theater Institute, so he went in that direction. Windows had been smashed in Secondary School No. 1, next to Government House, and a slow tide of tear gas flowed out of the dark building. Lights were on inside the Institute. The windows had been smashed out; broken furniture was strewn over the floor. Tear gas stung his eyes, and there was some other chemical scent as well. The merest hint of it brought him close to retching again.

Lamara was inside. She was crying softly, tears of grief and anger and not just from the gas, for she cradled a woman's head on her knees. Chanturia knelt beside her and felt for a pulse in the woman's throat, but she was dead.

"They murdered her," Lamara said.

"Did you see who did it?"

"No. You know who did it. Your god-cursed Union army did it!"

She wouldn't leave the dead woman. After a while he got up and went looking for an ambulance. When he returned, she helped put the body on the ambulance and then got in with it to go to the hospital. She refused to let him come and refused to talk to him.

After she was gone he walked back to the square and across it. There were hundreds of militiamen there now, patrolling in groups. No civilians were left. The army was gone. Militiamen who tried to stop him he stopped with his badge. He walked straight across the square, up the avenue where heavy tanks now sat with their engines running and with the heads of their drivers sticking from their hatches, and turned into the silent dark side street to his mother's apartment. She was asleep. Without turning on a light he flung his clothes—still thick with the reek of gas—onto the balcony and went to his bed, where he lay unsleeping until dawn.

He thought of his words about Georgi Mikadze—words spoken so long ago and recalled so lately: "He knew the rules of the game, and what to expect. He knew what he was choosing, and he should have been ready for it." And he knew they applied to himself.

Late the next morning he went to the apartment where Lamara lived with her mother and her sister, her sister's husband, and their twin children. She answered the door.

122

"How did you find me?" she asked. "I didn't tell you where I lived." Then she said, "Oh, your employers would know, wouldn't they?" and closed the door. She was wrong: he had asked after the family name in the neighborhood until he found her; but he had no chance to say that.

He knocked again, but she didn't answer, so he went back down the dark stairs and into the sunlight and walked back down to the avenue. All the streets entering the avenue were blocked by tanks and by troops on foot, but the side streets were crowded with cars, and every one of them seemed to be carrying a black flag or even a black scrap of cloth. Out on the avenue, white squares were taped to almost every tree—lists of the dead and injured. Troops kept people moving away from the lists but didn't tear them down. There were no militia to be seen. He walked along the avenue to the square. Down the steps of Government House fell a cascade of women's shoes, purses, blood.

A squad of soldiers ordered him away. He didn't bother to get out his credential. There was nothing to stay for.

· 23 ·

Sunday, April 9, 1989
9 A.M.
Tbilisi Central Police Station

CHANTURIA HAD NOT SEEN IRAKLY UNIANI SINCE THEY WERE IN THE SAME study group at the University of Tbilisi. Study groups were permanent, official arrangements that lasted all four years of undergraduate study, and he and Uniani had been close then. Still, it had been a long time, and he wasn't sure he would recognize Uniani any longer, or that Uniani would recognize him; but they both did. Uniani had a large office of his own in the militia headquarters just off Rustaveli Prospect, with windows full of Georgia sunshine. When Chanturia opened the door, Uniani leaned back in his chair and grinned. "Well, look what the cats dragged in! Sergo Chanturia. Are you here for the excitement, Sergo? Reinforcement for us helpless bastards in protecting Gorbachev's army from the Georgian people?" He got up and came around the desk to clasp Chanturia tightly in his arms and kiss him on both cheeks. "It's great to see you, Sergo," he said. "What does the Committee think of what's going on in this town?"

"I'm not here for the Committee, Irakly," Chanturia answered. "I'm just on vacation."

"From the looks of your eyes, you got more vacation than you need, Sergo. You've been partaking of the old wild lilac, haven't you? The bastards in the army are denying they used it, of course." "Wild lilac" was the army's name for CN gas, which had left him with broken blood vessels in his eyes.

"I was up on the avenue last night. My mother lives just one street over, you know."

"The excitement woke you up, did it? Lucky you didn't get a cracked skull. We still don't know how many dead we've got. At least a dozen. The stories on the street make it a lot worse, of course: people are claiming a hundred and fifty dead, pregnant women bayoneted by troops, the usual stuff. What a business we're in, Sergo! Incidentally, some of our men say they were ordered by a Georgian KGB officer to separate the army from the civilians last night. Local office of the Committee doesn't know a thing about it—they say it's evidence that the whole event was the work of provocateurs. They're all Russians, and between you and me, they're not the kind of guys who would worry about a few dead Georgians. Now that I see you, I understand it a little better. Don't I?"

"Irakly, do me a favor and don't talk about it."

Uniani looked at him closely. Then he reached over and took Chanturia's jacket sleeve and pulled it to his own face and sniffed it. "You should wash that stuff out of your clothes."

"Is there still some blood?" Chanturia asked, remembering the woman.

"No—were you hurt?"

"It was someone else's blood."

"I meant the gas. Long-term exposure isn't good for you."

"Nor to blood, either."

Uniani nodded sadly. "Well, it's great to see you anyway, Sergo. Want a cup of tea?"

"It's good to see you, Irakly." He sat down with Uniani on the two soft chairs in the corner of the office under the windows. "Life's a lot more comfortable here than in Moscow," he said, looking around the office.

"I hope so. We don't have the excitement of Dzerzhinsky Square, I'm sure. Or didn't until last night. The Russian bastards!" A woman brought a pot of tea, and they sat in the sun and talked about university days for a few minutes, before Uniani said, "You didn't come here to file charges for being gassed on the public street, did you?"

"No. I came looking for some information."

"Ah. About vacation spots in the region, I suppose?"

"I'm looking for a man. Or some men."

"It sounds like business to me. But tell me who you want. I'll have them dragged in within the hour."

"I don't know who, exactly. Maybe you can help me find out. Without telling the Committee about it."

Uniani's eyes blinked. "Seriously!"

"Seriously."

"This sounds like fun. Tell me what you need."

Outside Tbilisi, low, steep mountains rise in all directions, and the city has climbed the closer ones and covered the ridges and plateaus. Atop one of these ridges, overlooking the Kura River, the road ended at an iron gate in a stone wall. The gate was made in the old Georgian style, with ornate iron latticework. The wall was topped with broken bottles set in cement.

An old Zhiguli automobile halted at the gate. The two young Georgian men in it, roughly dressed, made a show of looking at a map of Tbilisi. The map did not show this road.

A young man came to the gate and stood inside it looking at them. He wore dark loose cotton trousers and shirt that almost formed a military uniform; but he was unarmed. Behind him the road turned out of sight to the right, and an even expanse of grass stretched up to another stone wall. A row of fruit trees blossomed along the wall. Behind it rose a white house with a red tile roof. The house was the size of an Institute.

The man inside the gate called to them: "You'll have to go back down! There's no way through here!"

"We want the Georgian Military Highway!" Uniani answered. "Isn't it over this ridge?"

"It is! But the road doesn't go through! Go back and take the first right!"

Uniani waved and turned the car around. "That's the place," he said to Chanturia. "I don't know if the man you want is there; but if he's in Georgia and he's Mafia, there's a man inside there who knows him. Knows all about him."

"Who is that?"

"Tomaz Broladze. Be careful where you say his name."

"I haven't heard it before."

"That's because people are careful where they say it. You've heard of Shevardnadze, I suppose."

"You mean the Foreign Minister?"

"You're well read in current affairs. When Shevardnadze was head of the Party in Georgia, Sergo, he vowed to clean out the Mafia. There were at least three attempts to assassinate him. It was impossible to prove who was behind them. We caught one assassin. He was found dead in his cell of a heart attack. Now Shevardnadze's in Moscow, and Broladze is still living up there." He motioned behind them with his thumb.

"Does Broladze have people working for him in Moscow?"

"I don't know; but if I headed a big organization, I'd want to have a branch in the capital of the empire . . . ah, the Union. Wouldn't you?"

"How do I get in to see him?"

"I'm only a captain of militia, Sergo. I don't get paid to think at that level. But I don't think even the army could get inside there. I know his men outgun the militia. He hires army veterans, and he arms them with the best weapons. Did you know that 7,300 automatic weapons were reported stolen from army installations in Georgia within the last year? Not to mention forty antitank rockets. What do you want to see him for?"

"I don't know yet. Sometimes you have to just go forward and see what happens. You don't have any of his people in prison? Anybody we could talk to?"

"I have to admit we haven't met our Plan requirements in this regard."

"You're a disappointment to me, Irakly."

"We did have his son once. Little Tomaz. I don't know the details: that was before I came back to Tbilisi. I believe he did time in one of the camps."

"Is he in Tbilisi?"

"Sure. Probably right back there in that house. But we wouldn't be able to touch him now."

"Do you have a file on Broladze? Maybe if I see it, I'll think of something."

"Do we have a file on him! Of course we have a file on him! We've got files on half the population of Tbilisi. And if we don't, I'll order it from the Committee's office. They have files on the whole population of Tbilisi."

It wasn't necessary to go to the Committee. The militia files had Tomaz Broladze, as well as his son Tomaz Tomazovich—"Little Tomaz"—and thirty or more of their associates.

Sergo started with the file on the father.

Tomaz Broladze had been arrested once in 1949 for black-market sales of machine tool parts stolen from a state factory where he worked. The charges were dropped before trial. Since that time, he had not held an official job—a crime in itself, but one for which he had never been charged. Nor had he ever been charged with another crime.

The son was arrested in 1979, at age twenty, when a woman charged that he had raped her. The original prosecutor died in an automobile accident before trial, but his deputy, protected around the clock by militia, obtained a conviction. Tomaz Tomazovich was sentenced to three years at hard labor; but he was released after little more than a year. He had never been charged with another crime.

Chanturia sat back and took a long drink of tea.

"Find something?" Irakly asked from his desk across the room.

"For Mafia chiefs, they don't seem to have done much."

"You won't find Old Tomaz's fingerprints on anything. He's a fox. The son . . ." Irakly shrugged. "The real work is done by the workers. It's like the Party. But let me call in one of my organized-crime people," Irakly offered. "Maybe he'll know something that's not in the files."

Mikhail Kavtaradze was the organized crime person. He was a lieutenant of detectives, apparently nearing retirement age. "Broladze?" he said. "No, you won't find much in his record. Old Tomaz doesn't like having things written about him."

"What about this machine-tool theft in 1949?"

"Ah, that was nothing. It's the business Old Tomaz is in: selling things. Sometimes stolen, sometimes not. He was just starting out then. I expect he sold the machine tools because they were available: the factory manager would have had to be in on it. Actually, he got his real start in flowers. Bought, not stolen."

"Flowers?" Chanturia said.

"Sure. Old Tomaz started as a truck driver, working for that same factory. Now, say he was supposed to drive a load of machine tools to the Ukraine. Five-day trip, ten if you break down. So he drives straight through in two days, arranges a 'breakdown' with a shop that's willing to fake the repair papers, drives straight back, buys a load of flowers and takes them to Moscow and sells them in a day in a parking lot next to an apartment building. Flowers are worth more than their weight in gold in Moscow in winter. You know that. And easier to sell than machine tools. He's home on schedule, with more rubles in his pocket than he'd make in ten years of driving. In a few years, every driver in Georgia is working for him—even the ones the KGB think they own. The Committee likes drivers—they're a big source of information. But you know more about that than we do. Trucks are still his biggest business: nothing moves in Georgia if Tomaz Broladze doesn't approve it."

"Is there a way to meet him?" Chanturia asked.

Kavtaradze looked at Chanturia for several seconds before he answered. It was a look of thoughtful assessment. "He might answer an invitation from the Committee," Kavtaradze said finally, "but I don't think he's going to answer one from us."

"I don't want the local Committee office in on this. This is special. From Moscow." He lied because he wasn't sure of Kavtaradze. He saw the caution in the man's eyes. Kavtaradze was Georgian, but who knew which side would win in a conflict of loyalties? Chanturia felt for the first time how the Russians he worked with daily must feel about him.

"The only way would be to find someone who knows him," Kavtaradze said. "You need a go-between he'll trust. Someone who has friends on that side. But I don't know who it would be."

"Your files say his son did time in the camps."

"Ah, that. Yes." He shrugged. "It wasn't for crime. For rape, actually." The shrug seemed to say, *You know young men.*

"Maybe I know someone with friends on *that* side."

128

· 24 ·

Monday, April 10, 1989
3 P.M.
Mikadze's Apartment

GEORGI MIKADZE SAT INSIDE THE BALCONY OF HIS APARTMENT IN THE OLD center of Tbilisi on a bench upholstered with faded green velvet. The balcony, fully enclosed, was like an extension of the apartment, overhanging a street no wider than a man could stretch his arms. The bench filled the narrow interior of the balcony, which was paneled above the bench with dark ancient wood carved in sinuous abstractions. At the sides of the balcony, narrow windows looked up and down the narrow street. Georgi sat leaning on his cane, sometimes turning to look up the street as if he expected someone. Chanturia faced him from a heavy carved armchair that almost completely surrounded him.

"Empires never learn, Sergo," Mikadze said. "Sometimes it seems that they're incapable of learning. They had a hunger strike on their hands: now they have a revolution."

"Don't divide the skin before the creature's dead," Chanturia said. "The Union won't go under so easily."

Georgi laughed. "Oh, the revolution's not here yet; not today. Not this year, perhaps. But already one can hear its footsteps."

"If so, you hastened its progress."

"A little more butter never hurt the stew," Georgi said. "Well, if I did hasten its progress, then I hope to die content. But the question is, what sort of revolution will it be? Will it be freedom this time, or just another change of governors?"

"Don't you worry about who may have been taking down your name, and for what reason?"

"At one time I worried about that. I don't any longer."

"You might not survive the camps this time."

"I know I can *bear* the camps, Sergo. Surviving is just a matter of extending that in time."

129

"I'm sorry I didn't make an effort to keep you out of the camps, Georgi Georgyevich."

The old man smiled. "As a KGB lieutenant? There was nothing you could have done. You'd only have wasted your *blat* for nothing. Endangered your career, perhaps."

"All the same, I should have tried. How often in life does one get a chance to do right in a way that matters? The chance shouldn't be wasted."

"One gets the chance every day, Sergo. We just don't always see the chance when it comes."

Chanturia thought about this. "I'd like your help on something."

Mikadze smiled again. It was fine summery smile for an old man. "If I can help you, I will."

"I want to meet a Georgian who was . . . in a prison camp several years ago." Chanturia said this hesitantly. He found it awkward that Georgi, who had been a prisoner, seemed to have no reluctance to talk about his time in the camps, while he himself, a jailer at third hand, could hardly bear to mention it. "He was not a political," Chanturia said with effort. "But maybe you know someone who knew someone who knew him."

"I didn't see many nonpoliticals, of course. But tell me who it is."

"The son of Tomaz Broladze."

Mikadze laughed. "Tomaz Tomazovich, is it? Maybe you were fated to meet, Sergo."

"Do you know someone who knows him, then?"

"We shared a cell for several weeks."

"How did that happen? I didn't think he was charged with a political crime." To avoid contamination, ordinary criminals weren't sent to camps that held politicals.

"No. He wasn't a political. But I was held in jail here in Tbilisi before my trial, while the Procurator prepared a case against me." He laughed. "It must have been a challenging case: I was a year in jail, waiting for a trial that lasted thirty minutes. While I was in jail, young Tomaz passed through, awaiting his trial. It was only a few weeks, and then he was gone. His trial took a day. A complicated matter, no doubt. He was charged with the rape of a certain young woman; but he denied it, and she was a woman of less than pure reputation. To put it bluntly, she was known to be a whore. Still, he was found guilty; but he was sentenced to only a year. Tomaz Tomazovich told me that the real problem was that he had been on too friendly terms with a different woman, the daughter of the district Party chief. Her father thought him unsuitable." He paused a moment in reflection. "H father died not long after the trial. Perhaps one can be too particular in the choice of friends for one's children." He smiled again. "Yes, I can help you meet Little Tomaz."

· 25 ·

Tuesday, April 11, 1989
2 P.M.
The Restaurant Ritza

IN ONE OF THE SIDE STREETS NEAR RUSTAVELI PROSPECT, OUTSIDE THE RESTAURANT Ritza, a motorcade of three black Volgas arrived at high speed. Each one carried on its radio antenna the red flag with a black and a white bar. An old woman scurried for safety as the cars swerved to the curb. Three men each got out of the front and rear cars and fanned out along the street before two men climbed out of the center car. These two came directly to the door of the restaurant without looking around. One opened the door and looked inside, then held the door for the other and waited near the entrance while the second man came back to the table where Chanturia was sitting with Georgi Mikadze.

"Tomaz," Georgi said, "I thank you for coming. I was expecting your son."

"My son was unfortunately called out of town," Tomaz Broladze said. "Rather than send his apologies, I came myself. It's been too long since we've seen each other." He introduced himself to Chanturia, and added, "You acted bravely on Rustaveli Prospect two nights ago, Captain."

"I'm surprised that you know about it." Chanturia had not told Georgi—nor anyone except Irakly—that he had been present at the army action. And he didn't think Georgi would have mentioned that he was a KGB officer. It could only mean that Broladze had his own sources of information in the militia.

131

"It's surprising how much one hears, if one listens carefully," Broladze said. He settled into a chair and, without looking to see if a waiter was there, caused a waiter to appear with a wave of his hand. "A bottle of wine before lunch?" he suggested. Without waiting for an answer, he sent the waiter off under orders.

Broladze rested his forearms on the table. They were thick arms, the arms of a truck driver still, with powerful thick hands, but uncallused. He wore a light blue linen shirt, open at the collar, under a cream silk jacket that hadn't seen the inside of any clothing shop in the Union. He appeared to be near sixty, but his thick hair was black and wavy, and though his face was lined, he was still handsome. It was a calm face; but the eyes were alight.

"So. What were your impressions of Sunday morning's military action, Captain?" Broladze asked.

"I'm not a military expert, I'm afraid."

"But I wasn't asking for your military opinion; only your impressions as a participant, and as a Georgian. Here we have our Georgian press crying murder, and the Union press telling of drugged-crazed drunken Georgians attacking helpless army troops. But you were there. What do you say?"

"It was a happy crowd, attacked because the authorities were afraid."

"Afraid? Of what?"

He looked Broladze in the eyes. "They were afraid the prisoners were escaping."

"You're a most unusual KGB officer, Captain." The waiter reappeared with the wine. Broladze poured three glasses without tasting it and offered wine to Georgi and Chanturia. "You'll like this wine," he said. "It's made for the Party big shots. You won't find it in any other restaurant, but they keep it here for me. So—to our meeting." He drank the glassful at a gulp and poured another. But Chanturia tasted it gratefully, let the smoke of it slide back through his mouth. Broladze smiled at him. "It's too good for Party hacks, eh? Here." He topped up Chanturia's glass, and Georgi's. Then he waved the waiter back and busied himself with the details of the meal. From his orders, it was clear that this was no ordinary Soviet restaurant; in any such place in the Union, his orders would have been a satire. He settled on a light soup, some local mushrooms, both creamed and pickled, a roast pheasant in wine sauce with rice pilaf, peppers and onions sautéed with cheese, for dessert, fresh wild berries with cream, and ended with another bottle of wine. "A simple lunch, but it should hold the pains at bay, eh?" he said with a wink at Chanturia, as if they shared some secret understanding.

Throughout the meal Broladze talked with Georgi about Georgian literature. It appeared that he had its folk poetry by heart, although he expressed no interest whatever in Russian poems. Chanturia showed astonishment that he could quote twenty lines together from any poem Georgi mentioned. "When I was driving," Broladze said, "our Georgian poets kept me alive many a time when otherwise sleep would have had me off the road; and they kept me always from boredom. There was no Western tape deck in the cab in those days."

They ended with a glass of Armenian brandy, "smooth as a virgin's bottom," Broladze said. "No one who drinks this could have hard feelings for our neighbors."

When it appeared that the meal was ended, Broladze said to Chanturia in a low voice—not too low for Georgi actually to hear, but as an indication that this was a private remark—"I'm sorry my son was unable to fulfill your request to meet with you. He'll not return until after your departure." Chanturia had not mentioned when he was to leave Tbilisi, but he let the comment pass. "Still," Broladze said, more loudly, "it was a pleasure for me to make your acquaintance. I knew your father. He was no good. And frankly, I see very few KGB officers whose company I enjoy. So my hopes were not high. I'm happy that I was mistaken. My thanks to Georgi for letting me share your company, even so briefly. It would be a pleasure to me, really, to invite you to my house for dinner while you are still in Tbilisi, if you have time. Could you come tomorrow?"

"I'd be pleased."

As they were leaving the restaurant, Georgi said to Chanturia, "It appears that you passed the first test. I don't know if you'll meet Tomaz the son; but without the father's permission, you never would have."

"And what should I expect when I do meet him?"

"I don't know. I haven't seen him in ten years; and the camps change some people."

"It doesn't sound as if he was a prize even before the camps."

"He was a wild young man. What he is now . . . ?"

· 26 ·

Wednesday, April 12, 1989
7 P.M.
The Hill

THE PLACE WHERE TOMAZ BROLADZE LIVED WAS CALLED "THE HILL." THE Hill overlooked the Georgian Military Highway, the old road traveled by armies moving from Turkey to Russia or Russia to Turkey. Once there had been a small fortress, and its foundations, dating to the thirteenth century, still clung to the south slope far above the highway; but the foundations now rose from the close-cut grass of a garden, and above the garden was Tomaz Broladze's house, and the house was a fortress too.

The entrance was on the north side, just below the top of the hill, through the gate where Chanturia had stopped with Uniani.

The black Volga carrying Chanturia sped toward the iron gate and did not stop. The gate opened ahead of it: someone had been watching. Inside the gate Chanturia saw the same young man, who gave no sign of recognition.

The Volga turned to the right inside the gate, where the drive ran for a hundred meters along the inside of the stone boundary wall, and then swung back around a rock outcrop that was the very top of the hill and down again behind the hilltop to the house. On the inside of the curve a guard post was cut into the rock outcrop. A young man stood there with a Soviet Army attack rifle in his hands.

At the house, Tomaz Broladze was waiting in the entrance porch. He welcomed Chanturia with the two cheek-kisses of Georgian friends.

The part of the house they entered was a large open room with walls of whitewashed stone. The floor was covered with Caucasian rugs and mounds of pillows scattered at random. Across the room, tall windows overlooked the valley on the south, where the city of Tbilisi clung to the feet of all the mountains. The city had managed to climb into the lower bowls and hollows not far above the valley floor, but there it gave up the effort, and the higher mountainsides were bare beginning far below this hilltop.

"You may want to see the garden," Broladze said. He led Chanturia across the room and onto a broad stone-paved patio bounded by a railing with carved stone balusters. Below a flight of marble steps, grass lawns and flower beds descended gently to the edge of a precipice, and beyond that was only air.

"The Russians used to watch from here for the Turks," Broladze said; "and at other times, the Turks for the Russians; and when they had the chance, the Georgians for both." They walked down through the garden to the precipice. Broladze stopped and with a wooden-handled folding knife from his pocket cut a rose, which he put in the buttonhole of Chanturia's jacket.

Below the precipice, two hundred meters down the mountain, the stone wall swung around the peak to close off the estate. In a tower built into the wall, a guard carrying an assault rifle was enjoying a cigarette. "That wall is the wall of the Turkish fortress," Broladze said. "And from this spot, it's said, the Turkish captain used to pitch his prisoners after interrogation." He added, with a smile, "The methods of your employer are more efficient, of course."

Chanturia wondered if he was thinking of his son.

As they walked back up to the house, Chanturia remarked, "It must have taken you a long time to build this," waving his hand around them.

"I didn't build it," Broladze said. "Your Party built it. It was for the use of the district Party Secretary here. He decided, however, that it was more grand than he needed." This seemed to amuse him in some dark way, but he said no more.

Dinner was in a smaller room that opened off the room they had come through. There was a long table of thick wood, dark with ages of polishing, and heavy old chairs upholstered in swatches of antique carpet. Four places were set at the table—set with antique china and silver—and between them, flowers in crystal vases and candles in antique silver candlesticks.

A man of Chanturia's age was standing behind the table with an empty wineglass in his hand. He came around the table to meet them, but warily, and he did not offer Chanturia his hand. He walked with curious care, as if afraid of losing his balance. "My son, Tomaz," Broladze said; but there was no need: the man was the image of his father; but there was a darkness in his eyes that was not in the father's. After his father spoke, he took Chanturia's hand briefly.

135

"Georgi Georgyevich sends his greetings," Chanturia said.

"My father said so already. But please tell Georgi I regret that I couldn't come to meet him yesterday. Business prevented it."

"What business are you in?" Chanturia asked.

"My father's business."

"I hadn't discussed with your father what that is."

"Now that private cooperatives are legal," the elder Broladze said, "I've begun a cooperative trucking company. We lease old trucks from organizations that no longer are able to use them, and we provide transport to organizations that are unable to get their products moved—frequently the very same organizations that leased us the trucks."

"That sounds magical," Chanturia said.

"Not at all. It's only a matter of hard work and good planning. For example, there is a heavy-equipment factory not far from Tbilisi. I was employed there once, in fact. This factory has its own fleet of trucks to deliver its products—parts and so forth. It drives a truck a hundred thousand kilometers, and by then it can't make the thing go any farther. It also has no way to dispose of the carcass. So it has a fleet of hulks going to rust out behind the plant. I said to the manager, whom I know, 'Let me have these. I'll take them away and pay you for them, and you'll have more storage space.' Well, you know, he couldn't do that: the law doesn't permit sale of state property. But it does permit leasing. So he leased me his wrecks for an annual fee, and I took pieces off one or another and made them into half as many working machines. And then I put them to work. I have to keep the remains of all of the wrecks—if I fully dispose of one, that's destruction of state property. But as long as there's something recognizable sitting out in my lot—even if it's only a number plate—then that truck continues to exist, and the state is satisfied. My lot is full of the relics; but somewhere their spirits are out on the road, working. And that's more than they ever did when the state had them. Some of them are working for the very factory they once belonged to, that had tossed them aside as useless. And in fact, it's the same with men. It's no trouble for me to find drivers: there are many men out of work. The Party denies it, of course; but I don't have to go looking for men who need work to feed their families—they come looking for me."

"Where do your trucks go?"

"Everywhere," the old man said. "Everywhere in the Union, and some places outside."

"It must be a very profitable business."

"Of course, the cooperative alone would not pay for such a house as this. I have a thing or two besides. No, only the Party has a single business that could bring its owners a place such as this."

"I hadn't thought of the Party as being in business."

Broladze laughed a long time. "The Party doesn't *want* you to think of it as being in business. But, of course, it is. Farming, that's the Party's business: farming the state."

A man in a Georgian peasant shirt appeared carrying a tray with two glasses of wine. Broladze handed one to Chanturia and took the other. "Your health," he proposed.

The wine was different from what they'd had in the restaurant, but as good. Old Tomaz watched Chanturia taste it. "I hope it's to your taste," he said. "It's also a special Party product." He looked at the fourth plate on the table and then at his son. "Is he not coming?"

"He said he was. He's reported not checked in yet."

The old man shrugged. "Let's eat. If he comes, he comes." He said to Chanturia, "We had expected another guest; but we won't stand on ceremony. We're an informal family."

Dinner was not Georgian but a mixture of dishes from the cuisines of the southern republics of the Soviet Union. There was spicy *kharchko* soup and Uzbek pilaf and Azeri shashlik and glazed fish. There was wine of three varieties, and Tanya would have traded frantically for any one of them at the KGB special stores. In answer to Chanturia's compliment, the old man said, "My cook was once the chef at a special Party hotel in Yalta. But he tired of the pace and the demands. Here, his life is simpler. And, I believe he views it as a promotion."

"He's paid more than Gorbachev," Little Tomaz said, returning from a trip to the toilet. They had drunk freely, and as he walked, Little Tomaz rolled with the roll of a ship in high seas. "More than Gorbachev is paid *officially*," he corrected himself. He came around the table to help Chanturia to some more of the glazed fish. As the meal went on, he had become more and more friendly, approximately in proportion to his consumption of wine.

It was then that Chanturia noticed for the first time what he had been seeing all evening—that Tomaz Tomazovich Broladze was left-handed. And the reason he noticed it now was something else he had just seen—that Tomaz Tomazovich Broladze didn't walk unsteadily just because he was drunk: he limped. And sudden recognition of the truth sank through Chanturia like a stone. Little Tomaz had walked so carefully before dinner not because he was full of wine, but because he was trying not to show a limp. And the Georgian prisoner, Akaky Shetsiruli, one of three men who had confessed to the murder of the American Charles Hutchins—he was a Georgian who limped; but he was not left-handed. When he had signed his prisoner-consignment papers, he had used his right hand. But the knife-thrust that had killed Charles Hutchins had been delivered with a left hand. Two witnesses had agreed that the thrust had been delivered from directly in front of Hutchins; and the knife wound was in the lower right rib cage. And the medical examiner was sure the blow had been delivered left-handed.

And therefore?

And therefore, Sergo Vissarionovich Chanturia, a captain of the Committee on State Security, was very probably having dinner with the killer of Charles Hutchins, agent of the Central Intelligence Agency in command of Moscow Station. And furthermore, there was nothing he could do about it, even if he could convince anyone that it was true; because someone had got Akaky Shetsiruli to agree to take the fall for Little Tomaz, and that meant that Akaky Shetsiruli knew that if he changed his story he would be dead.

And one more thing: Little Tomaz was well known to the Georgia KGB. Not only was his father the father of the Georgia Mafia, he himself had been in the camps. The files of the Committee's Tbilisi office must be full of Little Tomaz Broladze. The KGB officers here had to know that Little Tomaz Broladze limped and they had to know he was left-handed. But when they went looking for a Georgian who limped and who had killed a man with a left-handed knife thrust, they hadn't found left-handed Little Tomaz: they had found right-handed Akaky Shetsiruli. They had to know they should be looking for a left-handed man: that theory was in Chanturia's own notes on the case, which had been sent to them. But that meant they hadn't looked for Little Tomaz, but had looked the other way entirely. They must have thought that, with a confession, no one would notice; and until now, no one had. And the only question remaining was, who else in the KGB knew about it, and did that include someone in Moscow?

Chanturia knew he was going to have to live very carefully for a while. Not just this evening, but for as far into the future as he could see; because whoever at the Committee knew about this wouldn't be amused that he had found out.

If dinner left Little Tomaz unsteady, it left Old Tomaz quite unchanged even though he had drunk just as much. Chanturia himself—and it startled him—felt the mountain roll once like a very large ship in a quite small sea as he got to his feet. Old Tomaz smiled, but it might have been at some private amusement. "Let's have a brandy," Broladze said, "while Tomaz is arranging the car." Chanturia doubted that any "arranging" needed to be done to have the car appear, but he followed Broladze into the sitting room while Little Tomaz went in the other direction.

Broladze selected a pile of cushions and made himself a nest in them, motioning for Chanturia to do the same next to him. The waiter appeared with a decanter and glasses. Broladze held the bottle up to the light for a long time, as if looking for the future in its depths, and then poured two glasses. "I find you an unusual person, for an officer of the Committee, Sergo," he began. Chanturia did not answer. "I've made inquiries about you, of course. Georgi Mikadze thinks highly of you—of your character and of your intelligence and your good sense. Georgi is an excellent student of men—unlike many writers, who create what they need rather than recognizing what is before them. I find that you also have a good reputation in your business, except among some persons whose own reputation needs looking out for. You have shown me that you can see truth in front of your nose: your analysis of the situation here, in a sentence, said all that needed saying. And you were not afraid to say it. In all, a most unusual combination." He lifted his hand to cut off Chanturia's polite disclaimer of praise. "I don't say this without reason. If you've made any inquiries about me, in your turn"—he grinned as he said this—"then I hope you will have been told that I don't waste words. I'm a businessman, not a politician. Well, Sergo, the fact is this: good help is hard to find. I'd like to hire you for my business."

Chanturia sat for a long time, shifting among his cushions, and Old Tomaz was content to let him do so. At length Chanturia said, "I don't know that I'm qualified for the trucking business."

"There is perhaps such a thing as being too direct," Broladze said. "And we need not say *all* that there is to say. We understand one another. You know I don't want you to drive a truck. Still, there may be more to my business than you know, or think you know. The fact is this: times are changing. The world is changing. The Union is changing. In particular, Georgia is changing. You have eyes: you've seen it. Georgia is chained to a Union its people do not want, but they don't know what to do about it. What they should do depends

139

in part on what is being done elsewhere. I mean, of course, in Moscow. In this business, Sergo, information is important. I have many sources of information. In Georgia, my sources are good. In Moscow, not so good. I need to know what is being thought in Moscow.''

''I think you give me too much credit. I'm not important enough to know that.''

''No one knows everything, Sergo; but everyone knows something. You know that's true; information is your business, after all. And in your business, you must hear some unusual things. I'm not asking you to tell anything you think shouldn't be told. I'm only asking you, when you hear something that you think I should know, to remember me. And if you've inquired about me, I hope that you will have heard that I'm grateful to my friends.''

Outside the front door, a car arrived quickly and stopped. A car door slammed, then the house door. Little Tomaz came into the room. ''Ready,'' he said.

His father rose easily to his feet and held out a hand to help Chanturia. In the other hand he had a slip of paper. ''Here's a telephone number,'' he said. ''You should think about our conversation. A person at that number will know how to reach me at any time.''

He walked to the car with Chanturia and patted him on the shoulder as he got into the back with Little Tomaz, as if Chanturia were a favorite nephew he had loved all his life.

The Volga wound down through the avenues of Tbilisi. ''You're not ready to go home yet, are you?'' Little Tomaz asked.

A Georgian couldn't say his mother was expecting him. ''Can you suggest something else?''

Little Tomaz spoke to the driver: ''Atman, can you suggest something for us to do? We can't take our guest home this early.'' He said this in Russian, but with a strong Georgian accent.

The driver turned his head half toward them. He had a dark face that matched the Muslim name, but in profile it was severely flattened, as if at some time in his life a brick wall had suddenly jumped in front of him. ''Shavlego,'' he said.

Shavlego was the name of a Georgian patriotic song. ''The Arabs have romantic souls,'' Little Tomaz said with a grin. ''True connoisseurs of defiance, even when they don't understand the words.''

''You're an Arab, Atman?'' Chanturia asked.

The driver didn't answer. Little Tomaz said, ''Atman doesn't know what he is, except that he's one of us. He's from Romania; but his father was a Turk and his mother's a Kazakh, so we call him 'the Turk.' And you were late for dinner, Atman. Where were you? Working?"

"You shouldn't drink," Atman said. "You talk too much when you drink."

"We're not all Muslims, Atman." Little Tomaz added, to Chanturia, "I don't know if Atman's a good Muslim; but I know he drinks."

The voice from the front of the car was quiet: "But I don't talk too much."

"I need to be careful where I'm seen," Chanturia said.

"You mean who you're seen with. Don't worry: your Committee's people here are all Russian; and no one who talks to Russians will be at Shavlego." Apparently Shavlego was also the name of a place.

Atman speeded up and turned off the main avenue into a series of side streets, ignoring the traffic laws and seeming to ignore other traffic as well. Little Tomaz laid a hand on Chanturia's arm. He said in Georgian, "Don't worry. Atman has a sense for these things. He's my father's favorite driver. I'd almost say, my father's favorite son. He's not his son, of course; but as close as if he were. Atman and I were in the camps together."

They stopped in front of an unlighted building on a quiet street. Atman got out of the car and walked beside them to the door.

The room was dark, except for a woman in a black dress standing in a pool of light, singing. It was a song designed for tearing hearts out. "Not all the songs here are of war," Little Tomaz said. "But love's a little war, eh, Atman?" Except for the woman and the smoke, Chanturia could make out only the tops of heads at crowded tables, and the red points of cigarettes burning. The song floated among the layers of smoke drifting in the air. The song was like smoke, and the voice was like smoke.

A woman greeted Tomaz warmly by name, and he greeted her more warmly with a kiss, which she did not dodge but didn't respond to. She led them to a table, came back with a bottle of brandy. While Little Tomaz poured, the Turk sat staring at the singer, listening. Little Tomaz offered Chanturia a toast: "In the stirrups." It was a part of a long traditional Caucasian toast that was also a drinking game involving the story of a departing horseman. The participants were expected to drink at each stage of the story. Chanturia smiled. Little Tomaz nudged the Turk, who raised his glass to them without taking his eyes off the singer.

"He's mad for the singer, that one," Tomaz said, nodding at the Turk. He said in Russian to the Turk, "You must be careful: you'll find some Georgian knife in your gizzard if you look that way at Georgian women." The Turk only smiled.

"So many arguments about women," Tomaz said. "Look at a woman of the wrong nationality, and you get your throat cut. It's the same everywhere. Or maybe the KGB doesn't have that trouble. Are you allowed to have Russian women?"

"There can be problems," Chanturia said. It wasn't a conversation he relished.

Chanturia looked at the woman singing. She had dark eyes, and a mass of black hair pulled back into a knot at her neck. He knew she couldn't see him, outside her circle of light; but she seemed to be looking into his eyes as she sang.

"The Old Man had a Russian mistress once. Olga Viktorevna: now she's just a sweet old lady; but this was a long time ago. Some Russians didn't like it and tried to beat his face in; but they didn't know what kind of man they were dealing with when they started. They knew before he was finished. Then they wanted to make trouble for him with the militia; but he had bigger friends than the militia, too."

"Who were his bigger friends?"

Little Tomaz poured another round. "In the saddle," he proposed, and they knocked back the brandy. He smiled. "Forgive me that I can't tell you that."

Chanturia shrugged. "Of course."

The woman stopped singing and stepped back through the curtain behind the stage. With the spotlight out, the room was darker, but easier to see in. The Turk turned his chair back to the table. He said to Tomaz, "You talk too much."

Little Tomaz was unoffended. "You don't even know what I was saying."

"I know."

"I know my man," Tomaz said. "He'll be with us when we need him." He poured Chanturia and himself another glass. The Turk hadn't drunk his second. "For the road," he proposed. He and Chanturia drained their glasses again, and the Turk joined in with a critical smile.

"For the road" was not a closing drink. It was only another stage on the way through the toast. Chanturia breathed carefully, knowing he would have to pace himself the rest of the way. Clearly they were trying to get him drunk. For what purpose? To hear what words might slip from him? Was it a further test set by Old Tomaz? And if so, what was the penalty for failure? Better not to fail. One man on the other side drinking and one not: that could be a dangerous situation, if you drank with the one. And he was already a long way ahead of the Turk. He decided there was only one way out. He filled the glasses again. "Up the hill," he proposed—the next stage of the toast—raising his glass directly to the Turk. He had filled the Turk's glass higher: every gram would count now. Little Tomaz grinned at him. They all drank.

"Besides," Tomaz said to the Turk, "my father approved him. Even without you there."

"Only because I was late," the Turk said. He said to Chanturia, "There are only two ways out of The Hill." Chanturia knew he wasn't referring to the toast now, but to the Broladze fortress. "One is for Old Tomaz to approve you."

"The Old Man usually wants Atman's advice on it too," Little Tomaz said. "But Atman was out working." When he talked of Atman, he didn't sound wholly friendly.

"And the other way?" Chanturia asked.

The Turk smiled. Chanturia smiled back at him and refilled the glasses. He filled the Turk's first. The bottle had become empty: there was not quite enough to fill his own glass. Little Tomaz ordered another.

"Do you come to Moscow often yourself?" Chanturia asked Little Tomaz.

Tomaz retreated into a mocking look. "Sometimes. Not in a long time now, though."

"You should look me up next time."

"Can you find me a Russian woman?"

"If he can't, who could?" the Turk said. "But you've found enough woman problems here."

"That was a long time ago. I'm ready to try again. A nice round Russian woman. Like father, like son." The Turk frowned.

The new bottle arrived, and Chanturia captured it. He filled his own glass before either of the others could. He filled it low. He raised his glass to the Turk. "Behind the hill."

The brandy became a slow steady pressure at the front of his brain. Sweat formed around his eyes. The Turk was starting to sweat too; but Chanturia doubted now that he could last long enough to get the Turk out of control.

The singer came out again from behind the curtain, but the spotlight didn't come on. She sat down alone at a table next to the stage and lit a cigarette.

"And behind the hill was a girl," Chanturia said, quoting the next words of the toast. But he didn't drink. He took the bottle and his glass and left the two of them sitting. He felt the Turk's eyes on his back as he walked to the table where the singer was sitting. Her dark eyes inquired of him. He said, politely and formally, "Good evening."

She was a woman who more than enough drunks had assumed was available. She finished her cigarette and then answered him. "My singing tears your heart," she said. "You want to get to know me better."

He said, "You've been talking to Georgian men." He wished the pressure in his skull would subside, but it didn't. "Actually," he said, "I'm trying to escape from somebody. It would be a great favor if you'd let me sit here while you sing. Are you going to sing again?"

"Yes, I am. Who're you running from?"

"Two guys back there." She looked back the way he had come and must have seen them looking at her. "The Arab? Did he send you to hit on me?"

"That's one. But he didn't send me. I came by myself."

"You're in hard company, with those two." He thought she might be afraid; instead she seemed interested. "Why are you here?"

He shrugged. "We could say it's God's will, if we didn't have to be atheists."

"I wasn't asking about the meaning of life. Why are you at my table?"

"I don't completely trust those two, and the only acceptable excuse I can think of for leaving their company is to go looking for a woman. You don't have to take it personally. If you let me sit here for a while, maybe I can figure something else out, once my brain clears. I've had too much to drink."

She laughed. "Who ever heard of a Georgian man having too much to drink? Sure, sit here. I'll sing for you. If you won't take it personally."

"Kind of you. Would you like a brandy?" He sat down and put the bottle and the glass on the table. "I seem to be short a glass."

"No brandy. Order me a glass of wine. Brandy gets between me and my work."

She tasted the wine when it came, while he pretended to drink a brandy, and then she got up to sing. Yes, it was the kind of song that tore a man's heart out, especially if her eyes were locked on his. He was glad he didn't have to take it personally.

Halfway through the set, the Turk came to the table. Chanturia felt him there without having to look around. "We're going," he said. It was a voice you could use to chill melons.

Chanturia didn't take his eyes from the woman. "Go ahead. I'm comfortable."

"My instructions are to get you home."

"I'm glad to hear it; but I'm a big boy. This lady will see me home."

"No she won't."

"She said she would."

"I'll believe that when she says it." The sound of a saw cutting ice.

"She'll tell you, when she's done. Sit down so I can listen to her."

The Turk's hand touched his shoulder; but then Little Tomaz's voice said, "Let's go, Atman. He's my father's guest." Chanturia still didn't look around, but he knew they were gone.

When she came down from her circle of light, she said to him, "I was afraid you wouldn't be here when I came back."

"I was too." He raised his glass. "To the girl." Her wineglass had been refilled. She drank with him, but didn't empty the glass as he did. He was sorry for the other drinks he had taken, but not for this one.

"Are you sure they won't be waiting for you outside?" she asked.

"No. Do you think they will be?"

"The Arab one likes me. He's always in here staring. Who knows what an Arab will do?"

"Do you know Little Tomaz?"

"I know who he is. And what he is."

"What is he?"

"They aren't good people. Any of them. If you're part of their business, I don't want to know you. I've helped you; but I don't want to know you."

"I'm not part of their business."

"Then why are you with them?"

"I can't tell you that."

"I suppose you're a KGB officer investigating them?" She said this in the voice of a woman who has heard all possible stories more than once.

"Nothing so exciting. I just can't tell you."

"Well, I knew you weren't KGB, anyway. Who ever heard of a Georgian KGB officer?"

"Aren't there any?"

"Not in Georgia. They want Russians, to control us. Just like their Russian army."

"Do you sing again?"

"One more set."

"I'd like to stay and listen. I won't take it personally."

But he did. A dark-eyed Georgian woman, and a dark-hearted Georgian song. What chance was there of escape from that combination? The fact was, the woman was beautiful, and her words, even if not her own words, were magic. He wanted her.

When she returned, he said, "I love you."

"You promised not to take it personally."

"I didn't swear on Lenin's name."

"Next time I'll insist."

He touched her hand, and she didn't move it. "Let me take you home. I promise not to attack you."

"Swear on Lenin's name?"

"Yes."

"In that case, why should I?" She laughed at his confusion. "Come on. Either you take me home or I'll take you home. You need an escort: they may be out there waiting for you."

"Then I'll take you home. It will be better for my reputation."

He gave the taxi driver a wrong address first and then had him double back; but he saw no sign that they were being followed. The second time, he stopped the cab short of her apartment and they got out and walked. "It's such a nice night," he said, and it was, but she didn't entirely believe that was the reason. He stopped to tie a shoe that was not untied, and looked backward.

"You're a cautious man," she said.

"I try."

Her apartment was one room and a kitchen in a new Soviet-standard apartment building. The room was small and packed with things—cushions, pictures, a tall brass pot for Turkish coffee, one soft chair, a couch that was also her bed, against one wall a tall wooden wardrobe with a mirror on the door. They waded among the things to the kitchen, where she made tea.

The tea brought him back from too many brandies, but his alcohol-induced courage ebbed at the same rate. He was wondering how to excuse himself with the least embarrassment, when she said, "I should change out of my work clothes. Do you want to help me?" She offered her back, the zipper of the strapless gown. The skin on her neck was white and soft. He pulled the zipper down.

Holding up the front of her gown, she turned out the lights in the other room and went to the wardrobe. From behind its mirrored door came rustling sounds, and the gown fell to the floor. It was swept up again, apparently into the wardrobe. "I thought you were going to help," she said. "I'm over here."

When he went there, she was standing behind the door, quite naked, hanging her gown. She turned to him. "We'll hang your things too."

She laughed as she helped him undress.

"What are you laughing at?"

"I hope you're going to take *this* personally."

As she led him to the bed he cursed his professional training that made him suspect what might come next: the hidden cameras, the bursting open of the door . . . He had been led to her—the first sign to make a hunter wary. No, that was not quite true. He had been led to the club, but not to her. They had no way of knowing that he would approach her. And he was sure the Turk's anger wasn't feigned. Little Tomaz and the Turk had wanted to spend more time with him, to see what they could see. They hadn't expected to lose him to a woman.

He lost all that suspicion in her arms. Her eagerness was personal indeed. He wanted suddenly to whisper her name and realized he didn't even know it. The only name he could think of was Lamara. Sweet, brave Lamara who had no use for a Georgian in the KGB.

He got up to dress toward morning, and she did too. "I'll show you the taxi stand," she said. As they went to the door he took out his wallet to leave some money on her table. She caught his hand. "I'm not a whore," she said, with a flash of what looked like real anger. "If I liked you, and you liked me, isn't that enough? Would you want me to offer to pay *you*?"

He was ashamed and didn't know what to say. She smiled and kissed him. "You're forgiven." They walked together in the quiet warm night toward the taxi stand. Three cabs were there, all with their lights off, their drivers standing in the street talking and smoking. Their voices carried far up the quiet street. Football talk. She stopped. He held her in his arms and kissed her and felt her body still naked under the thin dress. She didn't offer her name, nor ask his; and although he knew how to find her, he knew that unless she offered, he never would. She didn't offer. She kissed him one last time and stepped back, still holding his hand, to the length of her arm, and with a smile dropped his hand and turned and walked away.

· 27 ·

Thursday, April 13, 1989
Morning
Tbilisi

CHANTURIA HAD INTENDED TO VISIT HIS FRIEND UNIANI AGAIN TO TALK about his meeting with Tomaz Broladze, but now he didn't think a discussion would be such a good idea. He had no reason to doubt Uniani's friendship; but even honest cops talked, and unsuspecting honest cops might talk in the wrong place. Somebody in the local KGB office had avoided having to arrest Little Tomaz, and Chanturia didn't want that somebody to suspect that he knew about it. If he told Uniani anything, he would have to tell him enough to keep him from getting into trouble by accident, and that in itself might put him in danger. Besides that, Chanturia himself had now met twice unofficially with Old Tomaz, without orders and without even an investigation he could point to as a reason. It wouldn't do now to have people realize he was still curious about the Hutchins case: "Curious Varvara got her nose torn off at the bazaar." And he'd been offered a bribe which he now couldn't report, and it wouldn't be any better to say he'd been offered a bribe on behalf of Georgian separatism than on behalf of the Georgia Mafia—if, in fact, that was what had happened. Old Tomaz was clearly smart enough to use Georgian nationalism to help his business along. But under the veneer of "Georgia free," Chanturia thought he saw something else—he saw the business Old Tomaz wanted to be in: the Party's business, the business of farming the State.

But after he decided not to see Uniani, Uniani telephoned him at his mother's apartment. As if he had come to the same conclusion, he didn't suggest another meeting: he had called to say goodbye. But he added, "I've learned one more thing you should know, Sergo."

"What's that?"

"Your Colonel Sokolov was assigned to Tbilisi once—early in his career."

"How do you know?"

"My organized-crime man, Kavtaradze, remembers him. He told me after you were into our files."

"What did he say?"

"Not much—he didn't want to talk about it, but I think he was worried because you work for Sokolov. He was afraid Sokolov would hear about your visit."

"Tell him not to worry. I'm not going to talk about it, if he won't."

"He won't—you can bet on it."

But if an open conversation with Uniani was out of the question, still there was Georgi. Chanturia stopped to say goodbye to him just before leaving for Moscow.

Georgi had acquired the prisoner's habit of discretion. He didn't ask any prying questions, but it was evident that he was curious about the meeting with Broladze. Sergo described it briefly, without mentioning his job offer. "I notice that Little Tomaz limps," he added at the end of his story.

"Yes, I understand so. I heard in prison that he had broken a leg. An 'accident.' The leg never healed properly. Health care for prisoners is not the highest priority of socialist society."

"You sound doubtful that it was an accident."

"Every Marxist-Leninist knows that accidents have causes. 'The objective correlation of forces was such that Tomaz Tomaz'ich's leg became broken.' It may have had something to do with the supposed rape of the daughter of the district Party Secretary."

"What?"

"I mentioned it to you once before. Perhaps you didn't notice. If the fact were a snake, it would have bitten you."

"Well, even an old woman can be enlightened. But if he was accused of raping the daughter of the Party Secretary, how did he get out in a year?"

"I didn't say he was *accused* of raping her. Her father would never have let that become public, of course. And as for whether it happened . . . who knows? In any event, he was accused of raping someone else, who had no reputation to protect. That was the weakness in the case, of course; but that was the only kind of woman who would be willing to testify to such a thing, at any price. One has to work with the material at hand."

"So you think he was framed."

Georgi shrugged. "Life is struggle. Part of life, here, at that time, was a power struggle—on the large scale, between the Party and the Mafia: on a personal scale, between the Party Secretary and Tomaz Broladze. Both had friends. Sometimes one had the upper hand, sometimes the other. Tomaz Tomazovich was accused and was found guilty: the Party Secretary seemed to be winning. In the sentencing, Broladze's power came to the fore; in the prison camp, again the Party Secretary's—or so it seemed at the moment. But shortly after young Tomaz's 'accident,' the Party Secretary happened to die."

"How did he 'happen to die'?"

"I understood that his car was forced off a mountain road by a runaway truck. But of course, I may be wrong. I was away at the time."

"And then young Tomaz was released?"

"It would have been not long after."

"So that ended the struggle."

Georgi said, "The house which Tomaz Broladze now occupies was originally built as a retreat for that Party Secretary."

No, there wasn't anyone he could tell all this. The only thing to do now was to go back to Moscow.

But he wondered: what possible reason could Tomaz Broladze have for letting him meet Little Tomaz? Was he just showing off, rubbing Chanturia's nose in the fact that now he could keep his son out of the KGB's hands? Was it another test, to see if Chanturia was suspicious? And if it was, did he know now that Chanturia was suspicious?

Chanturia threw away the slip of paper with the telephone number Tomaz Broladze had given him; but he memorized the number first.

· III ·

MOSCOW

· 28 ·

Thursday, May 25, 1989
Noon
The United States Embassy

THE CONGRESS OF PEOPLE'S DEPUTIES OPENED AT TEN O'CLOCK IN THE morning in the Kremlin, and the Union stood still. Although it was a work day, no one worked. The proceedings were televised. There was no other program on television anywhere in the country, and every person who did not have a genuine physical need to have his or her eyes somewhere else was watching.

They watched as Orlov, the Chairman of the Central Commission on the Election of the People's Deputies, gave his speech to open the proceedings—Orlov, not Gorbachev!—and they watched as the Latvian deputy Tolpezhnikov brazenly ran to the podium and called for an investigation of the massacre in Tbilisi, in Soviet Georgia, on April ninth, in which sixteen Soviet citizens were killed by the army. They watched as Andrei Sakharov, only recently out of his exile in Gorky, called for a decree of the Congress that would make its decisions permanent and irreversible.

The atmosphere penetrated even the American Embassy, where Soviet holidays were customarily ignored. But Martin, who had watched the proceedings on television all morning in his office, felt like a man locked in the funhouse at the fair, and so after the end of the morning session and before the start of the afternoon one, he left the Embassy and started to walk along Tchaikovsky Boulevard. He had no plan, but he told himself that it was his duty as special

153

assistant cultural attaché to observe the culture of the country. He walked south on Tchaikovsky and then Smolenskaya until he came to the beginning of Arbat Street at the Foreign Ministry building.

He turned into the Arbat pedestrian zone, but within fifty meters found it almost impossible to move between the knots of Russians clotting the street with their arguments. The street musicians and artists, normally the focus for small groups the length of the street, were pushed back against the walls of the shops on either side, or they left their wares forgotten and joined the political discussion that was the sole topic of interest that day.

"Tolpezhnikov, he's crazy!" a bearded man with fire in his dark eyes was thundering at an opponent. "They'll never admit that the Party was behind the decision to send the army into Tbilisi. Why go through a charade?"

"Because even if they don't admit it this time, they'll think twice next time, that's why!" his opponent retorted.

"Sakharov's a brave man," someone else said. "But it'll be back to Gorky for him before the Congress is even over if he doesn't watch what he says."

"They're both traitors!" was another opinion. "This Latvian, this Sakharov, all they can do is tear down what others are working to build. So all right, not everything has been perfect in the past; but it doesn't do any good to dwell on the bad. What's needed now is positive action for the future!"

To stand one's ground in these arguments was a struggle not only intellectual but physical. Martin found himself being squeezed, slowly but inevitably, toward the periphery, where, against the salmon-colored wall of a building freshly painted for the Congress, an artist had set up shop earlier in the day. The paintings now stood untended and ignored, facing the backs of the crowd, who did their best to keep from being pushed into them. At last a broad back bunted Martin nose first into the wall without so much as an *"Izvyenitye,"* and he had to do a standing push-up to keep from falling. As he pushed away from the wall he found himself staring into the vacant eyes of a mask painted on a blank canvas.

Palms against the wall, he stretched his arms out to keep from being pushed into the canvas and leaned there studying the face. This face was all red, a subdued but glowing red the color of the red gold popular in Moldavian jewelry. The eyes of the mask were dark, but in that darkness something moved. He couldn't quite make out what

154

it was, but it had a red tinge, and motion—perhaps it was red flags, the banners of a moving mass of people, seen through darkness.

Someone bumped into him. He pushed back, annoyed.

"Be careful of the paintings, damn you," the man who had bumped him said in Russian. Then, apparently seeing that he was dealing with a foreigner, he said in English, in a much friendlier tone, "Excuse me. The crowd is so much, I was . . ." Words failed him, and he made a pushing motion with his forearms. "Do you like the painting? It is very good. Very cheap." He braced himself with one hand against the wall so that he leaned facing Martin from the other side of the painting, his face only two feet away from Martin's. His breath had a tang of garlic.

Martin stepped back two steps against the pressure of the crowd. "It's interesting."

"Interesting! It is *good*. I am artist; I know!"

"Did you paint it?"

"Me?" He laughed. "I do not paint *that*! These are paintings of me over here." He gestured with his free hand under the arm he was leaning against. Beyond his armpit, Martin could see a row of the big-breasted nude fantasies which were becoming the staple of Arbat Street art.

"They don't look exactly like you. You mean they're your paintings?"

"Yes. Paintings of me!"

"Whose is this, then?"

The man laughed. "My girlfriend has painted that. That is her face. An *avtoportryet*. How you say *po-angliski*?"

"Self-portrait. Not much different from 'auto-portrait.' "

"Self-portrait. Her face."

"How much?"

The man looked Martin in the eyes, as if hoping the right price would appear there. *"Pyat sto rublei."* It was not quite a question, but almost; there wasn't much conviction in it. "Fife hundred."

"Five hundred? Too much!"

The man pursed his lips and then said in a lower voice, "You have dollars? I can sell for fifty dollars."

In spite of the man's get-'em-while-they-last tone, it wasn't a bargain offer: ten rubles to the dollar was the typical transaction price for street exchanges, although the offered price might start at three or five to the dollar; but changing money anywhere but at the Foreign Trade Bank was a violation of law, and Martin wasn't about to commit any economic crimes. "No. No dollars. Rubles."

The man shrugged. "How much you pay?"

Martin pondered. He wanted the painting, but he wanted information more. "I don't know . . . do you have any others like it?"

"No. This is only one."

"Your girlfriend only painted one auto-portrait? Most women like pictures of themselves."

He laughed. "She is not most women. But she painted one else. It was blue one. For the way she felt, she said. But it is already sold."

"That's too bad. Did you sell it today?"

"No. She herself sold it, long time ago."

"Do you know who bought it?"

"No. Some American, I think. You American?"

"Yes."

"Maybe you know him."

"It's a big country."

"Not so big as Soviet Union, though. How about four hundred?"

Martin looked into the painting's eyes, avoiding those of the seller. "It would have been nice to have two. One of her in a blue mood, and one in a red mood."

"You like her, eh? You see her for real, you would want one hundred pictures."

"Maybe she should sell them herself?"

"She does not sell them, only when I cannot be here. She is an artist."

"Well, you're an artist, too, and you're selling pictures."

The man grinned. "Sure. But I am businessman too. She does not know *'biznes.'* If she had to live on paintings *she* could sell, she would not eat. She would not sell any at all, if I did not . . ." He made a pushing motion again. "She paints, she is in her plays . . . She does not sell." He dismissed her activities with a wave of his hand.

"She's a playwright?"

"Play-write? What is 'play-write'?"

"Somebody who writes plays. Does she write plays?"

"No. She is actress. Ha. You want to see her, you go to the theater this weekend. Southwest Studio Theater. She is in play there. Molière's wife. That is who she plays. Tell her I sold you picture. Only three hundred rubles."

"Does she speak English?"

"No. But you speak some Russian, maybe? Or take a translator."

"There's no name on the picture. Tell her she should sign her pictures, if she wants big money for them."

156

"Big money? He calls three hundred rubles big money? What is big money, I know this. You know how much money makes my cousin in Chicago? He say to me, 'Hugo, you want money, you come Chicago.' My cousin, he drives taxi, he makes, you listen this, he makes sometimes two thousand dollars pro month! You know how much money makes an artist here in this Soviet Union? A member of Artists Union? It is crime!"

"Is she a member of the Artists Union?"

"No. But who wants to be member? I tell you, I, Hugo, make more here selling pictures on Arbat Street than 'official' artist makes. Let them have their union. Thank God for *perestroika*, I say. But all right, this woman needs this money. Three hundred rubles. Or maybe you have Marlboros? You pay me in Marlboros."

"How many Marlboros?"

He paused to calculate. "Ten cartons."

Three hundred rubles was 480 dollars at the official exchange rate. That was forty-eight dollars a carton. Martin could buy them at the commissary for ten dollars a carton, or from the Soviet hard-currency stores, the *Beriozka*, for just over twenty dollars a carton. And if he paid in cigarettes, was that any different from just handing over dollars? But the Embassy rule was, no paying Soviet citizens in real money (rubles not being real money), and no trading for merchandise. Anything could be an economic crime, and violations of the law got you sent home *persona non grata*. "Sorry. I can't do it. Anyway, all I have on me is fifty rubles."

Hugo looked at the painting and then at Martin. He could see a sale vanishing once Martin and his fifty rubles got far enough up the street to think it over. "Okay. Fifty rubles."

Martin had the feeling that he could have bought it a lot cheaper. But he took out his wallet and pulled out the ten blue five-ruble notes, which was, in fact, all the Soviet money he was carrying. Hugo started to wrap the picture in the front page of yesterday's *Izvestia*. "What's the artist's name?" Martin asked.

"Alina Obraz." He stopped wrapping. "You want this painting signed for you? I will sign her name. In Russian. Same as if she did."

"No thanks. Maybe she'll do it for me, if I go see her play."

That seemed to amuse him. "She signs pictures not." He tied the wrapped parcel in heavy brown twine—twine which Martin knew from experience was weak in spite of its thickness—and handed it over.

"Why not?"

He shrugged. "She says, 'Artists must be . . .' How it is said? Unknown. *Anonimnaya.*"

"Anonymous?"

"Ha! Anonymous. She says, 'Artists must be anonym. What is important is the work."

Hugo's offer to sign the painting had almost made Martin decide to back out of the sale. It made him doubt the whole story. Still, he had no doubt this picture was by the same hand as the one Hutchins had, and that one wasn't signed either. On the way back to the Embassy he stopped at a ticket kiosk and inquired about tickets for the Southwest Studio Theater. "An amateur group," the old woman in the kiosk sniffed. "I've heard of them. We don't sell their tickets. Their friends go, their neighbors . . . You have to know someone to get those."

One thing about being a special assistant cultural attaché: it gave one a perfect excuse to attend an amateur performance in southwest Moscow. It also gave one a lot of close personal acquaintances in the theater world. From his office, Martin telephoned Yuri Kulagin, who occasionally reviewed plays for the *Literary Gazette*.

"Yuri, this is Ben Martin. I was thinking about you. You remember we were discussing Bulgakov when you visited Spaso House for the film evening a few weeks ago? Well, our conversation moved me to reread some of his work, and one of the things I've been reading is his story "Molière's Young Wife." You know it well, I'm sure? Of course. Well, Yuri, someone chanced to mention to me that a Moscow theater group is performing a play which I'm sure must be based on Bulgakov's story. I'd very much like to see it; but you know better than anyone how it is trying to get tickets to Moscow theater. . . . Could you? That would be exceptionally kind of you. I'd hope you could come along, of course; and bring Olya. Oh? That's too bad; but of course you can't miss the reception for the Deputies. I certainly understand. Well, just one ticket then. I'm sure it will simplify your life, not to have to find a pair; and my social life is abysmally dull these days, unfortunately. Yes, many thanks."

· 29 ·

Saturday, May 27, 1989
7 P.M.
Southwest Moscow

MARTIN WALKED TO THE THEATER FROM THE SOUTHWEST METRO STATION. Behind the station was a foreigners' apartment complex—two buildings and a parking lot surrounded by a high guarded fence to protect the citizens outside from contamination. Far to the northeast, up Vernadsky Prospect, he could just see the tower of Moscow State University gleaming in momentary evening sunshine. None of the buildings close by looked likely to contain a theater, and it was only after asking twice that he found it in the basement of a nine-story concrete-block apartment building of the 1970s, a dirty-white prism overlooking an open field that progress had not yet deleted. At the edge of the field, half a kilometer up Vernadsky Prospect, a church closed for decades was half covered with a growth of scaffolding. On the unrestored half, cupolas dribbled rust stains down walls that had been white before the Revolution. But behind the scaffold, new paint gleamed salmon and white and green, and on one dome new gold glistened. Martin thought it a microcosm of the Union, struggling out of the rust and disuse of seventy years.

A new sign marked the theater entrance on the outside of the apartment building, and inside he found a box office at one side of a narrow hall. The woman in it smiled as she took his ticket and pointed to a door at the far end of the hall. He went through and stepped into blackness. There were no windows, and all the surfaces were painted black. It took a moment for his eyes to adjust to the dim lighting. Eight rows of fifteen or so chairs covered in red plastic fabric stepped up from a bare unpainted wooden stage that filled half the room. From the stage sprouted a forest of pillars—the supports for the nine stories of apartments above.

Faces turned toward him: he was late and had to step over people's legs to get to his seat, which was in the center of the front row.

159

Embarrassed, he stepped over feet and spring jackets along the edge of the stage, which was raised only inches off the floor. No sooner had he taken his seat than the house lights went out. They stayed out a long time; his eyes adjusted further to the dark. Silence rang in the darkness.

Light blazed forth.

There was a roar of music—he could not name it—which shook the tiny room, filled it as if with a physical presence.

And in the light, in the music, there was a woman.

She was so close he could have touched her.

She was dressed in nineteenth-century style. She had blond shoulder-length hair and dark eyes. Her face was a long face of the classic Russian model, with a long but finely-shaped nose and full lips.

She was beautiful.

And she was the woman in the paintings.

The play—he knew the story from Bulgakov. The young Molière, an actor, weds a young actress, who leaves her troupe to follow him. Late in life he replaces her, in art and in life, with another young woman. The first wife's part is a tragic one. The Russian appetite for romantic suffering could feed deeply from it. The woman's portrayal satisfied: when the stage went dark (there was no curtain), the audience called her back and back with the rhythmic clapping that was the highest mark of its approval.

Martin made a pretext of conversation with two other playgoers who lingered in the hall as the audience thinned and departed. They were man and wife—or, more accurately, woman and husband, as she responded first to his comment on the play and then carried the conversation without any help from him. They were pleased at the chance to talk with a foreigner: Aren't we, dear? We were surprised to see you come in. I don't think we've ever seen a foreigner here before, not even one of those who live up behind the Metro.

He was pleased to have the chance to see so unusual a play. He had read the story, of course, but he could not imagine it on stage. It had been beautifully done. Alina, who played Molière's wife, was especially fine. Did they know her, he wondered?

Of course. Ah, she comes here now.

The actors' dressing room and stage entrance was up the same narrow hall past the box office.

"Alina, this is *Gospodin* Martin. He's an American! He loved your acting—as did we all."

160

Onstage she had been striking, but, even when close enough to touch, distant: distanced by antique dress, by the force of words, by the sheer power of imagination. She had been fenced off by the spotlight's edge. But in life also she was beautiful. And he saw that the paintings told the truth: in her eyes was the same mystery, something compelling but undefined.

"*Ochen priyatno*," she said in thanks to the woman who introduced them. To him she said nothing, but she looked steadily at him, as if trying to see something hidden.

> *Look not in my eyes, for fear*
> *They mirror true the sight I see,*
> *And there you find your face too clear*
> *And love it and be lost like me.*

"Alya, are you ready?" the woman asked. "We're walking to the Metro."

"Yes, let's go."

"Mister Martin, are you taking the Metro?"

"What? Oh, yes. I am."

"Walk with us, then. It's so wonderful to find a foreigner who knows Russian literature."

Ten-thirty in the evening was still broad daylight in Moscow in late May, the middle of an evening that would linger almost until the early dawn. The street was still full of people walking: with a Moscow winter so shortly behind them, they could not get enough of daylight, and only exhaustion would drive them to bed.

As their little group walked southwest toward the Metro station, the woman occupied Martin with talk, and Alina Obraz said nothing at all, except short answers to the few comments the woman's husband addressed to her.

At the station, she fumbled in her purse for change and found nothing. Martin handed her a five-kopeck piece. She thanked him, pleasantly but without smiling. He followed the three of them through the turnstile and toward the stairs. The rumble of a train came up toward them. Although there was no hurry, they hurried, the thoughtless hurry of those who go because the train is there, not because they need to catch it: there would be another in four minutes. With the woman in the lead dragging her husband by the arm they clattered down the stairs, pushed back the closing doors of the nearest car, and struggled inside.

When they sat down, they were all laughing. "We have our exercise for today!" the woman announced. She sat next to Martin, with Alina on the other side of her husband, beyond both of them. It was impossible for him to talk to Alina over the racket of the subway.

The car was almost empty; but at the next stop a crowd thronged aboard, and all the seats filled. At the end of the crowd was a small old woman carrying thirty or more rolls of toilet paper strung together on two loops of cord, like strings of beads. She carried one loop over each shoulder and walked on her toes to keep the paper from dragging on the floor. "Look there," the woman said in a low voice to her husband, "I wonder where she found that toilet paper? Do you think there's any left? We could get off at the next stop and come back to buy some. No, but the shops will be all closed. She must have been visiting someone afterward."

The woman pushed past Martin but did not find a seat. He said to her, "Do you want to sit down?" She thanked him with a look of relief and took the seat he left for her. Martin stood to one side of her, then shifted closer to Alina. He said to her, "I'm also kind to dogs and children."

"Is that a custom of Americans?"

"Of the better ones."

"Is there anyone you're not kind to?"

"Well . . . policemen . . ."

"Why not to policemen?"

"They don't need kindness. They don't need help."

"I've seen plenty of them who need help."

"Oh? What sort of help?"

"Psychiatric help."

"You sound as if you've had more than enough experience with the police."

"It doesn't take experience. All you have to do is look around. Go to the railroad station and look at the policemen waking up people who have to wait all night for a train because there should be 'no sleeping in the station.' Anyone who does that needs psychiatric help."

The woman said, "It was said on our television recently that in America people are frequently murdered on your metro system. Is that true?"

"Only in New York. And not always then."

"Are you being ironic?" the woman asked.

"I have heard on our television that Americans are always being ironic," Alina said. "Even when they don't need to be. While here, Russians are always being ironic because they must be to survive."

"You sound as if you've had more than enough experience with Americans," Martin said.

"No. Very little. Although in strict logic, that could also be more than enough." She smiled at him, this time a truly dazzling smile, a smile to last a lifetime. He wondered whether she was also laughing at him.

"Was there anything you liked especially about the play?" she asked before he had time to come to an opinion.

"I liked it all. I guess I liked most the spareness of it—the way the staging forces the audience to use their imagination."

She did laugh now. "A bare stage is all we have; but one tries to make a virtue of poverty," she said. "Valery will be pleased to hear that someone thinks he succeeded."

"Valery is the director," the woman said. "He is a genius."

"Yes, he's a genius," Alina agreed. "Although it's tiresome to hear it too often."

"Not for Valery," the husband said. It was the first thing he had said all evening.

His wife frowned at him. "Here's our stop," she said. "We have to change to the Circle Line at Park Kultury. What about you, Mr. Martin? You must be going to Krasnopresnenskaya. It's closest to the American Embassy. Don't you change to the Circle Line?"

It did not appear that Alina was going to change. "No," he said, "I'll go on and change at Dzerzhinsky Square."

"Ah. Yes, you could do that. Well, then; good night." She dragged her husband from the train. He gave Martin a parting wave, hidden from his wife, and a sly grin.

Alina motioned Martin to the seat beside her. "They're an interesting couple," he said as he sat down.

"Is this frivolous American irony? Or serious socialist irony?"

"Beneath this laughing exterior, I'm a serious man. Is your stop on this line?"

"I change at Prospect Marxa."

Only three more stops, and one less than his own station. "And then?"

"I live near Kolomenskaya. I'll take the Green Line. And then a little tram ride. And then a little walk. But travel is an adventure."

"Especially walking in that area at night, as I understand from the newspapers. Would you permit me to share your adventure and walk you home?"

She looked at him for a moment. "Please don't trouble yourself. It's far out of your way."

"But what better way to spend my time? Anyway, I can add to my collection of Metro stations. I've never been in Kolomenskaya Station."

"Really, I'd prefer to go alone. I hope I don't seem rude; but I'm always exhausted, emotionally exhausted, after a performance. I'm afraid I wouldn't be sparkling company."

They rode in silence halfway to the next stop, Kropotkinskaya, located in the district of old town mansions—some still vacant ever since the Revolution—that Herzen had called the St. Germain-des-Prés of Moscow.

He could not think of a way to restart conversation as she rode vacant-eyed; but at length, seeming to rouse herself, she came to his rescue. "How did you find your way to our theater?" she asked him. "I've never seen a foreigner there."

"I heard of it from Hugo."

"And where did you meet Hugo?"

"On the Arbat. I bought a painting from him. I thought perhaps I'd see him at the play tonight."

"Why did you think that?"

"He said he was your boyfriend."

She frowned. "He's not. He's a friend. He won't be even that if he can't learn to stop talking about me. Hugo claims much more than he owns."

"Well, I'm glad he told me about the play. It was brilliant."

"Bulgakov's a great writer. Give ninety percent of the credit to him."

"There are plenty of great writers whose work has never made a worthwhile play."

"Well, give ten percent of the credit to Valery. He'd take more, if you let him. But he could make a 'worthwhile play' out of anything."

"I take it that he is a genius, then."

"Oh, yes. And the first to proclaim it, too."

Martin deduced that there was, or had been, more to the story of Valery and Alina.

"But how did you get a ticket to the play?" she continued. "We are not the most famous company in the world, perhaps, but Valery's work is well known in Moscow, and the theater is as small as you

164

saw it; ordinarily all seats are sold months ahead. You must have *blat*."

"I have dollars."

"But still, you have to know how to find our tickets. Did Hugo sell you one? No, he couldn't have. He doesn't know anyone but me well enough to get it. How *did* you get it?"

He was about to tell her when she went on, "Yekaterina Mikhailovna mentioned the American Embassy, I believe. Do you work there? I suppose they have means to get a ticket?"

"Yes, I work there."

"And what is your work?"

"I am a 'special assistant cultural attaché.' Which means I read Russian books and talk to Russian artists. And for this they actually pay me. And also, I meet people who have *blat* for theater tickets."

"How long have you lived in Moscow?"

"Nearly two years, in fact. I'm nearing the end of my term."

"And what happens at the end of your term?"

"I disappear like Cinderella."

"How is that?"

"*Cinderella* is an English fairy tale. A girl is given a magic dress and servants and other things by her fairy godmother, to try to catch a prince; but at midnight they all turn back to the original poor stuff."

"It's rather like me in the play, then. While it's going on, I'm magic; but afterward, I turn back into just myself."

He laughed. "But in your case, the magic lingers, because what remains is best of all. In Cinderella's case too, I suppose: the prince came looking for her."

"You have a honeyed tongue. Is this common among Americans?"

"I don't know. Have the other Americans you've known had honeyed tongues?"

"I've not known any Americans," she said.

"None at all?"

"I think not."

"Then I hope you're not disappointed in your first example." She did not respond to this.

"The painting I bought from Hugo," Martin said; "he told me you painted it."

"He also told you he was my boyfriend. You can't believe everything Hugo says."

"It was certainly a portrait of you, although an unusual one. Hugo said it was an auto-portrait."

165

"And do you like it?"

"It shows great talent."

She smiled.

"I had a friend who also had one of your paintings," Martin said. "He was an American."

"I wonder how he acquired it? Perhaps from Hugo as well."

"His name was Charles Hutchins. You didn't know him, did you?"

"I believe I said I have not known any Americans?"

"Did you?"

"But once a painting is gone, it has a life of its own. It travels where it wishes; who knows where? It's why I don't like selling my paintings. Do I want strangers seeing my heart?"

"Why do you sell them, then?"

"Everyone has to live. I can't live on what my job pays."

"Where do you work?"

"At Gorky Park. I make publicity posters for special events."

"An ad writer for the circus! I thought I'd never meet one."

"Yes, the circus, and other things. There are many events at the park."

They had come through the second station and were rapidly approaching her change. "Could I telephone you?" he asked, desperate not to lose contact.

She seemed to ponder this. "All right."

"Tell me your number."

"Do you have something to write on?" He found a business card in his wallet and handed it to her with his pen. Before writing her number she studied the card. "Do you have another I could keep?"

"Of course." He handed her a second card. She wrote a telephone number on the first and handed it to him as the train came into a station. "Here's my stop." They were at Marx Prospect, the center of Moscow.

As she rose to move to the door, he stood up beside her. "I hate to see you walk home alone."

She smiled. "It's quite safe. This is Moscow, not New York. What could happen to anyone in this city?"

She was swept off the train with the crowd. He watched out the window as she walked away along the platform, but she did not look back. Then the doors closed and the train started to move, and when he turned around someone had taken his seat.

· 30 ·

Sunday, May 28, 1989
11 P.M.
The United States Embassy

MARTIN DIDN'T KNOW IF SHE WOULD SLEEP LATE THE MORNING AFTER A performance. He didn't want to seem too impetuous—it would only make her more suspicious, he told himself, and certainly she was suspicious enough already—but after eleven o'clock he couldn't wait any longer. Tucking the card with her telephone number into his wallet, he left the Embassy by the side gate on the south and walked out onto Konyushkovskaya Street. He walked slowly north with the sun warm on his back. He turned to the east at the Stalinist-gothic apartment building north of the Embassy to give himself a chance to look behind for a tail, and walked around the building through empty Kudrin Square and back west up Barricade Street toward the Moscow Zoo.

Outside the zoo he bought a cup of ice cream at a kiosk and ate it reflectively while watching the way he had come. If there were any KGB in the area, he decided, they must have children with them. Crumpling the ice cream cup into a small ball, he tossed it into a trash can and walked a little way up the street to a vacant pay phone. He put a two-kopeck piece into the phone and dialed Alina's number, which he had memorized.

After two rings, a woman's voice answered: "This is not an assigned number."

"*Allio*," he said, but the voice simply repeated itself: "This is not an assigned number." It was a recording.

He hung up, got his two kopecks back, and tried again, with the same result.

He knew enough of the ways of the Moscow telephone system to be patient. He walked up the street a hundred meters to another phone and tried again. There was a busy signal. His hopes raised, he tried again and then again for five minutes. Then a solidly built man

167

walked by, and although he kept going, Martin dared not try any longer at that spot. He walked to the Metro Station Street of the Year 1905 (named for the failed revolution of that year) and boarded a train toward the city center. He did not think he was followed. He rode two stops and got off at Pushkin Square, on busy Gorky Street not far from Marx Prospect.

The square behind Pushkin's statue was filled with knots of people, at the center of each knot an argument: what had been said at the Congress, what should have been said, what was to be done. Although he felt that it was his duty as assistant cultural attaché to stop and listen at every one of these, instead he worked his way through the square, past the militiamen watching in uncertain fascination the sight of Soviet citizens expressing genuine political opinions. Outside the Rossiya Cinema he found a telephone and tried the number again. "This is not an assigned number."

He swore in Russian.

Walking away, he took out the card and checked the number, and found he had remembered it correctly.

Somewhere up Pushkin Street he found another telephone on the wall of a building. This one ate his first two-kopeck piece but accepted the second. It agreed that the number was not assigned.

Three out of four seemed to be reasonable agreement, for Moscow telephones. The number was in her own handwriting. She had given him a wrong number.

He cursed himself. He had lost her.

No, there was still the theater: surely he could find her again through the theater.

But suppose she took fright and didn't go back there? They might know where she lived; but suppose she left her apartment. If she knew people were still looking for her, she would have enough incentive to desert an apartment.

Or suppose . . . Well, was she KGB herself?

She didn't know any Americans, she said: but Hutchins had a painting of her, a self-portrait that she had sold to an American. And the description of the woman who had been with Hutch when he was killed was her description; Martin was sure of that.

But if she was KGB, wouldn't she have led him on to her apartment?

Maybe not. She hadn't known he was coming. Maybe she was surprised and had put him off until she could get further orders.

But then wouldn't she have given him a working telephone number?

Maybe she had just made a mistake.

About her own telephone number?

Maybe it was a special number, not her own, and she had just made a mistake.

Maybe the Moscow telephone system was as screwed up as usual.

He tried another phone, got a busy signal, then got the recording again. "This is not an assigned number."

Cursing himself in several languages, he walked on to Sverdlov Square, from where he took the Metro back to the zoo and then walked slowly back to the Embassy.

At least he was sure no one was following him.

· 31 ·

Wednesday, May 31, 1989
9 A.M.
The United States Embassy

MARTIN HAD ALWAYS SUBSCRIBED TO THE THEORY OF THE HEALING POWERS of art: it would be a poor special assistant cultural attaché who did not, he supposed. At the moment, however, he was not finding any solace in literature. But he concluded that perhaps what he needed was not precisely healing, but distraction, so that the theory remained unblemished—although, to tell the truth, he was not finding any distraction, either, in the book he was reading. The ringing of his office telephone relieved him of the necessity to decide whether that meant that the book wasn't art.

"*Gospodin* Martin?" It was a woman's voice, speaking Russian. It was muffled, as though speaking through a cloth. He immediately thought of Alina; but he couldn't be sure it was she.

"Yes, this is Martin."

"Add twenty and fifty to the number you have."

"What?"

"Twenty and fifty. Add them to the number you have."

169

The phone clicked, and then there was the hum of an open line.

"Wait!" Martin called. "I didn't understand!" But he knew he was talking to no one. He put the phone back slowly on its cradle.

Twenty and fifty. Add them to the number you have. What was that about? The number of what? Well, maybe not the number of anything. If it was Alina, she meant the telephone number she had given him, obviously. Obviously? Well, hopefully.

He took from his wallet the card with the telephone number written on it. He studied it. The number was 5924743, written without any breaks. Twenty and fifty: that was seventy. Add seventy? But she hadn't said that. She'd said to add twenty and fifty. Add them where? Telephone numbers were customarily divided into two parts: 592-4743. Maybe she had meant he should add twenty to the first cluster and fifty to the second. Hence, 612-4793. Well, it was worth a try. But not from his office. There was certain to be a tap on any outside calls. Of course! That was why she hadn't just told him a number— the KGB knew where every number was located. But why had she given him a wrong number in the first place? Maybe because she didn't trust him not to call back from a telephone that might be tapped?

He signed himself out of the Embassy and exited at the front gate, onto Tchaikovsky Street. He walked north quickly. He had to decide where to go. He wanted to call soon, in case she was at that number and might tire of waiting. She couldn't have expected him to call back immediately, if she had gone to so much trouble to give him a number without speaking it over the telephone; but she might think the Embassy had a secure line. Some of the Embassy staff thought so, too—the Embassy wasn't the Soviet Union: it was America. But America ended at its gates; and Hutchins had always emphasized that one had to assume that all wires connected to the Soviet Union were tapped.

He considered turning left toward the zoo and taking the Metro somewhere again; but he didn't want to repeat his steps from yesterday even though he was confident he hadn't been followed. Across Tchaikovsky Street in the opposite direction, the streets were a nest of foreign embassies. There was too much chance that someone he knew would see him using a public phone there. Finally he decided to walk on up the Sadovye Ring, the second ring road—of which Tchaikovsky Street was one segment—encircling inner Moscow, with the Kremlin at the center. Once, the Sadovye Ring had been the outskirts of Moscow. Hence its name, the "Garden Ring." Now it carried four lanes of heavy traffic in each direction. Along this street he walked.

He stopped once at a food-shop window to check for tails. He had not walked in this direction from the Embassy in months, but the window display was still the way he remembered it. Possibly it had not changed since Stalin's time. The window, three meters long, was unoccupied except for a stack of fifteen cans of squalid tomatoes, looking unappetizing enough on the label as pink blobs on a faded-chartreuse background, but from experience he knew they were probably worse in life. Perhaps the best that could be said for them was that they weren't for sale. (He had never seen anything in a Soviet window that was actually for sale.) Behind the window display, the shelves were even more bare than the window itself.

He pondered the tomatoes long enough to check for foot traffic behind him. Surprisingly for Moscow, there was little of it, and no one going steadily his way. He went on. At Great Bronnaya Street he crossed to the inner side of the ring and went up that street one block to the Aquarium Gardens with their green pond shimmering under the sun. At the near end of the pond, several pairs of old men were playing chess in the shade of the lime trees, on concrete tables inlaid with cut-stone chessboards. The pond had once been called Patriarchs' Pond, and at the far end was the very bench where in Bulgakov's novel *The Master and Margarita* the devil had appeared in Moscow. The bench was occupied by an old woman with a poodle. She had a sack of bread crumbs which she was throwing to a flock of pigeons. As Martin approached her, an elderly man came along from the opposite direction, leaning heavily on a cane. He stopped to observe the woman's work for a moment, then swung his cane at the scattering pigeons. "Why are you feeding those *parasites*?" he demanded, tagging the pigeons with one of the worst epithets of Party propaganda. "Food is for those who work!"

Stopping to observe this interlude gave Martin a chance to satisfy himself that no one had followed him. He quickly crossed the street— probably crossing the very trolley rails upon which poor Berlioz, after his unpleasant chat with the devil, had slipped and been beheaded by a streetcar—and went to a pay phone on the outside of one of the rank of apartment buildings that lined that side of the street.

He dialed 612-4793. It rang. It rang again and then again; but no one answered.

So now what, smart guy? he asked himself. Had he taken too long to respond? Had the KGB closed in on her while he walked up Sado-vye in the sunshine? (A stupid thought, he knew, but he was annoyed enough to aim stupid thoughts at himself.) He took out the number from his wallet and looked at it again, as if it might have changed in his pocket. 5924743. Add twenty and fifty to it. Was there another way to do it? What if he added twenty and fifty to the end?

Of course! There was another way! She had written the numbers all together, undivided. He had divided them himself. But he had done it the American way, in two groups: 592-4743. A Russian would normally use three groups: 592-47-43. Add twenty and fifty to that, and you got 592-67-93.

He plugged his two-kopeck piece back into the phone and dialed again.

The phone rang. It rang again. And again. Shit.

"*Allio.*" He knew it was she even before he asked.

"Is this Alina?"

A pause. "I'm listening."

"This is your friend." He supposed Bierman would have some fancier way to make contact, but this was the best he could do out of his own head. *Tradecraft,* Le Carré liked to call it. Did real agents ever call it that? Did they ever practice it? And if they did, what was it?

She seemed satisfied enough with his effort. She said, "You were slow to call."

"I'm sorry. I had to go out to do it."

"Of course. You must have gone far."

"Please excuse me. I tried very hard to call you yesterday, but the number was incorrect, it seems."

"I will explain it to you. Perhaps you would still like to add the place you mentioned to your collection? You remember?"

"Yes."

"I could meet you there this evening."

"Not now?"

"This evening. At the same hour we parted last time, if that's convenient."

"Yes. I'll be there."

"Goodbye, then."

He hung up the telephone and felt his heart beating fast.

· 32 ·

Wednesday, May 31, 1989
11 P.M.
Kolomenskaya

THE SUBWAY TRAIN EMERGED INTO THE REMNANT OF EVENING ON A FLAT, ugly industrial plain where empty trucks and busses were strewn like litter across unpaved vacant lots. After several minutes, the train climbed onto a bridge over the Moscow River. A tug pushing a coal barge was forging slowly upstream beneath the bridge. At its mast a red flag with the gold hammer and sickle flapped slowly, without energy. At that moment, across the river to the east, the last sunlight touched the array of new apartment towers that had gone up there, and at this distance they might have been the white city that socialism always claimed to be but, up close, never was.

It was an instant of light; then the train plunged back into the earth. A recorded woman's voice announced arrival at Kolomenskaya Station.

He did not know where to find her. He waited a moment on the platform for the crowd to thin, and then he saw her step out from behind a column at the far end of the station. Without coming to him, she went to the middle of the station platform where passengers from both directions mixed. He followed and saw her step onto the up escalator. When he reached the top of the escalator she was taking coins from a machine that changed twenty-kopeck pieces. As he approached she turned to meet him. "You're prompt," she said.

"I try to meet my obligations."

Outside the station the sky was the pale white of late spring evening at far northern latitudes. The sun had gone, and a shadowless light lay everywhere, over the broad street and the few trees and the square monotony of apartment buildings so ugly you knew they had no mothers—no one with a gram of compassion could design buildings so ugly to house his fellow humans.

173

Immediately behind the Metro station a hundred-meter-long billboard proclaimed in red letters, SLAVA KPSS. Glory to the Communist Party of the Soviet Union. The people might elect non-Party members to represent them at the Congress of People's Deputies; but the Party, or its propaganda apparatus, was on autopilot, and kept to its own course, not noticing.

"Do you live near here?" he asked.

"Not very near. Let's walk to the river. The evening is lovely, and the river is only a half hour from here."

They walked up Proletarskii Prospekt—Proletarian Avenue—with a silver evening around them. Beyond the billboard they turned into Nagatinskaya Street, which was more proletarian still. The sidewalks ended. Men in soiled gray jackets and cloth caps gathered on the dirt footpaths beside the road, watching the trams and the few taxis but not as if expecting anyone. Women with heavy legs carried home their shopping. Young lovers walked hand in hand.

There were trees here. This area had once been a forest outside Moscow, and when the apartments had gone up, the trees between them had been left, although not as parks but as waste areas, unkempt and cluttered with undergrowth. The apartments here were Improved Planning buildings of the late sixties, more spacious than the *Khrushchovki* of the early sixties, though no less ugly—four- and five-story buildings with buff tile exterior walls over a core of brick that was little more than rubble. Martin had seen plenty of them going up when he lived in Moscow as a student one summer in Khrushchev's era: bricks of a dozen different sizes thrown together as they became available, with gaps you could see through in the mortar work. Then they were covered with tile, and looked all right for a while; but you still knew what was under there. It was like Soviet society. The surface could be made to look acceptable, if a little rough and homemade, if you didn't look too close. There were even plenty of people, foreigners, who found that attractive. Or who saw the white city that was in their minds.

In the slowly fading evening light, four young men leaned against the front of a produce shop on the left of the road. They were passing around a bottle of *Sontse Dar*—"Gift of the Sun," a concoction distilled from spoiled fruits and sugar, the cheapest drunk the Union had to offer its citizens.

Alina took Martin's arm.

As they approached, one of the men handed the bottle to a comrade and came out to them.

A *setup!* Martin thought. Just like that, a setup. The guy was big: a real seven-by-eight, as the dissidents called the KGB thugs. "You sure know how to show a guy a good time on the first date," he said to Alina.

"Don't talk," she said through closed lips. "You don't sound like a Russian."

The man wore blue greasy coveralls and a blue greasy mechanic's cloth cap. "You got a light?" he said to Martin. He did not have a cigarette in his hand.

"Sorry. I don't smoke."

"You a foreigner? You got any Marlboros?"

"I don't smoke." Martin kept walking, half-propelled by Alina, who was looking straight ahead. The man followed.

"Hey, you a foreigner? What're you doing in this neighborhood? The militia don't like foreigners around here, bothering citizens."

Martin didn't answer and didn't look back, but he felt that the others were following too.

"Hey, I'm talking to you, foreigner! And you, slut, what're you doing with a foreigner?"

Martin tried to stop, but Alina had a firm grip on his arm. "Keep walking," she said in a low voice, looking straight ahead.

Martin felt a hard shove in the middle of his back. He stumbled forward, regained his balance, separated from Alina. He stopped and turned around.

The man stood facing him, feet apart and nostrils flaring, his head thrust forward and his fists clenched at his sides, a pose he might have seen on a propaganda poster—valiant youth defending the Motherland. His friends were there but several feet behind him.

Alina caught Martin's arm: "Come on!" she said.

Martin shook her off. It wasn't bravery, exactly: he didn't want to turn his back on these four again. Better to make a stand at the beginning, he judged.

"Better take him away, slut!" the man snarled.

"Fuck your mother!" Alina snapped.

The man stepped back as if he had been slapped. Then he stepped forward again. "So that's the kind you are!"

"Better than being a *gadina* like you!"

As the name she called him sank in, the man leaped forward. He was going for her, and not for Martin; but as he came, Martin hit him hard in the face. He sank to his knees, grasped Martin around the waist and tried to pitch him to the ground. Martin tried to push him away, couldn't, then got the heel of one hand under his chin and pried his head back until he had to let go. Martin shoved him sprawling onto his back.

The other three came for Martin then.

"Run!" Alina cried.

It didn't seem dignified to run. Martin stepped forward and hit the middle one in the face. He felt the crunch of breaking bone. The man dropped. The other two converged on Martin and knocked him to the ground, but there was no method to their attack. They all lay struggling on the dirt path in unscientific squalor. It was then that Martin realized, startled, that they were all four so drunk that without him or one another to lean on they were barely on their feet. This was more a pawing match than a fight. The first one was still lying on his back panting, and the other one he had hit was sobbing face down. Martin stood up and kicked the other two loose from his legs. Alina nearly pulled him over trying to get him free of them. "Come on, let's go!"

They ran half a block and then looked back. The quartet were still lying on one another. Alina pulled Martin to keep him moving. The adrenaline drained from him, leaving him shaky inside.

"You're a mess," she said. Looking down, he saw that it was true: his coat and shirt were smeared with blood, no doubt from the nose of the first one, and he was covered with the greasy dirt of the footpath. And his right hand hurt. He saw that it was beginning to swell, and this knowledge made it hurt more. "I think I broke something," he said, holding up his hand and flexing the fingers. A bolt of pain shot through the middle of the hand.

"You'll have to clean up. Come to my apartment."

"Some people will do anything for an invitation."

"I'm sorry. I don't understand."

"I'm sorry you don't too."

Her apartment was on the fourth floor of a building up Yakornaya Street, which ran off Nagatinskaya behind a closed sporting goods store and a small bread store. The building stood on a lane whose gutterless crumbling asphalt pavement paralleled the river, and short stretches of water could be glimpsed between the identical apartment buildings on the other side of the lane. The lane was lined with poplars, whose cotton would turn May afternoons into a snowstorm but now in the still evening lay in tenuous drifts like a remnant of winter across the bare dirt and the asphalt.

In the building entryway the concrete walls and stairs bore traces of the paint applied at their conception, apparently not renewed since. Decades of stains patterned the walls. Martin and Alina climbed slowly in darkness: there had been a light bulb on each floor, but two of the first three were out, and so was the one on her landing. In the dark she fumbled for a key. He pushed the door open for her. The door was soft—covered in padded vinyl, he saw, when she turned on the light in her entrance hall.

"Hang your coat there, and your tie." On the wall of her entry hall hung a rack with a dozen wooden pegs. Most of them already held coats of various kinds, but she moved one over to clear a peg for him. "You can wear these slippers." They were men's slippers, knitted wool, not much too big for him.

He had never got used to the Russian custom of changing from shoes to slippers at the door. "You seem to be ready for visitors of all sizes."

"Those were my husband's. They're still here."

"I take it your husband is gone?"

"Yes. We're separated."

"Oh." He tried not to put too much into the "oh"; he felt far more than he thought such a small word could carry.

She looked at him critically. "I don't think I can clean you up. There's too much."

"Next time I'll try to fight cleaner."

She laughed. "I can give you a raincoat to wear home."

"Great. I wear a raincoat on the only warm evening of the year. I'll look like the Moscow Flasher."

"What is flasher?"

He made a motion with his arms as if opening and closing a raincoat.

She smiled. "You'd better soak your hand. It's swelling. Come in the kitchen and do that. I'll wash the blood out of your shirt, and then I'll get you some tea. Take your shirt off."

"It's not necessary."

"It's very hard to wash with you in it."

"I mean it's not necessary for you to wash it."

"You don't want to draw attention on the Metro."

"If I have a coat over it, no one will notice."

"Are you ashamed to take off your shirt?"

He took it off and handed it to her. She padded up the hall and through a side door. He heard water running. She called to him: "Now your hand. Come in here, please."

Following her, he passed a door to a room on the other side of the hall, apparently her bedroom. There was a double bed and two chairs and canvases stacked everywhere. They were all painted, but he could not make out the pictures in the last evening light.

The kitchen was tiny, big enough for a sink, a stove, a small table and two mismatched chairs, and no more. There was no refrigerator. The walls were covered with tiny pictures, mostly oils but some enameled metal. "Those are nice," he said. He wanted to say something friendly to her. "Are they yours?"

"They're my student pictures." She ran water into a large, gray enameled pot and put it on the table. "Sit down. You can put your hand in this. The cold water will reduce the swelling." She ran more water into a battered aluminum kettle and lit the stove with a kitchen match. "You did yourself more damage than you did them," she said, looking at his hand.

He didn't think that was a fair comment, nor even accurate. "I think I broke one's nose," he said.

"And his nose broke your hand. Which is better? Is it more useful to have a working nose or a working hand?" But she touched his hand gently as she said this. She had a nice touch.

Well, so they weren't KGB goons, he thought. And, more to the point, she wasn't either.

She said to him, "Well, you're certainly no KGB man."

"What?"

"I was afraid you might be KGB. But you're no professional fighter."

"You sure know how to make a guy feel good, Alina. Why exactly would you think *I* was a KGB man?"

She looked steadily at him. "Because you came looking for me. Because you asked about Charles Hutchins."

"And you said you haven't met him. Or any other Americans."

"I lied." He could see that she was watching his reaction to this.

He tried not to have one. "Why would you lie?"

"Because I thought you were KGB. That's why I gave you the wrong number. I needed time to check on you. I'm sorry. I was so happy when there was such a person as Benjamin F. Martin at your Embassy; and also when it was you."

"I guess you're not KGB either."

She didn't laugh. "Why exactly would you think I was?"

"The last time Hutchins was seen, he was with a blond Russian woman of rare beauty"—he studied her eyes as he said this—"and he was stabbed to death in her presence."

She didn't flinch at the words. "I know. I was there."

"Do you know why he was killed?"

"No. I don't know."

"Do you know who he was?"

"He was an American. He worked at your Embassy." She was still looking into his eyes. "He was an agent of your Central Intelligence Agency."

"Why do you think that?"

"He told me."

Would Hutchins really have told her, against—Martin could only suppose it would be against—all his instructions and all his training?

"Did you believe him?"

"Yes."

"Did he show you any evidence?"

"What identification do agents of the Central Intelligence Agency carry in the Soviet Union, Mr. Martin? A spy card? A letter from your President? No, he didn't show me any evidence. Do you want to show me yours?"

"Didn't he have some identification of who he was? How did you know he was even with the Embassy?"

Her laugh had an edge of scorn that he didn't enjoy. "Even the KGB can't fake an American! I knew he was that. And he showed me his diplomatic identification. He left it here, that night. It doesn't say 'CIA.'" She opened a drawer and searched through it. "Here." She handed Martin a black leather passport wallet. When he opened it, Hutch's picture looked out at him.

"Why did he leave it here?"

"He said he didn't want to have it on him. But perhaps he wanted an excuse to come back here, after the meeting." She looked Martin in the eye as she said this—as if challenging him to deny he had thought it. "Maybe he thought he could get me into bed, with the romance of his business."

"Did he?"

"That's an impertinent question." She withdrew her eyes from his, and he was sorry he had asked, the more so because she hadn't answered. She went to a cupboard above the stove and got out cups and saucers, a teapot, and a gray cardboard box of tea. She spooned tea leaves into the pot and poured boiling water over them. "I don't have sugar," she said. "I traded my ration for the tea. But I have some jam." She set out a separate small saucer of jam with two tiny spoons in it. She sat down across from him and poured tea into the cups, adding water from the kettle. She raised her cup. "To your health." They drank Russian-style, taking a tiny taste of jam and sipping tea around it, making it last a long time.

"I've been waiting for you to find me," she said after a while.

"How did you know I was looking?"

"Not you, of course; your Agency." She did think he was CIA, then. Well, why not? What would he think, in her position? The CIA *was* looking for her. And they weren't the only ones, either.

"Do you want to tell me what happened that night?"

"Charles met me in the Metro late at night"—he noted that she was completely unselfconscious in using Hutchins's first name—"on the train that goes to Prospect Mira. We got off there and walked to the cafe where we were to meet my brother Yuri."

"Why were you meeting at that cafe?"

"I don't know. Yuri suggested we meet there. I don't think he'd been there before. Maybe that was why. As it turned out, Yuri didn't come."

"Why did Yuri want to meet Charles?"

"Because of what he—Yuri—was involved in."

"What was he involved in?"

"I don't know." Then she looked at him, strangely. "Didn't Charles tell you this? Or don't you keep files?"

He took a deep breath. "I don't work for the CIA."

She had been about to take a sip of tea. She stopped the cup midway and stared at him. "You're at the American Embassy, aren't you?"

"Yes. But we don't all work for the CIA. Believe it or not."

Apparently she had trouble believing it. She set down her teacup. "Then why are you here?"

"I told you: in the interests of culture."

"No. Why are you here, looking for me?"

"Aside from the fact that you're the most beautiful woman I've ever met?"

"Yes. Aside from that. Even if that were true, you didn't know it before you came to the play. Did you just happen to be there, from love of Bulgakov?"

"No," he admitted. "I came looking for you. But it *is* true."

"Thank you. Why did you come looking for me?"

"Charles was my friend. The investigation of his death has gone nowhere. I knew there was a beautiful Russian woman with him at the time of his death. I saw a painting, an auto-portrait, of a woman that matched the face in a painting he had, and I looked for her."

"How did you know he was with a Russian woman?"

"It was in the KGB report."

For the first time she looked as if she couldn't believe him. "How would you see that!"

"When they found out who Charles was, they agreed to cooperate with us. I guess they couldn't figure it out for themselves and supposed they might as well see what we could turn up. We didn't turn up anything."

"Who is 'we'? The CIA that you don't work for?"

" 'We' is the American side. Including the CIA, I guess. But I don't work for them. I don't even really work for the government; only temporarily. I really am just a special assistant cultural attaché." He added, "I guess that means I'll never get you into bed with the romance of my business."

She didn't laugh. "You've put us both in a very dangerous position," she said angrily.

"I'd have thought you were already in a dangerous position."

"I was. But now it's worse. Alone, I was just a part of the proletariat. Who looks at them? But everyone looks at a woman with a foreigner. As you've discovered. Do you think I want every militiaman in Moscow looking at me, wondering what I'm doing with you?"

"Did you consider that when you were with Charles?"

"Yes, of course I did. But I had a purpose."

"You wanted to help your brother meet Charles."

"Yes."

"Why?"

"Because he asked me to. Yuri was involved in something bad. Something really bad. I thought I should help him."

"What was he involved in?"

"I don't know."

"You don't know! Why did you want to help him meet Hutchins, then?"

"Because Yuri asked me to help him meet someone from the CIA. He knew I knew this American—Charles—who had bought one of my paintings. I saw Charles on Arbat Street sometimes. I knew he worked at your Embassy. So I asked him to help me meet a CIA

181

person. But he wouldn't do it. He said the CIA wouldn't come without a report from some other American, without knowing what was the purpose; and I wouldn't tell him, so finally he told me he was CIA."

"Did you believe him?"

"I already told you I did. And I didn't see any credentials."

"How did you know Yuri was in something bad?"

"I know Yuri. Bad things attract him."

"But why would you help him with this? Why get involved in what could be treason?"

"This wasn't just dirty business. This time was different. He was worried. I didn't see him often, anymore, but I still knew him—knew what he was feeling. He was worried. He was worried and attracted at the same time. Worried and greedy. 'It's important,' he said to me. 'Important to the world, Alya. Not just to me.' He knew I'd know he wouldn't do it just for the world: he only did what was important to him. But he knew I'd know he was telling the truth too. I guess he hoped if I wouldn't do it for him, I'd do it for the world."

"So what do we do now? Can we find Yuri?"

"I don't know. He wasn't often in Moscow, for a long time. He had a different life. But he'd have found *me* by now, if he wanted to be found."

"What do you mean, he had a 'different life'?"

"His life was easy money." She said this as if the words "easy money" had a taste she didn't like. "That kind of life. He was working for the Mafia."

"What did he do for the Mafia?"

"I don't know. I never wanted to know. Bad enough that he was doing it."

"Maybe it starts to make sense. Maybe Yuri was sent to set up Charles."

"What does it mean—'set up'? You don't talk like a Russian."

"I talk Russian like an American who doesn't know what the Russians would say and has to translate American into Russian. In American, to set someone up means to put him in a position to be killed."

"Who would send Yuri to do that to Charles?"

"To name one name, the KGB."

"The KGB wouldn't have to hire Yuri for that. They could do it themselves." She said this as if explaining to a child.

He realized then that for her to believe there was a plot to kill Charles, she would have to believe that she had unintentionally

182

become a part of it. It was a belief she resisted. But his sessions with Bierman, he realized, had left their mark on him too: his first assumption was that the KGB would want to kill the CIA station chief. Would they? Maybe it *was* the reaction of a child.

"If not that, then what?" he asked.

"Yuri wasn't 'sent.' Yuri was going to be there because he wanted to be. I know Yuri. He wasn't working for somebody else on this. He schemed for this meeting. He was too greedy to work that hard for somebody else. Yuri wasn't 'sent.' The others were 'sent.' They were sent to kill Yuri."

"Why? For what purpose?"

"For the purpose of keeping him from selling what he knew."

"Selling?"

"Yuri didn't give away things of value. And if he schemed to have this meeting, something of value had to be there."

"And what was he selling?"

"I've told you, I don't know. Yuri wouldn't have told me—that would have been giving away whatever it was he had. That was what he didn't like most about me, you see—I didn't see the 'value' of what he was doing. We had different ideas of 'value.' "

"He sounds like a charming man."

"He was once. He could be, when he had hopes of getting something he wanted."

"What did he want?"

"He wanted to be rich, and he wanted to get out of the Union, because you can't be rich in the Union—there's nothing to be rich with. The CIA could get him both, if he had something they wanted enough."

"Is there anyone else who might know what he was selling?"

"I don't know of anyone."

"Is there anyone else who might know where he is?"

She said after a pause, reluctantly, "There's Dmitri."

"Who is Dmitri?"

"He and Yuri were friends. They were friends all their lives. They went into the army together. They didn't come back together. . . . Dmitri lost his legs in the war. But Yuri still visited Dmitri. Dmitri was the only person Yuri visited without wanting something. Or maybe he just wanted something different from Dmitri. Dmitri loved Yuri."

"Do you know how to find Dmitri?"

"I don't know if I want to."

"Why not?"

The answer seemed to pain her more than the mere words warranted: "Dmitri may not know anything. Or whoever killed Charles may not know that Dmitri knows. I don't even know if they know who I am. But if they do, and if they find out I'm talking to Dmitri, they may decide they don't want Dmitri alive anymore. I want to stay away from anyone I can hurt."

· 33 ·

Thursday, June 1, 1989
7 A.M.
The United States Embassy

MARTIN FOUND ROLLIE TAGLIA EATING BREAKFAST IN THE CAFETERIA, reading unclassified cables over his coffee. Rollie pushed a sheaf of cables across to Martin. "Nothing like a good read before work. Washington doesn't know what to make of the Congress of Deputies. Should we let 'em in on the secret? What happened to your hand?" Martin was wearing a plaster cast that covered his right hand from fingertips to wrist.

"I broke a bone up here." He ran his fingers over where the middle of his hand would be.

"Now this ought to be an interesting story! Are you free to tell me about it?"

"The usual thing—slip and fall in the bathtub." Martin took the cables from Rollie and, while pretending to leaf through them, said in a low voice, "Rollie, I've found her."

"Her?"

"Her."

"Want to come up to my place to talk about it?"

"Sure. Why not."

"Let's plug in His Excellency. I'll bring him. And Bierman."

"Why Bierman?"

"He *is* the station chief."

"He's a schmuck."

"A condition not totally inconsistent with being station chief."

184

"Hutch wasn't a schmuck."

"True, but not logically relevant. I'll bring Bierman too."

They closed the door to the Bubble and turned on the noisemakers.

"What happened to your fist?" the Ambassador asked.

"He fell in the bathtub," Rollie said.

"I broke it on somebody's nose."

"You're not the fighter you once were."

"Probably I never was."

"Do you plan to tell us about this escapade?" Bierman asked.

"I haven't decided yet."

"Does it have something to do with 'her'?" Rollie asked.

"Yeah. It does."

"I can hardly wait for this," Bierman said.

"Is this the 'her' I think it is?" the Ambassador asked.

"If you think 'her' is the woman who was with Hutchins, then the answer is yes."

Bierman leaned forward across the table, looking awake for the first time. "The woman who was with Hutchins? When he was killed?"

"Yes."

"You mean to say you think you've found her, when the CIA *and* the KGB couldn't?"

"I've found her."

"Who is she?"

"A Russian woman. Artist, actress. A blond beauty, as advertised."

"She got a name?" the Ambassador asked.

Now that he had reached this point, Martin found himself reluctant to say her name. He looked up at the ceiling above the clear plastic of the Bubble.

"No use lookin' up there," the Ambassador said. "The KGB hide their mikes better'n that. Anyway, they're just as likely to have put 'em in the floor, or in the wallboard. And if they did, they'll get her name soon enough."

"Her name is Alina Obraz," Martin said.

"Is that her stage name?" Rollie asked.

"No . . . I don't think so. I didn't see her passport." But it hadn't struck him until now, and he was surprised that it hadn't: *obraz* meant "image" in Russian.

"Artist, actress, KGB agent," Bierman said. "A good collection. What makes you think all these women are her?"

"She told me." He told enough of the story to make it convincing, except to Bierman.

"A KGB plant could know all that, and more," Bierman said. "And we don't know if half of it's true."

"And she had this," he added. He handed Hutch's credentials to the Ambassador. The Ambassador looked at it and passed it to Taglia, who passed it to Bierman.

"A KGB plant would have been given that too," Bierman said. But he didn't sound convinced himself.

"But what was Hutch doing with her?" the Ambassador asked.

"Aside from the obvious?" Taglia asked.

Bierman asked, "What's the obvious?"

"Come on, Bierman. Didn't they teach you about the birds and the bees in CIA school?"

"I don't think he was doing the obvious," Martin said. "And other than the obvious, I don't know what he was doing."

"You say she wouldn't tell you what this meeting was about?"

"No . . . I said she doesn't know either. I think she's on the edge of something she doesn't understand, and Hutchins stumbled onto her. That's not very helpful, is it?"

"Could you give us a category for this unknown activity?" Bierman asked. "Animal, vegetable, or mineral? Sounds like . . . ? What is it this Yuri's trying to sell?"

"I don't have any idea," Martin said. "And neither does she. How about you? Is there anything in the company files that you'd care to share with us?"

"No."

"Nothing there? Or nothing you care to share?"

"You know I can't comment on Agency operations."

"So what we know," Taglia said, "is that she has a brother in 'easy money' who was supposed to meet her at the cafe, but didn't, and hasn't been seen since. What does she think happened to him?"

"She says she doesn't know. She didn't seem to want to talk about him too much." Martin decided not to mention Dmitri unless someone asked directly, and no one did.

"I don't blame her," Rollie said. "I'm surprised she would talk to you at all. If the KGB was after me, I'd be careful who I talked to, too."

"Unless you were KGB yourself," Bierman observed.

"What do you think?" Rollie asked Martin. "Is she?"

"I thought she was at first. For one thing, she denied knowing any

186

Americans, even though her 'boyfriend' told me she'd sold a painting of herself to an American.''

"Have you changed your mind?'' Bierman asked.

Martin knew Bierman was going to laugh, but he said it anyway: ''Yes.''

Bierman laughed.

"Why'd you change your mind?'' Rollie asked.

Martin shrugged. "She dragged me away from a gang of drunks, for one thing.''

"That's no evidence,'' Bierman said, and Martin knew he was right, but he couldn't think of any real evidence.

"That where you banged up the wing?'' the Ambassador asked.

"You ought to see what *they* look like today,'' Rollie said.

"Well, as I said, I broke it on one of 'em's nose.''

"They weren't KGB either?'' Rollie asked.

"They did a piss-poor job if they were,'' the Ambassador said. "Only one broken bone on our boy, and no bruises.''

"No, they weren't KGB,'' Martin said. "They were just honest Soviet workingmen, high on Gift of the Sun. Looking to take out their frustrations on the foreigners. I don't know: I can't prove she's not KGB; but I don't believe she is.''

"Well, boys, what do we do about her?'' the Ambassador asked.

"We turn her over to the professionals to handle,'' Bierman said. "You did a clever job finding her, Martin. I can't approve of your making a personal approach to her, but there's no evidence yet that it did any damage. Now it's time to turn her over to the pros.''

"Which, I guess, means to you?'' Martin said.

"Or else to someone we might bring in to handle her. I haven't made that decision yet. I'll have to consult Langley.''

"And what exactly is this person supposed to do to 'handle' her, Bierman?''

"Two things. One, determine what information she really has about Hutchins's death; and two, develop her as a source of further information.''

"What information she 'really' has? I take it that you don't believe what she told me—that she only agreed to introduce Yuri to Hutch. And what do you expect to 'develop' out of a woman who doesn't know any more than that?''

"Let's not be naïve, Martin,'' Bierman said. "This is the real world. Maybe she told you the truth, the whole truth, and nothing but the truth; and maybe she didn't. But we can't just assume she did. For

187

one thing, it will take a lot of convincing to convince me that Hutchins actually told an unknown indigenous female that he worked for the Agency. And as for what we can develop from her, I don't know yet. But things come to mind. Here's one: we reopen our KGB contacts and hit them with this new information, to see what that blasts loose. Or here's a better one: we get her to go to the KGB without telling them she's working with us. We'll get a pipeline into the Committee's investigation of this case without endangering any resources of our own."

"But not without endangering her life," Martin said. "Not that it matters, since she's not one of our 'resources.' "

"You can't make an omelet without at least taking the chance of breaking some eggs," Bierman answered.

"We're not talking about eggs, Bierman. We're talking about a woman. This is the real world; remember?"

Bierman turned to the Ambassador, with a look that said, *You see?* "We've got to have a professional on this," he said. "Someone who won't get emotionally involved."

"Does 'professional' mean the kind of person who doesn't get emotionally involved in risking a woman's life?" Martin asked.

" 'Professional,' " Bierman said, "means someone who's trained to handle this situation and who'll do what's best for the United States."

"Are you suggesting I'm short on patriotism?"

"Take it easy, Ben," the Ambassador said. "We know you're a patriot. They wouldn't have let you come here if there was any question of that."

"I was merely pointing out," Bierman said, "that you're not trained to evaluate situations of this kind."

"I've evaluated it," Martin said. "And I won't accept any arrangement that puts no value on the life of this woman."

"It's not a question of what you 'accept,' Martin," Bierman said; but the Ambassador cut him off. "There won't be any 'arrangements' that put her in danger, Ben," the Ambassador said.

"It *is* a question of what I accept," Martin said. "Do you think you can find her again by yourself, Bierman?"

"What? You're going to interfere with an official investigation of the death of an American diplomat? Ambassador," Bierman said angrily, "I've got to recommend that this man be sent home!"

"Oh, bullshit, Bierman!" Rollie Taglia said. "Let's not get overwrought. I can understand why Ben is upset, with you talking about tossing this woman to the KGB. Let's get realistic on both sides."

"I wasn't suggesting we 'toss her to the KGB,' " Bierman said. "Of course we want to protect her to the limit of our ability. At the same time, we have a duty to make use of the information she's able to provide."

"Why don't we break out the electrodes and see what they jolt out of her," Martin suggested. "Do we have a 'duty' to use the old electroshock treatment, Bierman?"

"Calm down, Ben," the Ambassador said. "We need to work out a sensible plan for what to do about this. Now, what's your assessment? You're the only one who's seen her up close and personal. Is she going to shy off if we put someone else on the case?"

"That's a risk," Martin said. "If she's afraid of the KGB, she should be more afraid of the CIA." He avoided a complete lie by making this prescriptive, ignoring the fact that she had been concerned because he *wasn't* CIA. He thought what he said was true, even if she didn't.

"Bierman?" the Ambassador asked.

"We've got to have a professional," Bierman said. "Martin's a good man"—*You're a poor liar,* Martin thought—"but this informant is too important to leave to someone who doesn't draw combat pay."

"Rollie?"

"The way I see it," Taglia said, "we've got to find Yuri. The 'informant' "—he made it sound as if Bierman had used a dirty word instead of a euphemism—"has some reason now to trust Martin, silly though that may sound to sensible people like you and me who know and love Martin. If we try to change horses now, she may shy off, if I can mix an equine metaphor into Bierman's omelet. I say we go with Martin."

The Ambassador turned to Bierman. "And the Agency says . . . ?"

Bierman could see which way the decision was going and hurried to get there first: "If we're using Martin, we'll have to have some operational controls on him."

"Sure, of course we will," the Ambassador said. "Whatever's fair."

Bierman turned to Martin, all friendliness. "You'll need a checkout from me," he said. "A briefing before every contact, and a debriefing after."

"Anything that keeps me on the rails," Martin said. "I wouldn't want to run amok."

"It's settled, then," the Ambassador said.

· 34 ·
Thursday, June 1, 1989
6:30 P.M.
Kolomenskaya

AT THE TIME THEY HAD AGREED UPON, MARTIN TELEPHONED ALINA'S apartment from a pay telephone outside a Metro station two stops beyond hers. She answered as they had agreed she would if there was no trouble: "It's me." He knew her voice. He hung up the telephone without speaking and walked slowly back to the Metro. He took a train to Warsaw Expressway. Across the street behind the tram stop was a *kulinariya* where he bought an unsugared doughnut and a cup of tea. His bandaged hand made him self-conscious: he knew people were looking at him, and he was afraid the hand made him too memorable. He stood at one of the chest-high tables where he could see out the window onto the street and made his tea last until he saw Alina come out of the Metro station. She was wearing jeans and a light jacket and carrying a basket. He walked behind her to the tram stop, where they waited separately, without speaking, for the trolley. They sat at opposite ends of the car. At Red Beacon they got down and walked separately for several blocks, until he was satisfied that they weren't being followed, and then caught up to her. Bierman had approved all of these precautions and had added none—which pleased Martin even though he didn't like Bierman. But in checking for tails, Martin was as worried about someone sent by Bierman as he was about KGB.

Moscow is circled by rings of new high-rise apartments, and although the construction quality is such that the north-side residents may find ice on their living-room walls in winter, in summer they have the advantage that from their balconies they can look onto the *les*, the Russian forest, for at the outermost ring, the city stops abruptly and the forest begins and runs to the horizon.

Martin and Alina walked together around one of these apartment towers, as if going to visit there, but in the back they continued past

190

the school next door and then on up the road and were out of the city altogether.

They had started early in the evening and had hours of daylight ahead of them. "What's in the basket?" he asked. It was an old woven-splint peasant basket—a *lubok*—that had seen better days.

She answered with a question: "Did you eat supper?"

"No. Just a doughnut."

"I hope it wasn't large. I didn't eat either, so I brought some things."

He was embarrassed that he hadn't done the same.

"Do you like chicken?" she asked. "It won't be a grand picnic, but we won't starve. And there's bread and some wine I had."

"It will be a feast. Here, let me carry it, at least."

"Maybe you should save your hand."

"I'll carry it in the other hand."

She gave him the basket but took his bandaged hand and looked at it. "Is it painful?"

"Not so much."

"*Molodyets*." It was a Russian word of praise, derived from the old word for a young hero but used to praise any accomplishment. For her to use it was a little ironic—as if she were praising a small boy—but serious too.

With a nod she directed him to cross the road, and then they were in the forest. He was surprised how open it was. There was a well-beaten path, and then another, and another crossed it—the kind of maze that a city of nine million makes next door; but she soon left the paths, and underfoot there was just the forest floor, soft and quiet and free of low growth. Most of the trees were old friends from home—birch and alder and big-leafed maple and sometimes a brief stand of larches: good Wisconsin trees, friends of his childhood. The light among them was so uniform, except in the dark among the evergreens, that he soon lost his sense of direction; but he did not feel lost: he felt at home. The lack of a path seemed not to disturb her; and so he trusted her and the trees to get them back. They saw no one else.

On a gentle slope she stopped him and took from the basket a flowered plastic tablecloth which she spread on the ground. She directed him to put down the basket and knelt beside it on the table-cloth. Every time she moved, there was a plastic crackle as she set out plates, a plastic box with pieces of chicken, a loaf of white bread,

191

two boiled eggs, two pieces of cake and a bottle of Georgian wine and glasses.

"This is just like the real thing," he said as she motioned for him to sit down.

"How is that?"

"It's like a real picnic, instead of a business discussion."

"We're here with the food and the summer evening. Is that not real?"

"In everything but emotion."

"You sound like a Russian."

He laughed: "Only once in life such a meeting . . ." It was the refrain from an old Russian song, known to everyone.

"You sound *very* Russian." She began to sing, unselfconscious as the forest; and after the first words he joined her:

> *Only once in life such a meeting;*
> *Only once fate breaks the thread;*
> *Only once in the cold, gray evening—*
> *So much I want to love.*

But on the last line, both their voices wavered. They stopped. Neither looked at the other.

She tore open the loaf and handed him a piece of bread. He opened the wine and poured two glasses. "Did you hear Sakharov's speech to the Congress today?" he asked at last, handing her a glass. The sound of his voice was like glass breaking in the silent forest.

"Yes, of course."

"What did you think of it?"

"Sakharov is a brave man, to say what no one in power wants to hear . . . about Afghanistan and about other things. But we've known his bravery for years. I was more impressed by what his opponent said—a man who thinks of himself as Sakharov's opponent. He rose to denounce Sakharov; but his heaviest charge just slipped out, and it wasn't against Sakharov. He said that the old comrades hadn't left the young people any ideals by which to measure our lives. Did you hear it?"

"Yes, I did."

"And he said he was for 'national strength, the motherland, and communism'; but he also remarked that in a Congress where eighty percent of the Deputies are Communists, he was the first one who had used the word 'communism.' Not even Gorbachev had said the word."

"He sounded like a lonely man."

She nodded.

Martin took a boiled egg and tried to peel it. He could just hold it in the fingertips of his wrapped right hand. He could see under his brows that she watched him as he struggled at it. She bit her lip but said nothing. At length he had most of the shell picked away. He handed her the egg. She thanked him seriously, but with a smile that made the effort worthwhile.

"You're welcome," he said. "I told the CIA about you."

"Who is the CIA, in this case?"

"I can't tell you that."

"Why can you tell them about me and not me about them?"

"I don't know. It's one of their stupid rules. A price I have to pay for being allowed to keep playing the game. He ... they ... one of them wants to meet you, though—kind of a check on what I'm doing."

"Then why didn't he come?"

"He's afraid to meet you, even while he wants to. He's afraid you'll find out who he is. He wants to know you without your being aware of it. It's a problem for him."

"I can see it might be. Maybe he could wear a mask. How is it the robbers do it in your country? I saw a movie once. He had pantyhose over his head."

"On this guy, pantyhose would be an improvement. I can see him with the legs sticking in the air, like asses' ears."

She wasn't sure she was supposed to laugh, until he did. Then she did too.

"Well, if he won't come meet me," she asked, "what am I supposed to do?"

"Tell me what you know."

"I've done that."

"I have to ask for more details."

"All right, ask."

Bierman had provided him with a small tape recorder—not the kind of thing that strapped on the body under the clothes, but just a tape recorder, like a dictaphone. She was shy, at first, of talking into it—surprising in an actress. She laughed when he played back her voice. "I sound like a two-kopeck piece!"

"It's this cheap recorder. Your voice is beautiful."

Martin went over her story again, asking all the same things and getting the same answers, only more so, and on tape.

"Do I pass?" she asked, after he shut off the recorder.

"With hurrahs." Though he didn't know what Bierman would think. What was passing?

"What next?"

"They want to know what Yuri was trying to sell."

"I've said I don't know."

"I think that means we have to look for him. Do you want to?"

She said, "I want to know what happened to him."

"He hasn't come looking for *you.*"

"If he has, he didn't find me."

"Why didn't you look for him before?"

"I told you: I didn't want anyone in danger because of me." She added, "To tell the truth, I didn't want to be in more danger myself. I wanted to stay in a hole and not be found." She sipped at her wine. "I've had dreams, ever since that night . . ."

"Do you want to tell me about them?"

"No. I don't want to think about them."

"All right." He drank the wine and ate the bread. He had the uncomfortable feeling that she looked on him as a rescuer—or had done so at first—and he didn't feel like a rescuer.

"You said we might find Yuri through your friend Dmitri?"

"Yes. I don't know how else."

"How about your family?"

"There's no one. My father died when I was young; my mother a year ago."

"Your husband?"

"I haven't seen him in two years. Anyway, Yuri despised him. And he Yuri."

"And Dmitri? How do we find him?"

"He doesn't have a telephone. I know where he lives. I was afraid to go see him. I didn't know who would be watching. And . . . there are other reasons."

"What are they?"

"It's not a happy story."

He waited to see if she would say more, but she didn't. He asked, "Should we go there?"

"I suppose it's the only way."

"When can we do it?"

"I don't know."

194

"Sooner is better."

"Yes, of course. All right; we'll go tomorrow." She didn't sound happy about it. She sat with her arms clasped around her legs, her chin resting on her forearms over her knees. She had come with her hair put up in a bun, but now she had let it down and it fell over her shoulders and down her back. He wanted to touch it, but didn't.

"You've had a hard time of it, with all this," he said.

"If that matters. It's not like it was in Stalin's time."

In the Union, that was an unanswerable refusal to accept comfort, so he said nothing. He lay back on the crackling plastic groundcloth and watched the light slowly fading from the trees.

It was nearly dark among the trees before they left the forest; but back outside, on the street, the sky was still light. They walked a little way together, then separated to take different public transportation. He supposed spies shouldn't look back, but he did, after a few steps. Her pale hair was a light mark on the darkness as she walked away. Then she turned to look back at him. He waved, and so did she.

· 35 ·

Friday, June 2, 1989
8 A.M.
The United States Embassy

BIERMAN HAD FINISHED LISTENING TO THE TAPE FOR THE SECOND TIME. "At least she's consistent," he said. "But certainly there are some things we'll want to go over again."

"I could meet her again tonight."

"It's going to be at least a week, maybe two weeks, before the next meeting. She's already been too much in public with a foreigner for my taste. Someone's going to notice it, and then the wrong people will get curious. No, Martin: I'll tell you when you can see her again—if at all. We'll have to get her story down in detail, before we decide how to handle her."

"I thought we'd already decided that."

"Nothing is forever, Martin."

195

Martin reflected that, if that was the way the game was played, he was glad he hadn't run the tape when they talked about Dmitri. Bierman could run this contact however he wanted to, for his own part; but as for Martin, he didn't take orders from the Company, and he intended to find out what had happened to Hutchins, and do it as quickly as possible. What Bierman didn't know wouldn't hurt him.

And also . . . he wanted to see Alina.

· 36 ·

Friday, June 2, 1989
8 P.M.
New Ryazan Street

THE ELEVATOR OF THE BUILDING WHERE DMITRI LIVED WASN'T WORKING— "again," Alina said—so they walked up nine stories to his apartment. The stair wound around the inside of a square shaft with the elevator cage at its center, in which lifeless cables hung like jungle vines in the dim light of the few working light bulbs. Martin and Alina stopped every two floors to catch their breath. It was like walking to heaven.

"I should have brought some food," Alina said. "I forgot about the elevator."

"Do you want to go back down?" Martin asked her.

"No. I want this to be over."

"What is it you don't like about Dmitri?" It seemed to him that she wasn't just trying to protect Dmitri: she really didn't want to see him.

"It's an old story and it's complicated," she said. "I do like him. But it's not something I want to talk about."

They came at last to the top floor and stood to catch their breath. Then she stepped up to the door, but hesitated before knocking on it.

After several knocks there was the sound of someone moving inside. "Who is it?" A man's voice, muffled by the door.

"Dima, it's Alya."

"Alya?" A shuffling of locks. The door opened.

"Alya, come in!" But when he saw Martin, he stopped, rolled back a little.

Martin also stepped back.

When Dmitri held the door open, his arm stretched out level from his shoulder to reach the doorknob. His head was at the level of Martin's waist.

Martin thought at first Dmitri was a dwarf. Then he realized his mistake.

Dmitri had no legs.

He was buckled to a small square platform of wood with roller-skate wheels under it.

Alina had warned Martin. "Dmitri lost his legs in the war," she had said. But he saw now that the warning hadn't been explicit enough. He had been expecting someone in a wheelchair, or on artificial limbs, not a Third World cripple.

The Third World cripple let go the door and pushed himself back a little farther with one hand, pushing against the floor with his knuckles. Dark eyes glittered under long black hair, tied back with a cloth band, that mingled with a flowing black beard. The eyes did not leave Martin.

"Dima, this is a friend, Benjamin Martin. He's American."

"American?" When Dmitri seemed finally to comprehend, he laughed. His laugh had the deep bass foundation of a Russian church choir. "I've never met an American. I thought you were probably the KGB again. Come in."

Both Martin and Alya stopped abruptly. "What do you mean, 'KGB again'?" Alina asked.

"They've been hanging around for weeks. It's that letter of mine. Come in; don't stand in the hall." He waved them in with one arm—it seemed absurdly long, but Martin saw that it was a normal arm, long only in proportion to Dmitri's height, not to his body. Dmitri closed the door and pushed himself up the hall ahead of them. One powerful thrust of his arms shot him past them in a rumble of wheels.

"What letter do you mean?" Alina asked.

Dmitri spun around at the end of the hall and motioned for them to follow him. They passed a closed door and then the open door to the kitchen, a narrow room once painted white but now gray—or maybe it was a trick of the evening north light through an uncleaned window. At the end of the hall Dmitri waved them into a room on the right. In it were a couch and a table—a dining table cut down to

197

be no higher than a coffee table—and a low easel with a half-started oil painting of a woman. The easel was on wheels. Dmitri spun it around so it faced the wall. "You don't know about my letter? The kiss of fame is fleeting. I thought I was becoming the center of the universe. My letter's brought me plenty of company at all hours. I've got KGB running up my ass."

"What letter, Dima?" Alina asked with an urgency that stopped him.

"I wrote a letter demanding rights for the handicapped. Seven of us signed it. It was published in *Izvestia*. You didn't see it? Since then, I never lack for companionship. Sit down, please." He waved toward the couch. "I'll make some tea."

"Let me do it," Alina said.

"You think I can't make tea in my own house? Sit down." He scooted out the door with another single push, put out a hand to catch the door jamb, and swung up the hall, accelerated by a pull at the jamb. They could hear his wheels rumble over the wood floor and stop as he hit the linoleum of the kitchen they had passed coming up the hall. Then there was the clatter of getting out a tin kettle and cups, and water running. Martin wanted to go to the kitchen and see how Dmitri got up to the cupboards and the sink, but he didn't dare. Dmitri's voice came back into the room: "It hasn't been so bad for me! Since I've got no job and no family, they don't have anyplace to get a hold on me! For the others it's been harder! The KGB go right for their families, you know: talk to the bosses of all the relatives, ask them whether they should really be employing people whose relatives have such an inadequate appreciation of the motherliness of the Motherland as to demand maybe a wheelchair or a way to get on a bus!"

Dmitri scooted back into the room. "Water's boiling. Won't be a minute. So, you're an American?" He offered his hand to Martin. Then he seemed to notice for the first time the bandage on Martin's right hand. He grinned. "A fellow invalid? Sorry." He offered his left hand. It was like a rock. The knuckles were callused down to the first finger-joint, and his grip was powerful. "Sorry I wasn't friendlier. I was taken by surprise. You aren't dressed like an American."

Martin was wearing an old Soviet suit and shoes he had bought a long time ago, soon after he came to Moscow, with the idea that cultural experience would come more easily if he wasn't a foreigner at first glance. But then he had still been a foreigner at first glance— but one trying, suspiciously, to look Soviet. He had hoped now he

198

looked less exotic. "I'm sorry we couldn't warn you we were coming," Martin said.

Dmitri shrugged—a motion that seemed to encompass his whole body. "Someday I'll have a telephone." He let Martin's hand go. "How'd you get that?" he asked, glancing at the bandage on the other hand.

"I slipped in the bathtub."

"Why are the KGB bothering you about your letter?" Alina asked.

"Why? Ask *them* why! It's like Stalin's time. I'm composing a letter now to Comrade Gorbachev, asking *him* why. We'll see if that gets them off me."

The kettle whistled, and Dmitri again shot out of the room like the star in a vanishing act. In a moment he called back, "All right, Alya, I surrender! You can come help now!"

She went out of the room and was quickly back with a Soviet tea set—a tray with mismatched cups and saucers, teapot, and little saucers of jam. Dmitri followed her. He scooted up to the low table and quickly set out the cups and poured tea. "I'll make someone a good wife," he said. "So, Benjamin Martin, American, what brings you calling at my door? Is Alya introducing you to all her friends? She must have come to the end of the list to bring you here." He didn't say it bitterly or any other way especially, but Alina turned away from both of them.

"You know that's not true, Dima," Alina said.

"Do I? Well, what brings you here, then?" He stared directly at her as he asked this. His long hair came down over his eyes, and he twitched his head to fling it back; but his eyes never left her.

"I came to ask if you've seen Yuri."

"Lost him, have you?"

"Yes. I've lost him."

"Brought an American to help look for him?"

"Yes." She sounded like a woman being purposefully patient.

"Is she introducing you to her family?" Dmitri asked Martin.

Alina didn't let him answer. "I'm afraid Yura may be in trouble, Dmitri," she said.

"You're a little late worrying about him, then."

"What do you mean?"

Seeing her agitation, he relented, but only a little. "I haven't seen him in months. He was here in the winter. He was in trouble then. You ought to have come then."

"Well, she's come now," Martin said. He knew he shouldn't interfere if he wanted Dmitri's cooperation, but he was tired of this.

"What does your American have to do with Yura?" Dmitri asked this of Alina, ignoring Martin.

"He isn't my American. And he wants to help Yuri. As I do."

"Is that true?" Dmitri asked Martin. At the same time he handed Martin a cup of tea. He held it briefly, so that their hands were on the cup together for a moment. Although their hands did not touch, Martin felt the presence of the other hand on the cup, as if for that instant something connected them. It was a powerful hand, but not steady. He looked into the eyes, the dark eyes under that dark hair; but they told him nothing. "Is it true? Or is it Yura's sister that you want to help?"

"There was another American," Martin said. "In the winter; before I ever knew Alina. Yuri was to meet another American one night; but he never did. Is that when he came here?"

"What if it was?"

"The other American was my friend. He was killed that night."

Dmitri looked thoughtfully at Martin. "I'm sorry to hear it," he said at last. "Do you think Yura did it?"

"No. But I think he may know something about it. And he wanted to tell something to my friend. I think he may still want to tell it to an American."

"And if he does, are you the one?"

"I seem to be. I seem to be the only choice."

"That isn't much." Dmitri sighed. He took a small spoonful of jam in his mouth and sucked tea around it. He spoke into his cup: "Alya, why didn't you come sooner? All these months you haven't come here."

"I didn't know what to do, Dima. I didn't know what had happened to Yura. I hoped you would know; but I didn't want to hurt you. And I didn't want to bring trouble to your door."

"Trouble? If you mean the KGB, they're already here."

"Why would she mean the KGB?" Martin asked.

Dmitri looked sidelong at Martin. "Did I say KGB? Maybe I meant the Mafia. But they're not here. Yet."

"Why would you mean the Mafia?"

Dmitri laughed. It was not, as before, a clear laugh of discovery: it was a dark laugh, with the sadness of Mother Russia in it. "Why would I mean the Mafia? Why would I not? Wasn't Yura in with them for all his life, ever since we left the army? And yes, since that's what you're thinking, American, that is where I lost my legs—in the Red Army, 'doing my internationalist duty' for the Motherland. Carrying out my duty to the People. That's what I got for my service to humanity: lost my legs, lost my best friend, lost my wife.''

"Don't talk nonsense, Dmitri!" Alina said, with a coldness that seemed extraordinary to Martin, considering the losses Dmitri had just listed.

"Alya, please, if you'd just listen!" Dmitri insisted; but Alina was not listening. "I won't hear this again!" she said. "We came to find Yuri, not to talk over history! Do you know where he is? We must find him!"

Dmitri, hunched over his teacup, shuddered as if physically pulling himself together. "Yes, I know where he is." He stirred his teacup. "Yuri came here one night last winter. He said he was in trouble and had to get out of Moscow. He wouldn't tell me what trouble it was—said it was better I didn't know."

"Did he leave any message for me?" Alina asked.

"No."

"He just left?"

"He stayed two days. Then he left."

"What did he do for two days?"

"Looked out the windows. He didn't know what to do."

"He didn't try to send me a message?"

"No."

"Where did he go?"

Dmitri paused before he replied. "I helped him find a place."

"Dima, Dima, you know I've got to find him. Why won't you help me?" Alina seemed on the edge of tears. Martin wanted to put an arm around her to comfort her.

Dmitri chewed at the end of his beard in frustration. "Alya, why wouldn't you come see me, when you knew he'd come here? Am I so disgusting to you?"

"Dima, you know that's not it! I love you. If I don't love you the way you want me to, I can't help it! I'm sorry. I wish I did; but I don't!"

Dmitri, hating what he was saying but unable to quit now, oblivious of Martin and Alina and the world: "I don't care how you love me, Alya. You know how I love you."

"Why is it always like this, Dima?" she protested. "Why?" She jumped to her feet. "I've got to know where he is, Dima!" she said.

"I'm going now; but I've got to know where he is! Will you help me?"

"Yes, I'm going to help you, Alya," Dmitri said unhappily. "You know I'm always going to help you. If you need help, call on Dmitri. What else is he good for?"

"Stop it, Dima! You're a fine man: you know you are! Don't pretend to be some crawling thing!"

"I *am* a crawling thing."

"You're not!"

"I'd be a crawling thing if it would please you."

"It won't. Please, now, where is he?"

"Bryansk," Dmitri said bitterly into his cup. "I have an uncle. He's a retired forester near Bryansk, out in the village of Stary Buyan. I got Yura a train ticket: up and down those stairs I went—the elevator was out then too—and sent him off in the middle of the night to Uncle Fedya. Not so nice, then, in mid-winter. Yura was used to better things than Stary Buyan in mid-winter. But he got used to that too, and now mid-summer's not so bad." He looked up at her. "You want to take your American to see him? He'll be alive, thanks to Dima."

"Thanks to Dima," she said. She said it softly, and stooped to kiss his hair quickly, then stepped away, hurried out of the room, not waiting for Martin to follow her.

· 37 ·

Saturday, June 3, 1989
2 A.M.
Kiev Station

THE NIGHT TRAIN TO BRYANSK LEFT FROM THE KIEV STATION AT 2:30 A.M., on a socialist schedule designed for the most efficient use of rolling stock, not the convenience of the passengers. The Union had plenty of people, but not nearly enough trains.

Kiev Station at two in the morning was a vast dim warehouse for groggy bodies trying to be as inert as possible, as if inaction would preserve the life force until a train did come. The bodies were draped over orange plastic chairs apparently designed for the express purpose of preventing comfort. The night was a struggle between orange plastic furniture and people bent on sleeping. The only movement was a policeman, tapping people with his baton to wake them. "The station is not a place to sleep, Citizens." The chairs had friends in high places.

"I didn't believe you when you told me about that," Martin said, meaning the policeman. "Even after a year in the Union, I didn't believe you." He and Alina had occupied two chairs far back against the wall, where they could see most of the hall and be seen from little of it.

"The highest good is correct public behavior."

They had come by Metro from Dmitri's apartment. They had talked on the way, when there was no one near, about whether they dared do what they knew they were going to do, to take the train to Bryansk that same night to find Yuri. Talking about whether they dared do it was a substitute for talking about whether they would, for they knew they were going to. If they didn't do it this night, too many arguments would bear them down: it was illegal for Martin to leave Moscow without special permission, which he did not have and could not ask for; it was a fool's errand (Bierman's voice, that), or one that demanded special training (Bierman's voice again) or detailed planning (yet again). But they knew they were going because the chance might never come again. As it was, events had conspired for them. It was Friday night—Saturday morning now. Martin would not be missed for more than a day. And, most fortunate of all—and against orders—something had kept him from telling anyone he was going to see Alina. It was a day when he could vanish and, with luck, not be missed.

"How can Dmitri live alone, so high up, with an elevator that doesn't work?" Martin asked, thinking back over the evening past now that, for the first time, he had time to think.

"He can't," Alina said. "But he doesn't have a choice. He inherited this apartment. He grew up there, with his parents and his family, and he'd never find another as good."

"There must be a thousand as good, for him—"

"No . . . there's no place, not for people with no money. This one, it's his, the state can't take it. It would take years to be assigned someplace else. Another place, he'd be just an illegal renter, if he could afford to rent. He gets seventy rubles a month as pension. For

203

an illegal place, he'd pay a hundred. He can't go; he can barely eat on what he gets."

"Seventy rubles isn't much of a pension for a war hero," he said.

"Seventy rubles isn't much for anyone. As for 'war hero' . . ."

"Didn't he lose his legs in Afghanistan?"

"Yes. He was riding on a tank, and he fell off and it rolled over him. Over his legs. It made as much sense as any other war casualty."

"He said he lost his wife . . ."

"He said a lot of foolish things."

The loudspeaker system announced the departure of the train for Bryansk. She got up and motioned for him to follow. They edged around the hall, avoiding the policeman. Martin hoped he didn't look too foreign, even in his old Soviet suit and shoes. "Keep your mouth shut," Alina told him. "We'll hope for the best."

He kept his mouth shut as they found their car. The conductress standing at the steps, a round-cheeked, motherly woman of fifty with two gold teeth, pointed them to their compartment. Alina had bought tickets in a two-person first-class compartment. It was only five hours to Bryansk, but their conductress had pulled down the upper bunk and made it and the seat into beds. They were traveling without luggage; but people often came into Moscow from Bryansk for a day of shopping or visits, so there was nothing suspicious in that. Still, he felt better after he closed the compartment door and drew the curtain on its window.

The train jolted out of the station on time and rolled at a walking pace through sleeping Moscow. It was the brief hour of near-darkness. To save electricity, the street lights had been turned off in all the back streets, and the city was only a collection of dark square shapes, like a giant village draped over the banks of the river Moskva.

There was a tap at their compartment door. It was the conductress, come to look at their tickets. "Do you want tea?" she asked Martin, ignoring Alina. He didn't think he could play dumb, so he answered: "No. We'll sleep a little."

Her gold teeth added a friendly wink to her smile. "Our beds are comfortable. And not too narrow for two." Alina blushed, and the conductress laughed. "It's wonderful to be on a train with a handsome man, dear." She slid the door shut again.

"I don't know about a handsome man, but it certainly is wonderful to be on a train with a handsome woman," Martin said.

"Don't get any ideas," Alina told him. "You're not getting me into bed with the romance of your profession. It isn't even your profession."

"My profession is culture," Martin answered. "There's nothing more romantic than that. Why, I'm the confidant of great writers of two languages! Three, if you count my lousy French. Any actress should be moved by that."

She didn't say anything, but busied herself with arranging the blankets on the top bunk. He took it that she intended to sleep there. "You and your writers can go out into the corridor," she said. "I'm going to get undressed and get into bed. When I knock on the wall you can come back in. Leave them outside. Especially the French ones."

"What do I do? Undress in the hall?"

"You can undress in here after I'm in bed. I won't peek."

"That's what I was afraid of."

"Get out."

He stood in the corridor and watched the southwest Moscow suburbs slide by—tall white apartment towers spaced far apart in a vast emptiness that in the first dim light might have been a park, though he knew day would show it to be wasteland. Already at 3:00 A.M. he could make out people walking, workers trudging to the Metro a kilometer or two distant to ride to early jobs. The spacing of the buildings was intended to preserve natural surroundings, he supposed; but it hadn't done that. It had only separated people from one another and sprawled the city over more and more ground. It was mere empty space—not an amenity, but a desert to be crossed on foot. It was a Los Angeles without cars.

The train was moving a little faster now, with a steady click at the rail joints.

Alina knocked on the wall, but Martin stayed where he was, watching Russia. The apartment buildings ended abruptly, and then there were suddenly little clusters of houses—old villages that had not yet been razed to make way for modern living. They clung to the banks of little streams with white ducks asleep on the water. In the damp summer foredawn, the warm houses steamed like cattle dozing in a meadow.

The conductress came up the corridor. She had the easy air of an owner in possession. "Can I get you anything, Man?" she asked, using the only informal way of addressing him left since the Soviets had destroyed the old title "Mister."

"No, I'll just watch the land a little and then get some sleep."

205

"Men aren't what they used to be," she said. "My husband, though he's dead now, if he'd been off with a *dyevochka* like the one in there"—she nodded to Martin's compartment—"I'd have had heartburn for a week with the thought of it. Apparently, she's your wife."

Martin liked the woman's friendly impertinence, so typical of Russian women, ready to talk about personal matters—yours or theirs—on the slightest acquaintance. Still, he had to avoid talking too much. "She's tired," he said.

"You don't know much about women. The way she was looking at you? Hah!" She nudged him toward the compartment door.

He stayed at the window until she went on to her own little room with its samovar and travel supplies, and then he slid the door open and entered the compartment quietly. Alina had turned off the light, but the early dawn was coming in the window. He started to undress with his back to the beds. He hung his coat on the hanger on the opposite wall and put his shirt and tie over it.

"What was she asking you about?" Alina asked behind him. "You must be careful talking; people will know you're a foreigner."

"She wasn't asking anything," Martin answered. "She's a true Russian woman: she was giving advice."

"Don't be too smart. What was she advising you?"

"She suggested that you had been looking at me with lust in your eyes."

He heard her turn over to face him. "Like all foreigners, you're a liar! The Party warned us about you!" Her tone of voice, however, did not make this a very heavy accusation.

"It's God's truth." He turned around so that she could see him cross his heart, Orthodox-style.

She looked out from the darkness of the upper bunk like a cat in its lair. Her face, just at the level of his, was only inches away. Her eyes were darker than the night around her.

He leaned forward and put his arms on the edge of her bunk and rested his chin on them. "She also accused me of insufficient manliness for leaving a girl like you alone in here."

"You're a foreign liar." She added after a moment, "What is 'a girl like me'?"

"A beautiful brave woman who makes a man's heart turn to mush."

"I see now why they warned us. A foreign liar with a sweet tongue."

He leaned closer and touched his lips to hers. It was not a kiss, really, only a touch, but she drew back—only an inch, but out of contact. "No," she said. It was only a whisper. Was there finality to it?

He sat down on the edge of the lower bunk and took off his trousers and laid them on the table at the window and stretched out on the bunk and covered himself with the blanket—the combination sheet and blanket found everywhere in Russia, a sheet made into a pocket with a blanket stuffed inside. The sheet was white and fresh and cool. He watched the dawn slowly brighten the window. After a little while he heard her voice from above him: "Sweet dreams, Benjamin." He doubted he was going to sleep; but eventually he did.

· 38 ·

Saturday, June 3, 1989
4 A.M.
New Ryazan Street

DAWN TOOK A LONG TIME COMING THROUGH DMITRI'S WINDOW. THE WINDOW had not been washed in years, except for the efforts of the rain, and the pattern of overlapping gray streaks made gloomy suggestions about even the clearest dawn. It did not help that the window looked out onto a gray dirty courtyard. The courtyard was designed as a playground for the children who lived in the complex; but it was so deep and narrow that only in midsummer did the sun penetrate to the bottom of it, and the rest of the year it was cold and abandoned. Also, a spring dawn in Moscow was a complicated affair, a sort of propaganda campaign that began announcing great things long before any result was evident—and then too often the only result was cloudy confusion.

Dmitri poured himself another hundred grams of vodka.

Drinking alone was no fun, but he had no visitors, and it was better than not drinking alone.

He knocked back the vodka and set the glass down hard on the table, which had jumped up to meet the glass. The bang of the glass on the table echoed down the hall. After a minute it echoed again,

207

and then he realized that the echo was someone knocking on his door.

He listened, waiting to see if it would happen again. When it did, he rolled his cart as quietly as possible out into the hall and up to the door, where he sat waiting. When the knock came again he decided it must be Alina. He opened the door.

There were two men in the hall. They weren't his usual KGB guardians. The one with the dark, lean face and the mustache stepped forward to keep him from closing the door again. The other asked, "Where did your friends go?"

Dmitri answered, with unfeigned sadness, "Into the void, mostly. That's the problem, being atheist, isn't it? Not only is there nothing to look forward to, there's nothing for friends to fasten on but memory."

"Don't be a wiseass," the man said. "The American and the woman: where were they going?"

Dmitri tried to slam the door in spite of the one blocking it, but he had nothing to brace against, and so he simply spun in a circle on his board. He stopped with each of the men holding one of his arms. The spin added to the vodka made him want to vomit. One of the men kicked the door shut. "It would be less painful for you and for us if you tell us now," he said. "But especially for you." Dmitri tried to shout, but the dark man clamped a hand over his mouth. "Being an afghanyets"—the word meant Afghan War veteran—"you've probably heard stories about what the Afghans did to captured Russians," he suggested. "You should consider them to be true, and think about what to do. Now, do you want to cooperate? Nod for yes."

Dmitri nodded. When the hand was taken from his mouth, he shouted as loud as he could for help. Even before he felt the first blow he reflected sadly that the one thing he had always liked about this apartment, alone at the top of the stairs, was that he never heard his neighbors.

· 39 ·

Saturday, June 3, 1989
6 A.M.
Lenin Prospect

CHANTURIA JOLTED AWAKE. CLOUDS OF VAPOR HAD ROLLED THROUGH HIS sleep, but he opened his eyes to the clear white dawn filling his Moscow apartment. "What?" he demanded. He didn't know whom he demanded it of.

"Telephone," Tanya said sleepily. The curve of her side rose beside him under the blanket, sleek as a beached seal. She didn't move. The phone rang again. He reached across her to pick it up.

"It's Belkin," the telephone said. "I have a report we should discuss."

"Yes, all right. At the office." He dropped the receiver back and stayed slumped across Tanya.

"Work again?" she asked.

"Yes."

"Tell them where to put it. The damn Constitution guarantees no more than forty-two hours a week."

"Our socialist Constitution guarantees a lot of things." He got up scratching himself thoughtfully and wandered toward the bathroom. Whatever Belkin had, it must be important to call him at home.

For the center of secret knowledge of a world empire, the KGB headquarters was quiet on Saturday morning. There were few names on the roster when Chanturia signed in, and Belkin's wasn't one of them.

He spread some papers on his desk to look busy, and within a few minutes Belkin looked in. He was carrying two cups of tea.

"You're not here," Chanturia said. "According to the roster."

"Sometimes I forget to sign in," Belkin said.

"How do you get the guard to permit that?"

"Distract him with food. He's like any other watchdog."

209

The tea was too hot to drink. Chanturia blew on it. "You didn't give him all the cookies, did you?"

"No—no cookies this morning."

"I was afraid of that. Well, what's going on?"

"Our *lastochka* is flying." The word meant "swallow." Belkin had turned Martin's name into the name of the most similar bird that Russian had to offer. But ironically, the word could also be used as a term of endearment—"darling." "Our darling is flying." Belkin loved that sort of thing. The poetry of the secret community.

Ordinarily Chanturia didn't care for code words and tried to forget them promptly; but this one he recognized. "Migrating?"

"A short flight. He had company."

"Who?"

"We don't know the name yet. A very beautiful blond Russian woman. She bought them tickets on the train to Bryansk."

"When?"

"This morning. They'll nearly be there by now."

Now what the hell was this? "Does he have permission?"

"Not that I can find. But you know how the records are. I didn't want to make too big a deal of it. Who knows who'll be interested."

"Yes, you're right." His tea had cooled enough to drink. He sipped at it. "This place needs cookies on Saturday morning," he complained. "How did we get onto this?"

"Good planning, of course. But mostly luck. Well, all luck, to be truthful. The Tatar was assigned to watch a dissident because somebody in another section was sick. The Tatar recognized Swallow coming out of the dissident's apartment with a woman and followed them."

"Dissidents! *Now* what's going on? Who's the dissident?"

"His name's Dmitri Kassin. I've checked what I can without asking any direct questions. He's some nut-case Afghan veteran going on about medical care. I'm afraid to ask too many questions of the other section."

"You should be. Did the Tatar make a report?"

"He called me first. I told him I'd report it. I sent him back to watch the dissident. He didn't even tell anybody he'd been gone. Don't worry. The Tatar doesn't ask questions."

"Well done. Do we have any idea who the woman is?"

"Not yet. It was only early this morning. Should we question the dissident?"

"No. We'd have to explain that to the section he belongs to. The fewer people who know about this the better." He thought for a minute. "Did they buy return tickets?"

"Yes. But didn't make a reservation to return."

"You'll watch the trains from Bryansk?"

"That's being done."

"How many people?"

"Two, of course. They might return separately."

"*Molodyets*. Did you assign the right people?"

"People with good eyes and no brain. They won't ask any questions we don't want them to ask."

"All right. You'll have Swallow and the girl followed when either of them returns."

"Of course."

"Did you put someone on them at Bryansk? Or ask the train crew to report where they get off? They may not go to Bryansk. Maybe they'll get off at Moscow Commodities and come back to town."

"The train's an express. It doesn't stop until Bryansk. But I thought it was too dangerous to try to have them followed at Bryansk." He was sad-eyed at this one defeat. "We could possibly still do it. Do you know anyone you trust at Bryansk?"

"No. My friend Mashkin used to be there. We trained together. But he's long gone. No, you're right: it's too dangerous. Especially if they learned he's American. It would surely raise questions. No, we'll have to find them when they come back."

· IV ·

THE OLD HELL-RAISER

· 40 ·

Saturday, June 3, 1989
7:45 A.M.
Bryansk

BY THE TIME THEY GOT DOWN FROM THE TRAIN IN BRYANSK, THE SUN WAS already high, although it was not yet eight in the morning. Sunshine had driven the dew from the concrete station platforms; but the air was still full of a cool silver haze that turned everything more than a mile away into a single blue distance. Silver air and a blue world. The conductress had got out a step stool for her passengers to use in getting down from the car. She winked at Martin as he stepped down. She said to Alina, "I wish I still had a handsome man like yours to travel with." Alina walked off ahead of him. When he caught up to her, she was smiling but wouldn't look at him. "Foreigners don't always lie," he said after a while.

"Not always."

"Usually."

"But not always."

She asked directions from a cab driver, and they walked to a bus stop and took a city bus to the intercity terminal. There they ate cabbage-filled *pirogi* and drank tea while they waited for a country bus. By now it was near ten and the air was becoming hot.

The haze dissipated with the afternoon heat and the world turned from blue to green, with vast yellow swatches where the winter wheat was already ripening.

215

The country bus groaned like another aged Soviet worker as it climbed slowly up the long, low hills and eased gingerly down the other side. Whenever the driver shifted down to a lower gear for the hills, the bus belched a cloud of disagreeable black oily smoke that swirled for a long time in one spot, like an unpleasant memory.

"Stary Buyan!" the driver called out. "Any hell-raisers on board, this is your stop." This was the driver's little joke: the name Stary Buyan meant "old hell-raiser."

They stood in the street, waiting for the stink and dust of the bus to settle out of the air, and then looked around. "Where might Uncle Fedya live?" Alina wondered. But there was not much for wonder to focus on: Stary Buyan was a clearing in the forest. There were only five houses, three of them ramshackle log affairs that looked never to have been painted, and the other two also built of logs but painted the bright chrome-yellow that was the color most recently offered in the Bryansk universal store. All of the houses had large yards fenced with wooden rails, and four of the yards were filled with vegetable gardens that looked fit to overcome the inhabitants; the fifth was a jungle of weeds. "I know where I hope it isn't," Martin said; "but it shouldn't be hard to find out." But he had a bad feeling that he knew where Uncle Fedya lived. At four of the five houses, women had come into the yard to take in the show as the bus stopped, and in one of them two young children as well. At the fifth, the house with no garden, no one had come out.

Alina walked to the youngest woman, the one with the two children, and asked after Feodor Nikolayevich. "Oh, Uncle Fedya!" the woman said. "He lives over there," shading her eyes with one hand and turning to point with the other to the fifth house. When she lifted her arm, the swell of her dress made it clear she was pregnant. Martin thought at first that the woman must be Dmitri's cousin, or his sister; but then it appeared that "Uncle Fedya" was just a name that everyone there used for Feodor, son of Nikolai. "He's there. Bang on the door until he answers. Maria Pavlovna, she's there too, poor thing; but she won't often answer. And their nephew, Dima, I think he's gone to the forest. I saw him leave early this morning."

"Dima?" Alina asked.

"Yes, he's their nephew, he came this winter to stay with them. It's kind of him. Not many people would put up with them." She added quickly, "Not that they're bad neighbors. Really, they're sweet people." It was obvious that she thought—now that she thought at all—that she was probably speaking to other relatives of Uncle Fedya. Who else would come to Stary Buyan to visit?

The gate to Uncle Fedya's garden was off its hinges. It leaned against the fence to close the opening. A few chickens scratched unhappily along the edge of the weeds, all the time eyeing the riches of the gardens next door. Martin lifted the gate to one side and then set it back in place behind them.

The door was of dry boards, so warped and cracked that from the inside you could see winter through them. Alina knocked politely. There was no answer. She knocked several times. Martin saw the neighbor woman watching them. She grinned at him and shook her fist. "Harder," Martin said. Alina banged on the door.

"Who in the hell's that?" demanded a voice not entirely steady on its feet. Rather than answer, Alina banged again, and shortly the door opened and an old man stared out at them, white-faced as if he had not yet seen summer. "Who are you?"

"Feodor Nikolayevich?" she asked.

"I doubt it. *I'm* Feodor Nikola'ich. So probably you're not." His breath was rich with recycled alcohol.

"I'm Alina Obraz," she said. "I'm looking for my brother Yuri. Is he staying here?"

"Yuri? No Yuri's here. Dima, my nephew, he's here. He's not here, but he's here, so to speak. He's out in the forest."

"May we wait for him?"

It seemed that this concept took a while to penetrate to the active part of his brain. "Wait? Why wait? Wait where?" He looked her over closely; but even then, courtesy could not get the better of whatever caution or confusion had charge of his brain. He seemed to see Martin only as an afterthought. "Who's this?" he said to Alina.

"A friend of Yuri's—my brother's. His name is Benjamin Martin. He's American."

The old man staggered back a step. Some miscalculation in the step made it almost a small dance. "American? I've met Americans! In the war, my unit fought all the way to Berlin, and there we met— Americans! The Army of the United States of America! You're American? Come in, please!"

Alina looked from Martin to the old man and back, astonished. Martin shrugged. "The brotherhood of arms is a powerful influence," he said.

The room the old man let them into was a tiny parlor furnished with an upholstered bench facing a pair of chairs. To one side of these, a fireplace full of cobwebs challenged the guest to name the year in which it last held a fire. "Wait, wait," he said. "There'll be tea." He pointed out the bench to them and went on through a doorway to the back of the house, calling out, "Marusya! Marusya, company! Where's the teapot?"

"Well!" Alina said. She seemed not to know what else to say.

The old man popped back through the door. "And a little little drink," he said to Martin. "Of course. For our meeting."

"Of course," Martin agreed.

"Of course." The old man vanished again.

"Of course," Alina said to Martin.

"The brotherhood of arms," Martin said.

The old man came back into the room. He did not have tea, but he had an unlabeled bottle and a glass. He held the bottle up for Martin to see. "A nice little drink, a sweet little drink, for our meeting." He pulled the cork with his teeth, poured out a glass of the liquor full to the brim, handed the glass to Martin, took the cork out of his mouth with the hand that was now free, and held the bottle up in toast: "To my American colleagues! And," he added, "to our meeting!"

"Certainly, to your colleagues. And to our meeting."

Even though he only sipped it, the vodka burned its way down inside Martin. He tried not to gag, saw Alina smiling a tender little smile at him, saw the old man pull a long drink directly from the bottle and then point the bottle at him: "Good, eh? Made it myself. Secret recipe. Have another." He refilled the glass, not seeming to notice how little was gone from it. He poured until it overflowed. "To your health!" He took another long pull at the bottle. He noticed this time how little Martin had drunk. "What's wrong?" he asked, concerned. "Has it gone off? I'll get another bottle."

"No, no, it's perfect," Martin answered. "It's just . . ."

"Perfect!" The old man beamed. "Well, then . . . to the vodka!" While taking another pull at the bottle, he watched Martin out of the side of his eye to see that justice was done to his concoction. He wiped his mouth with the back of his sleeve. "Perfect! Yes, it is good, isn't it? Perfect!"

Martin found that the vodka burned less now that the first shock was over. Or perhaps his tongue had died. Even now he thought he could feel brain cells winking out one by one like stars at the death of the universe.

The old man sat down suddenly on one of the chairs opposite Martin and Alina—an act that was a somewhat controlled fall ending mostly on the chair. He leaned forward confidentially. "When I was in the army," he said, "the Americans I met were not extremely good drinkers. I can see that you, however, are a man of substance. A man who has perfected his taste through long practice. Perfect!" He took another swig from the bottle, unencumbered by a toast.

Alina laid a hand on Martin's arm, as if to keep him from proposing the toast he had no intention of proposing. "About your nephew, Dima," she said to Uncle Fedya.

"Dima? Who . . . ? Oh, yes. Dima." He waved a hand grandly at the forest surrounding them. "Out. He's out . . . there." He said to Martin, "It was May of 1945, when our company took Berlin. We drove to the very back wall of the whatchamacallit, Hitler's own house, and there the Americans were, coming from the other direction. And that was the end of the war, you see. We had smashed the Fascists flat, until there was nothing left to smash. There was fire everywhere, and smoke, and the smell of burning meat. I'll never forget it. It was Germans, burning in their houses. I'll bet you've never smelled that, American though you are. No, those days are gone now. But it was sweet then, victory was. To victory!" He raised his bottle, but the bottle was empty. "I'll be right back," he whispered, as if conspiracy was required, and got to his feet and crossed the room like a man climbing the deck of a ship in heavy seas.

"Now what?" Martin asked.

"God knows. You're not helping. Can't you stop drinking that stuff?"

"I'm afraid to stop. If I stop, it'll overwhelm me. As long as I keep drinking, I can stay ahead of it."

"You're making no sense." She took his glass and went to the front door and threw the rest of the vodka into the yard. The chickens came running from all sides of the yard, but then backed away and scattered again.

She handed the glass back to Martin. "You think he hasn't got more?" Martin asked. "I'll bet he's been stockpiling this stuff since 1945, waiting for the next American to show his face."

She ignored him. "I wonder where Marusya is, or who?"

"The unseen mystery, Maria Pavlovna."

"I'm going to go look," Alina said; but Uncle Fedya came back. He had a fresh bottle in hand, still corked, but now his face was ash-gray and he dragged his right foot as he walked. "Got to . . . rest a little," he said, sitting down heavily. "Then we'll go again."

"Go where?" Alina asked.

Uncle Fedya held up the bottle.

"No," she said. "Uncle Fedya, we need to speak with Dima. Or with Yuri."

Fedya waved his hand, a motion as if chasing flies from his face. "He'll be back. Plenty of time for a drink." He leaned back in the chair, his head fell forward, and he was asleep.

Alina got up and went through the door where Uncle Fedya had kept disappearing. In a moment Martin heard voices. Uncle Fedya showed no signs of coming back to life, so Martin followed after Alina.

The door opened into a bigger room, perhaps four meters square. A single back window looked into the forest, where night was already gathering among the trees, although evening sun still shone through the window. The glare from the window made it hard to see anything in the room for a few seconds. As his eyes adjusted, Martin saw that the room was dominated by a built-in Russian brick stove with an iron top, made both for cooking and for heating. The stove took up more than a fourth of the room. The only other furniture was a bare table and two chairs, and in one of the chairs was a woman dressed all in black, so that she seemed little more than a part of the darkness in the room.

Although Alina was talking to her, the woman didn't move or even look around. She was frail and shrunken as a dried cornstalk. She had short gray hair that had been cropped any old way to avoid the trouble of putting it up: it stuck out in odd tufts and bunches around her ears and neck. She must once have been a large woman, for now flaps of skin hung under her chin, as baggy as her black, long-sleeved dress. She wore her skin exactly the way she wore the dress—like something from another life that no longer fit her but was still in use because it was still hanging around. But her eyes, her luminous eyes seemed too large, too alive, for her withered face.

"Are you Maria Pavlovna?" Alina was saying; but the woman had no answer. As Martin came into the room, Alina said, "This is Benjamin Martin. He's an American." The woman turned her face then. She fixed her eyes on Martin and said with great determination, as if saying it were the most important thing in the world, as if delivering a message of great urgency, "I don't know you."

"I'm Benjamin Martin," he said. "The American."

"I don't know any Americans," she said. She turned her face back to Alina. "What should we be doing now?"

"Well, I don't know," Alina said. "What do you want to do now?"

"I don't know. What should we be doing?"

"Maybe we should be looking for Dima," Alina suggested. "Do you know where Dima is?"

"I don't know Dima. Do I know Dima?"

"I don't know. Do you know Dima?"

"I don't know Dima."

"I don't think she knows Dima," Martin said. He asked her, "Do you know Yuri?"

"I don't know Yuri."

"I don't think she knows Yuri either." He asked her, "Who *do* you know?"

She puzzled at this for quite a while. "I don't know. What should we be doing now?"

"We should be looking for Yuri," Martin said. "But I'll be damned if I know how to do that. Go back to the neighbor woman, maybe."

"Maybe if you stay right where you are, he'll come to you," a man's voice said. Both Martin and Alina spun around, startled. A bearded man in a broad-brimmed hat was standing in the kitchen door behind them. In his hands he had an old double-barreled, outside-hammer shotgun that was pointed at Martin.

"Yura!" Alina cried. Her leaping embrace knocked the hat to the floor and jostled the shotgun.

"Be careful with that thing!" Martin demanded. He stepped forward and pushed the gun barrels aside.

The man pushed off Alina's embrace and stepped back to free his gun. "Alya, what are you doing here? Who's this?" He gestured with the gun, again aimed at Martin. He seemed ready to retreat through the door, or to do something wild with the gun.

"He's a friend, Yura. He's American."

"CIA?" Yuri asked.

"No," Alina said.

"Yes," Martin said at the same time.

"Which is it?" Yuri demanded, clutching the gun.

"Temporarily CIA," Martin said. "I was sent to look for you." If this wasn't quite true, at least it would save explanations. "Now, would it be too much to ask of you to point that somewhere else?"

Yuri turned the gun toward the ceiling, but kept it ready.

"I don't understand what we're doing," the old woman said. "What should we be doing?" Her plaintive cry was like the calling of distant crows down the wind, just a sound without human meaning. She hardly moved as she said it, did not look at anyone, or at what they were doing.

· 41 ·

Saturday, June 3, 1989
Evening
Stary Buyan

"THAT WAS THE FIRST REAL MEAL I'VE HAD IN SIX MONTHS, EXCEPT FOR what Katya cooks for me sometimes," Yuri said. Alina had cooked the supper—potato pancakes and a rabbit in sour cream. The rabbit Yuri had shot at the edge of a clearing that day. The three of them sat at the table. Maria Pavlovna, the old woman, occupied the fourth chair but out in the middle of the room, where she preferred to sit, and where Alina had fed her a bite at a time. Uncle Fedya was still stretched out on the bench in the sitting room, his feet hanging over at one end and his head at the other. His head drooped backward almost to the floor, so that his taut neck muscles dragged his mouth open. His snores echoed from the bare log walls.

"Is Katya the woman next door?" Alina asked.

Yuri nodded. "Her husband objects to her cooking for me, though; so it's been a slim six months. Whatever she can fix at lunchtime when he's too far afield to get back. Otherwise, we eat what I cook. Uncle Fedya's always drunk, and Maria Pavlovna is crazy."

"I don't understand what he means," Maria Pavlovna said, apparently to someone other than their group, although no one else was there.

"He means, old fartress, that you're crazy," Yuri said to her. Seeing the shock on Alina's face, he said, "Don't worry about her. She doesn't understand anything, and wouldn't remember it in two minutes if she did. Look here," he said to the old woman by way of demonstration. "What did I just call you?"

Her brows furrowed, then the fit of concentration passed on. "What are we supposed to be doing?" she asked.

"It's a good question," Martin said. "We're supposed to be finding Yuri. And now that we've found him, we're supposed to be finding out what he knows."

"What I know about what?" Yuri asked.

"What happened the night you were supposed to meet your sister and my friend Hutchins, for one thing."

"Well, as I wasn't there, maybe you should tell me."

"What happened was Hutchins was killed and the KGB was set after your sister," Martin said angrily. "So maybe you should tell me why you weren't there."

"I decided not to go."

"What was it that made you decide not to go?"

"I went to visit my friend Dmitri. That's all."

"Dima said you came there late that night," Alina said.

"Late that night and scared," Martin said.

"Dima squealed on me easy enough, the coward."

"Dima told your sister where you were, for God's sake!" Martin said. "It's not as if he'd turned you over to the KGB!"

"Sure, he would tell Alya, wouldn't he? There's nothing Dima wouldn't do for Alya; and nothing Alya would do for him. Dima was always sick for love of Alya; did she tell you that, American?"

"Keep your mouth shut, Yuri," Alya said. "It's got nothing to do with Dima, what we're here for."

"I'm not blind," Martin said. "It's not hard to figure out."

"And did she tell you what she did to him, while he and I were serving the Motherland in fuck-your-mother Afghanistan? Did she tell you she married another man, when he knew Dima would try to kill himself when he heard of it?"

"God damn you, Yuri!" Alina shouted. "I don't owe my life to Dmitri! I didn't ask him to fall in love with me! I don't have to jump just because he says he loves me!"

"The least you could have done is marry someone worthwhile. That prick Obraz who married you for a Moscow address—what was he?"

"I'm not going to justify my life to you, Yuri. If I made a mistake in my marriage, it hurt me more than it ever will you. Or Dima. So stay out of my troubles. I'll take care of them myself."

"Tell me what happened to you that night, Yuri," Martin said. He saw what Yuri was trying to do, and he wasn't going to let it happen.

"I don't have to tell you anything."

"No, you don't have to. But you wanted something from Hutchins. You wanted money and you wanted a way out of the country. I can get that for you—if you make it worth my while."

"How much money?" Yuri said, suddenly all business.

"I don't know. It depends on what you're going to tell me."

"Oh. And then when you know, suddenly it's worth nothing?"

"Well, I'm not giving cash in advance; so you'll have to trust me."

"What I know would be worth a lot."

"What's a lot?"

Yuri looked at him for a moment. "A million dollars." Martin had a feeling he had picked the number without any plan, because it sounded big.

"That's a lot, all right."

"And a way out of the country. A way to America, and protection there."

"I'd have to ask. It's not easy to arrange." Martin supposed this must be true. He couldn't imagine himself how it would be done. But that was what Bierman got paid for. Bierman would have an orgasm thinking about it.

"All right," Yuri said. "I'll tell you half. A million dollars and out of the country. You get the other half when I'm out."

"I don't have authority to make the deal. I can relay your offer. That's all. But news six months old is pretty stale."

"This news isn't stale. They'll want it, when they hear what it's about." Yuri was playing the big shot now, and he enjoyed it. It was how Yuri saw himself. Not stuck in a cabin in the Russian forest, but making deals that carried a million-dollar tag.

"What's it about?"

"Plutonium."

Martin knew Yuri was right: this was going to catch Bierman's attention. "Plutonium?"

"The people I worked for . . ." Yuri corrected himself: "The people I worked with were in many lines of business. Have you heard of Semipalatinsk?"

"Yes. Soviet nuclear tests." That was the limit of Martin's knowledge, and no more than anyone could read in the papers; but it seemed to satisfy Yuri, who nodded.

"About two years ago, there was very big excitement in the Semipalatinsk region. Big but quiet excitement. You want to know why they kept it quiet? It was because they'd have been embarrassed to admit that a sizable amount of nuclear material was found to be unaccounted for. Not just nuclear-reactor stuff, either—weapons-grade enriched plutonium. It was never found. Your people can probably confirm this if they're as active as the KGB always claims. In fact, I heard that the KGB were afraid that the CIA had found a way to get the material; but I know this wasn't so."

"How do you know?"

"My colleagues have it."

" 'Colleagues.' That's good. They sound like lawyers. So what do your 'colleagues' plan to do with enriched plutonium? It's not much good unless you want to make a bomb."

"Exactly."

"The Mafia?" Alina said. "What would they do with a nuclear bomb? Extort money? That's crazy. The Mafia may think they're tough; but they don't have an army. They'd be hunted down to the last man."

"Of course they would," Yuri said. "Although not all of them are smart enough to know it. But the Old Man sure was."

"Who is the Old Man?" Martin asked.

"Never mind that. He's somebody even smarter than you. Smart enough to know what to do with the stuff. And I know too. And I know the United States would want to know. That's why it's worth a million dollars. A million and out."

"Yuri, this is scandalous!" Alina said. "If what you're saying is true, you should tell what you know at once! This is the fate of thousands of people you're talking about! Maybe millions!"

"I know it is. That's why it's worth a million dollars. A million people—that's only a dollar a nose. Maybe I should raise my price."

"We should just turn you in to the KGB!" Alina said.

Yuri smiled. "That's not a good idea. I was told the KGB may be in on it."

"Well, I'm getting out of here," Alina said. "I don't have to listen to this." She banged out of the kitchen door, going straight for the woods that began not ten steps away. Martin called to her, but she didn't stop. When she disappeared among the trees, he started after her. "We'll be back," he called back to Yuri. "This isn't over."

What should I be doing? Should I be doing something? The voice of old Maria Pavlovna, like a withered conscience, followed him.

· 42 ·

Saturday, June 3, 1989
Late Evening
Stary Buyan

ON THE HILL ABOVE STARY BUYAN WAS A BASSWOOD GROVE, AND IN IT ON summer nights a nightingale sang. Most nights the grove was deserted except for the nightingale, for it was a long way from anywhere to Stary Buyan, and few people lived there.

Martin caught Alina halfway up the hill; and although she wouldn't talk to him, she let him walk with her. She gradually slowed; and then, amid the thorns of a raspberry thicket, she let him take her hand and help her.

They came to the basswood grove before the end of daylight. The bird was trying a few varied notes; but they were not ready yet to listen.

"I'm ashamed that Yura's my brother," Alina said. "If what he says is true."

"Why would he lie?"

"He'd lie for the money. But I don't think he is lying. That's the shame. He's refusing to tell a terrible secret, except for money. But I'm afraid he was always that way: his own advantage was the most important thing to him." She moved closer to him as they walked. "What if the KGB is in it?" she said.

"I don't know. What if? We haven't told them anything. Mainly because we had nothing to tell. Now we do; but we still can't. It's as if nothing's changed."

She sat down at the foot of a basswood tree. Its flowers sent a delicate scent into the night air, like the perfume a young girl should wear. "I'm sorry for all the mess," she said. "About my life, I mean— all the emotion, all the . . . It's not as bad as it sounds. Or maybe it is."

"Your brother is a gifted liar."

"No. Or, yes, he is; but not this time. He was telling the truth."

226

"All of it?"

"You mean about Dima?"

He nodded.

"Yes, all of it, I guess. I'm sorry; I didn't want to get you into any of this."

He sat down and leaned against the tree too. It was too small a tree to sit beside her: he was facing half away from her, but one shoulder touched hers. "He said he lost his wife. Did he mean you?"

"Yes. Although we were never married. He was in love with me."

"He *is* in love with you. I knew that already. Anybody could see it. Is that your fault?"

She didn't move her shoulder away from his. "Dima's in love with me. He's a sweet person. He'd do anything for me. I don't love him. I can't stand to see him, with love for me eating away at him. He thinks I can't stand to see him because of his legs . . ."

"Were you going to marry him? Before that?"

"No. I was never going to marry him. But I never had the heart just to tell him that. So he built his own castles. He and Yuri had to go off to the army. I married somebody else, the wrong person . . . Yuri told you all about that."

"Somebody who needed a Moscow residence permit."

"It wasn't quite that way. Yuri thought so, because that's the way Yuri thinks. It's what he would have done."

"You said you were separated from your husband?"

"Yes."

"Not divorced?"

"No. We just never got around to it. I didn't have the energy to do it. Is it all right if we don't talk about my marriage?"

"It's all right if we don't talk about any of this."

"Some of what Yuri said is true, though. In part, I did get married so that I wouldn't have to tell Dima I couldn't marry him. I haven't got divorced so I won't have to tell Dima I won't marry him."

"So let's not talk about your marriage."

"Maybe if you hear all the bad things at once, we'll have them all out, and I won't have to be afraid what else you might hear about me."

"In that case, is there anything else you'd like to confess?"

"Don't laugh at me, please."

"Believe me, I'm not."

"I think it's true that Dmitri tried to kill himself, when he heard about my marriage."

227

"Is that when he fell under the tank?"

"Yes."

"I was joking. Was it really?"

"The army said it was an accident. He went to sleep riding on a tank, and fell off. Yuri thinks he tried to kill himself."

"Or so Yuri says?"

"Yes."

"Your brother's a peach."

"He certainly has a stone in his heart." She sighed. "I keep trying to convince myself that I love him because he's my brother. I never quite manage. I only convince myself that I *should* love him."

The bird found a few longer phrases, tried stringing them together in combinations, looking for a song.

"May I ask you something?" she asked.

"Of course."

"Are you . . . married?"

"Me?" He was astonished.

She asked it so hesitantly: what did that mean, he wondered. Questions in Russian had a kind of natural hesitation in the middle—that was how you knew they were questions and not assertions. Was it more than that?

"I . . . I just wondered. What it's like. Your life, I mean. It's hard to imagine a Westerner's life. Do you have a wife here . . . in Moscow?"

"I'm not married."

"Oh."

"I was once. It was a long time ago." Naomi. He could hardly remember her now. She'd had a terrific grasp of eighteenth-century English narrative; but that no longer seemed as important to him as it once had.

"What was she like?"

"Professorial." It was hard to explain about eighteenth-century English narrative.

What was she like? Passionate, when she wasn't being professorial; professorial, when she was done being passionate—which happened more quickly as time went on. After that, she just drifted away, into another time.

"Did you love her?"

"It seemed so at the time." He doubted that Midwestern reticence was going to match up with the Russian love of personal details. He doubted that it would try.

"Are you in love with anyone now?"

"No." *Only once in life* . . . No. Not yet.

There was Mallory. She'd come to visit him for a month in Moscow last summer, but left in a week. After a lifetime of campus socialism, she didn't care to have her convictions measured against the Moscow standard.

The warmth of Alina's shoulder flowed into his. "What do we do now?" Alina asked him.

"Well . . . it's a good opportunity for a little fooling around."

"No—I mean about Yuri's story. Can you really get a million dollars for him?"

"Hell, I don't know. You know this isn't my business. Who knows what the CIA will pay for that kind of information, if they think it's good? Your brother's right: it's worth a lot to keep a nuclear weapon out of the wrong hands."

She said, "This 'fooling around'—what is that?"

"I beg your pardon?"

"I wondered what 'fooling around' means. You don't talk like a Russian."

"Well, it means . . . enjoying each other's company, in particular ways."

"What ways, for example?"

"Well, for instance, my shoulder is touching yours." When he said this, she moved her shoulder away. "You hadn't noticed?"

"Yes . . . I noticed. I thought you didn't." She put her shoulder back against his. "Is that 'fooling around'?"

"Not exactly. But it's a start."

"What comes afterward?"

"Things your mother told you never to do."

"Oh."

"Would you like a demonstration, for example? Just in the cause of international cooperation, of course."

"Yes, all right. For international cooperation."

"Of course. Turn around here, then." She turned to face him. Her face was close to his, as close as it had been on the train. Her eyes were large and dark.

"Is this how it starts?" she asked.

"This is how it starts." He kissed her gently. Her lips were parted. He felt her tongue touch his lips and enter his mouth. She put her arms around him.

The bird was singing. It sang some sad songs and some happy ones. He felt it had been singing for a long time, but he couldn't be sure.

Her breasts were warm against his chest. He cupped one breast in his left hand. She moved against his hand. He clumsily tried to unbutton her shirt, but his left hand was no good for that, and his right hand was bandaged. She kissed his bandaged hand and helped him. There was a little cloth flower on her bra between her breasts. He touched it with his lips. Then he unfastened her bra at the back and pushed it up, and she unbuttoned his shirt and he felt her skin against his. She pushed her breast into the pit of his stomach and moved it in a circle as he kissed her.

"Is this 'fooling around'?" she asked, her lips at his ear.

"Did your mother tell you never to do this?"

"Not specifically."

"You have a liberal-minded mother."

"I think she didn't imagine I would be doing this. She didn't know American customs. How sweet they are."

He put one hand on her leg. She was wearing cardboard-stiff Soviet jeans, but the warmth of her leg came through them. When he slid his hand farther up her leg, she moved to meet it. She swayed her hips gently, thrusting herself against his hand. "I want to make love with you," he said.

"I was hoping you did. I want to make love with you."

They both moved gently, in no hurry to be done. She shuddered against him and started to cry out and bit her hand to keep quiet, and then she moved again, breathing hard, and cried, "Oh, *Lastochka!*" and shuddered again and again, and then he let himself go and she did cry out.

After a while she kissed his neck and moved away from him. It was quite dark. There was a rustle as she put on her clothes. She knelt beside him and kissed him.

They walked slowly, carefully down through the raspberry-filled woods toward Stary Buyan, where there were no lights at all.

They had only a general idea where the village was, but knew that if they kept going downhill, they would at least come out onto the road. Then the only question would be which way to turn. Martin walked ahead to plow a way through the raspberry thorns, while Alina stayed close in his track. Once when they paused she turned him around and pulled his arms around her and kissed him.

"What's that for?" he asked.

"That's for you."

They plunged on. A little way farther, light showed through the trees, and they came out onto the cleared strip of land along the road.

The grass there was deep in dew. They waded the grass and stepped out into the road. "I think we must be west of the village," Martin said. "If we walk east, we'll come to it."

She took his hand. "Let's walk. It'll soon be light."

"We'll need some sleep," he said.

"We won't get much. The bus is at six. It'll be a half hour late; but we should be on the road at five-thirty in case it's a half hour early."

"Soviet scheduling?" he asked.

"Yes. For the convenience of the citizens."

They started up the road, which lay almost white in the moonlight. Martin and Alina walked hand in hand, not talking. Nightingale song like a distant memory drifted down from the hilltop. She squeezed his hand. Then the song faded behind the curve of the hill, and the night was silent except for their footsteps. Even the crickets had fallen still. Sometimes above the summer odors of the forest he could catch the scent of her perfume, still distinct after more than thirty hours.

Martin was listening to the sound of their footsteps come back to them from the trees when behind them he heard another sound. He stopped and turned back, alert.

"What is it?" she asked.

"I don't know. Wait."

They both stood still in the middle of the road, and then it came again—the sound of a car on the road.

"Let's get out of sight." He kept her hand in his and went down through the grass and into the trees on the other side of the road where they would be on the inside of the curve and out of the vehicle's headlights.

Within thirty seconds the machine arrived, rolling slowly and without lights. The only sound was the low rustle of tires: if the driver had not shifted down for a short grade behind them, they would never have heard it.

It was a black Volga. Martin could make out two people in the front seat. He could not tell if anyone was in the back. It vanished around the curve.

"Now *that's* strange," Martin said.

"Who could it be?"

"I can't think of anyone we'd want it to be." He stepped out of the trees and listened carefully, but there was no sound. "All right, let's go on. But we're going to keep to the edge of the woods." They walked on in the grass, the dew soaking through their shoes and pants legs.

Within four hundred meters they rounded the curve, and he was glad they had stayed off the road, for not far ahead the Volga was stopped down in the grass on the other side. It had been turned around and was facing them. Just beyond it was the edge of the clearing in which Stary Buyan stood: the houses loomed dark in the pale moonlight. The closest house was Uncle Fedya's. Martin pushed Alina back into the trees. "I don't think there's anyone in the car," she whispered. "Where could they have gone?"

"I don't think we want to find out." They watched for five minutes, but there was no movement around the Volga. Martin waved his hand, and they moved on slowly among the trees.

They had gone past the Volga and almost as far as the houses when the angry cackling of geese erupted from the darkness. They heard a man shout, then the crash of breaking glass followed at once by a boom that rolled echoing along the valley. Shotgun pellets ripped through the trees over their heads. Martin pulled Alina to the ground behind a tree. There were two soft pops, and then almost at once a *whoof*, not an explosion but the sound of sudden spreading ignition. Martin rolled to look around the tree and saw the whole perimeter of the house engulfed in flames that seemed to start everywhere at once. In one window appeared the silhouette of a man with a shoulder weapon. He raised the weapon. Before he could fire, there were three quick pops, and he fell out of sight behind the windowsill. The sound of running feet came toward them. Feet slapped the road; legs hissed through the grass; and two men crashed in among the trees not ten meters away.

Tree trunks slowly emerged from darkness, tinged with the red glow of the fire; but the light did not reach to the ground where Martin and Alina lay in a pool of shadow behind the bank of the roadway.

The two men had stopped, looking back across the road, their faces now bright in the fireglow. Standing in the low shadow of the roadway, they seemed to be up to their knees in dark water. "Did you get him?" one asked. He shifted uneasily from foot to foot. His face was ruddy in the firelight, marked in bold strokes by a thin black mustache, black brows, black hair.

The other man had a lean dark face that, in profile, looked as if it had been flattened by a blow from a board. "You saw him fall," he said. "He's still in there. He won't be coming out." As he said this he held up one hand. There was a pistol in it, an automatic pistol with what Martin at first thought was a long, ungainly barrel but then realized was a silencer.

"What about the other two?" the first man asked. He did not take his eyes from the burning house.

"There won't be anybody coming out of that." The light was growing rapidly brighter. A sigh of wind moved suddenly in the trees, moving from the forest to feed the fire in the clearing.

"Did Vanka cut off the other side?"

"Yes. Nobody got out."

There were shouts across the road. Martin could not make out the words. Men's voices, two or more, and then a woman screaming.

"Let's go," the first man said. "The peasants are waking up. Let's get out before somebody sees us. Get Vanka moving."

The second man brought up from a belt holster a small two-way radio of the kind carried by Soviet militiamen. He spoke into it, too low for Martin to make out the words.

The two men turned and moved off through the woods in the direction of the car. The first one was limping. Martin wondered if Yuri had got some shot into him before he died.

Martin and Alina lay for what seemed a long time, although it might have been only a few minutes. The light around them grew steadily stronger, as did the air flow in the trees above them. It changed from a breath to a breeze to a hissing wind. "What's happening?" Alina asked.

"The house is burning."

"We've got to go try to get them out—Yuri and the two old people!"

"Stay down. I'll see what it looks like." He hugged the trunk of the tree and drew himself up to his knees as close to the trunk as possible.

Heat struck his face.

He could see the whole village. There were lights in the windows of all the other houses now, but they weren't needed—the roaring blaze lit up the whole village and the edges of the surrounding forest. Fire was boiling from all of the windows, the door, and through cracks in the roof. The fierce heat had set on fire the outbuildings and the weeds in the yard and the trees and part of the wooden fence. It had singed the forest trees closest by, but it had not been enough to set on fire the forest itself nor any of the other houses. There was a small crowd of people over by the next house, perhaps twenty of them, their faces made hollow masks by the glare of the fire. Children ran back and forth, pointing and shouting. The adults stood staring blank-eyed, the women hugging themselves with their arms.

Alina pulled herself up to kneel beside Martin. As she did so, the house shifted, sagged to one side, and then collapsed into itself. A volcano of embers burst skyward in a swirling vortex that rose and rose and seemed never to stop. Children screamed in excitement. Alina made a shuddering intake of breath, close to a sob. The fire had no shape any longer. There still was a fierce towering blaze, but the house no longer existed. Its old dry logs burned with a steady roar. The house had been built long ago of pine logs, and the pitch pockets deep within the logs began exploding, sending out new volleys of sparks. The crowd of neighbors moved back and then suddenly dispersed in four directions as men and women ran to the wells for buckets, to try to wet down their own roofs, to protect their own homes.

Alina tried to pull herself to her feet, but Martin held her arm. "We've got to go help!" she said.

"No. I don't want anyone to see us."

She sank back beside him. "Of course. You're not supposed to be here."

"It's not just that."

"What else?"

"The men who were here—they said 'the other two' didn't get out. I don't think they meant the old people."

"You mean they were after us too."

"We'd better assume that, if we want to stay alive."

He half expected her to fall apart; but she only knelt quietly, leaning against the tree. After a minute, she asked in a steady voice, "Who do you think they were?"

"I don't know. We have two choices."

"The KGB and the Mafia?"

"I'd say so."

"We shouldn't have come. The KGB must have seen us at Dima's apartment. We should have known. All we did was get Yuri killed. And Uncle Fedya and Maria Pavlovna. Not just killed. Burned alive."

He didn't know what he could say. Probably she was right. So he said nothing.

She sat down, drew up her legs and clasped them in her arms, and rested her forehead on her knees. After a while she said, "They didn't think of them at all. They didn't matter to them. They were just . . ." She shrugged. "They were just furniture, or . . ." She began to cry softly at last.

He let her rest a few minutes. Then they started walking away from the village, toward Bryansk, walking at the edge of the woods. When the sky lightened, they came to a small stream where Alina washed off all her makeup: when she was finished there was no longer any trace of tears on her face. He felt exhausted; but she looked rested and fresh as the dawn. He hoped he looked half as good himself.

As they waited, a militia car sped past toward Stary Buyan, its blue lights flashing.

"They're late enough," Alina said.

They chose a resting spot with a clear view of a long stretch of road so they would see the bus far off and could stay out of sight in the forest until it arrived. Six o'clock came and went, the hour when the bus was due in Stary Buyan, only a few minutes drive away. It was nearly seven before it topped the distant rise and slid down toward them, trailing a smog of diesel fumes. When it was half a kilometer away, they climbed up onto the road and waved. The bus came on and came on until they thought it was going to pass by, but at the last moment it slowed and ground to a halt just beyond them.

They had agreed in advance that a good attack was the best way to deflect questions. Alina carried it out. "You're late!" she snapped at the driver. "What are schedules for, if citizens can't rely on them?" The bus was half full of passengers, peasants off for a Sunday in Bryansk, and many of them muttered in agreement. Any group of three or more Russians instantly formed a collective, and every collective had a collective opinion, which most likely was the opinion of its one strongest member.

The driver, a moon-faced man of thirty with protruding dark eyes, protested: "It's not my fault! It's the fire back there, you know!"

"Fire!" an old woman snorted. "He was late before he ever saw that fire."

"What fire?" Alina asked, all curiosity. She certainly *was* an actress, Martin reflected.

The driver grinned, relieved to deflect attack so easily. "Back in Stary Buyan. A house burned in the night. Everybody inside burned up too, they say. Five of them. The old man and woman and their nephew, and two guests."

"And then this driver sat and gossiped about it with the militia for half an hour, while we all stewed," the woman said.

"Ah, you were happy to get off and see the ashes yourself," the driver grinned at her.

"Ashes!" the woman snorted. "Such ashes! They were still too hot to get within ten meters of the walls!"

The driver pounded at the gearshift to get the bus into gear again, and with a profound groan the machine started up one more hill.

· 43 ·

Sunday, June 4, 1989
Late Morning
On the Moscow Train

THE LADY CONDUCTOR WITH THE GOLD TEETH HAD THEIR RAILCAR AGAIN. The train came from Bucharest, but she had gone only to Kiev and stayed over, and now she was on her way home to Moscow. Politely ignoring their disheveled clothing, she said to Martin, "I didn't *think* you lived in Bryansk. Did you have a good visit?"

Alina answered for him: "Yes, we saw our uncle."

"The changes in our country are wonderful," the conductress said to her. "Once you wouldn't have been able to take a foreign husband to Bryansk, dear."

"The changes are certainly wonderful," Martin agreed, but unhappily: he took pride in his Russian and he had never really believed Alina when she warned him that he would be taken for a foreigner.

The seats in their compartment were folded down for daytime use. Martin sank into his, supposing that he intended to sleep sitting up; but Alya had another idea. She made him move and folded the seatback up into its double-berth configuration.

"Would it be all right if I stop playing the strong woman for a while?" she asked, climbing into the top berth. "I don't think I can stay in character any longer."

"I didn't know it was an act."

"If only you knew how hard I've been working. I want just to climb up here and hide."

"I'll stretch out down here." He lay across the seat and closed his eyes.

He didn't expect to sleep, but there was a sudden crash and he struggled from a dream of the house collapsing and found that the train was moving and the crash was the conductress opening the compartment door. While he fumbled for their tickets, she gave him a pitying smile and came back with an armload of bedlinens and showed him how to lock the compartment door from the inside. "Nosy woman," Alina said from the top berth when she was gone.

He sat down again with the pile of linens on his seat. "That's not a charitable thing to say about a woman who's trying to take care of us."

"She's spying on us."

"Why should she be?" Martin asked, although he knew the answer before she gave it.

"It's the way our system works. Everybody spies on everybody."

"Who do you spy on?"

"Nobody. But if they could find me, they'd want me to. To spy on Yuri, to spy on Dima, to spy on you . . ."

It was no comfort that her words reminded him of Bierman, of Bierman's demands that he had never told her about.

"Somebody knew we'd gone to Bryansk," she said. "Somebody knew we got off at Stary Buyan."

"Maybe they found Yuri independently."

"And just happened to come along the night we were there? Do you believe in that much coincidence?"

"No. No, I don't. You're right. Somebody knew. Probably the KGB. They could have seen us at Dmitri's apartment. It was stupid of us to go from there to the train, when we knew he was being watched. Or would he have turned us in?"

"Dima wouldn't do that."

"No? Not even to keep you from me?"

There was a long stillness. Her hand dangled down from the top berth. "I don't know."

He took hold of the hand. "I'm sorry about your brother." He had said nothing before. He had felt then as if it should wait, as if everything had to be concentrated on escape. Now, Bryansk was behind

237

them, and he had a feeling of—not security, certainly, but relief, even if it was founded on nothing.

"I'm sorry too. I wish I could cry more for him. It's terrible to know your brother's dead and no one cares. The most terrible is when you know it's the best thing."

He couldn't argue, so he changed the subject. "Look, she brought us all this bedding. Let me make up a bed for you. You'll sleep better."

"I don't know if I want to sleep. I keep seeing fires. Poor Yura. Poor old people." There was a break in her voice, but she didn't cry.

He unfolded the bed linen and started making up a blanket. "If you want to sleep up there, you'll have to come down while I make your bed," he said.

She slipped down to the floor and started helping him. They spread and tucked in the crisp bottom sheet and stuffed a blanket into the pocket of the top sheet. Her hand touched his again, and her side was against his, and so he turned to her and kissed her, and she returned the kiss. He reached behind him to lock the door and found her hand already on the lock.

She was wonderfully surprising. Before, he had expected her to cower before the fate the system was trying to impose on her, but she had refused to cower. Now she made love with a despairing passion. "*Lastochka!*" she whispered to him. "You're my *lastochka!*"

"Do you know what that means in English?" he whispered back to her. "It's a swallow—a kind of bird. My name in English means a kind of bird, almost the same kind."

"That's good," she said. "That's a good omen."

And when all passion was spent at last, he looked in his heart for the stale mistrust, and examined it. What did he really know about this woman? He lay with her sleeping lightly in his arms in the rocking coach of the Bucharest–Moscow Express, a woman who was sweet and brave and beautiful; and what did he know of her, really? That she had been at the death of Hutchins, and escaped; and now of Yuri? Could she be, still, as Bierman surely would say, a KGB torpedo aimed at him, at all of them? What could he ever hope to know of her, truly, in a country which hid from strangers by reflex, a country in which women conductors knew him on sight for a stranger? How could he ever know?

But, drugged by lack of sleep and the train's motion, at last he fell asleep; and when he woke, he did know. He woke, though it was not morning, recalling the Russian proverb "Morning is wiser," sure in his heart's deep core that he truly loved her, and certain that she was not a faithless woman, and that against the sureness in his heart, the void—mere lack of proof—could not prevail.

· V ·

MOSCOW

· 44 ·

Sunday, June 4, 1989
Evening
Moscow

AS THE TRAIN ROLLED SLOWLY THROUGH MOSCOW'S WESTERN SUBURBS, they spoke for the first time of what to do.

"You can't stay at your apartment," Martin told her. "Whoever it was, KGB or Mafia, we've got to assume that they knew who you are, and that they know where you live. They may think you're dead, but they may come looking for information at your apartment anyway. We don't want them to find out you're still alive. Is there anywhere else you can stay?'

"What about you?" she asked, ignoring his concern for her. "They'll have much less trouble knowing who you are."

"I'll be safe enough at the Embassy," he said. "Maybe the only answer is to get you out of the country. I can ask for asylum for you."

"That doesn't get me out of the country. It only gets me into your Embassy."

"Yes, you're right. And as foreign as I look, you look just that Russian. We can't even get you past the militia at the gate—at least not without some preparation. I could get you some American clothes, and of course you're a whiz at makeup . . ."

"There's another problem with this," she said.

"What's that?"

"I don't want to leave my country."

243

Although he took pride in his sensitivity to things Russian, Martin was startled. It had never occurred to him that anyone faced with a genuine opportunity would refuse to trade the Union for the United States.

She saw the look. "What would I do?" she asked. "I'm an actress. I don't speak English. And my life is here."

"You could be my wife," he said. The words came without premeditation. He had never thought them before that moment.

She sat back, startled, and then smiled and kissed him. "We don't know each other that well yet," she said. "Love should come first, and a little more acquaintance."

"I do love you," he said. "We'll work on the acquaintance."

She lowered her head. "I think I love you too. We will work on the acquaintance. But . . . in the meantime, I'm going to go on living my life."

"How can you do that? Why?"

She shrugged. "It seems to me like living under Stalin. If everyone had refused to cooperate, Stalin would have been nothing. Well, whoever this is, I'm not going to cooperate."

"*Molodyets,*" he said, admiring, and sad, and afraid.

In the early evening they walked arm in arm up Yakornaya Street. At first he tried to hold her hand, but she wouldn't let him. "We don't want to look like foreigners," she said. "Here, this is the way." She slipped her hand under his arm. After a minute, she laughed. "Now we look like an old married couple."

"Someday we'll *be* an old married couple."

"Don't eye it," she said.

"What?"

"I have to turn aside the curse," she said. "If you say something too good, I have to turn aside the curse—the 'eye.' *Nye sglazit.*"

"*Nye sglazit.*"

Against the sun, the leaves of the poplars had the glow of green water, and a blizzard of their drifting cotton filled the air with a shining haze.

They did not see the black Volga automobile that stopped among the lilac bushes half a block behind them, where the dark knobs of old unfallen flowers still hung among the leaves.

They climbed the dark windowless stairs to her apartment. Opening the door was like entry into a new life, the rooms were so full of light.

"Do you want tea?" she asked.

"No. I want you."

"I think that comes after the tea," she said, but she didn't resist when he put his arms around her from behind. He felt the swell of her breasts against his forearms, and when he turned her around she answered his kiss without hesitation.

The air drifting through her bedroom window was sweet with unknown flowers, and the curtain, restless on the breeze, came to touch her face. He ran his fingers over her cheek in the track of the curtain. She smiled without opening her eyes. "You did get me into bed with the romance of your business."

"Is that what it was?"

"No. It was you. I've waited so long for you," she said. "Now you're here. My *lastochka.*"

"*Nye sglazit.*"

"*Nye sglazit.*"

He rose and started to dress.

"Are you going away?" she asked.

"I'll be back soon."

"Where are you going?"

"To my apartment at the Embassy. I'll bring some food, and get a change of clothes. I'll stay tonight here. If you don't mind."

"Of course I don't."

"I don't want to leave you alone tonight. In the morning we can decide what to do next. I think we should move you into the Embassy."

"I've said I don't want to go."

"If you don't, my people will think you're KGB."

"I don't care what they think. Are you going to tell them about us?"

He pondered this. He hadn't even considered what he would do. "I don't think so."

It took Martin a long time to climb the stairs to Alina's apartment. Clutched in each arm he had a bag of groceries from the Embassy's weekly shipment from Helsinki, and a bouquet of roses between one elbow and his ribs. He leaned against the door and tried to push the doorbell with his thumb, and nearly fell over when the door opened first. "Grocery man," he said. She didn't answer, and when he looked at her, she "had no face," in the Russian saying.

245

"You're pale as an aristocrat," Martin said, trying out another Russian phrase she had taught him. "What's the matter?"

She motioned with her head into the apartment. "Someone's here."

"Who is it?"

Sergo Chanturia stepped out of the kitchen into the hall. Martin recognized him even though he was dressed in civilian clothes. "Hello, *Gospodin* Martin," Chanturia said.

"He saw you from the window," Alina said. "I didn't have a chance to warn you."

"Well, we're not breaking any laws," Martin said, hoping that mattered. He hadn't seen any suspicious cars or people outside, but then, he hadn't really looked, either. We grow too soon old, he thought, and too late smart. Sooner or later, our laziness kills us. He asked, "Is this a social call, Captain?"

"Let's say that it is, for now," Chanturia said. "If we treat it as such, we may have a conversation of use to both of us."

"About what?"

"I'd ask you that. I understood that our agencies had agreed to share whatever information each one possessed about the murder of Mr. Hutchins."

"So we did. But I thought that matter was solved. Three men are in prison for it, and the fourth dead."

"Yes. But the men who went to prison claimed to know nothing of the woman who was with Mr. Hutchins, and who mysteriously vanished. Nor did the CIA, you said. Yet, here you are with her."

"She had nothing to do with the murder." He wished immediately—too late—that he had denied that Alina was the woman. Did Chanturia know, or was he guessing? Well, he knew now. A glance at Alina showed that she didn't know whether Chanturia knew either. Martin was thankful for that. She couldn't definitely blame him for giving it away.

"That's interesting," Chanturia said. "I'd like to hear more."

"Well, if this is a social call, take one of these bags, before I drop them both." Chanturia did come forward and take a bag. He held it in both arms, and when both his hands were occupied Martin felt a little easier. At least Chanturia wasn't going to draw a pistol and execute them. Martin took out the flowers with his free hand and gave them to Alina.

"Thank you," she said. Her voice was like an injured bird's. It made him suddenly want to fight someone.

They all went to the kitchen. Martin went to the window to look out; but Chanturia, who had stayed in the hall—there wasn't space for three in the room—said, "There's no one out there. I came alone."

"Really?" Martin doubted it; but when he looked, he couldn't see anyone at all outside.

Martin started handing groceries to Alina while she hunted for places to put them. Chanturia said nothing, but Martin could see him watching as each item came out of the bags. It was the same stupefied look that every Soviet citizen had when first confronted with a Western supermarket. He hadn't expected it from a KGB man, who had access to the special stores. But probably the impact was exaggerated for Chanturia, who was seeing only the little fraction of the West that fit into two paper bags and imagining the rest. Chanturia started going through the bag he was holding. "What's this?" he asked, handing Martin a can.

It was a Swedish ham. There was a picture of the ham on the front of the can, but it didn't look much like a ham that had ever seen the inside of a Soviet food store. Martin told him, and added, "Are we being arrested for possession of ham?"

"No, you're not, Mr. Martin," Chanturia said with sudden crossness. "Possession of ham has not been a punishable offense since Comrade Stalin died." Martin could not help smiling. Chanturia added, "And I'm not here to arrest you. I told you this was a social call."

"No. You agreed that we'd say it is, for now."

"Well, I correct myself. Please think of it as a social call."

"It's hard for me to think of it that way, since we don't know you socially."

Chanturia, holding half a bag of groceries in both arms, suddenly smiled. "Let me introduce myself, then. I'm Sergo Vissarionovich Chanturia. Yes, to forestall the question I see in your eyes, I do share a patronymic with the late unlamented Josef Stalin. Our fathers had the same first name. It doesn't mean I agree with his policies, in spite of what you may think about my employment. You know that I'm a captain in the KGB. I also love football, Georgian poetry, and good food. My mother thinks that I'm not a bad person; but that may be more a function of her being my mother than of any genuine merit. I'll let you judge, when you know me better." He shifted the groceries and held out his right hand to Martin. Martin, reluctantly, accepted it. Chanturia said nothing about the bandage, but held Martin's hand

247

lightly and continued, "And you are Benjamin Martin, assistant cultural attaché of the United States."

"*Special* assistant cultural attaché," Martin said.

"Quite right—*special* assistant cultural attaché. What does that mean, exactly, by the way?"

"It doesn't mean I work for the CIA."

"No, it's obvious you don't work for the CIA—no offense intended. But I don't quite understand your position."

"You're not the only one. All the real diplomats wonder what the hell I do, and suspect I'm a spook; and the spooks wonder what the hell I do and wish I didn't. Except Hutchins. Hutchins and I got along. Neither of us worried about what the other was doing."

"You *are* special then. And my research indicates that you are a genuinely cultured man. I'd already concluded, contrary to the opinion of some of my colleagues, that you're not employed by your Central Intelligence Agency." Chanturia dropped Martin's hand and went on, "Your friend Alina I've already introduced myself to. I'm sorry to say that she's even more suspicious of me than you are, if that's possible. But, we have to start somewhere. So, here we are. 'The dancing starts from the stove.' " He went back to handing over groceries. He came up with a can of Danish butter cookies. "What's this now, if you'll excuse my curiosity?"

"*Pechenie*," Martin said.

Chanturia turned the can back and forth in his hands. "Cookies. The material excesses of the West are certainly disgusting. Don't you agree, Alya?" Alina looked at him with an expression approaching stupefaction, until he sighed. "Nobody ever understands irony," he said. "Even here, in the world's capital of ironic situations. We should open a ministry. Ministry of Ironic Situations. Ironically, however, that would almost certainly cause production of such situations to decline." He held out the cookies to Alina. "Are these any good?"

"I don't know," she said; "I've never had any. Would you like to try them?"

"I thought you'd never ask."

They sat at the small table in Alina's living room drinking tea and eating Danish cookies. "These are not bad," Chanturia opined, "but not so truly decadent as I'd hoped. One hates to give up one's illusions."

"I'll bring the chocolate éclairs from Paris to our next party," Martin said. "Then we'll talk decadence." In spite of the circumstances, he was starting to like Chanturia, who had a certain stealthy charm. And he remembered that Chanturia was the only one on the KGB side who had laughed at his one joke, at the long-ago meeting in Dzerzhinsky Square. "But pleasant as this is, you didn't come here just to socialize."

"Truth," Chanturia said. "No, we do have some business among us. I don't want to spoil the party; but maybe we should discuss it."

"I don't know anything about the murder," Alina said.

"No, I'm sure you don't. On the other hand, you were with a CIA agent that night. And from your lack of surprise now, I take it that you did know that he was an agent. So I'm curious what was going on."

"In fact, I didn't know what was going on," she said.

"That's certainly not impossible; but of course, it's surprising."

Martin, with a hand on Alina's arm, cut off her response. "Captain, whether or not Alina now knows what's going on, I do know. As you suggested, I don't work for the CIA. But I am a diplomat. As such, I'm immune from arrest. The Embassy knows where I am now, and when I'm due back," he said, lying, "so if I don't return as scheduled, they're going to know where to start looking for me. The dancing starts from the stove—now, maybe we can make a deal."

"What deal would you suggest?"

"I'll tell you what's going on, if you give me your word to leave Alina out of it. I mean completely out. No arrests, no interrogations, now or in the future."

"That's a lot to ask for, Mr. Martin. I have to tell you that if this were the ordinary investigation I'd be forced to refuse, because the fact is, I don't have authority to make such a promise, which might involve waiving the laws of my country. Still, I give you my word. But I stress that it is only *my* word—no one else's. I want you to know that this is outside my authority, because it may happen in the future that someone else on my side may not feel bound by my promise, and I don't want you to think then that Sergo Vissarionovich Chanturia lied to you. On the other hand, right now only one other person—someone I trust deeply—knows that I'm here, or that I'm even interested in this subject, and I'm certainly going to do my best to keep anyone else from finding out. I tell you this for a good reason: I don't want you to tell anyone else on your side, either. You must promise me that. If you won't, I'll walk out right now, and forget about this meeting and hope that you do too. Because if you do tell anyone—I mean *anyone*—we could all be in deep shit, as I believe your saying goes. I don't know what news comes back from your side to ours, and in this case I don't want ever to have to find out; because if I do find out, it's likely to happen shortly before I become permanently deceased. That's how serious I am about this. Now, you have my promise. Do I have yours?''

Martin looked a long time at Chanturia. He said at last, "I don't think I understand what's going on here."

Chanturia said, "I'm ahead of you only in that I *know* I don't understand what's going on here. I do know something that you don't; and I think you know something that I don't. If we put the two together, maybe we'll have something. Maybe not. But I'm willing to trust you. I know you can be trusted, because you've given me a hostage—Alya here. Well, I've given you a hostage too, although you aren't sure of the value of that yet. The hostage you're holding is me. I'm completely serious, Bendzhamin. Somebody in my own organization is going to try to kill me if he, they—whoever—learn that I know what I'm about to tell you. Give me your promise, and I'll tell you what I know.''

It was the use of his first name that decided Martin, although he knew that was a stupid thing to base a decision on. Bierman would have been eager to tell him that.

The hell with Bierman.

"All right," he said. "I promise. I don't tell anyone on my side. Or on yours either, if I need to add that. And you can call me Ben."

"Then you can call me Sergo. The truth is this, Ben and Alya. The men who confessed to killing Charles Hutchins didn't do it. Or at least one of them didn't. Two of them may have been involved. The fourth might be dead, or his reported death might have been a fiction, although it was confirmed by our office in Tbilisi."

It was several seconds before Martin said anything. Then he asked, "Why would someone confess to a killing he didn't commit? You mean your side blew the investigation? Decided you had to have a quick result, and . . ."

"And beat a confession out of some poor bastard? You have a low opinion of us, Ben. No, in fact we do try to enforce the laws. It has to be something more important than the mere killing of a foreigner—however important you may seem to yourselves—to get us to frame someone. No, this isn't something we cooked up to get you off our backs; this was cooked up to get *us*—some of us—off someone else's backs. I know who, or in part who—the outsiders, not the insiders—but I don't know why. Until recently, I didn't think it mattered much

250

why. I thought it was probably what it seemed to be: the Mafia attacked the cafe for protection money; your guy got killed by accident; and the guy who did the killing was too important to go to prison over a little thing like that, so someone was paid to go in his place. But something still didn't seem right. What was your CIA station chief doing risking himself on a stupid frolic with a Russian woman? People do get carried away, of course; and if I had seen Alya before I started looking into this, I might have concluded that it was no more than that. But I hadn't seen her, and so I kept looking. And what I found out was this: the two of you met with a political dissident living in New Ryazan Street, and then went off on the Bucharest train. You didn't stay long. Looking for someone? All right: I've showed you mine. You show me yours." He hadn't shown them everything; but he didn't think he had to say that.

There was another moment of silence. Then Alya said, "We've been looking for my brother."

"For what purpose?"

Martin took a deep breath, like a man preparing for the highest dive of his life. "Hutchins's meeting that night was with him."

"And have you found him?"

"We found him and he's dead."

It was Chanturia's chance to be silent for a moment. "I'm sorry," he said then to Alina. He said to Martin, "What happened to him?"

"He died in a fire last night."

Chanturia sat up, startled. "Last night? Where?"

Martin didn't answer.

"Bryansk—was that where?"

When Martin still didn't answer, Chanturia said, "I know you went to Bryansk."

"They *were* KGB, then," Alina said.

"Who were KGB?" Chanturia asked.

Martin said, "Yuri—Alina's brother—was living near Bryansk. There was a fire last night. He died in it. Along with two old people. The people who set it probably think we died in it too."

"And the 'they' who were KGB—they are . . . ?"

"Three men who set the fire." Martin added, "You've already said that somebody in your organization may be in on this."

"Yes, but . . . well, if my organization knew you were at Bryansk, then the people involved may be closer to me than I'd have thought possible. I knew you went there. Only two other people know, and I trust both of them. But, of course, what we knew, others could

251

have learned the same way. Others either in the Body or outside of it."

"How did you find out?"

"One of my men saw you leaving the apartment of the dissident Kassin."

"He's no dissident!" Alina flared. "He's an army veteran who's been abandoned by his country!"

"I beg your pardon," Chanturia said. "And I'm sorry to hear it. So then, you were seen leaving the apartment of an abandoned army veteran, the unfortunate Kassin."

"Dmitri doesn't need your condescension," Alina said.

"Forgive me; but I didn't mean it as condescension. I meant it sincerely. Kassin is dead too."

When she spoke, it was with the calm you see on a clear winter dawn. "Dead? How?"

"He fell on the stairs from his apartment. My man who saw you leaving there went back to talk privately with him, after seeing you off on your train. He found him halfway down the first flight at the top. He had hit his head—apparently trying to descend the stairs. The elevator was inoperative."

"*Apparently* trying to descend the stairs."

"Apparently." Chanturia took her hand in his. "This puts me in an awkward position. We hadn't seen a reason to believe it was anything but an accident. Now we see a reason—but I can't point it out to my organization without putting us all in deep danger."

They all sat silent. Finally Chanturia said, "Now we have to assume the worst. And the worst is that everyone knows you found your brother: not only that I know, but that the Mafia knows, and that someone else in my organization knows. The only saving grace is that the others may think you are dead."

Alina and Martin said nothing. It was tacit acquiescence in the death of another person; but there was nothing else to be done.

Chanturia said to Martin, "I believe you were going to tell me what is going on. What is this all about?"

The second high dive was easier. "It's about plutonium."

"Plutonium!"

"Alya's brother, Yuri, knew that the Mafia had some stolen plutonium—enough to make a nuclear weapon, or maybe a lot of them. He was trying to sell the story to the CIA; but someone killed his contact."

"Hutchins."

252

"Yes."

"What more?"

"No more. That's all he'd tell us. He wanted a million dollars for the rest. A million and out."

"It's a fantastic story!" Chanturia said. "How would the Mafia make a nuclear weapon?"

"I don't know; but that's the story. You're the expert. You figure it out."

Chanturia said to Alina, "What did your brother do for the Mafia?"

"I don't know. He never admitted to me that he did anything for them. He held a real job, for cover. It took him away from Moscow a lot. He could have done anything while he was gone."

"What was his cover?"

"He was a truck driver."

"A truck driver?" There seemed to Chanturia to be a dawn in all this, somewhere. A long way off still, but surely there. "Where did he say he drove?"

Martin interrupted. "I said no interrogations, Captain! Not now or ever!"

Chanturia threw up his hands. "This isn't a game, Bendzhamin! This is . . . this is . . ." He knocked his forehead on the table in frustration. Then he sat up, looking sheepish. "That was stupid, wasn't it."

But it was enough to break the antagonism. Martin looked at him with a sort of friendly concern for someone flaky enough to do that.

"This is important," Chanturia said. "Please."

"He told me he drove all over the country. Sometimes outside the country—but only to other socialist countries, of course."

"Of course."

"I never knew what to believe from him. Does it matter?"

"I don't know," Chanturia said. "I don't know what matters. It's all such a . . ."

Martin interrupted suddenly. "Did he ever drive to Kazakhstan?"

After puzzlement, understanding suddenly showed in Alina's eyes. "Yes. He said he did."

"Kazakhstan," Martin said to Chanturia. "Yuri said the plutonium was stolen at Semipalatinsk, from the nuclear test range, in Kazakhstan." He said to Alina, "What if Yuri really was a driver? If he really did drive to Kazakhstan, and outside the country?"

Chanturia asked Alina, "Did your brother ever mention the Turk?" Kazakhstan: that was why the name had popped into his head.

Kazakhstan was one of the Soviet Muslim republics. And the Turk was half Muslim. Half Kazakh.

"Yes, I think so," Alina said. "The Turk. Yes. He was a driver too . . ."

"Did you ever meet him?"

"No."

"Did your brother drive with him? For him?"

"I think so. With him or for him—I don't know which."

"What do you know about it? What cargo, what routes . . . anything?"

She thought; and then, looking from one to the other of them, said with quiet triumph, "Romania. He drove to Romania with the Turk. Yes, I remember. When he wanted to meet Charles; he told me he was going to Romania soon. It was his second trip there. He was excited about it."

"His second trip?"

"Yes. He had gone once before—with this Turk, or for him."

"What cargo?" Martin asked.

"He didn't know, I think. He didn't say. He wasn't excited about it, that first trip."

Chanturia: "Where did they go the first trip?"

"I don't know. I remember he said they didn't go to any city. That seemed strange to him. They stopped at a camp somewhere, some sort of military camp. And he brought back oranges."

Martin: "Oranges?"

"Yes. He said he got them from the Iraqis."

"He got them from the Iraqis," Chanturia and Martin echoed her. And it all fell into place. There was a dawn.

"The men who set the fire," Chanturia said. "Three men, you said. Did you see them?"

"We saw two," Martin said. "But there was another; they called him by radio."

"They called him? Did they say any name?"

"I think so. I don't remember."

"Atman?"

He shook his head. "It was a Russian name. I don't remember."

"The ones you saw, what did they look like?"

Martin thought. "One had a very strange face. Flattened. Not misshapen, but . . . well, flat." He saw the look on Chanturia's face. "Do you know him?"

"It's possible. And the other one?"

"He had a mustache, dark hair . . ."

"He limped," Alina said.

"Ah."

"You do know them," she said, asked.

"Yes, I think so."

"It *was* the KGB, then!"

"No. *They* weren't from the Body." He rubbed his hand over his face. "*They* weren't. But they're not the only wolves in this forest."

"Who were they then?"

"One was your brother's friend, the Turk, I think. And the other . . . well, we'll let that wait." He looked at her squarely, in a way that made her uncomfortable. "I'll try to find out," he said to her. "I'll try to learn what happened to your friend Kassin. But I can't ask too much. If the wrong person hears the question . . . You understand: I can't make it an investigation."

She nodded silently—to lose his eyes, not to cry.

Outside, the brief darkness was almost at hand. "We've got to get Alya out of here," Chanturia said. "You'll be safe at the Embassy, Benjamin; but she can't stay here. Not now that we know someone else knows of her connection to this. If they realize she's not dead, she'll be dead. Maybe she'd better go to your Embassy?"

"We've discussed that," Martin said. "She's against it."

Chanturia looked to Alina, who nodded. "There are a lot of strange people in the world," Chanturia said. "Still, you're right, Alya. If you go there, our friend Mr. Bierman will ask you a lot of questions, and I've already explained that I don't want to find any of the answers coming back to my side. You've got to disappear."

"Isn't somebody going to miss her?" Martin asked.

"Stop talking as if I'd already disappeared," Alina said. "I'm still right here. I can decide for myself what to do with me. But nobody's going to miss me for a while. The play has closed. No one will look for me for a few days."

"What about your work? Public relations for the circus?"

"This is the Union, Benjamin. Who asks if workers come to work? Some of them don't even exist, except on the account books so the boss can keep the wages. But I don't know where to go. If they knew Yuri, they can know my friends. I can't put anyone else in danger." Not even the voice of an actress could fully hide fear.

Chanturia was thoughtful. "There's a place I can put you."

*   *   *

255

Tanya's apartment was on the eighth floor of a Stalin-era building on Chkalova Boulevard, a part of the Garden Ring circling inner Moscow. Chanturia telephoned her from a public phone on the way there to let her know he was coming with some friends. He didn't want to mention his purpose on the telephone, but he also didn't want to spend any time at her door waking her.

When they arrived, at two in the morning, after a winding drive through southeast Moscow to lose any pursuit—although they saw none—Tanya looked ready just to start out for the evening. Chanturia was not a man in the habit of dropping in at late hours, and so, not knowing what to expect, she had decided to look her best for whatever was coming. She was dressed in a gray skirt and black angora sweater. Her hair was so artfully piled that at an earlier hour Martin would have thought she had just come from the hairdresser.

She was a contrast to Alina, who was dressed in faded jeans and a man's old sweater with a tan polyester jacket over it. The stress of the last two days now showed in Alina's face. But still she would have turned men's heads in any city in the world. Martin was glad Tanya was dressed for the occasion. He would have thought most women would feel threatened by Alina; maybe the finery would help Tanya feel more equal. The meticulous luxury of her apartment, astonishing in Moscow, was a contrast to the studied poverty of Alina's. Martin began to worry whether Tanya would cooperate when she heard Chanturia's plan.

His worry was groundless. The mother instinct was as strong in Tanya as in most Russian women. When Tanya heard what was needed, within minutes the relationship between the women had moved on to "Alya" and "Tanyechka." They made the couch in the spare room into a bed and Tanya shooed the men out the door. "This girl is going to get some sleep now. Yes, we know she's not to go out on the street. She'll only speak on the phone to a voice she recognizes. Now go away. You look like you need some sleep too, Bendzhamin."

He felt that way too.

· 45 ·

Tuesday, June 6, 1989
7 P.M.
The Lubyanka

BELKIN CAME INTO CHANTURIA'S OFFICE QUIETLY AND CLOSED THE DOOR behind him. It was long enough after hours that few people were around, but not late enough for anyone to be surprised that he was still there. He placed a briefcase on the floor beside Chanturia's desk.

"Anything interesting?" Chanturia asked.

"All you ever wanted to know about trucks. During the last week in January, thirteen trucks traveled from Moscow to Romania. Ten of them were TIR trucks—Transportul Internazional Romaniya. Three were Soviet. Eleven of them crossed from the Union into Romania at Chernovtsy, on the usual route to Bucharest. Two, traveling together—one Soviet truck and one TIR—left the Union at Ungeny in Moldavia, reported destination Izvor. The Soviet truck returned through the same checkpoint two days later, alone."

"What do you make of that?"

"For one thing, he probably didn't go to Izvor. He *could* have got there and back from the border in two days, but he'd have been plowing to do it."

"Do we have any information on the truck?"

"The Border Guard has a permanent record of every vehicle that crosses the borders of the Union."

"Except for Matthias Rust's airplane," Chanturia suggested.

"They have that one now, too. The registration number of the truck was KGK 4198."

"K as in Kazakhstan?"

"That's right. It showed a cargo of cotton goods. It returned empty. The same truck had crossed the border there once before, on June 25, 1987. Also back in two days."

"Who owns the truck?"

257

"It belongs to a state cotton processing plant near Alma-Ata; but a year ago it was leased to a cooperative."

Chanturia sank a little deeper into his chair, as if to get a good purchase on the world. "It was leased to a cooperative." He did an imitation of a walrus sinking under the ice of this information; the nose was the last to go. "Any information on the cooperative?"

"I've only been on this for thirty hours, Captain."

"You're doing well. What about my two friends?"

"Not much news. Tatar reports that a source says they were in Moscow two days ago and they're not now. He's not sure it's true. You told me not to ask too much. Do you want more?"

"Yes. *No*—don't get us killed."

Chanturia met Martin later that evening at Alina's apartment. It wasn't a good place to meet. It might be watched. But they had tried for hours to think of somewhere else, and in the end, everything else was worse. There were no public places safe from observation, and private places were hard to arrange.

When Chanturia arrived, Martin was wandering along the walls of the small living-dining room that also served as Alina's studio, studying the paintings that were spread along the walls.

"She's a talented woman," Chanturia said.

"So I'm beginning to understand. What's in the bag?"

"A key."

"It's a big bag."

"It's a big key. The key to this case. Number KGK 4198." He took out Belkin's report and held it up for Martin to see.

"You want to stop being a smartass and explain this to me?" Martin asked.

Chanturia handed the report to Martin and sat down at the dining table to explain what Belkin had learned.

"Any information on the cooperative that owns the truck?" Martin asked after his explanation.

"I've only been on this for two days, and I can't put a full team on it—just one Jew in his spare time."

"You're doing well. Lucky for our side your government is chasing out all your Jews. Any idea where KGK 4198 was going on these trips?"

"The TIR trucks are normally driven by the Securitate, as you know. It seemed logical that they might have sent one of their boys along to guide our half-Turk driver, or to keep an eye on him. I

258

checked with our First Chief Directorate about what the Securitate might have going on along the Izvor road."

"Find anything?"

"First Chief Directorate won't say anything officially; but a friend of mine over there in the Socialist Countries Liaison Department says the Securitate is running a special training camp in the forest east of Munten. That's maybe three hours short of Izvor."

"What sort of special training?"

"The usual stuff. Middle Eastern terrorists."

"Iraqis."

"Probably."

"Could it be a front for a nuclear weapons facility?"

"You know that anything can be a front for anything. Oh, pardon me, I forgot that you aren't in the business."

Martin tossed the report onto the table with a shake of his head. "Listen, Sergo, I've got to get the Agency in on this."

"What?"

"It's getting too big for me. I can't handle it, not anymore."

"You son of a bitch, Bendzhamin, you promised me! The only reason I trusted you is that you're *not* the Agency! Your Agency station here may be so clean there's no place to spit, but your station chief has to report; and somebody has to read his reports; and somewhere, somebody who reads that report is going to be one of our guys, and he'll have to send it back to our side. And when that happens, you and I and your sweet Alya are going to be dead in minutes, I guarantee you!" Martin sat down dejectedly across from Chanturia. "At least wait until we've got some proof," Chanturia said.

"What *is* proof?"

"I don't know. The truck—that seems most likely. They've been making deliveries of plutonium with it. They must have modified it to protect the driver. Maybe there'll be some contamination. I don't know."

"How are you going to find one truck in the Soviet Union? It's a big country."

"We know who owns it. They have to keep trip tickets for every trip the truck makes. You don't think we let people wander around unaccounted for, do you? We'll find it."

"How soon?"

"Soon. Trust me."

259

· 46 ·

Wednesday, June 7, 1989
1:30 P.M.
The Lubyanka

BELKIN STOPPED BESIDE CHANTURIA'S TABLE ON HIS WAY OUT OF THE CAFE-teria. "I talked to a friend in Alma-Ata recently," he said.

"Oh?" Chanturia was sitting alone. Captain Solodovnik was two tables over, but the cafeteria was noisy enough to cover their conversation. "You seem to have friends all over the Union, Belkin. What does this friend have on point five?" Identification of nationality was point five of all Soviet job applications.

"The Star of David; does that worry you? We're the one nation the Union doesn't have to worry about: we've got no place to call home, no little bit of territory we can tear off and keep for ourselves. If we don't leave for Israel, we have to stick with the Union. Do you want to hear this?"

"Sure. I'm sorry."

"The Committee office in Alma-Ata doesn't want to talk about this officially. My friend called me at home. The registered owners of the cooperative are a bunch of drivers from the cotton mill; but my friend believes there's a secret interest owned by some people whose names are too important to go on the certificate. *Really* important people. People whose names would curl your toes."

"Is that the mill that the former Party secretary for Kazakhstan used as his private capitalist empire?"

"The Procurator charged that the Party secretary stole five hundred million rubles in goods from the state, if you count that as a capitalist empire."

"Really? Imaginative devil, wasn't he?"

"I wouldn't have said so," Belkin said. "Why bother stealing cotton from the state, when he could have been stealing the state itself? These cooperative people are going to end up owning the state's enterprises legally."

260

"Except for the hidden ownership technicality."

"They'll get around that. You'll see. One day it will all come out in the open, and the people will be sucking hind teat. Again."

"I didn't know you were a Communist, Syoma."

"The Russian Jews have always been Communists. Ask Pamyat. Ask your Colonel Sokolov."

This was too serious for Chanturia. "Any chance that the Mafia has a piece of this cooperative?" he asked.

"There's no evidence. But, to quote a friend of mine, does the wild bear shit in the woods?"

After close of business, Belkin came again to Chanturia's office. Before he could say anything, Chanturia said, "I apologize for what I said at lunchtime."

"I don't hold it against you," Belkin said. "You're a good man, Sergo Vissarionovich. What I said about Pamyat stands, though."

"I know."

"As for the fuck-their-mother Iraqis, good Communists shouldn't be dealing with them. They're enemies of the United States, okay; but they're enemies of the rest of us too. They'll try to kill us all before this is over."

"Where's the truck?"

"On its way to Moscow from Omsk."

"Why Omsk?"

"It went there from Alma-Ata."

Chanturia sucked at his mustache. "Semipalatinsk is on the way from Alma-Ata to Omsk."

"Yes."

"Does the trip ticket show a delivery or pickup in Semipalatinsk?"

"No. But what's a few hours to a truck out on the road? You can't measure time closer than days on those roads."

"Why Moscow?"

"I don't know. It's on the road to anywhere west. My guess would be that he's meeting a Romanian truck here—a guide. Someone to ease his way into Romania."

"How did you find out where he is without letting them know we're interested in him? From a friend?"

"Sure. I asked someone to do a 'random check' of all the trip tickets in the cooperative's files. He asked them some questions about a lot of other trip tickets. About this truck, he just read the tickets. No questions asked."

"Good. Now. How do we stop this truck for a check?" Chanturia asked.

"That won't be easy, Captain."

"These aren't sugar times."

"Well, if he's en route from Omsk to Moscow, he's got to cross the Volga. His trip ticket showed he planned to take the shortcut from Ufa to Kazan instead of going around by Perm. But the Kuibyshev Reservoir is in the Volga on that road. There's no bridge; he'll have to cross the reservoir by ferry. The lineup will be five kilometers long. It wouldn't be hard to find him. Or we could have a 'special crewman' right on board the ferry. There'd be plenty of time to check him out during the crossing, without raising any suspicion."

"I like that. But we don't know when he might arrive, closer than a day plus or minus. How long can we keep someone on board?"

"Checking security on a strategic river crossing? Forever, if we want to. The only thing is—what are they checking for?"

Chanturia knew then that he was going to have to let Belkin in on this all the way; but he still couldn't bring himself to say it directly. He asked, "Can you get us a radiation counter, Syoma?"

"A radiation counter! Is that really it?"

"That's really it."

"I don't know how to get one without answering some serious questions. It'd be easier to get one out of the CIA."

"I already tried that, Syoma."

Belkin laughed, until he saw that Chanturia wasn't laughing.

"They have even more questions," Chanturia said.

Belkin reflected. "I had a friend in Kazan," he said. "It's been a long time since we talked. Maybe he's still there."

"Is he reliable?"

Belkin shrugged. "Who knows who's reliable these days?"

"Nobody knows," Chanturia answered him. "What are we willing to risk to solve this? That's the question. All right, call your friend. And if it's not going to work, tell me at once."

262

· 47 ·

Friday, June 9, 1989
3 A.M.
The Magpie Mountains

THE VOLGA RIVER FLOWS FROM THE HEART OF RUSSIA—IS THE HEART OF Russia. Springing from arctic lakes far to the north of Moscow, it swings east and south across a whole continent and at last in the subtropics empties into the Caspian Sea. It is a wide powerful river, tamed at intervals by dams.

The dam in the Volga at Kuibyshev backs up a vast reservoir, too wide to bridge, that stretches some four hundred kilometers upstream. At the little town of Sorochi Gory the reservoir cuts the road from Ufa to Kazan. Sorochi Gory means "Magpie Mountains": perhaps a joke, for there are no mountains in Sorochi Gory, only a line of low hills above the valley of the Volga.

At the Magpie Mountains at 3:00 A.M. in June, the river Volga was already silver in the dawn. Across the river on the east bank, the line of dew-covered trucks waiting at the ferry station stretched up from the water's edge out of sight over the bank. The deck hand at the ferry's bow, waiting to hand down the lines, knew that there were trucks for three kilometers or more east of the ferry station. He had walked the line the night before, and he knew that KGK 4198 was in it, inching forward for a half hour as the ferry loaded and then sitting an hour, and then inching forward again. Sometimes trucks waited two days to get over. But KGK 4198 was getting close.

On the ferry and on the shore a yammer of truck engines arose like bellowed greetings of relatives as the ferry tied up; and then the bow ramp went down and the trucks on board began to rumble down onto the shore and hurry away to the east, toward Asia; and the long line of trucks on shore began to ruffle itself forward, extending and contracting like a great, slender, olive-drab worm.

KGK 4198 was the last truck to board. The deck hand watched it

263

snort up the ramp and lurch into place. The ramp came up behind it, the deck hand cast off the lines, and the ferry slid out into the river dawn.

There were two men in the cab of KGK 4198. They sat there for so long the deck hand began to wonder if they would stay in the cab for the whole crossing; but finally they got out and wandered up to the other end of the ship—now the bow, as this end had become the stern—to watch the river go by with the rest of the drivers. The deck hand walked to a locker outside the ship's cabin, unlocked it with a key from his pocket and took out a package wrapped in yesterday's *Pravda*. Returning to his post, he partially unwrapped the package and took out a chunk of white bread and some pieces of sausage; and then, since no one else was at the stern of the ship, he also took from the package a small metal box and, chewing on his sausage, walked down alongside KGK 4198, where he passed the box along the frame, the fenders, and the bumpers. Frowning, he checked to see that he was still alone, then crawled under the truck and moved the box carefully along the chassis members. He stopped at a spot under the back of the cab. From a meter away no one could hear, above the roar of ship noises, the steady crackle that the box was emitting.

The deck hand crawled out from under the truck and wrapped the box back with the remains of his breakfast. A few minutes later the ferry began to slow and the truck crews started coming back to their trucks. The deck hand said a few words to the two men who came to KGK 4198. "Nice to be on the river so early," he said.

"Better to be on the road," the driver replied. He was a Muslim from the look of him, a lean, dark man, but with the face almost grotesquely flattened in profile; but he spoke good Russian. The other man looked Russian.

"Where you headed?" the deck hand asked. "Moscow?"

"Sure. But farther than that, too," the Russian said. "All the way across country."

"Is that right? Where to?" But the Muslim stopped him from showing off any more. "Let's be going, Vanka," he said.

"Moscow," the deck hand said, with speculation in his voice. "I've never been there. What's it like?"

"It's an armpit," the Muslim said.

"Nice," the Russian, Vanka, said. "Everything in the world there. You can't imagine."

"Hotels, I'll bet," the deck hand said. "Where do you stay? Big fancy hotels?"

"They're all armpits," the Muslim said. "Except for where the foreigners stay."

"Well, that's the way it is," the Russian said. "Keep the best for our 'foreign guests.' They're used to it. We're used to this. We can get along."

"It's that bad, is it?" the deck hand said.

"Nah, it's not so bad. Us, we stay with the foreigners. The Ukraine Hotel. If you ever get to Moscow, try to get in there. It's full of East German women, mad for some strange cock."

After the last of the trucks disembarked, the deck hand walked down the ramp in the stinking haze of diesel smoke behind them, still carrying his breakfast package.

He walked half a kilometer up the main road to the village. It was a little past 5:00 A.M.

On a side street in Sorochi Gory, a single car was parked, a beige Volga. The deck hand unlocked the car and got in and drove away.

It was more than an hour's drive west to Kazan, a drive made slower by the long line of trucks he had to pass. Passing KGK 4198, the deck hand was careful to pull his cap far down over his face.

The beige Volga arrived before six-thirty at the Institute of Physical Sciences. The deck hand, carrying a small leather bag, walked to the entry hall of the Institute. The guard said that Dr. Bernstein was already there: he always was early when he had an experiment running. In a few minutes, Dr. Bernstein came to the reception area. The deck hand turned over the bag to Dr. Bernstein.

"Was it still working?"

"Yes, very well. I wonder, could I use your telephone?"

"Of course. Come in." They walked back to an office that opened onto a large laboratory full of experimental apparatus. Neither of them asked any questions of the other. The deck hand went into the office and closed the door.

The Institute had a good line. It took only a few minutes to get through to Moscow. "Syoma," the deck hand said.

"Is that you, Misha? How goes it?"

"It goes well. I met our friends. They have the package, as you thought. They put it under the seat—maybe inside, maybe outside, I couldn't tell. They left this morning for Moscow. They might stay at the Ukraine Hotel." That was a lucky thing, the Russian's saying that. If it was true.

265

"Were they people I'll know?"

"One was Vanka—Russian. He was with a Muslim, I think."

"I'll watch out for them. Thank you."

"It's nothing."

As the deck hand left the office, he waved to Dr. Bernstein, but they didn't exchange any further words.

· 48 ·

Friday, June 9, 1989

7 A.M.

Moscow

CHANTURIA RECEIVED THE CALL FROM BELKIN BEFORE HE LEFT FOR WORK. "Our friends are on their way. They might stop in Moscow, maybe at the Ukraine Hotel. But maybe not."

"Do you know any dates yet?" Chanturia asked.

"No."

"Well, when we find out more, maybe we can arrange a party. Let's talk about it."

On his way to the office he telephoned Martin at the Embassy from a pay phone. It was a prearranged signal. He babbled some Russian lunacy into the telephone and then hung up. It wouldn't fool a voice-print machine, but he hoped it wouldn't have to. If there was one, it was more likely to be his own side's than the Americans', and that would be bad news indeed.

· 49 ·

Friday, June 9, 1989
9 A.M.
Alina's Apartment

"NOW," CHANTURIA SAID, "WE'VE GOT TO CHOOSE. AFTER THE VOLGA River, there's no place we can be certain of finding a moving truck."

"I thought the KGB covered this country like a blanket," Martin said.

"Using its official resources, of course, the Committee would have no trouble tracking one truck. The highway patrol could be assigned to watch for it every few kilometers, if necessary. But that would require an official order; and getting an official order would require explanations. And explanations may be hazardous to my health. And they might also result in a warning to our target. And of course, with that many people watching, someone's going to wonder why. There's a big chance of a leak."

But without those resources, a single truck would vanish in the vastness of Russia.

"But what if they transfer their secret to another truck?" Martin wondered. "If they follow their past practice, they're going to meet a Romanian truck in Moscow, with someone to serve as guide and as guard. Could they move the cargo to the Romanian truck—or to any other truck, for that matter—and let it go on alone? How hard can it be to transfer a few kilos of plutonium? How much plutonium are they carrying, anyway? What kind of container is it in? Surely it must be shielded; but it might not have to be immovable."

"I don't know the answer to any of those questions," Chanturia said. "And it would be scary to ask, right now."

"Well, here's another. If we only get this truck, we've stopped one shipment; but Yuri said there are others. Can we prevent the Mafia from shipping them, or from stealing more the same way, if we don't roll up the whole ring?"

"I don't know the answer to any of those questions either."

267

Martin sighed. "Maybe we should just grab these guys while we've got the chance, and get the others if and when we can. Maybe it's time to risk your health, Sergo."

"That's easy for you to say."

"Well, think of what's at stake. Remember where this stuff is coming from. A Soviet Muslim republic. And where is it going? To the Iraqis. For what? Only one answer makes sense: the Muslim bomb. Maybe the plutonium is going direct to Iraq to be manufactured there; or maybe it's being worked on in Romania—I don't know. Ceausescu is crazy enough to be willing to share with the Iraqis if it helps him get nukes of his own. But who's in favor of a Muslim bomb? There's your Kazakhs and your Uzbeks and your Tadzhiks and some others who are Sunni Muslims, the same as the Iraqis . . . And then there's your Azerbaijanis, who are Shiite Muslims whose land used to be part of Iran and want to rejoin it . . . How many nuclear weapons would it take to break the whole of the southern U.S.S.R. out of the Union? How many people would die in that cause? There's a limit to secrecy, Sergo; and I think we're at it."

Chanturia stared unhappily at the floor. "I never asked to be a hero," he said.

"Well, you're not one yet."

"I hope I never will be. If I am, a dead one is likeliest. Well, so what do you think we do?"

What should I be doing now? Should I be doing something? The voice of poor old Maria Pavlovna rang suddenly in his memory, so clear that he looked around, startled. What was it they were doing? It seemed suddenly a crazy undertaking. Was it just his crazed imagination, that they could do this? But what choice was there? "I think you put out an arrest notice for the truck, and you take your squad and whoever else you can round up and you arrest the sons of bitches who're driving it, and then you get your boss to come down on the truck's owners and the plutonium-plant guards and anybody else who might be involved like stink on shit."

"That's an interesting phrase! Is it an American idiom?"

"Yeah. Stick with me, Sergo, and you'll learn a lot."

" 'Like stink on shit.' Yes, that's good! I hope I live to use it."

"If you don't, Sergo, we'll always say you should have." Martin thought a little while. "The trouble with our position now, Sergo, is that we're working in secret. I know that's what you're trained to do; but I'm not, and I don't like it. And maybe it's *because* I'm not

268

that I can see the weakness of the position. Because right now it is weakness. We're afraid to move, because if we do move, somebody might see us and kill us. But the only reason they can kill us is because right now nobody else knows what's going on. We've reached the limit of secrecy, Sergo, and the limit is its weakness. If we just come out in front of God and everybody and say, 'Look, you dumb shits, this is what's going on,' what can they do to us? Look what happened to Alya's brother, Yuri; look what happened to Hutch. They died in secret. In public and yet in secret. If somebody just stood up and announced what's happening, we'd be safe. Nobody could touch us. Secrecy kills, Sergo.''

"Have you ever read anything by Georgi Mikadze?''

"Nope. Heard of him, but never read any.''

"He hasn't been published much, thanks to my organization. Literary criticism is one of our main efforts. He's been published in Georgian, mostly, and then in French once: *The Book of the Dead*. And he spent ten years in prison for it. But he said the same thing, Ben, in that very book he went to prison for: 'secrecy kills.' When we allow our acts to be made secret, he said, we are playing the executioner's game.

"Maybe you're right, Ben. Maybe we've had too much secrecy. All right: let's set our plan. Where do we go from here?''

"This is where it gets hard. I don't know anything about the spy business.''

"It wouldn't help much if you did. Well, if you're right, then we'd better try to get *everything* out in the open. Let's try to flush all the birds at once.''

269

· 50 ·

Friday, June 9, 1989
10 A.M.
Frunze Embankment

CHANTURIA, DRESSED IN CIVILIAN CLOTHES, STOOD AT A PAY TELEPHONE on the wall of the Aeroflot building on the bank of the Moscow River opposite Gorky Park. There was a long line at the Aeroflot entrance, people starting the long wait for tickets to anywhere—wait here for reservations, wait around the corner to pay for tickets, wait at the airport for a flight, wait in the airplane for the flight to take off. Sometimes flights were a day late. Patience was a socialist virtue. Socialism wasn't built in a day.

He had waited patiently in line for this telephone, too. It was a popular telephone, with so many lines of people standing in the vicinity; plenty of people calling to say they'd be home late for dinner. Nobody would listen long to a tap on this phone. Now, at the telephone, he dropped in his two kopecks and was impatient as the telephone rang. The woman in line behind him, a tired barrel-shaped woman with a string bag dangling from each hand, looked through him with nothing in her eyes.

The telephone at the other end kept ringing. He was sure he remembered the number, and he had checked that it was a Moscow number.

The woman's lips pursed—a signal that he had tried as long as was fair. Sometimes numbers rang on the calling end but not the receiving. That could go on for days. Sometimes no one ever answered.

Someone did answer. *"Da."* That was all. Chanturia turned away from the woman's pursed disapproval. "I'm calling for Old Tomaz," Chanturia said in Georgian.

"Who is this?"—also in Georgian.

"A friend from Tbilisi."

"He's not here."

"He'll want to talk to me. My name is Sergo. I had lunch with

270

him two months ago, and also dined at his home. I was thinking of our interesting talk. Tell him I called and that I have to speak to him personally. I can't wait here, but he can call me after one hour. I will be at 243-57-40." It was his own apartment number. Probably no one would be listening on it, but it didn't matter now. Try to flush all the birds at once.

In his apartment, while he waited he looked through an old copy of Georgi's forbidden book: looked, but did not read. It was the original book in Georgian, not in French, on the flimsy paper, insubstantial as smoke, that *samizdat* typists used to make eight copies at one typing. This appeared to be about a seventh copy: it was barely legible. It had been confiscated in Tbilisi. A friend of Chanturia's who had been in the KGB's Tbilisi office at the time, and knew that Chanturia knew Georgi, had saved it for him as a curiosity. He sat looking at the brave words, words that were in themselves brave deeds when set on paper, and wished that he had ever been worthy of them, that he had found a law of honor to live by as Mikadze had.

The telephone rang at last, and when he answered it, Tomaz Broladze was on the line. He didn't identify himself, but Chanturia knew the voice. "It was good of you to call me," Broladze said. It was the voice of a man in command of his world.

"I was thinking of our last conversation, and I heard something I thought would interest you."

"I hoped you would."

"I've been told of an opportunity to deliver cargo from Kazakhstan to one of our sister socialist countries. It occurred to me that such a transaction would be of interest to you as well. In fact, I understand that a delivery is underway. But perhaps you know of it already, through your old channels?"

Broladze cleared his throat. "Tell me more."

"Perhaps your old channels are drying up. I'm told that a shipment will pass through Moscow in the next day or two. There could be complications in Moscow, though."

"What kind of complications?"

"Safety inspections, that sort of thing. They could hold up the shipment for a long time. The people of Moscow are becoming very sensitive about safety."

"What do you recommend?"

"It's a delicate matter. Before I could make a recommendation, I'd need to be certain you were serious about pursuing this . . ."

"Yes, I understand." There was a long silence, which Broladze broke at last: "How would the people involved be convinced of my seriousness?"

"Some token of your interest would be helpful."

"Mm. What would be the size of this token?"

"A hundred thousand rubles would be adequate." Thirty years' salary—that should seem sufficiently greedy.

"It's possible. Someone will speak to you."

Now there was nothing to do but wait.

· 51 ·

Friday, June 9, 1989
1 P.M.
The Lubyanka

CHANTURIA HAD NEVER BEEN GOOD AT WAITING. EVEN AS A BOY—ESPE-cially as a boy—he had hated waiting. The days before a birthday were agony. New Year's never came. The Revolution Day fireworks were ages arriving, too quickly out.

The old channels are drying up, he had said. Well, the "old channels," whoever they were, would open up when they heard that. If the news ever got to them. The danger was that Old Tomaz would abandon the old channels entirely.

But Broladze had said someone would speak to him. That didn't sound as if he were abandoning his old channels. But it had to be done quickly. The shipment was on its way.

So he waited for someone to speak. And if no one did? Then he would have to arrange a meeting with the Americans, before the truck could come and be gone. It was impossible to wait long. If someone was going to speak to him, it would have to be within the day.

He stayed alone in his office, to offer every chance; but no one came. At lunch in the officers' cafeteria, he sat alone with his body wire (provided by Martin, from CIA supply), trying to look as if he

272

was not waiting. No one joined him. Solodovnik raised his hopes by stopping to chat—although Chanturia would have been disappointed to think that Tomaz's man in the Committee was Solodovnik. That would make him give up the Mafia as a lost cause altogether.

His heart sank when he saw Sokolov coming toward him. *Let him pass by.* But instead he came over, with his bowl of solyanka and his cabbage-roll—the same thing he had eaten every noon Chanturia could remember, but normally he ate alone, or with officers of his own rank. Now he established himself at Chanturia's table—an event that had not happened before in Chanturia's years at the Committee. *Why now?* he thought. *There's so little time to find this person: come another time to talk. Why now?* But the Colonel had settled in.

He talked of this and that. Things were better when he was young. He had been stationed once in Tbilisi: did Chanturia know it? He'd had some good years there. "There was a man I knew," the Colonel said. "I wonder if you've met him? His name was Tomaz . . ." He paused, as if trying to recall, while Chanturia stiffened.

"Broladze?" Sergo asked.

"Yes . . . perhaps it was." Password given and answered. "A remarkable man. Do you know him?"

"We've met."

"He started with nothing, except his wits and a friend or two; and now he governs a province. In all but name. A man of great influence, which runs in various channels. I understand it has been said that one channel or another is drying up." Sokolov paused. Chanturia said nothing. He wondered if the pounding of his heart would be heard on the tape. Sokolov continued, "It's my view, on the contrary, that other channels may be opening up, but that the old channel is not about to be displaced by the new." He slurped down a spoonful of his soup, muttered about its temperature—too hot—but took another. "Still, what would it take to satisfy this new channel?"

"I heard one hundred thousand rubles mentioned."

"Your friends must be very hungry."

"Everyone has mouths to feed."

"Of course. More than they know, sometimes. Well, a hundred thousand—less twenty-five for the *old* channel, eh?"

"Tell me how to arrange this."

"A parcel will come to your office. It's very simple. The twenty-five can be deducted in advance. And if Tomaz should ask—it's all well. Right?"

"Of course."

"How did you learn of the shipment, and who else knows?"

"I'll need his permission to tell you that," Chanturia said.

Sokolov looked at him coldly. But he had been in a military organization long enough to know when rank had been invoked successfully. He said nothing.

· 52 ·

Friday, June 9, 1989
3 P.M.
The United States Embassy

BIERMAN'S OFFICE, ONCE HUTCHINS'S, HAD ALL THE PROPS AN AGRICULture attaché could need—maps of Soviet crop production, rainfall predictions, the USDA Yearbook for years to which the memory of man runneth not. Martin entered and closed the door behind him. He motioned for Bierman to turn on the noisemakers. It was an inside office, and the most nearly bugproof that the Embassy could offer outside the Bubble.

"What?" Bierman asked.

"What do you know about Hutchins's last meeting?" Martin asked. "Is there anything in your files, like what he thought it was about?"

"No."

"You're a lying sack of shit, Bierman. I want the truth."

"There is no 'truth': there are various truths. Some truths you're not cleared for, and the content of this station's files is one of them."

"Then let's see if the Ambassador will ask you."

"The Ambassador might; but the Ambassador's not cleared to see this station's files either."

"You like playing God, don't you, Bierman?"

"No, Martin. I like *being* God. There's a difference."

"True; but I'm not sure you know what it is. What do you know about shipping plutonium?"

Bierman paused an instant too long before he answered: "Why do you want to know about how to ship plutonium? Do you plan to send some home as a souvenir?" Bierman never sounded friendly, not even when he wanted something; but the way he sounded now had crossed the threshold of hostility.

"I believe that there's a danger that terrorists are obtaining weapons-grade plutonium illegally from the Soviet Union. I wondered, if they did, how we might recognize a shipment. What would it look like? How would they package it to avoid radiation? Is this something you could carry in your pocket, or what?"

"Where did you get this idea?" Bierman asked.

"I have a fertile brain. Does it matter?"

"Yes, it matters. I've always been worried about the security of the Agency's files here, Martin. Now I'm more worried."

"I don't see what the Agency's files have to do with me, Bierman. I'm not an employee. I'm not cleared for them. As you like to point out."

"Yes, that's exactly my point. You're not cleared for them. Where did you get this information about terrorists?"

Martin considered what he was hearing. "Wait," he said. "Do you mean that the Agency files here already have information on this?"

"I don't *mean* anything. I'm asking where you got this information."

"If you really want to know, I got it from the KGB."

"Don't play games, Martin. I'll have you arrested for breach of security, for . . ."

"Hey, you're serious about this, aren't you, Bierman?"

"I'm a serious person. I don't play games."

"Don't you? How long has this been in your precious fucking files? Did you know about it from the beginning? That this was what Hutch got killed over? If that's not a game, what is it?"

Bierman suddenly sat back in his chair. "What do you mean, 'what Hutchins got killed over'?"

"You sat right there and lied to us," Martin pressed on. "Not just to them, but to us! To me, to Rollie, to the Ambassador! We asked, what was Hutch up to; and you said you didn't know! And all the time you knew what he was after: stolen plutonium. A terrorist bomb!"

For an instant Bierman turned pale. "So that was it!" Then he seemed to catch himself, and turned red. "You must be crazy, Martin! To think that you can steal classified information and then to threaten govermental officers over its content!"

"Why do you think I stole anything from you?"

"How else could you know about the plutonium?"

275

"The Agency isn't the only source of knowledge in the world, Bierman. You aren't really God. I'll tell you what I've done, Bierman. I've single-handedly set a meeting with the KGB to further discuss some aspects of the murder of Charles Hutchins. It starts two hours from now. They agreed to it because they think I'm the Agency, or that *maybe* I'm the Agency. It doesn't matter which, because the meeting's on. If necessary, I'll attend as the special assistant cultural attaché of the United States Embassy. But I'll tell you one thing, Bierman. There's going to be a joint action that will not only solve the murder of Charles Hutchins, it will save the world from the first serious attempt to build a terrorist bomb, and if you know anything that would help the effort along and don't contribute it, there are going to be a lot of questions about why you didn't."

· 53 ·

Friday, June 9, 1989
5 P.M.
The Lubyanka

MARTIN WASN'T SURE THE MEETING WOULD REALLY HAPPEN UNTIL IT started. It was the miracle of having power: sign your name, and things happen because you've signed your name, whether they make sense or not. After Chanturia's telephone call, Martin had called Dushenkin; and here they all were, back again in the conference room at 2 Dzerzhinsky Street. On his side of the table were Bierman and Rollie Taglia, and on the other, Chanturia and the two colonels Dushenkin and Sokolov. The Major Translator was not there.

"We're told that you wish to report a development to us," Dushenkin said, leading for the Soviet side. "We'll be glad to hear it. Although, since the murderers are in prison, we're puzzled what it may be."

"More than one development, actually," Martin said. "Probably three developments."

"Three? You've been busy!" Dushenkin did not sound completely enthusiastic about an active CIA.

276

"Developing this case has taken longer than we expected," Martin said. He hoped Bierman appreciated his bravado on behalf of the Agency. "But the case was more complex than we had thought. Indeed, we haven't reached the bottom of it yet. We appreciate your cooperation, however: we couldn't have reached even this point without the efforts of your personnel."

It was hard to tell whether Dushenkin or Sokolov struggled harder to look not caught by surprise.

"This case," Martin continued, "is now known to involve four threads. First, there is the well-known theft of nuclear material from your weapons factory at Semipalatinsk; second, there is the death of our colleague Charles Hutchins; third, there is the smuggling of the stolen material out of the Soviet Union to a facility where, fourth, we believe it will be manufactured into weapons of terror—nuclear weapons—which may be used against the Soviet Union as well as the United States."

Dushenkin's eyes widened; Sokolov's narrowed. Dushenkin looked to Sokolov to proceed. "You mentioned four 'threads,' Sokolov said. "Yet you said there have been only three developments. The 'thread' having no new development, presumably, is that concerning the murder of your Charles Hutchins, which has already been solved."

"No. There have been new developments concerning the murder. What is missing is the means by which the nuclear material was stolen. The rest we are certain of."

"This is fantastic!" Sokolov objected. "What connection have you made between the Semipalatinsk theft and some Mafia attack on a cafe, let alone on weapons of terror?"

Sokolov was apparently going to say more; but Dushenkin held up a hand, and Sokolov stopped talking instantly. "You mentioned a 'well-known' theft at Semipalatinsk," Dushenkin said. "I'm sorry to say it is not well-known to me. Could you elaborate, please?"

Martin turned to Bierman.

Bierman was in his element, and he made the most of it. If the Russians were going to know what was in his files, he was going to make them green with envy. "Over the course of a year or more," Bierman said, "supplies of certain nuclear materials—weapons-grade plutonium, to be precise—at the nuclear weapons factory named for V. I. Lenin, near Semipalatinsk, were found to fall short of previously reported quantities. The shortages were carefully concealed, but a detailed investigation by the Committee on State Security eventually led to the conclusion that enriched plutonium was being systematically diverted from the factory. The means by which this was done were not discovered. I believe they have not been discovered to this day."

"If this is true, it's an outrage!" Dushenkin snapped. He looked at Chanturia—a look that, had Chanturia been combustible, would have ignited him at fifty meters. "Captain, have you verified this?"

"No, sir. I have not been authorized to inquire into this subject."

"Nor have I. Sokolov, you say you've heard of this. What about it?"

Sokolov sat back carefully in his seat. "I have heard of it. I'm not familiar with the details."

"Colonel Sokolov asked what is the connection between the Semipalatinsk thefts and the murder of Charles Hutchins," Martin said. "The connection is this: Charles Hutchins was an employee of the Central Intelligence Agency, and he was killed on the night he was to interview someone—a Soviet citizen—who was familiar with the rest of the scheme, the plan to smuggle the stolen material out of the Soviet Union."

This was news that sat both colonels up in their chairs—not just about the plan to smuggle plutonium, but about Hutchins. It was no news to them that Hutchins worked for the Agency; but they had never expected to hear an American official admit it.

They recovered their composure. "But the men who committed that murder are in prison," Sokolov said. "And they did not give any such reason for the murder. They were engaged in extortion, pure and simple."

"The man who committed the murder is not in prison," Martin said.

"We have multiple confessions from the murderers," Sokolov said. "How can that be, if they did not do it?"

"They lied," Martin said.

"Why should they lie?"

"Because someone paid them to. Either that or they were afraid to tell the truth. Either way, a lie was in their own best interest; so they lied."

Sokolov's next question should have been who committed the murder; but he didn't ask it. Chanturia noted it well: Sokolov didn't ask. Instead, he changed the subject. He said to Bierman, "What is the source of your information about the supposed theft of materials at

278

the Lenin factory? We can hardly accept a report we're unable to evaluate."

"I'm sure your own files will confirm what I've said," Bierman answered. "We don't have to burn our sources to tell you what's happening in your own backyard."

Dushenkin interrupted. "And if our confessed murderers didn't kill Hutchins, who did?"

So, Chanturia noted, Dushenkin wasn't in on the story. If he had been, he would have tried to talk about something else too, as Sokolov had. This was a relief to Chanturia. He would have been unable to deal with both of them.

"I would refer you to Captain Chanturia," Martin said.

Dushenkin's eyebrows went farther up; Sokolov's went farther down.

Chanturia composed himself. Now was his time. "The killer was a left-handed Georgian who limped," he said. "The persons who confessed to the murder consisted of one Georgian and two Russians. The Georgian limped; but he was not left-handed."

"Why is it that we are now hearing this for the first time?" Dushenkin demanded.

"I was led astray by the man's confession. I failed to notice at the time, even when I obtained his signature, that he was right-handed. Only when I became aware of a left-handed Georgian with a limp, a man who is a member of the Georgia Mafia, did I consider that we may have arrested the wrong man. Members of my section have established conclusively that this second person was in Moscow on the night of the murder. Moreover, his identity establishes a very strong motive for the man who was arrested to falsely accept the blame, and the sentence, in his place."

"Who is this person?" Dushenkin asked. Sokolov was silent as a distant storm.

"He is Tomaz Tomazovich Broladze." As Chanturia said this, he watched Sokolov. Sokolov showed not a flicker of recognition, nor of anything else. Chanturia went on, "He is the son of the head of the Mafia in Tbilisi. He was too highly placed to go to prison: so someone else went for him. All of the men who confessed work for him or his father. Two of them may, in fact, have been present at the murder. The third certainly was not. He gave a false confession in order to protect the young Broladze."

"Fantastic!" Dushenkin and Sokolov said this simultaneously; but they meant two different things entirely.

"So we have two threads," Dushenkin said. "What of the other two?"

"Captain Chanturia will explain them," Martin said. "But before he does, let me furnish some additional information.

"Our agency became aware very recently that Mr. Hutchins had an appointment at the cafe on the night he was murdered. The man he was appointed to meet never came. The murderers came instead. But we found the man. His story is interesting. He was a member of a Georgia-based Mafia group, though not Georgian himself. He was employed by Tomaz Broladze, the father of the man who murdered Hutchins. As you may know Tomaz Broladze began his career in illegal trucking operations, and he continues today to operate trucking throughout the Soviet Union. Your Committee is known to employ him from time to time to obtain information.

"The man I speak of was employed by Tomaz Broladze as a truck driver. He became aware that one of his duties was to be the transport of stolen plutonium to a foreign country, by means of a specially modified truck. He decided to report this to the CIA, and it was for this purpose that he arranged a meeting with Charles Hutchins."

"Why with the CIA and not the Committee on State Security?" Dushenkin demanded.

"We pay better," Taglia said. He flashed Martin a sorry-I-couldn't-resist grin.

"Capitalist money!" Sokolov said with a show of distaste. "How much did he ask?"

"He asked for the world. He wanted money; but he asked for the world. He wanted us to get him out of the Soviet Union, into the Free World."

"And where is this man now?" Sokolov demanded. He turned to Chanturia: "Have you interviewed him? I've seen no report of it."

"I haven't," Chanturia said.

"Why not?"

"Because he's dead," Martin said.

"But *you* have spoken with him?"

"I have, Colonel."

"The CIA finds a key actor in this play, and interrogates him, and he then dies before he can be interviewed by the KGB? How convenient!" Sokolov said, again to Chanturia, "And do you believe this?"

"There is some additional evidence which is relevant," Chanturia said.

"Of what sort?" Sokolov was becoming more and more demanding, while Dushenkin sat silent, seemingly willing to let Sokolov test this case.

Chanturia took a file from the briefcase at his side on the floor. "My section has reviewed the trip tickets of a truck which the deceased drove for some months before the murder of Mr. Hutchins."

"Does this dead man have a name?"

"Yes. Yuri Volkov." Chanturia handed a small stack of papers to Sokolov. "He is one of the drivers named on these trip tickets, which show that he is a regular driver of this vehicle. They show that in January of this year, the vehicle left from Alma-Ata, in Kazakhstan, bound for Romania. In Moscow it joined company with a truck of the Romanian International Transport Service, a truck that was driven by persons known to us to be agents of the Romanian Securitate."

Sokolov snorted. "All the Romanian drivers work for the Securitate!" He turned angrily on Chanturia: "Is this all there is? Trip tickets to Romania? Do you know how many trucks of the Soviet Union visit Romania regularly?"

"Yes, sir, I do." It was not the response Sokolov wanted, but he didn't dare shut Chanturia off with Dushenkin there. "In the last week of January—the week after the Hutchins murder—there were three, as well as ten TIR trucks. Nearly all them crossed into Romania by the usual route, via Chernovtsy. Only two—Volkov's vehicle and the accompanying Securitate vehicle—took a different route. They crossed into Romania at a little-used border crossing at Ungeny, in Moldavia, and the Soviet truck returned alone, less than two days later—hardly enough time to have reached its announced destination of Izvor.

"As it happens, on the road to Izvor there is a Romanian military installation. Forgive me if I do not say more, in the circumstances"— he glanced meaningfully toward the American side of the table—"but we do know that forces of a certain Middle Eastern nation are sometimes present at this installation."

"Don't mind us," Bierman said. "We know they're there." He didn't say what else he knew, what Hutchins had known from the CIA station files, a story that had come first from the Israeli intelligence service, the Mossad: that the Iraqis were there because in Romania they were out of reach of Israeli fighter-bombers. The Iraqis had lost one nuclear weapons plant to an Israeli raid: they didn't wish to lose another.

"And is this the story, then?" Sokolov said with quiet malice. "A dead man's tale, and some Iraqis in Romania?"

"I don't believe I specified that they were Iraqis, Comrade Colonel," Chanturia said.

"No? I believe you did. But whatever you did or did not say on that point, I still see no reason to conclude that your dead witness, if he said these things, was telling the truth. I have another theory, Captain Chanturia. You may not want me to describe it, but I'll do so anyway. My theory is that you are lying. You have violated your duty to the Committee and to the People. You say that you know another man, a Georgia Mafia member, who killed the American, Hutchins? How convenient. But what proof is there? Your own testimony, and nothing more. You're a Georgian, you've recently visited Georgia, and you admit that you've been in touch with the Mafia there. Furthermore, we know now what our American 'colleagues' have not admitted before, that Hutchins was an American spy. You've been working closely with American spies, it appears . . ."

"It was my assignment," Chanturia said.

"It was your assignment to investigate the death of Hutchins. You've continued long after that case was closed. For what purpose? I'd suggest that this case has gone astray because you've chosen to lead it astray, Captain. Maybe your dead man wasn't the only one who wanted something from the Americans! I suggest that you're in their pay yourself!"

The strength of Sokolov's attack surprised Chanturia. He had planned a scene of easy entrapment of Sokolov. He saw now how naïve he had been. He played his ace: "You know I'm not, Comrade Colonel. You know that, in fact, you are the one who arranged for the wrong man to be arrested. You are in the pay of the Georgia Mafia yourself."

Sokolov's face went red with rage. "I was doing the People's work before you were born, Captain; and I expect to continue doing it long after you're shot for treason!"

"You need not deny it, Colonel," Chanturia said, more calmly than he felt. "Here is the evidence." He threw on the table the CIA tape recorder. As he did so he was aware for the first time how foreign it looked.

"So your friends helped you, did they?" Sokolov snarled. "Well, they needn't have bothered. Here's my evidence!" He threw on the table a tiny Soviet-made recorder, one of those that Chanturia had been afraid to try to check out, for fear of questions. Sokolov switched it on, and Chanturia heard himself at lunch, agreeing to a bribe on behalf of the Georgia Mafia.

Dushenkin seemed to have sunk into himself. "That's very interesting," he said when the tape ended. "What's on yours, Captain?"

"The same."

"And what is the point of it?"

"I knew that someone in our Committee was in the pay of the Mafia. I let it be known to the Mafia that I knew about the plutonium shipment and could be silenced, in order to find out who their friend is. I was approached by Colonel Sokolov. He knew of my contact with the Mafia. He could only have learned of it from one source—the Mafia."

"Clever," Sokolov said; "but the truth is exactly the contrary. I had reason to think that the Mafia were trying to penetrate the Committee, and I went looking for their agent. Fortunately"—he nodded toward his miniature recorder—"I went armed."

"We'll not discuss this further here," Dushenkin said to both of them. He looked at the Americans across the table. "I'm sure you'll excuse us." He didn't smile as he said it.

"What about the plutonium?" Martin asked. "Are you going to let it go?" He wanted to help Chanturia directly; but he knew that anything he said would only make Chanturia's case worse.

"Of course not. If there's a truck, we'll find it. And then we'll know the truth of this matter."

"The truck is on the road from Kazan to Moscow," Chanturia said.

"How do you know that?"

"It occurred to me that a truck that is used to carry plutonium must have special facilities for the safety of the crew. It probably would be reused and not be risked for ordinary activities—low-value smuggling and the like. Therefore, I obtained the registration number of the truck that made the earlier trip and inquired further into its whereabouts. I learned that it is at this moment en route from Kazakhstan to Romania, via Moscow." It appeared that Sokolov was about to try to cut Chanturia off, but Chanturia was concentrating on Dushenkin, so that he would not have to recognize anything Sokolov said. "I had the truck tested, discreetly, Comrade Colonel. It exhibits a substantial amount of radioactivity."

"How did you have this done?" Dushenkin asked. "Surely the crew would be alerted?"

"The test was carried out while on board a ferry crossing the Volga at the Kuibyshev Reservoir. The truck's crew were watching the river."

283

"Admirable!" Dushenkin said—as much praise as had ever passed the lips of the Silent Death. Sokolov knew it too, and said nothing.

"And where is this truck now?" Dushenkin asked.

"On the road from Kazan to Moscow, as I've said. We don't know where, exactly."

"What? Why not?"

"The story, as Colonel Sokolov has correctly pointed out, is highly unusual," Chanturia said. "I'm sorry to say it, but I was afraid of interference from within the Committee, without strong corroboration of my suspicions."

Dushenkin sat a long time looking at Chanturia. At last he spoke. "We'll discuss this further in my office." To the Americans, he said, "We'll advise you of developments."

"This was a stupid idea, Martin," Bierman said as they drove away from the building in the Embassy car, "and now that it's blown up, I'm going to see that you get full credit for it."

"We've got to help them find the truck," Martin said.

"How the hell can we do that?" Rollie asked.

"I was hoping you'd tell me."

"They'll find it," Bierman said. "If they want to. They've got two hundred thousand men they can use; more, if they bring in the army. But what if they don't want to find it? What if this whole thing is a KGB deception? There goes my career."

"That's pretty tough, Bierman," Taglia said. "There goes your career. Not to mention the rest of the world, when the Iraqis get the bomb." He added, "I wouldn't want to be either of those bastards."

"Who?" Martin asked.

"The Colonel and the Captain. One of their two asses is going to be grass: and it wouldn't surprise me if both were."

"Why both?"

"Because if they can't decide which one is lying, they're going to have to proceed as if they both were. Probably it will all straighten out in time. Maybe not in time to do *them* any good, though."

"Christ, you're right! Then I've got an errand to run, Rollie."

He stopped the driver.

"Where are you going?" Bierman asked.

"Someplace important. Don't wait up for me."

He got out at the square Fifty Years of October, just past the National Hotel, and walked back to the Metro station. He didn't think he would be followed from the KGB headquarters, but he was in too much of a hurry to be careful. He took the quickest route, a train to the station Red Gates and, looking over his shoulder, a change to the Circle Line to the Kursk railway station.

Not fifteen minutes had passed before he was outside Tanya's apartment.

When no one answered the bell, he came near panic. He was sure Chanturia wouldn't have turned in Alina. But Chanturia was going to have some hard questions to answer now; and Alina's name would have to come up in the answers to those questions; and then somebody higher than Chanturia was going to want to talk to Alina personally. With Chanturia up against a full colonel, there was no guarantee what would happen. It was certain that Chanturia would not resist having Alina brought in. After all, she would support his story. But would mere truth be enough to protect either of them?

He leaned harder on the doorbell.

Was there even a reason to be sure about Chanturia? No, of course not. She could have been taken in already.

Was Bierman right? Had he really blown the whole thing?

She had been here that morning. That much he knew. Everything had gone smoothly, right up to the end of the meeting at the Lubyanka, fifteen minutes ago. Or so it seemed. Was anything as it seemed?

She opened the door. "Ben! What—"

He put his hand to her mouth and closed the door behind them. "We've got to get you out. Let's go."

"I'll get my things."

"Leave them." An array of Tanya's raincoats hung on pegs on the wall. He shoved her into one of them. It was made by Burberry. He found a broad-brimmed hat—French label—and stuck it on her head. "Great. We'll both look foreign." He pulled her out the door. The elevator was still there, so he got them into it, but he pushed the button for the second floor and got off there instead of at the ground. The elevator went on down. Someone got on it below, and it went up past them and stopped somewhere above.

She started to say something, but he said in a low voice, "Don't talk. You sound too Russian. We're foreigners now." They walked down the stairs and out the door.

There was a beige Volga sitting just outside the door. A large man was in the driver's seat watching the door. He looked at them hard. Alina took Martin's arm. "We're an old married foreign couple," Martin said in English. The man looked away. Maybe he was nobody. They walked opposite the direction he was facing, toward the Kursk station.

Now the problem was to get into the Embassy. Martin wished he had been smart enough to arrange for Rollie to meet him somewhere with a car. If wishes were horses . . .

They rode the Metro for an hour, changing trains three times, and then Martin telephoned Rollie's apartment from the Metro station opposite the zoo, not four hundred meters from the Embassy. "Hello, Rollo. It's certainly pleasant that you don't have a social life. I knew I could count on you to be home on a Friday evening. Look, I've had a bit of car trouble. I wonder if you could have yours pick me up. How soon could you start out?"

"Where the hell are you?" Rollie asked.

"If this is really inconvenient, I could call back at another time. But if you could start right away, that would be great. You know what I mean? Really, really great."

"Well, if it's like that, I can come myself. I'll start right away. Say where and when."

"At the zoo in four minutes? Be heading west." Even if someone was listening in, they'd have trouble reacting that fast.

He was looking for Rollie's Volvo; but it was the Ambassador's Cadillac that he spotted coming up Barricade Street. Rollie was driving, and wearing a chauffeur's cap. Martin and Alina strolled out of the entrance to the Moscow Zoo as the car swerved to the curb, as Muscovites stared. Martin opened the door, handed Alina in, and got in beside her; and the Cadillac rolled away.

"I thought you might need the room," Rollie said, grinning. "You must be Alina. As lovely as your reputation. I wish I could kiss your hand, but I've got to concentrate. Somebody's behind us. I don't think they'll dare stop us, though. Where to, sir?"

Martin kept Alina from looking back, and resisted the temptation himself. "Quickest way home, please."

"Oh. Well, then, let's do this." Rollie made a tire-squealing illegal U-turn in the face of traffic that cut off their tail from doing the same. Only two traffic lights separated them from the Embassy. If someone was supposed to be controlling those lights, he was asleep at the switch. The Cadillac hit them both on green and was back at the Embassy in two minutes. The Soviet militia at the gate weren't in on the game. They barely glanced at the Cadillac. Rollie waved at the security camera; the gate went up; and they were home.

"Just one request," Rollie said.

"You name it."

"Don't ever tell the Old Man that I took his car without asking."

· 54 ·

Sunday, June 11, 1989
1 A.M.
The United States Embassy

MARTIN WAS SURE HE HAD BEEN DREAMING, BUT WHEN HE WOKE HE could recall not a single fragment of the dream. His telephone was ringing, and the ring had crazed the surface of the dream and it had become opaque, like shattered safety glass still hanging in its frame. He fumbled the telephone to his ear but couldn't find the mouthpiece.

When he turned, Alina's eyes startled him, dark in the gray half-light of the bedroom. He had forgotten she was there, forgotten in his dream.

"Who is it?" she asked him.

"Don't worry," he said. "You're safe here."

"Are you there?" an annoyed voice asked on the telephone. It was Chanturia's voice.

"Sergo! Are you all right?" Alina laid a hand on his arm.

"Yes, I'm all right. Did you get her home safe?"

"She's safe."

"You were as smart as I thought you'd be. I couldn't help giving her name; and the minute I did, Dushenkin sent to haul her in. They aren't quite sure what happened to her. They suspect the CIA got her, of course. It was a little tough on me that she was gone; but better for her."

"I didn't dare call about you, Sergo. What's happened?"

"It's all gone wrong."

"What? How could it?"

"They can't find the damned truck. Now they think Sokolov's right—that I've taken a bribe, or that it's all made up, somehow, that I've fallen for a CIA trick."

"You should know you can't trust the CIA, those clever bastards. So where's the truck?"

"How should I know? I told you they can't find it. Every GAI

287

militiaman in central Russia has spent a day looking for it, plus the KGB and half the internal security forces. A million eyes watching, and nobody seeing."

"Are you drunk?" Martin became suddenly aware that Chanturia's words were about thirty degrees off his intended course. "Where are you calling from?" Or maybe they'd drugged him.

"A Georgian is never drunk. Emotional, yes. Drunk, no. I'm calling from my office. I'm supposed to be taking a piss. I'm not under arrest. Yet. Not until they find out I've just called the American Embassy."

"Is Sokolov under arrest?"

"No. And if we don't find this truck, he won't be, but I will. You've got to help find this thing. How can the whole fuck-your-mother KGB not find a single stinking truck?"

"I'd think that was a question I should ask and you should answer. You're in the KGB, after all, not me."

"All right, you ask me."

"How the fuck can the KGB not find a single stinking truck?"

"Horseradish knows! Maybe somebody warned them. Want to lay a bet on who it was? Maybe they stopped and hid out somewhere along the road. Maybe they turned aside. Maybe they turned back to Kazakhstan—but they wouldn't make it: the Volga crossings are all being watched."

"Maybe they got out of the country."

"No chance. There aren't many ways out, and they're a long way from any of them; and every border post is looking for this license number."

"Maybe they changed trucks," Martin suggested.

"Too hard. Remember, they had a special compartment built into this one to protect the crew from the cargo."

"So they don't tell the crew. Remember Chernobyl?"

"What are you getting at? Suggesting that the great socialist state doesn't protect the working man?"

Martin sat up on the edge of his bed. His drapes were open, and outside, the gray light was either coming or going: he couldn't tell which. "What time is it?"

"Just past one."

Going, then. His bedroom faced the Moscow River. On the other side of the river the craggy tower of the Ukraine Hotel was more than a silhouette: the night was still so light that he could see the gray face of the tower. If the Russian Republic building had not blocked the view, he thought he could have seen pedestrians along the Shevchenko Embankment on the hotel side of the river, and the queue of parked socialist-country trucks that was always waiting there. Waiting for what, he had never understood.

Trucks waiting. "Maybe they didn't turn aside," Martin said.

"Why would they not?"

"Why would they? Didn't they have an appointment here? Maybe they couldn't get into Romania without their guide. Maybe the Romanian truck has a secret compartment too. Maybe . . . who knows what?"

"They didn't come to Moscow. A fly couldn't have got into Moscow carrying that license number."

"Maybe they changed the license number."

"That's too easy."

"Well, you know the first rule of fixing an English sports car."

"Of course I do. What is it?"

"Always check the easy stuff first."

There was a long silence. Martin broke it: "Your people did consider that they might change the license number, didn't they?"

"Of course they didn't," Chanturia said, angry at the obviousness of it. "They're looking for KGK 4198."

"You see, they do know the first rule for fixing an English sports car. They're checking the easy stuff. And nothing else, apparently. How hard would it be to change the number?" But Martin knew the answer before Chanturia said it.

"They'd just have to paint over the old one." The numbers were painted on the tailgate of every truck in the Union, and on a small plate at the front. Most of them already looked hand-painted, or stenciled at best.

"So what did this truck look like? Could you find it by description?" He knew the answer to that too.

"Brown. With black letters. A Kamaz."

"Could be worse. You don't have to look for every truck in the Union. Just half of them." The others were blue Kamaz trucks with black letters.

"They'll pull everybody off the search, if I suggest that. We've got to narrow it down somehow."

"Then if we can't watch every road in Russia for this one truck, maybe we can watch some roads for some trucks. Where do you think they were supposed to meet their guide? Somewhere in Moscow, but where? It's a big city."

"I don't know," Chanturia said. "Our man in Kazan said the crew talked about the foreign woman at the Ukraine Hotel."

"What?" Martin stood up and stared across the river. "Do you know what I'm looking at, Sergo?" he asked.

"The beautiful Alina, and I wish I was."

"Wrong. From where I'm standing right now, I can see the Ukraine Hotel. Do you know what's at the Ukraine Hotel?"

"Foreign women. But I doubt they'd meet your standards. I know I wouldn't trade Alya for one."

"And besides foreign women, foreign trucks. Socialist, yes; but foreign. The big long-distance jobs, not your little Kamazes. Probably all made in Czechoslovakia, and sold to every socialist country in Eastern Europe. I'm willing to bet there's one from Romania. And since I'm not sleeping anyway, I might as well go have a look around. You want to join me?"

"I think they want me to stay here."

"So don't tell them. Or send one of your people. Are you finding the damn truck sitting there? I've got to pick up some equipment. Look for me on the bridge. If you don't see me, I'll be down on the embankment looking at trucks."

Martin telephoned to Doc Snyder's apartment. "Sorry to wake you," he said to Snyder's sleepy mumble. "I need to borrow a Geiger counter."

"A what? Can't you wait until morning to go prospecting?"

"You know how I am with a new toy. Anyway, you haven't used the thing since right after Chernobyl. I'll have it back before breakfast so you can check the milk in my cereal."

"You serious? Shoot, I was afraid you were. Okay, I'll meet you at my office."

In fifteen minutes Martin was on the Kalinin–New Arbat Bridge crossing the Moscow River toward the Ukraine Hotel.

He had come out without a jacket, and now he was sorry, because even in mid-June a cold front could put the nighttime temperature into the forties, and now a cold wind was blowing off the river and the light was going quickly.

He kept checking back over his shoulder for a car to slow for him, but none came. When he reached the west end of the bridge he took the steps down to the embankment. There was a small park between the river and the hotel, with a statue of the Ukrainian poet Taras Shevchenko facing the river. Beyond the park a single line of trees ran along the embankment between the river and the hotel, beside a paved street that ended in dead-storage winter parking for Muscovites' cars; along this street under the trees stretched the line of big rigs. "Balkancar," was written on the first one: Bulgarian. They were dark and silent in the last light. The drivers, he supposed, were off looking for the foreign women.

He was near the end of the line, a quarter mile upriver, when he found a gray semi-trailer truck with the big letters "TIR" on its sides. Behind it was a brown single-axle Kamaz. The light was too far gone for him to make out the license number painted in black on the tailgate of the Kamaz. It was the ordinary Soviet-standard truck, the size of an American farm truck, with a canvas-covered frame over the bed, closed by a canvas drop flap at the back.

Martin had walked up the river side of the street, away from the parked trucks. He walked on upstream a little way and leaned against the rail, contemplating the water and also looking for anyone behind him. There was no one in sight on the embankment. He crossed the street and started back toward the hotel, walking along the line of trucks. He stopped at the rear of the Kamaz, wishing he had a cigarette to light so he could loiter without looking as conspicuous as he felt. The air carried the smell of warm oil and diesel fuel: the Kamaz had arrived not long before: it was still cooling. There was another smell he couldn't place. He stepped in between the Kamaz and the truck behind it. The license number painted in big black letters on its tailgate was ARK 9998. But he recognized the smell now. The paint on the Kamaz's tailgate was dry to the touch; but it still smelled of volatiles: it had been painted not long ago.

He took the Geiger counter from the paper bag he had carried it in, turned the volume to low as Doc had showed him, and turned it on. There was a spurt of static, as from a mistuned cheap radio. He stepped back into the street, and as he walked forward along the truck the static increased in intensity, though not in volume.

"What are you doing?" The voice startled him. He found himself looking into a dark lean face—so dark he could barely make out the features now, even though the man was facing into the last of the evening. Martin didn't want to speak: he knew his voice would give him away as a foreigner. "I asked you what you're doing." This was no worker drunk on Gift of the Sun.

"I was just tuning my radio," Martin said, trying to sound Lithuanian. "It's this Japanese thing I bought in Praha last trip, but it won't

291

bring in these Russian stations." He held out the Geiger counter—but not far enough to be seen clearly—in demonstration.

"Well, take your radio somewhere else: I don't like Russian music."

"Who does, these days?" He turned to go around the back of the truck; and as he turned he heard the click of a pistol slide being worked.

Two days ago he wouldn't have thought twice about a click in the dark, wouldn't have thought *pistol* when he heard it. Now he did. And then he heard a car coming.

He turned back. The man had turned back too, for an instant. A car driving with parking lights only was coming slowly along the embankment. Martin leaped behind the truck and then ran. He heard the man coming after him. He dodged behind the next truck after the Kamaz as there was a pop and a bullet cracked past him. Out in the street the car jolted to a stop. Car doors opened. "State Security!" someone shouted. The popping noise again, then real shots, a steady hammer of shots that hurt his ears. A man's incomprehensible shout. Out in the street he saw the car stopped at an angle, the driver's door open. Someone was lying in the street beside it.

"Look out, he's got a silenced gun!" Martin yelled, and listened to another bullet crack past him for his effort. Then more unsilenced shots that seemed to be coming his way too, and he dived under the truck. He shut off the Geiger counter and stuffed it up above the back axle and started to crawl forward under the truck, back toward the Kamaz; but he stopped when he saw someone crawling toward him. He ducked back behind the truck's dual rear wheels and waited. It was full dark now and he could see only a few meters. The man stopped and turned his head and shoulders back the way he had come. He raised his arm and waited. Footsteps were coming carefully along the line of trucks. There was the explosion of a shot and a simultaneous flash of light that illuminated the man's face ahead of Martin: Chanturia. A gasping curse: the footsteps retreated, limping.

"Good shot, Sergo," Martin said.

"Ben, is that you?"

"I hate to admit it."

Chanturia ducked in behind the other rear wheels on the street side. "What have you done to make these people cross with you?"

"They're protecting the truck ahead of us. It's radioactive."

"How do you know?"

"Geiger counter. It's up there. What do we do next?"

292

"Next we come down on these people like stink on shit." Chanturia laughed without sounding happy: "At least I lived to use it!"

"Great. I hope we last a while longer. Where are your troops?"

"It's you and me, Ben. They shot poor Belkin. He was a good Jew, too."

"You mean there were only the two of you?"

"I couldn't bring a whole section down here, on a crazy idea like this, could I? But don't worry. Someone will be following me. I'm out without permission. And the militia will be along now that they've heard the shooting."

"Can we get to your car?"

"What for?"

"Well, to drive away from here, for instance."

"No good. It's dead. Bullets through the block, I think. They must be using armor-piercing. That's a machine gun they've got up there, in case you missed it."

"Who are these guys, anyway?"

The allusion was lost on Chanturia. "Securitate, I'd say," he said. "That's heavy stuff they're shooting. Although the Georgia Mafia has stolen enough automatic weapons to start an army, if they need to."

"Do you have a radio in your car?"

"That's not a good place to sit. Armor-piercing stuff goes through the doors. Not to mention the glass."

"Maybe you could fire off a few more rounds to get the militia moving this way."

"I've got only five left."

"You guys came prepared for a major campaign, didn't you?"

"Belkin had a gun," Chanturia said. "You take this, and I'll go get it."

"How are you going to do that without getting killed?"

"I wish I knew." He slid his pistol toward Martin.

"I haven't shot one of these in twenty years, Sergo. And I've never shot one left-handed."

"Probably it doesn't matter. It's so dark out that you couldn't hit anything anyway. I know I couldn't."

"That makes me feel just great."

"On the other hand, maybe they can't either. Otherwise I wouldn't be going out after this weapon."

"Do they need to see you, to get you with a machine gun?"

"We'll soon know." Chanturia slid out from under the truck and

293

darted into the street toward the car. Its parking lights were still on, but its vital fluids were pooling on the street around it.

The *whap* of the silenced pistol and the whine of a ricochet that missed. Chanturia, still running, reached the sprawled figure on the ground beside the car. He bent down, then turned and came back toward the truck, running low. A burst of machine-gun fire struck a pinwheel of sparks from the pavement around him. He stumbled, bounced hard off the truck wheel and fell onto Martin.

"Are you alive?" Martin asked, convinced he wasn't.

"I don't know. What kind of proof would you accept?"

"Try sounding lucid."

"I can't do that on my good days."

"Shit, Sergo, I thought they'd got you!"

"They did. My foot's gone numb."

"Let me see it."

"No time. We've got to keep them pinned in against the trucks. If they get outside, they can get a clear shot at us." As if in warning, a blast of machine-gun fire ripped past them. The weapon had been set up under a truck ahead and was firing back between the wheels to keep anyone from crawling forward under the trucks.

The starter of a truck ground, and an engine banged into life.

"Now what?" Martin asked.

"They're getting ready to go. The worst thing they can do is get caught here." A second truck started. It was the Kamaz.

"Can we stop them?"

"I don't see how. What ideas do you have?"

"Maybe we could get up in the back of the truck, before they start."

"If you don't mind the machine-gun fire."

"They'll have to move the machine gun before they can move the trucks. When they do, we can crawl forward and get aboard."

"After you, please?"

Chanturia didn't expect the American to accept; but he did. Martin waited for the hiss of air brakes from the bigger Romanian truck as it started to move, and then he rolled out between the wheels of the truck he was under and crawled forward as fast as he could move. There was space enough between the front of this truck and the back of the Kamaz for him to stand. He half-expected to feel the bullet then, but nothing happened. He felt for an opening in the flap that closed the back of the truck and was surprised to find one: he had expected the flap to be secured. The truck began to roll forward. He grabbed at the top of the tailgate, hoisted himself onto his extended arms, and fell into the bed of the truck. As the truck roared forward, someone fell on top of him. Inside the canvas, with the flap dropped, all was blackness.

"What's going on out there?" a voice asked. It wasn't Sergo, and it wasn't the body on top of Martin. It came from the front of the truck box.

A dim flashlight beam from the same location fell on the face of the body on top of Martin. It was Sergo's face.

A laugh from the location of the flashlight. "Captain! It's wonderful to see you!" The light went out.

Chanturia rolled off of Martin. He knew the voice. "Tomaz Tomazovich," he said. "I didn't know you'd be here."

"My father said you had contacted him. He told me to make sure the trucks got through Moscow. But how did you find us?"

"Comrade Colonel Sokolov told me where you'd be."

"Sokolov? Of course, he'd have known: he arranges our contacts with the Securitate." Then the tone changed from puzzled frankness to suspicion: "But why would Sokolov tell you? My father wouldn't have told you about him."

"Correct. Your father wouldn't. But you just did."

"I don't understand."

"Understand this: you're under arrest." As he said this, pistol fire came from the front of the truck—not from one place, but from two. Chanturia dropped suddenly. He fell hard on top of Martin again and then rolled away. Martin tried to get to his feet, but the truck, gathering speed, lurched suddenly. There was a grinding crash and he shot forward along the truck bed and ended in a pile of struggling bodies. There was shouting outside, but he could make out no words. A soft light swelled—some light outside that was strong enough to penetrate the canvas. The shouts again: "Get out! Get out!"

A ripple of flame ran up inside the corner of the canvas.

In the tangle of bodies, faces turned fireward, eyes big. There was Chanturia, and there were two faces Martin recognized in the firelight—faces he had seen in the firelight at Stary Buyan: the mustached Georgian face of Little Tomaz, and the lean dark face of the man who had shot at him—he recognized it now in profile, a face that looked to have been flattened by a board: the Turk. He and Chanturia had been struggling for his pistol when the flame caught them by surprise.

Martin dived and got the pistol while they were looking at the flames.

And the other pistol—he looked for it, but by then Chanturia had it from underneath Little Tomaz.

"Who's in there? Get out! Put down your weapons!" The tailgate dropped and the canvas flap was torn away. There was a crowd of police and security troops around the rear of the truck. Martin threw down the pistol, threw it out the back of the truck where the dark-faced man couldn't get at it. Chanturia did the same. They jumped down with their hands in the air, explaining simultaneously in a jumble of words which no one listened to.

The truck had crashed into a barricade of police cars that closed this, the only street exiting from the embankment. It had buried itself into the rear flank of a car, and the car was on fire, a gasoline fire that spread along the right side of the truck and had leaped to the canvas and was now working its way toward the truck's gas tank.

"This thing's going to blow up!" Martin shouted. He said it to everyone; but only Chanturia and Little Tomaz and the Turk understood what that meant.

"We know it!" a police captain shouted back. "Get away from it!" But by then Martin was running for the driver's door of the truck. "Halt!" the Captain shouted, tugging at his holstered pistol, but Chanturia stepped in front of him, prevented the Captain from getting the pistol out while he tried desperately to explain that an explosion in this truck was going to contaminate the whole Moscow River and make Chernobyl look like a Young Pioneers' picnic. The captain knocked Chanturia down, and three other militiamen converged on his prostrate body, nightsticks swinging. But by then Martin had reached the truck.

Although a sheet of fire glazed the passenger window, the driver's side was clear of flames. The door hung open where the driver had been dragged out by soldiers, who now stood back in a circle watching as Martin dived into the cab. The light of the fire shone mesmeric in their eyes.

The engine had stalled. At first Martin couldn't find the starter. He located it at last on the floor, an old-style foot starter. He stabbed his foot at it. The starter ground, but the engine wouldn't start. The fire had starved it of oxygen; it was not coming back to life. Desperate, Martin rammed the gearshift into what he hoped was reverse. Pain lanced through his injured hand. He straightened his leg against the foot starter as if he could push the truck backward by the sheer effort of pressing himself into the seat. The starter strained, unable to turn the engine against the load of the gears and the police car that clung to the truck's front bumper. The truck shuddered. Martin released the starter and hit it again, and the truck staggered back with the police car on its bumper and then broke free and shot backward barely missing the soldiers and police who scrambled out of its path. It lurched thirty meters and came to a halt against a lamp post. By the time Martin was out of the cab, a squad of soldiers had torn the burning canvas from the frame. The truck's right front tire was aflame. A blanket of police jackets snuffed it out, and the truck sat smoking wearily in the lamplight.

· 55 ·

ASSAULT WITH A TRUCK;
OR, DRAMA ON A JUNE NIGHT

ON THE NIGHT OF 10–11 JUNE, SHORTLY AFTER 0200, A LONG-DISTANCE TRUCK belonging to the Transportul Internazional Romaniya sped in a hail of bullets from the area of the Ukraine Hotel on the Shevchenko Embankment. It was followed closely by a second truck, a Soviet Kamaz vehicle with guns blazing. The two trucks were met by a barricade of police and military vehicles. Seeing the way closed, the driver of the first vehicle attempted to smash through by sheer mass, but the force of the impact was so great that he instead lost control and ended by breaking through the guard rail and plunging into the Moscow River. The driver and a passenger drowned in the wreckage.

The second truck was stopped by a collision with a police car, which burst into flames. Several persons were observed to have been pulled from the truck by police, and the truck was then driven backward from the flames and successfully saved from the conflagration.

A guest at the hotel, Mr. W. Johnson of the United States, said to our reporter, "My room overlooked the embankment, and the noise woke me from a sound sleep. It sounded like a war going on out there. Machine guns fired for five minutes solid, and then these two

297

trucks roared up the street. Police cars had moved into place just seconds before the trucks arrived at the intersection under the bridge. The collision was tremendous."

Neither the police nor military personnel on the scene would make any statement as to the cause of the wild chase. The office of the Procurator later issued a statement that the shooting and chase arose during the course of clarification of relations between competing criminal groups. Several persons are in police custody, and prosecutions are expected shortly. Other organizations also cooperated in the investigation and arrests.

The presence of military personnel at the scene has not been explained.

I. Klima

Izvestia no. 165, June 14, 1989, p. 8.

· 56 ·

Wednesday, June 14, 1989
1 P.M.
The Prague Restaurant, Moscow

NO CEREMONY MARKED THE SUCCESSFUL CONCLUSION OF OPERATION X. IN place of that, Martin and Alina met Chanturia for a private lunch at the Prague Restaurant at the end of Arbat Street. For once, they didn't care who saw them.

"Oh, your face!" Alina kissed Chanturia's bruised cheeks.

"If I hadn't been at the festivities," Martin said, "from the marks on your face, I'd say, 'Let's see what the other guy looks like.'"

"The other guys all looked Russian," Chanturia said. "And to a Russian, all Georgians look alike. That's what the militia told me. 'How were we to know you were an officer of the Committee, Captain?' Anyway, knowing I work for the Committee wouldn't have slowed them down—as long as nobody could prove they knew. Probably it's better they *didn't* know. Mafia hooligans they can pound on anytime; but how often does a militiaman get a clear chance to beat the crap out of a KGB officer?"

"Not often enough, apparently. When they took you off in the ambulance, I thought I'd never see you again. How's your leg?"

"My leg's fine. The bullet missed it completely—it just took my boot heel off. It numbed me for an hour. Probably it's a good thing— I couldn't feel the police sticks on that quarter. The rest of me still remembers them."

A table was ready for them in a small private room on the third floor looking out on Kalinin Prospect, where in the June sun the square concrete buildings of modern Moscow were looking as good as they ever could look. Chanturia groaned as he sat down, hoping for more sympathy from Alina, and getting it. She put a hand on his arm.

"Another kiss might ease the pain, Alka," he said.

"How about being a major—doesn't that ease the pain?" Martin asked, glancing at the new insignia on Chanturia's collar.

"Being a major—that's just a burden. Now I have to decide what to do about it."

The table was already stocked with vodka, mineral water, and *zakuska*. They waited until the waiter had opened all the bottles and retired.

"What are your choices of what to do?" Martin asked.

"Oh . . . a Chekist does what he's ordered." He used the old name for the KGB, a name made from the initial letters of the organization's original name: "Che Ka"—the "Extraordinary Commission." The people of the Extraordinary Commission, the Chekists, had kept the old name alive all these years. The name and too many other things, Chanturia thought. He poured two glasses of vodka. He offered to pour another, but Alina shook her head. He handed one to Martin. "But right now," Chanturia said, "I'm in a good position to ask for orders. The question is, what to want? What I've said I want is to be posted to Tbilisi."

"Will Tbilisi be safe for you? The father of Little Tomaz isn't going to be your friend."

"Is the danger more there than here? I doubt it. But maybe I could do some good there. If they'll let me: the orders aren't cut yet. Maybe it's my duty. Or, maybe I should resign. Maybe I should be a real person for part of my life."

"Who could be more real than you, Sergo?"

"Well, Mikadze for one. He can speak for himself, instead of saying

299

what he's ordered to say. And in speaking for himself, he speaks for others."

"On the other hand, every nation needs some honest cops."

"Every nation does."

"Did you read the paper this morning?" Alina asked Chanturia.

"Of course."

"Someone should tell them the full story, and see if they'd print it."

"Someone should—I'd feel a lot safer. 'Secrecy kills.' But not everyone is ready for the full truth yet. About the murder there's nothing secret. Little Tomaz admitted he killed your friend Hutchins, Ben. He didn't know who Hutchins was. Little Tomaz and his gang went to the cafe looking for Alya's brother because the Turk had learned Yuri was trying to sell what he knew. They planned to make the murder look like part of a general attack on the cafe. They didn't find Yuri, but they knew Yuri was going to meet his sister and a foreigner there, and they knew who the sister and the foreigner must be—there were no other choices, in that room. They killed Hutchins to keep him from getting the information, or from passing it on if he already had it. Out of a certain Georgian gallantry, he didn't kill the sister. He didn't consider her a threat anyway. Even if she had received any information, where could she go with it?

"But about the information itself—plutonium stolen from a nuclear test site—*that's* a secret, and it's going to stay one. The CIA may know it, but the public's not going to. And so," he said to Martin, "we didn't get your name in the paper, Bendzhamin. We couldn't even make you a Hero of the Soviet Union. But you can't expect the Committee to admit that the CIA saved its bacon."

"I'm not CIA," Martin said.

"You're not supposed to say things like that to me. Unless it's not true."

"Sorry. It's hard for civilians to keep the rules straight."

"It's hard even for professionals. Anyway, the Committee's not going to admit that an American citizen saved its hide, either."

"That's more credit than I deserve. You did the work. I just stumbled along behind Alya."

"Behind the hill, there was a girl," Chanturia said, raising his glass. "To the girl."

As the vodka went down, Martin couldn't help thinking of Uncle Fedya, bad as his vodka had been.

Chanturia refilled the glasses. "But Belkin did the work, more than any of us. He'll get a decoration: 'Honored Chekist—posthumous.' His widow will get a pension. Poor Belkin. He was a fine officer. Better than we deserved. And Sokolov—he was worse. But let's forget the bad. To my comrade Syoma Belkin."

They drained the glasses again.

"Do you know what's happened to your Colonel?" Martin asked.

"I'm not supposed to tell you, of course. And I don't know exactly. He's arrested. He admitted to a long-standing relationship with a certain Mafia leader. They met, it seems, through the daughter of Sokolov's foster mother, who by all accounts was a fine woman. After the Great Patriotic War, when men were few in Moscow, the daughter met a handsome Georgian in Moscow and became his mistress."

"Tomaz Broladze," Martin said.

"Yes."

"And Little Tomaz was their son?"

"Oh, no," Chanturia said, sounding surprised. "The mother of Little Tomaz was Georgian, and married to Tomaz Broladze. Georgian men don't *marry* Russian women, Bendzhamin. Oh, forgive me," he said to Alina, who had blushed. "I didn't mean any disrespect . . ." He stopped in confusion.

Martin took Alina's hand. "Go on."

"Broladze was building a Mafia gang around illegal transportation. As the Party declined, the gang rose; and Sokolov, a true Russian traditionalist, transferred his loyalty to the stronger party. He was a great convenience for Old Tomaz, being where he was. Let's hope he was the only one."

"Do you think there are others?"

Chanturia shrugged. "If there are, life's going to be uncomfortable. But probably it's going to be uncomfortable anyway. And not just for me. What are you going to do about Alya?" He asked this of both of them.

"Russian women don't *marry* American men, it seems," Martin said, and Alina blushed again.

"I'm not being quite so personal. But what are your plans for her?"

"Are you asking the CIA's plans? I don't intend to let them use her."

"No. She won't be any use to them. I mean your plans—the two of you."

"I start rehearsing a new play in two weeks," Alina said.

Chanturia nodded. "I understand you'll be leaving the Union soon, Bendzhamin. Your tour is almost over."

"Did I tell you that?"

"We have our sources."

Martin shrugged. "You're right. I'll be gone in a month. I'm trying not to think about it."

"I hope it doesn't seem out of place for me to make a suggestion. But maybe you could leave sooner. Any maybe you could persuade Alya to take a vacation outside the country."

"Outside? Why?"

"Some powerful people have reason not to like either of you. Old Tomaz, for one, is not the kind of man you want to be cross with you. He has the means to get as even as he wants."

"You mean the Committee can't keep us safe?"

"The Committee is not the greatest power in this country any longer. A lot of us don't believe that yet; but me, I've interviewed Lev Bok."

"Who's Lev Bok?"

"The manager of the cafe where this all started. There are people Lev Bok fears more than he fears the Committee, Bendzhamin."

"You mean you think the Mafia is taking over?"

"No. I mean the Committee is losing out. The Committee and all it stands for. Nobody's taking over: not yet. If we're lucky, the people will take over, as they should have long ago. But for now, the Committee can't keep Alya safe. The Committee—parts of it—may still be her greatest danger. Sokolov's arrested; but Old Tomaz may have other people on the Committee; and certainly he has plenty of hands on the outside."

"This is odd advice from a man who wants to enter the lion's den. If you think Old Tomaz doesn't like Alya and me, what can he think about you? If he's as strong as you say, what chance do you have?"

Chanturia shrugged. "Tbilisi's where I belong."

"How can you say that? You told me you don't even know if Georgia should stay in the Union."

"I *don't* know. But while I'm figuring it out, maybe it's better to have me in the Tbilisi office rather than someone else, someone who's *sure*. There's too much certainty in the world, don't you think? Things are not good in Georgia, but the Mafia's not making them better. Nor, I'm afraid, is the Committee—not there; not now. Someone's got to try to make things better."

"There's not much I'm certain of, Sergo; but one thing is that it will definitely be better to have you in the Tbilisi office than someone else. Well, maybe you'll even be able to keep Old Tomaz so busy he won't have time for us."

"He's got time." He said this looking at Alya.

She said, "I'll talk with Ben about it."

Martin smiled. "We'll talk about it, Major."

Chanturia made a show of looking over his shoulder. "Major! Where? Did he hear us? Oh, you mean me. I haven't got used to this exalted status yet."

"Get used to it, Sergo. I'll talk with Alya." He took in his left hand the hand Chanturia offered him.

"How *did* you hurt that hand, Bendzhamin?" Chanturia asked.

"I told you: I fell in my bathtub."

Chanturia looked to Alina.

"I understand he fell in the bathtub," she said.

"This is not a woman," Chanturia said; "This is a treasure. Protect her well, Bendzhamin."

· 57 ·

Wednesday, June 14, 1989

4 P.M.

The United States Embassy

"THE BAD PART OF THIS JOB," BIERMAN SAID, PUTTING DOWN THE NEWSPA-per, "is that you never get credit for your good work. You only get blamed for the screw-ups."

"You're money ahead," Taglia told him. "You may never get another chance to be a Hero of the Soviet Union; but it wouldn't look good on your record, anyway. And Martin did all the work for you. Plus, think of all the good feeling you engendered by this inter-service cooperation. You can't expect the Committee to go ahead and actually make it public that the Americans kept their virtue intact—such as it was; especially when one of their own officers was in on the scam."

Bierman said, "The KGB are laughing up their sleeves, just at knowing who I am. And then this 'report' they gave us." He picked

303

up a thin typed document. "Broladze didn't know who he had killed. What kind of idiots do they take us for?"

"The average kind, I suppose," Martin said. He knew Bierman would never accept that the CIA station chief had been killed without special malice. "But look at the bright side: it could have been you instead."

Bierman, tossing the KGB report back on the table, answered him sourly, "I assume that your house guest will be moving out, now that the heat's off?"

"Sergo doesn't think the heat's off."

" 'Sergo.' You seem to be real buddies."

"I've had worse friends."

"You've been in this country too long, Martin. Well, I can't recommend to the Old Man that we let her stay here. A foreign national inside the Embassy is too much of a security risk."

"Don't worry. She doesn't want to stay in the Embassy. But Sergo doesn't think she'll be safe even now, in this country. Old Tomaz Broladze apparently is not the kind of guy you want to have cross with you. I think I've convinced her to take a vacation trip outside. My tour's about up: with any luck, she won't want to come back."

"You intend to commit marriage?" Taglia asked.

"If she'll do it."

"If the Committee's worried about her, they should tell Old Tomaz what they're going to do to his kid if he doesn't toe the line," Bierman said.

"Ah, for the good old days when you could pull out people's fingernails in peace and quiet," Taglia said. "It won't work anymore. Old Tomaz knows how to use the newspapers. Harm his kid, and there'd be things in *Izvestia* that nobody would want to see published, not the KGB or us. But what about Sergo? Just being a major now isn't going to keep him safe, either."

"Sergo wants to go back to the lion's den," Martin said. "He's asked to be posted to the KGB office in Tbilisi. That's not something you have to report," he added, seeing Bierman hastily scribble something on the side of his hand.

"If you don't want something reported, don't say it," Bierman said. "This isn't amateur night, Martin."

"I thought you said he was ready to favor Georgian independence," Rollie said.

"I said he didn't know what to think after his last trip down there.

Maybe he wants to go back to decide what to think. Could be he'll resign, after a while. Or maybe he's going to try to straighten out their operation there and see if there's a way to keep the Georgian Republic in the Union. Whatever it is, I wish him luck."

"I wish them all luck," Taglia said. "This whole nation, if there's enough luck to go around. They'll need it."